PROTECTING BREE

SEAL OF PROTECTION: ALLIANCE
BOOK 7

SUSAN STOKER

This book is a work of fiction. Names, characters, places, and incidents are products of the author's imagination or used fictitiously. Any resemblance to actual events or locales or persons living or dead is entirely coincidental.

Copyright © 2026 by Susan Stoker

No part of this work may be used, stored, reproduced or transmitted without written permission from the publisher except for brief quotations for review purposes as permitted by law.

Without in any way limiting the author's [and publisher's] exclusive rights under copyright, any use of this publication to "train" generative artificial intelligence (AI) technologies to generate text is expressly prohibited. The author reserves all rights to license uses of this work for generative AI training and development of machine learning language models.

This book is licensed for your personal enjoyment only. This book may not be re-sold or given away to other people. If you would like to share this book with another person, please purchase an additional copy for each recipient. If you're reading this book and did not purchase it, or it was not purchased for your use only, please purchase your own copy.

Thank you for respecting the hard work of this author.

Edited by Kelli Collins
Cover Design by AURA Design Group
Manufactured in the United States

CHAPTER ONE

Jude "Smiley" Stark stared at the woman sleeping on his couch. He couldn't believe he'd found her...or rather, she'd found *him*. And for the second time, she'd played a huge part in saving the lives of his teammates' loved ones.

Without Bree Haynes, Ellory and Yana might have ended up in a shipping container, sold for their organs. The two kids owed their lives to Bree for leading the bad guy away when they were hiding from him. Smiley hated that she'd taken a beating for her heroic actions. He could still see the almost-healed bruises on her face...and he was sure she had more all over her body, as well.

Then there was yesterday, when she'd snuck into the backseat of the car owned by the man who'd kidnapped Kelli, texting Smiley directions as to their location, thus allowing him and Flash to arrive in the nick of time to prevent the asshole from killing his teammate's woman.

Bree was reckless. Impulsive. Didn't think before she acted.

And he'd never been more in awe of anyone in his entire life.

Ever since he'd met her in Las Vegas—after Josie's dead ex-boyfriend's psycho mother sold her to a man who had connections in the sex slavery industry—he'd been hooked.

There was just something about Bree that had captured him and wouldn't let go.

And now she was here.

In his living room.

Sleeping on his couch.

He'd actually demanded she take his bed, but in the end she'd proven more stubborn than he was.

Smiley had been looking for her ever since that fateful night in Vegas, when she'd been tied up in the back of a car, scared out of her mind. He freed her—and then she'd disappeared into the chaos of that night. And even though Smiley had been irritated and frustrated that he wasn't able to find her after months of searching, he was also impressed. She'd done a very good job of staying under the radar. In fact, he'd venture to say that if she hadn't come to Riverton, hadn't gotten involved in the lives of his friends, he might never had found her at all.

Which led to the question...why had she done it?

Why come to Riverton? Why track him down? Why help his friends?

Why not run to the opposite side of the country?

And why was the man who'd "bought" her—Smiley *hated* that in today's day and age, humans were still buying and selling other humans—so bound and determined to get his hands on her?

Smiley had so many questions, and the only person who might be able to answer them was Bree.

A part of him wanted to shake her. Make her sit up and talk to him again. But now wasn't the time. She was exhausted. He'd seen it in her face and body language while questioning her earlier, even though she'd tried to hide it.

Smiley was tired too, but he was afraid that if he went to bed, he'd wake up in the morning and Bree would be gone. He'd lose his mind if that happened. So he was going to keep his ass right here in the living room and watch her sleep.

"Why are you called Smiley?"

He jerked in surprise, caught off guard. Bree was awake. And he'd had no clue. Her breathing hadn't changed. She hadn't shifted.

Making a mental note that this woman was more observant than he'd given her credit for—which was stupid, considering all the things she'd done recently— Smiley leaned back in the easy chair and shrugged. "Because of my outgoing personality?"

Bree's eyes opened and even in the dim light of his apartment, Smiley saw her hazel gaze zero in on him with an accuracy that made him realize she'd probably been awake for much longer than he'd thought. "No offense... but no," she said with a small smile.

Smiley blinked. Had he ever seen this woman smile before? Nope. She'd never had any reason to smile the few times they'd interacted.

And very suddenly, he wanted to see her happy, smiling, more than he wanted anything. More than he wanted information. More than he wanted to catch bad guys.

3

More than he wanted to be a Navy SEAL.

That was...disconcerting.

"It's sarcasm," he blurted, sounding more curt than he'd intended. "One of my drill sergeants commented on how I wasn't exactly Mr. Smiley, and it stuck. How long?"

She frowned, and went to sit up on the couch.

"No, stay. Don't get up," Smiley ordered. He couldn't stand seeing the small wince she made when she'd tried to move. To his relief, she settled back on the cushions and snuggled into the blanket he'd given her earlier.

"How long, what?" she asked.

"How long had you been visiting Kelli? Here at my place?"

Bree shrugged. "About a week. Not long."

"Why now?"

"You know, you're a big boy, you could use your words. More of them, I mean. It would prevent me from having to ask for clarification every time you ask me something," Bree said with another small grin.

Even that little twitching of her lips made satisfaction swim through Smiley's veins.

"Why reach out to me *now*? After all this time. And why didn't you come directly to me when you found out I wasn't staying here, that Kelli and Flash had moved into my place because of their situation? What changed?"

"Right, so...that was maybe *too many* words," she joked.

But Smiley wasn't amused. He felt itchy and unsettled. He needed to understand this woman, and right now he was so far from understanding it wasn't even funny. "Bree," he said, his tone communicating that he wanted answers.

She sighed. "I don't know."

Smiley scoffed.

"I'm being honest. I admit that I came to Riverton because you were here. That awful night in Vegas, I remember you telling me your name, Jude Stark, and that you were a Navy SEAL stationed in Riverton. When things got...intense back home, the first place I thought to go was here. Where *you* were. Except once I got here, I had no plan, and no idea how to find you. And I realized how ridiculous it was to come. You didn't know me, and I didn't know you. We'd met once for like five seconds. So I felt stupid. But that didn't stop me from hanging out around the gates of the naval base in the hopes I'd get a glimpse of you...and I did."

"So you followed me."

Bree shrugged. "Yeah."

Smiley was glad she wasn't prevaricating. Wasn't trying to lie about what she'd done.

"Honestly, it kept me sane. Living out of my car was boring. I didn't have much money, so it wasn't as if I could go out to eat or stay in hotels. I *have* money, I'm just afraid to use it because I have a pretty good idea that the guy who thinks he owns me can track me that way. So I watched you. Figured out who your friends were. Followed *them* as well. You can learn a lot about a person by watching them without their knowledge."

Smiley should be upset. Pissed that she'd spied on him. But for some reason, he wasn't. "What did you learn about me and my friends?"

"That you're loyal. And kind. And that you work hard and play harder."

She wasn't wrong.

"So why'd you come to my place? Kelli said you came right up to the door and knocked."

Bree snorted. "Not my finest moment. For all the watching I'd done, I hadn't even realized you weren't here anymore. Stupid. And I thought she was your girlfriend at first, so I was mortified."

"Why?"

Bree stared at him with tired eyes. Then she took a deep breath and blurted, "Because in all the time I'd watched you, I hadn't seen you with a woman. I had this little fantasy in my head that I'd knock on your door, you'd be thrilled to see me, would solve all my problems and find out you like me in the process and we'd live happily ever after." She finished by rolling her eyes.

Her words were a little defensive and a lot sarcastic. But they still sent an electric buzz shooting through Smiley.

He leaned forward, resting his forearms on his knees, holding eye contact with Bree as he spoke. "There *is* something between us," he said simply. "I wouldn't have spent the last several months of my life doing everything in my power to find you if there wasn't."

She stared at him for a long moment, the air between them charged. Smiley had never felt anything like it before. The hair on his arms and legs felt as if every strand was standing straight up. Something was happening here. Something he didn't understand. But he'd learned through his time as a SEAL that sometimes you just had to go with the flow. Even if what you were doing made no sense whatsoever...if it went against everything you'd been taught.

"I was going to leave, but Kelli was...persuasive. And she lured me inside with the promise of a shower and a meal," Bree said a little quieter. "I used to take showers for granted. And when I was hungry, I ate. They weren't even questions in my head. Just things I did. But when you get to a point where you can't just go to a bathroom and turn on a shower, or go to the pantry and grab a snack, you realize how important those things really are."

"Yeah. It's not the same, not at all, but after a two-week mission, where we've been crawling through a jungle or walking through miles of sand, or even swimming hours in the ocean...there's nothing better than that first shower or meal."

Bree nodded. "Right. So, I came inside when Kelli invited me. Then I found myself coming back. I knew I shouldn't. That I should just leave. Go east. Somewhere. *Anywhere*. But Kelli was so nice. And being in here, surrounded by your stuff...it made me feel normal again."

"I'm going to figure this out," Smiley told her.

Bree snorted.

"I am," he insisted.

"I've been racking my brain trying to decide what to do. Figure out how my life came to this point. With no luck. I don't know how you can possibly find the guy who's looking for me."

"I have connections," he said simply, his mind spinning with the things he needed to do. The people he needed to contact. "You have family?"

"A sister in Washington. But I don't want to involve her. And we aren't close," Bree told him.

"Parents?"

"Well, I wasn't hatched, if that's what you're asking," Bree told him with a slight grin.

There it was again. Smiley was already addicted to this woman's smiles. Because he had a feeling that, like him, she didn't smile often. Each one was a gift. A reward. And he craved them like he craved the adrenaline rush he got while on a mission.

"You close to them?" he asked, returning to their discussion.

"I was. But my mom got colon cancer a few years ago and passed. My dad was hit by a drunk driver just a couple months later."

"Shit, Bree. I'm sorry."

She shrugged. "Yeah, it wasn't a good time in my life."

Smiley figured that was a massive understatement.

"My dad used to beat the shit out of my mom while I hid under the bed in my room," he blurted. "I should've done more to stop it. Stop *him*." He wasn't sure why he was telling her this, except that she was sharing painful memories, and he felt as if he needed to reciprocate.

"How old were you?"

"Six. Seven. Ten. It went on for quite a few years."

"Smiley, you were a *kid*. What could you have done?"

But he shook his head. He'd *never* forget those mornings, finding his mom in the kitchen the next morning, making him breakfast, covered in bruises. Sometimes still bleeding...and smiling at him, pretending nothing was wrong. All while his dad was passed out on the couch, snoring loudly, still drunk from the night before.

He did his best to push the memories to the back of his mind. "I'll make sure your sister is covered, that no one will go through her to get to you. I'm going to need as much information as you can give me. The name of your ex—that asshole who sold you—what he did, where *you* worked, friends...everything."

Bree sighed and closed her eyes. Seeing the frown on her face made Smiley's insides twist.

"Sometimes I can't believe this is my life. I had a job that I didn't love but was at least good at. A boyfriend. People I hung out with and considered friends. And now I'm homeless, on the run from a man who wants to use and abuse me in the worst ways, and wondering where I went wrong."

"Most of the time it's not *you* who went wrong, it's just life. It has a way of shitting on you when you least expect it."

Bree's eyes opened, and Smiley could feel the weight of her stare as she asked, "Do you truly believe that?"

"Yes."

"You need more fun in your life, Smiley."

He snorted. "Fun? Killing terrorists is fun. Blowing up ships full of people who want nothing more than to kill innocent civilians is fun. Seeing evil people get what's coming to them is fun."

"Um, that's not the kind of fun I was talking about," she told him. "I meant...bowling nights. Picnics in the park. Lying on the sand at the beach, soaking up the sun."

"That's not fun. That's torture. I hate sand," Smiley said.

"Of course you do," she said, laughing.

Fuck. He was doomed. Every time he made this woman smile, he felt a surge of pride and contentment coursing through him. He'd spend the rest of his life saying stupid things and making a fool of himself if it meant seeing the current look on her face.

And if having a job, a roof over her head, and friends to hang out with was all it took to make her happy, he could easily give her all those things. He wasn't sure he was boyfriend material, he was too...hard. Too cynical. But if having a boyfriend was also something she wanted, he'd bend over backward to be the kind of man she could rely on.

Smiley wasn't even freaking out that he was thinking long-term when it came to this woman. She'd been the center of his world for months now. He'd worried about her every minute of the day and night. And now she was here. Safe. On his couch. It was no wonder he didn't have any concerns about giving her anything she needed to be happy.

"How about you get some more sleep," he suggested grumpily.

"What about you?"

"What *about* me what?" Smiley asked.

"Are you going to sleep? You can't sit in that chair all night, watching me. I promise not to leave, Smiley."

The hell he couldn't stay here all night. He'd slept in this chair more times than he could count. And damn straight she wasn't leaving—he wouldn't let her. She needed help. Help only he and his connections could give her.

Bree Haynes was about to find out that coming to Riverton was the best decision she'd ever made. She wanted friends? She was already close with Kelli; it wouldn't take much for her to be integrated into the fold with the other women, especially Addison. She would want to meet the woman who'd saved her daughter and stepdaughter. And Caroline Steel and her crew would definitely take her under their wings too.

Bree had no idea how much her life was about to change.

"Smiley? Did you hear me? I promise not to sneak out in the middle of the night."

"You think you could? I *am* a SEAL, after all," he told her.

"Is that a challenge?" she asked, with a lift of her chin.

"No!" he barked, suddenly afraid she'd decide to prove that she could sneak out without him knowing.

"Relax," she told him, laughing again, "I'm too tired to do anything more than sleep...*tonight*."

"Fuck," he swore, realizing the can of worms he'd inadvertently opened.

Bree giggled.

Honest-to-God *giggled*—and Smiley knew he was a goner.

He'd spent the first thirty years of his life being annoyed by giggling. And now he found himself getting hard by the sound of *this* woman doing that exact thing.

Settling into the chair, Smiley pulled a blanket hanging off the back over his lap. The last thing he wanted was to have Bree notice his erection. It was inappropriate, and given everything happening with her life, it would probably scare the shit out of her.

"Sleep, Bree," he ordered gruffly.

"Smiley?"

"You aren't sleeping," he told her.

She smiled again. Each one burrowing further and further into his heart.

Then her smile disappeared. "I appreciate any help you can give me, but if things don't work out, if he finds me... you aren't allowed to feel guilty."

Guilt was a part of Smiley's life. He carried the mantle

of guilt that he hadn't done anything to help his mother, and it wasn't about to disappear now.

As much as he wanted to tell Bree that whoever was after her wouldn't find her, he couldn't. He knew better than most people that bad shit happened in life. Hell, she did too, which was why she was bringing this up now. But he could make her a vow.

"If he finds you, I'll come after you. I won't stop until I've found you—and he's got my bullet in his forehead." It was a violent and depressing thing to say, but Smiley didn't regret it.

"Promise?" Bree whispered.

"Promise."

CHAPTER TWO

Bree looked through her lashes at the man sleeping in the chair across from her. He'd left a light on in the kitchen so she wouldn't wake up in the middle of the night and wonder where she was.

As if that would happen.

Bree knew *exactly* where she was. In Jude Stark's apartment. On his couch. And she'd never felt safer. At least in the last several months, that is.

Her life had been turned completely upside down, and she still wasn't sure how it all happened. One day she was at her job, having just broken up with her boyfriend, and the next she was kidnapped, hogtied, and informed that her ex had *sold* her—and that she now belonged to an organization that had every intention of selling her for sex.

It was unbelievable. And yet it had happened. To *her*.

She'd been extremely lucky that the man who'd kidnapped her had stopped to pick up a second woman that night, before taking her to his contact. And even luckier that the second woman, Josie England, had a Navy

SEAL boyfriend who wasn't about to let his woman disappear into thin air, as so many people did year after year.

She'd had a terribly close call, and the fact that Smiley's face was the first one she'd seen when he'd opened the kidnapper's car door and found her...

It had a profound effect on Bree. Yes, some would say she only felt a connection with him because he'd saved her that night. And maybe it started off that way, but as she'd followed him and his friends around Riverton, Bree had gotten a pretty good insight into his character.

She'd been watching him for quite a while now. He didn't drive like an asshole, opened doors for people—men *and* women—tipped generously, if the smiles on the faces of anyone who served him were any indication. And while it was true, most of the time he had a scowl on his face—was resting bitch face a thing for men?—he'd been nothing but kind and accommodating to her.

She really *had* almost turned around and run when Kelli opened his door about a week ago. Bree had truly thought he'd gotten a girlfriend, and she'd somehow missed it. But it shouldn't have been a surprise that he'd given up his apartment for his friends because they were in danger.

Bree had a feeling if she pointed out all the good things about Smiley, he'd simply scowl at her and say she was wrong, that he was an asshole.

Well, if he thought he was an asshole, so be it. She knew differently. And the fact that she was lying on his couch, warm, clean, and with a full belly, hammered that belief home.

His words before he fell asleep echoed in her brain.

If he finds you, I'll come after you. I won't stop until I've found you—and he's got my bullet in his forehead.

One of her worst fears was that she'd disappear and no one would notice. Or care. She didn't know why Smiley had developed an obsession with finding her after that night in Vegas, but she wasn't upset about it.

Bree smiled as she stared up at the ceiling. His promise was such a...Smiley thing to say. He was very rough around the edges, saying a lot of things that most people would consider inappropriate, but knowing that he wouldn't hesitate to inflict harm on the man who was hunting her felt *good*. Comforting. Other people's opinions on the matter be damned.

The truth was, she was at the end of her rope. She put on a good front, but inside she was dying. She had no idea how she'd ended up in this situation. She'd been a good girlfriend...loving, supportive. Then out of the blue, Carl had asked her to participate in a three-way, and she'd said no. An *unequivocal* no. He was pissed, and he began to bug her about it almost daily. Calling her a prude. Claiming it would make their sex life better. Telling her that if she *really* loved him, she'd want him to be happy, and fulfilling his fantasy of sleeping with two women at the same time would do exactly that.

So Bree dumped him. Because she realized that she *didn't* love him. She could never love a man who wanted to be intimate with someone else when he was with her, as if she wasn't enough.

And that's when her life had taken a sharp turn.

Carl hadn't taken her rejection well and vowed that she'd regret it. And it was true—she *did* regret it. But not for the reasons he'd probably thought.

She regretted not dumping him much sooner.

He'd *sold her*. Like she was nothing. Property. A piece of trash.

And thanks to him, she was on the run, and nothing she did could shake the man who was after her. Bree figured he was probably pissed about losing not only her, but Josie as well. But if that was the case...why wasn't he after the other woman? Why just *her*?

She was nobody. Mid-thirties, average height for a woman at five-five. Her reddish-brown hair and hazel eyes weren't anything special. Neither was her body. She was utterly normal. She worked hard, liked puppies and kittens, went out of her way to be kind to people.

And yet, here she was.

Turning her head, Bree looked back over at Smiley. His mouth was slightly open as he breathed deeply in his sleep. His hair was flat on one side, where he'd been sleeping on it, and his facial hair looked a little too long to be a five o'clock shadow, too short to be an actual beard. His brows were furrowed even in his sleep, which gave off angry vibes.

She should be afraid of this man. She didn't really know him, after all. But she wasn't. She felt safe. Which was crazy, because she wasn't really safe *anywhere*. Not until whoever wanted to add her to their stable of women had given up or was dead. So maybe it was just that being with Smiley gave her the *illusion* of safety. She'd felt it all those months ago, when she'd first met him, and she felt it again now.

It was the reason she was here. In Riverton. On his couch.

She recalled his words from earlier.

There is something between us.

He wasn't wrong. There was definitely something between them. It was confusing and kind of scary, considering she didn't know him. Not really. But she knew she couldn't leave Riverton before figuring out exactly what it was that drew them together.

It was dumb. And she was weak. She was bringing danger to his doorstep, yet she couldn't bring herself to leave.

Sighing, she turned onto her side.

That small sound made Smiley open his eyes. "You good?" he asked sleepily.

"Yeah," she whispered.

"You uncomfortable? You could move to my bed."

Lust shot through Bree so fast, it made her suddenly uneasy. Thinking about being in this man's bed came with visions of sharing it with *him*, both of them naked and having wild, crazy sex. He wouldn't be an easy lover. He'd be demanding and forceful. And she'd love every second.

"I'm fine here," she croaked.

He made some sort of noise in the back of his throat that she took as acceptance.

"Why aren't you sleeping?" he asked.

"I just...habit," Bree explained quietly. "When I slept in my car, I was constantly on alert. Every light I saw, I thought it might be *him* coming to get me. Every noise was him breaking into my vehicle. It's hard to trust that I'm safe. He's out there. Waiting. Watching."

Smiley sat up, and Bree realized she shouldn't have said anything. Should've just made up some lame excuse and let him go back to sleep. It was still a couple hours until the time he normally left for the base, but Smiley looked wide awake now, and she hated that she'd disrupted his rest. He didn't get enough as it was.

"I hope he *does* show up," he said in a low, menacing tone.

It should've freaked her out; instead, it ramped up her arousal. This man...he was *intense*. And apparently she was a sucker for a bad boy. For a dangerous man.

No, that wasn't true. She normally didn't go for assholes. Or men who made her nervous. Smiley was both, and yet she knew down to her core that he wouldn't hurt her.

"Anyone who contributes to the assault and exploitation of women—hell, of humans in general—is the lowest of the low. The scum of the earth. We're all on the same rock trying to live our lives, and no one has the right to use or abuse someone else for their personal gain. Whether that be money or to sate their lust. And rape is the worst offense a man or woman can commit in my eyes. I *want* the guy who's after you to find you. So I can rip off his head and shit down his throat."

Bree couldn't help it. She chuckled.

"You think that's funny?" Smiley asked, scowling.

"No. Yes. I don't know! I mean, I've heard that quote in a few movies, but never heard anyone say it in real life."

"I'm being serious," he insisted.

Bree sobered. "I know. Thank you."

"Shit. I can't believe we're having this conversation," he bitched under his breath.

That made Bree struggle to hold back another chuckle.

"And she's *laughing*," Smiley said with a roll of his eyes.

But Bree could tell that he wasn't upset. In fact, if she was reading him right, it seemed as if he was...pleased? She had no idea what he was so happy about, but after spending so much time with Carl and rarely being able to please him, making Smiley happy, even in the middle of the night when they should be sleeping, felt amazing.

"Can you tell me what the plan is? I mean, to try to fix this mess I've found myself in?" Bree asked in a small voice. She needed to know. Was the kind of person who didn't do well with surprises.

"In the morning, I'm going to call a former SEAL named Tex Keegan. He's a computer genius. Get him on this. Try to figure out who your fucktard ex sold you to. Get a tracker or two, so if the worst happens and you *do* get taken, Tex'll be able to tell us where you are and we can come get you. Need to get your car detailed too, even though you aren't going to be driving it for a while.

"As soon as possible, I'm going to introduce you to Addison and MacGyver, to set up a meet-and-greet with Ellory and Yana. I'm sure all the other women will want to meet you too. And I want to call Fiona and Cookie. Maybe Julie and Hurt. Both women were kidnapped by human traffickers and taken to Mexico quite a few years ago. I feel like talking to them might be of some use to you. And Josie, Blink, Remi, and Kevlar are getting married in a couple weeks, and they're having a huge shindig at Aces Bar and Grill. We'll go to that. You can meet and get to know everyone."

"To each other?"

"What?" Smiley asked.

"The four of them are marrying each other?" Bree joked. She was overwhelmed with Smiley's plans for her. Not upset about meeting his friends officially, but overwhelmed all the same.

It was his turn to smile. And when he did, Bree's world shifted.

Broody and angry-looking Smiley was hot. But smiling? The man was *lethal*.

"No, not to each other. They decided to have a double ceremony. Blink and Remi are really close after an ordeal they went through, and since both couples would be inviting basically the same people to their receptions, they figured they might as well have the ceremonies at the same time. And I have it on good authority that Kelli and Flash are gonna go to the courthouse and tie the knot, so it'll probably turn into a *triple* wedding reception."

"Why?" Bree asked.

"Why what?"

"I don't know them. Not really. I mean, following you and your friends around doesn't really qualify me to go to the most important day of their lives."

Smiley tossed back the blanket he had over his lap and stood. Walking over to the couch that Bree was lying on, he sat next to her hip. She stared at him as he braced himself with a hand by her shoulder and leaned in close. She should've been alarmed at the way he was all up in her personal space. But after that smile, it was taking all her control not to tackle the man and have her wicked way with him.

"You should know something."

Bree waited, but when he didn't continue, she got up the courage to ask, "What?"

"You're under my protection now. And where I go, *you* go. To the store, to the base to work, to Aces—everywhere. Until we catch this asshole who's after you, I'm not leaving you alone. I'm not going to take the chance that he'll get his hands on you. And since I don't want to miss my friends' reception, you're coming too. But even if you *weren't* in danger, you'd go anyway, because Addison would insist on inviting you. As would Kelli, Remi, Josie, Wren, and Maggie. And when you meet Caroline's crew, they will too.

"You've entered a whole new world, Bree. One where friends have each other's backs. Where we don't look the other way when shit goes south. Until this asshole is caught, you aren't going to be alone. Ever."

His words soothed a part of Bree that she didn't even realize needed soothing. "Even to pee?" she joked with a smile.

"Fuck...that smile. It slays me," Smiley muttered. Then he shifted, brushing a lock of hair off her forehead. "Even to pee," he confirmed. "Never know when someone will slip through the window. Desperate people will do desperate things. And I'm not willing to risk anyone putting one fucking finger on you."

Now Bree wanted to cry. How had she invoked such... intense loyalty in this man?

"That okay?" he asked.

She nodded, speechless.

"Good. Can we sleep now?"

Bree had a million questions. About Tex, trackers, why he was so sure all his friends would want to meet her. But instead, feeling overwhelmed, she simply nodded again.

Smiley stared down at her for a long moment, long enough that Bree thought he might actually lean down and kiss her. But to her disappointment, he sat up, nodded once, then went back to his chair.

Damn. The sexual tension between them was larger

than life. Bree wanted nothing more than to find out if what they had was a fleeting thing, caused by the tension of her situation...or if it could be something more.

But in the middle of the hell that was her life wasn't exactly the best time to start a relationship, if that's what this even was. She didn't think so. Smiley felt responsible for her, that much was obvious. But could he feel more? After this was over—and please, let it end sooner rather than later—would he even want her around? He might send her back to Vegas and her old life without a second glance, satisfied that he'd tied up all the loose ends from the night he'd met her, once and for all.

Sighing, Bree snuggled back down under the warm fleece blanket Smiley had given her. "Can I say one more thing?" Bree asked, after Smiley had gotten comfortable once more.

He sighed as if irritated, but she could see his lips curled into a small grin. "What?"

"Thank you—"

"Nope."

Bree frowned in confusion. "Nope *what*? Words, Smiley."

"You don't get to thank me. I'm not helping you for your gratitude."

"Then why *are* you?"

"You don't know?"

"Obviously not," she told him, a little miffed.

"Then I'll tell you after."

"After what?"

"After this is done. After the asshole is caught and you're safe."

"You're annoying," Bree blurted.

Smiley chuckled. "I know."

"And cocky," she added.

"It's not cockiness that has me so sure whoever is after you will pay for terrorizing you, and however many others. Or has me knowing that whoever is ultimately behind this—not the goons after you, but the man at the top of the chain—will regret his chosen path in life. It's the bone-deep knowledge that we were meant to meet. To be right here, right now, at this moment in both our lives. And that we have a future together. We can't have that with this threat hanging over us. So we'll resolve it and move on."

Goose bumps broke out on Bree's arms. She'd never met anyone like Smiley before. He didn't beat around the bush. Went after what he wanted. And it seemed as if he wanted *her*. Little nobody Bree Haynes.

The truth was, she wanted him too. More than she'd wanted anything in her life.

She'd do whatever she had to do in order to survive this. Whatever "this" was. She'd wear a hundred trackers, let him stand in the bathroom door while she peed. Meet all his friends. Whatever he asked, she'd do it. Because the truth was, she was terrified. And she wanted to make it to the other side of whatever was happening, if only to experience one night in Smiley's arms.

"Sleep, Bree. Tomorrow's going to be busy."

Instead of worrying about exactly what that meant, Bree dutifully closed her eyes. She thought she'd lie awake thinking and worrying, but instead, she fell asleep almost instantly. And had dreams that alternated between terrifying images of her being thrown into a trunk of a car, and standing on the sand by the ocean, staring into Smiley's eyes as they said their marriage vows.

CHAPTER THREE

Bree's face hurt from smiling. Which was weird, because it felt as if it had been years since she'd been this carefree. Oh, her life was still a shitshow. She could practically *feel* she was still being hunted. But for right this second? She felt free.

Smiley hadn't been kidding when he'd said he wasn't letting her out of his sight. She figured it was *mostly* because he was worried about whoever was after her...but also a little because he didn't completely trust she wouldn't take off again.

She wasn't going to do that. For one, she'd promised. But more importantly? She'd be a complete idiot to not take the help Smiley was offering. She needed his assistance and wasn't about to do something idiotic...like think she could hide out for the rest of her life.

And for the moment, she was having more fun than she'd had in years.

Smiley had woken her up at the ass crack of dawn and dragged her out to his Ford Ranger, bringing her to the naval base, where he'd met up with the rest of his team for their morning PT workout.

It was a little awkward meeting the team officially, especially since she'd been stalking them for quite a while now. She knew where they all lived, what they drove, what their girlfriends and wives drove. She'd followed them to Aces Bar and Grill, and to what she assumed were some of their other favorite restaurants in Riverton. Hell, she even knew where Addison and MacGyver's kids went to school.

Everyone was polite, and Bree expected there would come a time when they'd want to ask her questions. They were all extremely protective, and she figured they'd want to make sure she wasn't a danger to their teammate—which was funny, as she was certainly no harm to anyone.

Well...maybe everyone except MacGyver and Flash would question her. After making sure she was all right with it, those two men had actually given her long, heartfelt hugs, which had felt amazing. But she hadn't helped their loved ones for any kind of thanks. She'd kind of been on autopilot, only doing what instinct told her to do. She was relieved that her actions had helped save others...but the fact remained, she'd only been in the right place at the right time because she was stalking Smiley and his friends.

Figuring she'd have some explanations to make later, Bree was relieved when Kevlar announced it was time to start. To her surprise, Smiley led her over to an ATV parked next to one of the lifeguard towers. He'd handed her the keys and told her to keep up.

He hadn't asked if she'd ridden an ATV before, or if she knew how to operate it—she hadn't and didn't, but managed to figure it out pretty fast—just gave her a look she couldn't interpret and turned back to his friends.

That's how Bree came to be cruising down the beach as the sun came up, watching seven incredibly in-shape men run, skip, and even crawl through the sand and surf. They took their workout very seriously, and it wasn't a hardship to watch their muscles flex and strain as they did what they needed to do in order to stay in shape, ready to save the world.

She had no idea how Smiley had gotten permission for her to use the ATV the lifeguards obviously used while they were on duty, but she was grateful. There was something so freeing about racing over the sand this early in the morning, without having to worry about running over any sunbathers or swerving around little kids who weren't paying attention to their surroundings.

She was currently sitting still, soaking in the breathtaking morning sunrise and watching the team do some sort of sadistic burpee combination that involved pushups, rolling in the sand to the right, jumping jacks, and then more rolling—when Smiley abruptly stopped what he was doing and jogged toward her.

Sitting up straight, Bree frowned and looked around. Was something wrong? Why was he stopping?

He walked over to where she was sitting on the ATV while his teammates continued their workout and asked, "You good?"

Bree frowned. "Uh...yeah. Why?"

"Just wanted to check in. This probably wasn't what you had in mind for your morning. Getting dragged down to the beach and being bored out of your mind, watching me and my teammates work out."

Bree couldn't stop the small chuckle. "Oh, yeah. It's tough, but I think I can manage," she said sarcastically.

Smiley tilted his head as his brows furrowed, clearly trying to figure out what she meant.

"Smiley, it's fine. Trust me. Watching you and your friends roll around in the sand and flex your muscles isn't a hardship. Not at all."

She could practically see said muscles relaxing at her words.

"Other than wishing I had a cup of coffee, this is the perfect way to start the day. The sunrise, the beach, the beautiful weather, and watching guys I admire and respect put their bodies through hell, simply to stay in the best shape possible so they're ready at a moment's notice to go off and save people? Yeah. It doesn't suck."

"I'll see what I can do about the coffee thing tomorrow. We'll stop on the way back to my place and get you one this morning though."

"That's not—"

"You want coffee, you'll get coffee," he interrupted. He wasn't smiling, was still staring at her with the same intense look he always wore. "I just wanted to make sure you were good. I know this can't be all that exciting."

"Smiley, I've been living in my car. The only thing to do was people watch—and those people rarely looked like you guys. *That* was boring as hell. This is perfect."

"Okay."

"Okay," she echoed.

"Have to say...I'd do just about anything to see that carefree smile on your face every day. Just wanted to come over and see what caused it, so I can replicate it in the future."

Bree was stunned. She wasn't sure how to respond.

"Shit. And now it's gone," Smiley muttered.

"Smiley! Get your ass back over here!" Kevlar shouted. He was standing with the rest of the guys near the surf. "We're gonna do some shuttle sprints before heading back."

"Oh joy," he sighed.

Bree's lips twitched.

Smiley's gaze locked on her lips. He gave her a chin lift, then turned to head back to his morning workout. He turned around after a few steps and warned, "We're all on watch, but keep an eye out, just in case."

That sobered Bree up. He was right. Here she was, pretending she was on some sort of vacation or something, when in reality there was a reason her ass was on this ATV and Smiley didn't want to let her out of his sight.

Looking around, she saw nothing but a few die-hard morning runners along the beach and the beautiful coastline. His words were a good reminder that her life could change in a split second. She knew that better than anyone.

* * *

PT that morning was shit. Smiley hadn't been able to concentrate on anything except the woman riding the ATV alongside them as they ran. Every time he looked over at Bree, she was smiling as if she was having the time of her life.

By all rights, she should be a mess. Someone was after her, wanted to lock her up and force her into a life no man, woman, or child should ever live. And yet, she was able to find pleasure in the smallest things.

And when Smiley had stopped on the way back to his

apartment and gotten her a vanilla latte, she'd acted as if he'd bought her a freaking diamond or something. But again, that smile on her face was enough to ensure she'd have her sugary coffee drink every morning from here on out.

He'd slipped up that morning with his comment about seeing her smile every day. On top of his assertion last night that they'd have a future together...he was pushing her too hard, too fast. Shit, she'd only known him for a fucking day. But he felt as if he'd known *her* forever. He'd spent so much time looking for her, finding out as much as he could about her life, being with her in person felt like the natural progression.

Thank goodness she hadn't questioned him. Or told him that he was being ridiculous. Or obsessed. He *was*, of course...but he was relieved she hadn't called him on it. With every second he spent with her, it was getting harder to keep his hands to himself. To not throw her onto his kitchen table, his couch, up against the nearest wall, and *beg* her to give him a chance. To let him love her the way he ached to after all these months.

Taking a deep breath, Smiley tried to ignore the small sighs of satisfaction she made while drinking her latte...the memory of hearing his shower this morning, and knowing she was naked inside...the thought of her addictive smiles.

He assumed once he'd found this woman, his obsession would go away. Instead, it had only increased tenfold.

"Why are we meeting with your commander again?" Bree asked, as she and Smiley walked down a long hallway toward the room the team usually used for conferences and meetings.

"Because he knows all about you and your situation.

I've kept him briefed over the last several months," Smiley told her. "He has the ability to take me out of deployment rotation, and I need him to agree to do so. The best chance I have of getting him to do that, is by letting him hear your story firsthand."

Bree stopped dead in the hall and turned to him. "Wait—why would you *not* want to be deployed?"

Smiley couldn't tell if she was kidding or not. "Seriously?"

"Yes."

"I already told you, until this asshole is caught, I'm not letting you out of my sight. And if I get deployed, I can't make sure you're safe."

"I'm not your problem, Smiley. I mean, yes, I'd like your help but in the end, what happens to me *isn't* your responsibility. We don't even know each other!"

"You once made a three-layer birthday cake for your neighbor's five-year-old daughter because she couldn't afford to buy one."

Her brows instantly scrunched down. "Huh?"

"You always worked overtime for coworkers when they needed time off. You regularly went in early and stayed late," Smiley continued. "You visited the retirement home down the street from your apartment every other week."

"Smiley..."

"I know you," he told her. "I've spent the last several months learning *everything* there is to know about you. I've talked to your neighbors, your coworkers...everyone and anyone I could, trying to figure out where you could've gone. Where you were hiding. Not one person had anything bad to say about you."

"Then you must not have talked to the old fart who

lived in the apartment beneath mine. He always complained that I walked too heavily. That I stomped around purposely just to disrupt his life," she murmured.

"I *did* talk to him," Smiley countered. "He was shocked that you'd disappeared. Yeah, he told me that he bitched about you walking too loudly, but admitted that he only did it because you'd bake him homemade cookies to apologize. And since his wife died a few years ago, and he can't cook to save his life, he missed having home-baked sweets."

"Oh my God," Bree whispered.

"I *know* you," he repeated. "And as far as you not being my responsibility, I suppose you're right. But that doesn't mean I don't *want* you to be. The man who's hunting you was going to take Josie away as well. Anyone who hurts one of our own isn't allowed to get away scot-free. And the *last* thing I'm going to do is allow him to take someone else who's important to me—you. So I'm going to circle the wagons, use every resource I have to make sure you're safe, and take that asshole down. But in order to do that, I have to be *here*. Not in a foreign country taking out some terrorist."

Bree blinked—and Smiley was alarmed to see tears in her eyes.

"Oh shit, don't cry. I can't handle it."

She let out a cross between a snort and a chuckle. "You take out terrorists on a regular basis and don't bat an eye, but you can't handle a few tears?"

"No."

"If you ever have a daughter, she's going to have you wrapped around her little finger."

"I don't want kids," he blurted—then wanted to smack

himself in the head. This wasn't the time or place for a conversation about hypothetical future children.

"You don't?"

"No."

She stared at him for so long, Smiley shifted uneasily.

"Are you saying that because of all the research you did on me?"

Smiley frowned. "I don't understand."

"I don't want children either. Most people think I'll change my mind once I fall in love. That my biological clock will start ticking or something. But...I don't think I will. I've never felt a need to have kids. I love them, like playing with *other* people's kids. But don't want any of my own."

That was the moment Smiley knew this woman was meant for him. He already lusted after her. Was intrigued by her. Was desperate to make sure she was safe from the asshole searching for her. But hearing that? Hearing her say exactly what he felt in regard to kids?

He was done for.

"I didn't know that about you," he said.

"Smiley? You gonna stand in the hall all morning or get your ass down here?"

Looking up, he saw his commander's head peeking out from the meeting room. He sounded irritated, which wasn't a good thing.

"Coming, Sir!" he called out.

"Smiley?" Bree asked.

"Yeah?"

"Thanks."

"Nope. What did I say about thanking me? Come on. Let's get this done," he said gruffly, uncomfortable with the feelings coursing through his body. He wanted to snatch Bree up and run away with her. Stash her in a cabin in some remote mountain region, so no one could touch one hair on her head. But he also wanted to integrate her with his friends. Make certain she didn't even consider going back to Vegas once her pursuer was caught.

His fingers brushed the small of her back as he urged her to continue down the hall. He opened the conference room door and gestured for her to precede him.

Entering the room, Smiley wasn't surprised to see not only the commander, but his entire team as well. He hadn't known they'd be there, but since he'd told them about the meeting that morning, it wasn't a huge leap to think they'd want to be here to have his back.

But Bree obviously wasn't expecting to come face-to-face with so many people. She stopped in her tracks just inside the door.

"Oh," she said under her breath.

"I've got three more meetings this morning," the commander said brusquely. "I should've stayed in the field, it would beat sitting on my ass all day, talking to idiots. Not you guys," he added quickly, to clarify.

Smiley led Bree to a seat and took the one next to her. And for the next twenty minutes, Bree went over her story —how she'd broken up with her boyfriend, then was abducted in the parking lot of her apartment complex, ending up in the car where Smiley and Blink had found her. How she'd gotten scared and run from the scene during the capture of her and Josie's kidnapper...and that she'd *been* on the run ever since.

She also explained that she was no longer able to access her bank accounts because every time she did, she suspected she was being followed. The men she'd noticed following her often changed, and that's why she assumed it was some sort of organization after her, determined to get what they'd paid for.

Her ex-boyfriend, Carl, was found dead in Vegas shortly after she'd escaped the city, something Bree only discovered after Kelli had googled the man for her.

All-in-all, she didn't have a lot of concrete information that would help figure out *who* was after her. The *why* they knew: someone had paid a lot of money for her, and he or she wasn't happy that they'd been stiffed. They were obviously determined to retrieve their merchandise—Bree.

She also had a lot of feelings and speculation about being followed, but not a lot of hard evidence. Some people would dismiss her as being paranoid. Would scoff and tell her that she was being ridiculous. But since Smiley and his team often staked their lives on those kinds of "feelings," they were the last group of people to tell her everything was in her head.

"So, Smiley, you want out of the deployment rotation?"

"Yes, Sir."

"For how long?"

"Until we figure this out," Smiley told him without pause.

"That's what I thought. You're talking to Tex this morning?" he asked.

"Yes, Sir. Immediately after this meeting."

He nodded. "With Tex on this, hopefully it won't be too long before it's finished. I assume the rest of you want off the schedule as well?" the commander asked, looking at the other men.

Sounds of "yes, Sir" rang out around the room.

"I *have* been working your team pretty hard, haven't I?" he said, smirking. "And rumor has it that three of you are getting married soon. Figure you might want some time off for honeymoons, huh?"

Smiley's lips twitched as everyone agreed with their commander.

"Fine. Two months. I'll be able to take you out of rotation for two months—but any longer than that, I can't guarantee. Will that be enough time, Smiley?"

"Yes, Sir."

"If you need me for anything, you know where to find me. But being out of rotation doesn't mean time off. You're still expected to be at PT every morning, and you'll have to participate in more meetings."

Everyone groaned but nodded.

"Good. Miss Haynes, I'm glad you're all right. You've found yourself some damn good champions. Do yourself a favor and don't hold back any information about your situation. No matter how uncomfortable it might make you."

"I won't," Bree said softly.

With that, the commander nodded at the men around the table, then stood. "Tell Tex I said hello," he added, before walking through the door, shutting it behind him.

The room was quiet for a moment before MacGyver broke the silence. "I haven't said it officially, and this seems as good a time as any. Thank you, Bree. For what you did for Ellory and Yana."

Bree gave him a small smile. "I didn't do much," she told him.

"Bullshit," Safe said sternly. "From what we understand, you took a hell of a beating for helping the kids get away."

"I can never repay you," MacGyver said. "But anything you need. Anytime. You've got it."

"Same goes for me," Flash added. "Getting into that car with Kelli and her kidnapper was reckless, dangerous, and stupid—and one of the bravest things I've ever seen. If you hadn't been there...hadn't given Smiley updates as to where Kelli was being taken..." His voice trailed off.

"You guys have to know, I was only in both those places because I was stalking you and your girlfriends," Bree admitted. "The commander said not to leave anything out. Well...there you go. I started following you guys around because I wanted to know the kind of people Smiley hung out with, trying to decide if I could trust him. Then I *continued* following you because I was bored. I saw all your cars racing away from MacGyver's house and joined the caravan, that's why I was at that shipyard at the right time. I snuck in through a hole in a fence and just happened on the two girls. I hadn't planned on doing what I did. And I was in the parking lot of Smiley's apartment complex because I was going behind his back and hanging out with Kelli."

"Don't care how it happened, just that it did," Flash said firmly.

"Same," MacGyver agreed.

"Anytime you want to stalk Josie, go for it," Blink added.

Bree's lips quirked up.

"But how about instead of stalking us behind the scenes, you join us instead?" Kevlar said. "Blink and I are getting married in a couple weeks, and we'd love to have you there. If Smiley hasn't already told you, we're having a party afterward at Aces Bar and Grill. I'm assuming you know where that is?"

Bree nodded.

"Good. Our families will be there, Blink's twin brother and his Night Stalker team, Wolf Steel and his team... everyone," Kevlar said.

"I...I'd like that. Thank you. If I'm still here," she added.

"You'll still be here," Preacher said confidently. "Once the women get their claws into you, you won't be able to escape."

Everyone laughed except Smiley. He frowned. Not sure how Bree would take his friend's words.

To his relief, he saw her trying to hold back a smile.

"Maggie's pregnant, right?"

Preacher looked surprised for a moment, then he grinned. "Forgot you're a stalker. Yes, she's pregnant. As is Addison."

"Babies. Who would've thunk it," Kevlar said with a shake of his head. "Now that we've gotten the thank yous out of the way, let's call Tex. He's probably chomping at the bit to talk to Bree."

Blink leaned forward and pulled the phone toward him. Before long, they could all hear it ringing through the speaker.

"About damn time," a man said shortly as he answered.

"Tex. Good to hear from you."

"Whatever. Smiley, I've sent you a package. It's got a few trackers. You should get it today. Bree, you wear them —all the time. I'm not taking any chances with you. Too many women have disappeared, and it's a bitch to find anyone without trackers."

"Um...okay," she said, looking at Smiley with a frown.

"Tex, I'd like to formally introduce you to Bree Haynes," Kevlar said. "Bree, Tex lives out east with his wife and kids and dog. He's a former SEAL turned computer genius. He's nosey as hell, and I have no idea what we'd do without him."

"Hi," Bree said.

Tex went on as if Bree hadn't spoken.

"I'm on this," he said. "I tracked a large sum of money that appeared in your ex's account before you were taken. I traced it back through a series of other accounts to find the source. The organization that wants you is no joke. It's bad news. And unfortunately, it's tied to an asshole who was taken out a few years ago. Del Rio was at the top of his game in Peru before the Mountain Mercenaries and Silverstone took him out."

Smiley looked at Bree to see how she was taking Tex's no-nonsense talk. She was staring at the phone with no expression on her face. Without thought, he reached over and took her hand in his, resting their clasped hands on her thigh. She looked at him briefly, squeezed his hand, then turned her attention back to the phone.

"Tied how?" Safe asked.

"From what I've been able to dig up, the man in charge was one of the guys who used to supply del Rio with women."

"Fuck."

"Are you shitting me?"

"Damn."

Smiley agreed with his teammates. They all knew about del Rio and how ruthless his operation had been. They didn't know any of the Mountain Mercenaries personally, but they'd heard how the leader's wife had been kidnapped while in Las Vegas and held for an entire decade. It was only Rex's relentless determination to find out what happened to her that led to del Rio finally being taken out.

"Yeah, and worse—wait. Who's there? Just your team, Kevlar?"

"And Bree. Why?" Kevlar said.

"Because what I'm about to say will open up a can of worms I'm not sure needs to be opened."

Smiley held his breath. If Tex didn't think the information was good, it had to be very, very bad.

"Mateo Castillo. Has anyone heard of him?" Tex asked.

Everyone replied in the negative.

"He's the head of this particular organization. The one who paid for Bree. The reason I asked if you guys were the only ones there is because...I have reason to believe years and years ago, he was a low-level player in a Mexican trafficking ring—the very one Fiona and Julie were rescued from."

Smiley's breath caught in his throat. *Holy shit*. Could that be true?

"Cookie's going to lose his mind," Flash muttered.

"Not to mention Hurt," Preacher added.

"I don't understand," Bree whispered to Smiley.

But he didn't have time to explain how huge this was. How really, *really* not good this information was.

"Right. Bree? You listening?" Tex asked.

"Yes," she said dutifully.

"You do what Smiley tells you to do. The organization after you is one of the worst. Under no circumstances do you want them to find you. I'm doing what I can behind the scenes to take them out, to hit them where it hurts the most—their bank accounts. But that isn't going to stop what's already in motion. Be smart. Be alert. It's impressive that you've managed to stay one step ahead of them all this time, but it's probably made them more determined than ever to find you and bring you into their organization. Trust me, you don't want that."

Bree nodded, and even though Tex couldn't see her, he went on.

"If the worst happens, *do not panic*. Do whatever you have to in order to stay alive. Understand me? I'm on this. As is every man around that table with you."

Smiley's belly churned. He didn't want to think about Bree falling into this Castillo's hands.

"Okay," Bree agreed.

"No one leaks this info to Cookie, Hurt, or anyone on Wolf's team. I'll talk to them myself when I have more information. I do *not* want Fiona or Julie to have to deal with this until I have confirmation Castillo was involved in the group that abducted them. *And* until we have good news we can give them. Namely, that we know where this asshole is and any threat that might exist is mitigated."

"Do you think Fiona or Julie are in danger?" Preacher asked.

"Honestly? No. It's been years. If Castillo wanted to get his hands on them, he's had more than enough time and money to make a move. And they're outside the age range of women he can easily sell. But just knowing he's out there will send Wolf's entire team on a rampage, and I'd rather concentrate on what I need to do in order to make Bree safe than worry about reining in Cookie and Hurt and the rest of that team."

Smiley wasn't sure he agreed. If he was Cookie and Hurt, he'd want to know about a past threat rearing its ugly head again. But he needed Tex and his expertise, and the last thing he wanted to do was piss the man off.

He'd give Tex some time—but not much. SEALs stuck together. Period. And while Wolf's team might be retired, they were as much Navy SEALs today as they were years ago.

"I'm *going* to tell them," Tex said, as if he could hear the disapproving vibes coming from the seven men around the table through the phone line. "Wolf and his team are some of my closest friends. I don't want to alarm them if it's not necessary. I just need a little bit of time to get more intel. To find this asshole. To make sure he isn't a threat. If I truly thought Julie or Fiona were in danger, I'd be the first one calling them."

That made Smiley feel a little better. Though, very little.

"So, Bree. You did good, girl. But don't let down your guard. I'm on this. As are my people. I have a partner in New Mexico and another in Texas who are doing what they can to track the money trail from Castillo to the people he has looking for you. We'll find them."

"Thank you."

"Don't thank me. I fucking hate thank yous. Just be smart. My blood pressure is already high enough, don't do anything that will make it go even higher. Tex out."

The room went silent after he hung up.

"Fuck. This is not good," Kevlar said after a moment.

Smiley thought that might be the understatement of the century.

"How are you holding up?" MacGyver asked Bree.

She shrugged. "I'm alive and safe. I'm good."

"How much more emotional shit can you take?" he asked.

Smiley frowned at his friend, not sure where he was going with his questions.

"Well...considering the emotional shit I've been through recently, you might as well pile more on."

MacGyver grinned. "This time, hopefully it's *good* emotional shit. Addison is chomping at the bit to meet you. As is Ellory. Thought maybe you and Smiley could come over tonight for dinner."

Bree looked at Smiley, as if checking to see what he thought. He saw the eagerness and excitement in her eyes. He could no sooner deny her anything she wanted than he could kick a defenseless puppy.

He turned to MacGyver. "Six good?"

"Six is perfect. I'll tell Addy."

"I'm going to take Bree to the store to pick up some stuff she needs and stock up on groceries. I also want to be home when the package from Tex arrives. Get Bree set up with the trackers. MacGyver, I'll see you tonight. Everyone else, tomorrow?" Smiley was suddenly eager to get Bree home. Behind locked doors. Of course, they were probably safer here on the base, but there was no telling who Castillo had working for him. After all, look at what happened to Preacher's woman. Maggie's tormenter was under their noses the entire time. Right there. On base.

They all nodded and agreed.

Smiley and Bree headed for the door before anyone could come up with anything else to talk about.

His mind was spinning. If what Tex said was correct, and he had no doubt it was, this Mateo Castillo was even more bad news than he'd originally thought. And Bree was definitely in danger. Anyone who'd survived in the sex slavery industry for as long as Castillo had was obviously cunning and smart. He'd learned to stay under the radar. Probably had tons of connections.

Bree wouldn't be safe until Tex found him and ended him once and for all.

And that couldn't happen fast enough for Smiley's peace of mind.

* * *

Mateo Castillo sat in a parking lot across from the main entrance to the naval base. He'd been so close. *So close* to getting Bree Haynes in his clutches. But the Navy SEAL she was shacking up with wasn't letting her out of his sight. It wasn't going to be as easy as he'd thought to get his hands on her.

Navy SEALs had disrupted his life years ago in Mexico, and they were continuing to make things much more difficult than they needed to be now.

The only reason he was in Riverton at all was because the men he'd sent to retrieve his property had fucked up time and time again. They'd let Bree Haynes slip through their fingers more than once. He knew it was time to step in personally.

And in researching the bitch and the area of California where she'd fled—and the men who'd interrupted his sale in the first place—he'd learned that the two women responsible for fucking up his life so many years ago were *also* living here.

Fiona Storm and Julie Lytle were property of the organization he'd worked for in Mexico. Then the women had been rescued by Navy SEALs. Now they were married to SEALs, as well.

When Mateo realized Bree Haynes was connected to the bitches from years ago, via the man she'd run to for help, he couldn't shake the idea that formed—he'd take *them* too.

All three women would be where they belonged. On their backs, making him money.

He wouldn't keep them, oh no. He already had buyers lined up. Buyers who didn't care how old the bitches were. One in North Korea, one in Russia...but Bree Haynes would stay in Ecuador. Where he was currently located. She'd join the stable he'd set up that closely mirrored the one del Rio had run. He already had most of the police force in his pocket, and in Ecuador, it was easy to bribe government officials.

He had no need for the fourth woman. Josie England. The woman who'd sold her had demanded next to nothing. It was an insignificant loss.

But Bree's ex had negotiated a significant sum. And the other two women...that was personal. Mateo just had to be patient. Eventually the SEALs would let down their guard. Or, more likely, the women would do something stupid. They *always* did.

Right now, the fact that everyone's attention was focused on Bree Haynes could work in his favor for snatching Fiona and Julie, but if he did that, the SEALs would lock down the third woman. No, he needed to wait. See if an opportunity arose to get all of them at the same time. That would be ideal. Swoop in and snatch them before anyone was the wiser.

In the last few weeks, his men had already learned that all the SEALs and their families hung out at a bar called Aces. He figured it was only a matter of time before all the women gathered there together. The more they hung out, the more opportunities he'd have to grab them.

And while he didn't have designs on any others...if he was *able* to get a bonus woman or two? All the better.

Mateo spotted the smaller pickup truck owned by the man Bree Haynes had latched herself to, narrowing his eyes as it exited the base. Her time was coming, he just had to watch and wait. When she least expected it, she'd be his.

CHAPTER FOUR

Smiley looked over at Bree from behind the steering wheel. They'd just parked outside MacGyver's small house. "Are you sure you want to do this? We can put it off."

"I'm sure," she told him. "I'm a little nervous, but it'll be good to see the girls happy and not scared out of their minds."

Honestly, Bree was looking forward to officially meeting Ellory and Yana. When she'd seen them at that shipping yard, they'd been so terrified. From what she could tell from a distance, they'd been doing well since their ordeal. But she wanted to know for certain, to talk to them in person.

And she couldn't help but want to meet Addison too.

Who was she kidding? She wanted to meet *all* the women. She'd been watching them from afar for so long, she felt as if she knew them.

But the truth was, she *didn't* know them. Not at all. She was the creepy stalker who'd watched them from her car, who'd spied on them. If they knew that, they'd probably not want anything to do with her.

She was well on her way to changing her mind now, telling Smiley that she wanted to leave, but it was too late. He'd gotten out of the truck and was walking around to her side.

Taking a huge breath, Bree tried to give herself a pep talk. This would be fine. She'd meet the kids, Addison, eat what was going to be a much better meal than she'd had while living in her car, then go back to Smiley's apartment. She had nothing to be scared about. She didn't need to be best friends with Addison or her kids. People didn't click all the time. It wasn't a big deal if all the women didn't like her.

Shit.

Except it was.

At least to her.

She had no more time to worry because Smiley was opening her door. Like a complete dork, she tried to get out of the car with her seat belt still on. It wasn't the best start to the evening.

Smiley chuckled, and Bree felt her cheeks heat. When she got herself straightened out, she stood. But he didn't step back. In fact, he crowded her against the car, getting into her personal space. One of his hands came up and smoothed a lock of her hair behind her ear. Bree couldn't do anything but stare at him.

"Breathe, Bree. This is going to be fine."

She nodded.

"If I didn't think so, there's no way in hell you'd be here," he went on. "I'd never expose you to any kind of situation where there was the slightest chance you'd be hurt...physically or emotionally."

"Smiley," Bree protested, feeling overwhelmed all over again.

"This is new to me," he told her.

"This?" she asked, when he didn't elaborate.

"Being with someone I can't stop thinking about. Who I constantly worry about. After I've spent months wondering what she's thinking and doing, at all hours. It's...disconcerting."

She couldn't help it. She snorted. "Yeah."

His head tilted. "You feel it too?"

Bree nodded.

"Does it make me a dick to be relieved that I'm not the only one?"

She smiled up at him. "No."

"Fuck. That smile. You have no idea what it does to me. Come on, we need to get in the house. I don't like standing outside like this."

And just like that, the reality of her situation hit home once more. She wasn't a normal woman on a date. She was the target of a scary man who wanted to find her and force her to have sex with men for money. And that *sucked*.

"Damn, I didn't mean to scare you," Smiley said, as he led her toward MacGyver and Addison's front door.

"You didn't," Bree tried to reassure him.

"Bullshit. Don't lie to me. Don't say what you think I want to hear. Be honest with me. Always. Because I don't know how to be any other way."

Bree looked at the man at her side as they approached the door. He was so rough around the edges. A little paranoid, if the way he was eyeballing their surroundings was any indication. He was honest to a fault and didn't seem to give a crap how he looked...but then, he looked good no matter what he was wearing, or even if he hadn't remembered to brush his hair—which he hadn't. It was kind of sticking up all over his head in a way Bree assumed he might look after sleeping.

But she couldn't deny that with every minute they spent together, she was drawn to him more and more.

"Did you hear me, Bree?" he asked.

"Yeah. You didn't scare me, but I *am* a little nervous in general. About tonight, about this Mateo guy, about everything."

Smiley nodded. "I'd be worried if you weren't. But we're on this. All of us. My team, Tex, the commander, everyone."

Bree opened her mouth to thank him once more, but the door in front of them was jerked open and a girl stood there. Ellory. Bree would recognize her anywhere.

To her absolute shock, the girl threw herself at her.

Bree went back on a foot to keep herself from falling, and she wrapped her arms around the girl, who was hugging her as if her life depended on it. Thankfully Smiley already had his hand on the small of her back, because he kept her from literally falling on her ass with Ellory in her arms.

"Ellory!"

Looking through the door, Bree saw a tall redhaired woman shaking her head but smiling at Ellory with love. "I'm sorry, she was so excited to meet you. I'm Addison. Come in. Please."

Ellory let go of Bree and took a step backward. "I'm sorry too. I couldn't wait another second to thank you."

"El, back up, let them in," Addison scolded gently.

"Sorry, yeah! Come in, come in. We've been cooking nonstop since we got home from school. I can't eat a lot of what we made, but it smells delicious. And Yana helped too."

Bree smiled at the enthusiasm of the young girl. She'd heard about her Crohn's disease from Smiley, so she wasn't surprised at her mention that she wouldn't be eating the same as everyone else.

She stepped into the house and saw Smiley give MacGyver a chin lift, and that made her grin. It was such a guy thing to do. But before she could comment on it, Ellory took her hand. "Come on, Yana's excited to meet you! And so are Artem and Borysko."

"*Ellory*. You're being rude," Addison told her with a frown.

"Oh, she's fine. I'm excited to meet everyone," Bree said.

"But *I* haven't even gotten a chance to officially meet you yet," the woman grumbled.

It was a weird feeling to be the center of attention, to be the one people were arguing about meeting first.

"I'm Bree," she blurted, sticking her hand out toward Addison.

The other woman ignored it and stepped toward her, hugging her just as hard as her daughter had moments earlier.

Bree felt, more than heard, Addison's breath hitch as she hugged her.

"Thank you. You have no idea what you did," Addison said softly.

"I didn't do anything anyone else wouldn't have," she protested.

Addison pulled back and ran her gaze up and down Bree's body. "Are you okay? Ricky said you were hurt. That the man hurt you."

"I'm okay," Bree assured her. The genuine concern she sensed in Addison's words felt like a warm blanket after basically being an outcast for so long. After being on the periphery of life.

Tears filled Addison's eyes and she sniffed loudly. MacGyver wrapped his arm around her waist and pulled her against him. She went willingly.

"She cries at the drop of a hat lately," he explained. "Pregnancy hormones."

Bree smiled. "Congratulations."

"Thanks. And I'm not crying because I'm pregnant," she complained. "Okay, not *entirely* because of that. I just… you got hurt protecting my kids. I'm allowed to cry about that."

"Mom, I'm *fine*. Yana's fine. Can I please bring her to the kitchen to meet her now? Besides, I probably need to check on her anyway, make sure she's not about to burn down the house."

"She's fine," MacGyver said. "And she's in the living room now, watching TV with her brothers."

"Whatever," Ellory said with a roll of her eyes.

Bree couldn't help but laugh out loud. This meeting wasn't anything like what she imagined it would be.

Ellory smiled at her and reached for her hand. "Come on. We'll see if we can peel everyone away from the TV."

Bree looked back at Smiley and saw him watching her

with a look she couldn't interpret, but the pleasure in his eyes was easy to see.

She let herself get dragged into another room, where two boys and Yana were sitting on the couch, staring at the TV as if mesmerized. Her belly growled at the delicious scent of Italian seasoning coming from the kitchen. Whatever Addison and Ellory had been cooking smelled divine.

"Yana, this is Bree. She's the woman who helped us when the bad man took us. Remember?"

Yana looked toward them, and her eyes widened. She made a little squeaking noise in the back of her throat, and she practically flew off the couch, toward Bree.

Surprised once more at the exuberant greeting, Bree went to a knee and held the little girl, who was shaking as she hugged her. "I guess she remembers," she told Ellory quietly.

The preteen was beaming and nodding. "Yeah. We talked about what happened a lot with our therapist. And while everything was scary, the best part was when you appeared and helped us get away."

"Thank you for saving our sister. I'm Artem."

"And I'm Borysko. Yes, thank you."

The two boys had stood, and each put a hand on their sister's shoulder to try to comfort her.

Bree felt overwhelmed. She'd just been in the right place at the right time. And the only reason she'd been there at all was because she was a stalker. Had been spying on Smiley and his friends. Wondering what was happening and why everyone was racing to the shipyard. Besides, she hadn't actually saved anyone; she'd just led the asshole kidnapper away to give the girls time to get to the SEALs, who'd been desperately searching for them.

Yana lifted her head and looked at Bree. "Wanna see my dolls?"

Blinking at the abrupt change of subject, she nodded.

"Not her dolls again," Borysko said in disgust.

Artem simply shrugged and turned back to the TV.

"Ten minutes," Ellory told her sister. "Then it'll be time to eat."

Yana nodded, and Bree found herself following the little girl toward her room. It was obvious she shared it with Ellory, because half the room was filled with books and toys appropriate for someone Yana's age, and the other half was more fitting for a teenager.

Ten minutes later, something made Bree look toward the door.

Smiley was propped against the doorjamb with a hint of a smile on his face, watching her. She was surrounded by what felt like a hundred Barbie dolls, and Yana had been babbling nonstop ever since she'd plopped down on the floor and began introducing Bree to each and every one. She spoke in a mixture of Ukrainian and English, and it was absolutely adorable.

Even though Bree could only understand half of what the girl said, she continually nodded and smiled. The little girl was open and loving, and Bree figured that was because MacGyver and Addison were great parents. They made Yana feel safe, which was probably the most important thing at this point in her young life. Smiley had told Bree all about how the three Ukrainian children had come to live with MacGyver and Addison, and she could only be amazed at how well adjusted they seemed after their ordeal.

Bree touched Yana's arm and said, "I think dinner is ready."

Smiley nodded, letting her know her assumption as to his appearance was correct.

"Sketti!" Yana exclaimed, jumping up and running toward the door. Smiley scooted out of her way at the last second to avoid a collision as the little girl disappeared into the hallway.

Bree was slower to get up; she wasn't old, not in the least, but she wasn't quite as nimble as Yana. By the time she got to her feet, Smiley was in front of her.

"Wanted to check on you."

"I'm fine."

He studied her face for a long moment before nodding, then put his hand on the small of her back and urged her toward the door. "I don't know about you, but the last ten minutes have been torture smelling that dinner."

Bree grinned. "You too?"

"Oh yeah."

They walked into the living room, and Bree headed for the kitchen. "Anything I can do to help?" she asked Addison.

"Nope. You and Smiley can sit. The kids are responsible for setting the table and bringing food in."

Bree looked toward the large table just off the kitchen, smiling when she saw the name cards the kids had made. She was apparently sitting between Ellory and Yana, which was fine with her. Smiley was directly across from Bree. Perfect. She could stare at him all she liked without seeming too obvious about it.

Except, as the meal progressed, every time she looked up, Smiley's gaze was already on *her*. It was both nerve-racking and exciting to be the center of his attention.

Conversation around the table was lively, and by the time they'd all finished eating the spaghetti and meatballs with garlic bread and cheese-crusted broccoli, Bree was not only full, she felt as if she'd known this family forever.

After dinner, she helped Artem and Borysko with the dishes, and then everyone settled into the living room to talk until it was time for the younger kids to go to bed. Bree found herself reading a book—or three—to Yana in her room, and by the time she arrived back in the living room, found Ellory sitting at the kitchen table wearing a pair of headphones, working on a laptop, and the adults chatting quietly on the couches.

Bree sat next to Smiley, loving how their thighs touched as the cushions sagged, pushing her closer to him.

"So...welcome to our crazy," Addison said with a small laugh.

"It wasn't so bad," Bree said immediately.

"Well, it'll just get crazier with the addition of this one," she said, putting a hand on her belly.

Talk turned to Addison's pregnancy, then to the kids' improving English, then to Ellory's current Crohn's treatment, and finally to the other women in their SEAL family. Ellory got up and kissed her mom, hugged MacGyver, said good night to Smiley and Bree then disappeared down the hall. And still the adults talked.

There was never a lull in the conversation, and Bree discovered that MacGyver was actually funny—and very much in love with his wife and family. He might not be the biological father to the four kids living under his roof, but he adored them as if he was.

Bree had no idea how late it had gotten until Addison said something about PT in the morning. Looking at her watch, she was startled to see it was almost midnight. Smiley and MacGyver—and her too, since she was going everywhere Smiley went—had to be up in four and a half hours.

"Thanks for coming over," Addison told her, when everyone had stood. She gave her a heartfelt hug as she said it.

Bree loved being included. It was a heady feeling.

"Thanks for having me."

"I said it before but...thank you. Seriously. You have no idea how much what you did means to me and my family. If there's anything you ever need, it's yours."

Bree gave her a small smile. "They're great kids. All of them. You guys are doing an amazing job."

"It's all Addison," MacGyver said.

His wife rolled her eyes, looking so much like Ellory that Bree couldn't help but laugh.

"Sorry. My daughter is obviously rubbing off on me," she said.

"We'll see you tomorrow," Smiley told MacGyver.

"I'll walk you out," the other man said in a firm tone.

The easygoing evening suddenly shifted for Bree. MacGyver's words were a reminder that she wasn't a woman on a casual date with her new boyfriend. Because Smiley *wasn't* her boyfriend, he was...what was he? Her protector, her bodyguard. But she had deeper feelings for him than she'd had for any man before. It was so confusing.

She walked out between Smiley—who had his hand on the small of her back, which she was already getting way too used to—and MacGyver. Both men's heads were on swivels as if expecting the boogeyman to jump out from behind one of the bushes in the yard. Smiley got her settled in his truck and shut the door. He and MacGyver exchanged a few words, then he joined her inside the vehicle.

"Is everything all right?" she asked, as soon as he started the engine.

"Yes."

"Would you tell me if it wasn't?" she asked, a touch sarcastically.

He turned to her with a brow raised in surprise.

Bree sighed. "Sorry. That was rude."

"No, it wasn't. You're allowed to feel what you feel."

"I just...the night was so good. I forgot exactly who I was for a moment."

Now Smiley was frowning. "Who you are...?"

"Yeah. A homeless stalker who forced myself into your life and the lives of your friends. I'm bringing danger to *everyone*. Even Fiona and Julie, women I haven't even met but who could be in this guy's crosshairs because of me. I should leave, Smiley," she finished, her tone low and anxious.

He just stared at her for a moment...then backed his truck up without a word and headed for his apartment.

Bree bit her lip and stared out the side window. He hadn't disagreed with her—which spoke volumes. Maybe her blunt statement managed to put things in perspective for him.

She was a huge headache to *everyone*. Smiley didn't

want to let her out of his sight, which had to be a pain in his ass. Hell, he'd had to ask his commander not to deploy him just so he could babysit her. The man couldn't even do his *job* because of her.

By the time they arrived back at Smiley's place, Bree was a mess.

When he turned off the engine, he got out, then motioned for her to climb across the front cab and exit on his side.

Still lost in her own misery, Bree didn't even ask why. She simply did as he said. As soon as she was close enough, Smiley took her hand in his and helped her step out. He quickly walked them through the front door and into the elevator, all without saying a word.

Depression swamped Bree. This was it. He was obviously waiting until he got inside his apartment to tell her that she was right. She was too much of a liability. That she should go.

Feeling a sense of loss that hurt more than any actual breakup she'd ever had in her life, Bree watched him unlock his apartment door and swing it open for her. She stepped inside...

Then gasped slightly when Smiley took her shoulders in his hands and backed her against the closed, locked door.

"Listen to me, Bree. Are you listening?"

She stared up at a very frowny Smiley and nodded. She didn't know where to put her hands. So she pressed her palms against the door behind her.

"You aren't going *anywhere*. You aren't homeless—you live *here*. You didn't force yourself into my life—hell, woman,

I've been searching for you for months. I *wanted* you in my life, and yet you were too smart to let yourself be found. If Fiona and Julie are in anyone's crosshairs, it isn't because of you. It's because some asshole is an asshole. Got it?"

She stared up at him. Speechless.

Smiley took a deep breath. "I don't want you to go. I've just found you. And now that I'm getting to know you, watching you with my friends, with the kids tonight, I'm already realizing that I've been missing out on a fuck of a lot. You light up a room when you enter, and you have a way of making everyone your friend. Within seconds of meeting you, Yana wanted to share her most prized possessions with you—her dolls.

"You need me, Bree. Need my expertise. Need my friends to help find this Castillo fucker and take him out once and for all. But more importantly, I need *you*. I can't tell you how long it's been since I've hung out with one of my teammates at their homes. I...I've missed it. MacGyver is a great guy, and seeing him with his family was nice, and eye-opening, and overdue. I need you to remind me that there's more to life than working. That there are people out there who are good and kind. Who aren't just all about themselves."

Somehow, Bree's hands had moved from the door to Smiley's shirt, gripping it at his waist.

"Will you stay? With me? Let me find this guy and make sure he understands you're off-limits?"

Bree couldn't say no to that. She nodded.

"Good. And no more talk about you being anything except an amazing friend, a brave-as-fuck person who's willing to step in and help perfect strangers, and the woman I'm becoming addicted to, who fascinates the hell out of me."

"Um..."

"And no arguing. I'm right. Just ask any of my friends. I'm *always* right."

"Cocky," Bree muttered, but she couldn't stop the smile that crossed her lips.

"I swear I'd slay dragons and make a complete ass of myself if only to see that smile on your lips," he murmured. Not giving her time to respond, he eased back and pushed her gently toward the hall. "Go get ready for bed. I have to get up way too early. And since I have to get up, so do you."

"I like watching you guys work out," Bree admitted. "As long as I don't have to run alongside you and can ride the ATV, I'm good."

"I'm glad, because until we find Castillo, your ass is gonna be on that ATV right by my side. We have to leave before the coffee place is open, but I'll make you a cup to go before we leave in the morning." When she just stared at him, he added, "Well? What are you standing there for? Go get changed, woman!"

Fighting another smile, Bree headed for the bedroom, where the few things she owned had been stashed. They were washed and folded, and seeing them stacked neatly in her suitcase on the floor in Smiley's room gave her heart a little twinge. The man she was living with was more than a badass SEAL. He was considerate and went out of his way to make her life as easy as possible. She could get used to having him around...except this was probably temporary. Once he found this Mateo person, she'd likely be moving on.

He said that he wanted more, that he was "addicted" to her, but once her situation was solved, and she prayed that would be soon, he might feel differently. Get tired of her. She hoped not, but Bree didn't want to get her hopes up and be crushed if he decided she wasn't what he wanted after all.

The thought hurt, so she pushed it down. She needed to worry about today, not tomorrow. Thinking about the future was a useless endeavor. She had no idea what tomorrow would bring, so she had to live in the moment. And for now, she was going to do what she could to enjoy being with Smiley.

CHAPTER FIVE

The next few days went by quickly. Smiley brought Bree with him to PT every morning, then they'd go back to his apartment, shower and change, eat breakfast, and head back to the base.

He had plenty of meetings, but Bree seemed content to settle herself in one of the unused offices nearby.

The trackers Tex had sent arrived the same day as their call with the man, as promised, and Smiley was pleased with the assortment. Bree didn't seem as excited, but she'd admitted that was more because she couldn't help thinking about the *reason* why she needed to wear the earrings with the trackers embedded. Or the necklace. Or the barrette. Tex had even sent a belt that had a tracker in the buckle. The note included in the box instructed her to switch up which tracker she wore each day, in case anyone was watching her.

That had freaked Bree out. It wasn't as if she was being naïve and refusing to believe she was being hunted. She'd spent time on the run for that very reason. It was more about how blunt Tex had been, and that, along with the trackers, apparently had the situation sinking in that much more. She'd admitted as much to Smiley but, thankfully, wore the trackers without complaint.

Now, today was the day Bree was set to meet Julie Hurt and Fiona Knox. They were getting together at Julie's secondhand clothing store, My Sister's Closet. Bree had been resisting getting more clothes, saying she had plenty back in storage in Las Vegas and she didn't want to spend any more of Smiley's money than she had already.

But Smiley was determined to see her expand her wardrobe. It wasn't that he actually cared what she wore, but seeing the same four outfits over and over hurt his heart...because it was a reminder that those few items were all she owned in the world.

Well, all she had access to at the moment.

He strode out of the conference room he'd been holed up in for a few hours with his team and headed straight for the office where he'd left Bree. When he opened the door, he panicked when he didn't immediately see her. Then every muscle in his body relaxed when he saw she was lying on the small couch, curled into a ball, fast asleep. Her hands under her head as a makeshift pillow.

They'd been staying up late talking, playing cards, watching TV, as if neither of them wanted to end their time together. And of course, they'd been getting up early for PT. It was no wonder she was napping. He wanted to let her sleep, but if they were going to get to My Sister's Closet to meet with the women, they needed to leave.

He'd taken a single step toward her when his phone

vibrated. Stopping to look at it, Smiley frowned when he saw Cookie had texted.

Cookie: Change of plans. We're meeting at Caroline's house instead of the store.
Smiley: Why?
Cookie: My job is not to ask why, it's simply to show up when and where I'm told.

Smiley wasn't happy about the change. He was used to going with the flow while on missions, but he'd been looking forward to finding some new outfits for Bree. He started to reply, but was interrupted.

"Why are you frowning? What's wrong?"

She sounded stressed. That was no way for Bree to wake up.

He immediately wiped all expression from his face and shoved his cell in his pocket. Soothing Bree was more important than arguing with Cookie. "Nothing's wrong. I was just about to wake you."

"Don't lie to me," she said, sitting up.

"I'm not. I promise, nothing's wrong. Cookie was just telling me that instead of meeting at Julie's store, we're going to Caroline's house."

"Why?"

"I don't know. But it's not a big deal. Caroline is probably just anxious to meet you. She gets a little cranky when she has to wait too long to meet new members of our crew."

"You looked upset," she pressed.

"Because I wanted to get you some new outfits. And I wanted to ask Julie to source some things she thought you'd like and send them to the apartment. I figured if they simply arrived, you wouldn't be able to say no."

To Smiley's relief, Bree's shoulders relaxed, and she lost the concerned expression she had a moment ago.

"I won't lie to you, Bree. I don't know how many times you need to hear it, but I'll keep reminding you as much as necessary. And if I find out something about Castillo, I'll tell you. It's in your best interest to be as informed as you can be."

"Thank you."

"Would you rather go back to my place and nap? We can meet Julie, Fiona, and Caroline another day."

"You don't have to buy me clothes," she said, instead of answering his question.

Smiley sighed. "I know. But I hate that you only have four outfits. You should have a closetful of clothes."

"I do," she reminded him. "But at the moment, they're in boxes in storage in Vegas. You said yourself that it wouldn't be smart to have someone go there and get them, in case the unit's being watched."

He *had* said that. Frustration ate at Smiley. He wanted to give this woman the world. Wanted to see her clothes overflowing out of his closet. Wanted to give her space in his drawers.

Needed to see her occupying more of his life than the simple corner of his bedroom where her suitcase currently sat.

Bree stood and walked over to him, putting a hand on his arm. "Is it that important to you that I have more clothes?"

"Yes," he said simply.

"Okay."

"Okay?" he asked.

"Yeah. I'll talk to Julie. See if she can pick out some stuff—but I'm *not* going overboard."

Smiley's lips quirked upward. "Great."

"I think you should do that more often."

"What?"

"Smile."

"Then we're even. Because seeing you laugh or grin, when it's obvious you haven't had reason to recently, makes me feel ten feet tall."

"You mean you aren't already ten feet tall?" she joked.

This woman. She was killing him. "You didn't answer my question," he reminded her. "Are we going to Caroline's house or my apartment?"

"Caroline's," Bree said. "I want to meet Julie and Fiona. From everything I've heard about them, they sound amazing. They survived what Mateo has in store for me. I think it's important to hear their stories from their own lips."

"That isn't your future," Smiley growled.

"I know. I just...I think seeing them, knowing they survived hell, it'll give me confidence that *if* something happens, I can too."

Smiley wanted to protest again. Tell her that nothing was going to happen to her. That he'd rather die than see her in the clutches of an asshole like Castillo, but he knew as well as she did that he couldn't promise her safety. He couldn't read the future. All he could do was make sure she was as prepared as she could be for the worst, and use every ounce of his training and connections to ensure she never had to experience anything remotely like what had happened to Fiona and Julie.

Looking her in the eye, Smiley said, "I have no doubt that if the shit hits the fan, you'll kick some major ass."

She smiled up at him, and again his heart skipped a beat. "Thanks. That means a lot coming from you. The badass Navy SEAL that you are."

Smiley shook his head and gestured toward the door with his head. "You ready to go?"

"I'm ready," she said, sounding a little lighter than she had after waking up and seeing him scowling at his phone.

Twenty minutes later, they were pulling up in front of Caroline's house. Except they had to park three houses down because of the number of cars lining the street. Smiley should've known the reason for the change of venue was because *all* the women on Cookie's team wanted in on the meeting with Bree.

"Um...there are a lot of cars here," she said, after they'd gotten out of his truck.

Smiley sighed. This being social thing wasn't easy. He'd gotten used to his solitary life. But in the less-than-a-week since he'd found Bree—or rather, she'd found *him*—he'd spent more time with his fellow SEALs and their women and families than he had in months.

"This was *not* my idea," he told her. "I thought this was going to be Fiona, Cookie, Julie, Hurt, Caroline, and Wolf. But apparently word's gotten out and everyone wants to meet you."

"Everyone?"

Looking at Bree, Smiley was relieved to see that she didn't look freaked out, simply curious.

"Yeah. From the cars, it looks like Wolf's entire team is

here. And who knows if any of them brought their kids or not. It's gonna be a mad house in there even *without* them. We can still leave." He held his breath, hoping she'd take him up on that offer.

To his surprise, Bree stepped in front of him and tilted her head back to keep eye contact. She put a hand in the middle of his chest and said, "If you need to go, we go."

Smiley frowned. "This isn't about me."

"It's about both of us. And you forget—*stalker*. I already know you aren't very comfortable in social situations. You're always the first to leave any kind of get-together with your friends. You stand off to the side, and you don't often initiate conversation. You're more of a stand-back-and-observe kind of guy. It wasn't very cool of your friends to spring this on us. We can go, I can meet Julie and Fiona another day."

Smiley closed his eyes, afraid if he looked into her bottomless gaze, saw the compassion and concern for him one second longer, he'd grab her, haul her back into his truck, and take her back to his apartment to keep her all to himself forever. But he wasn't a selfish man, or at least he tried not to be. And Bree needed to meet the other women. See for herself that life moved on, things worked out, adversity could be overcome.

"Smiley?" she asked in a quiet, concerned tone.

He opened his eyes—and couldn't stop himself from burying one hand in her hair and wrapping his other arm around her waist. She fell against him with a small *oof*, her other hand joining the first on his chest. But she didn't push him away. Simply continued to look at him with that empathetic and gentle way she had. She made him feel as if they were the only two people in the world.

"I'm a little...*miffed* that Cookie didn't warn me that they'd all be here. But they mean well. And they're my friends. I look up to these men. They're legendary in our circles. The things they've been through, that their women have been through, it's enough to bring lesser people to their knees. I can handle them. I just want to make sure no one is pushing *you* too hard. This is all new to you. You've been living a very solitary life for months. If this gets overwhelming, just tell me and we'll leave."

"Does the reverse also apply?"

"Meaning?"

"If *you're* feeling overwhelmed, will you let me know you want to leave?" she asked.

It was in that moment when Smiley understood he was going to do whatever it took to make sure this woman never wanted to leave him—ever.

He'd always known he wanted her, didn't want her to leave Riverton, either now or when her troubles were over. But in the back of his mind, he figured if she insisted on leaving, he'd have to let her go.

Now, he knew he'd fight to keep her. Turn his entire world upside down for her. He'd leave his grumpy disposition behind, turn into a social butterfly...hell, change everything about himself if it meant somehow convincing Bree to stay with him forever.

He needed her. It was that simple.

"Smiley? I'm serious. I admit that I want to meet your friends, especially since I've heard so much about them, but not if it makes you uncomfortable."

"I'm fine. And yeah, if I want to go, I'll let you know."

"Good. Should we have a code word? Oh! I know, how about a signal? Tugging on our ear? No, that's too obvious. Maybe I can, I don't know, blow my nose or something?"

Smiley chuckled. "How about you just tell me, or I'll tell you."

She wrinkled her nose. "That would be rude."

"Trust me, Bree, the men and women you're about to meet won't think it's rude. They'd appreciate you coming out and saying what you feel."

She looked doubtful, but she nodded. "All right. Deal. Then I'm thinking we should probably get inside and stop standing out here like a couple of psychos."

Her words snapped Smiley back to reality. He was an idiot. Castillo's men were out there somewhere, probably watching and waiting. Maybe even the man himself—and he had Bree standing out in the open as if they didn't have a care in the world.

To his surprise, Bree went up on her tiptoes and kissed his cheek. "If I forget to tell you later, thank you for this. For introducing me to Fiona and Julie. For letting me meet your friends. Being on the inside, instead of the outside looking in, is a gift."

"Anything you want or need, I'll do my best to give it to you," he vowed.

She gave him a grin, then turned toward the house.

He was forced to drop his hand from her hair, but he kept his other arm around her waist as they walked toward the door. It opened before they got there, and then Caroline was beaming at them.

"It's about time!" she said happily. "I thought you were going to stand on my lawn forever. Then I thought you were going to bolt. For the record, this wasn't my idea. Fiona told me about meeting you, and I suggested that maybe it would be more comfortable for you to talk here at the house instead of Julie's store. One thing led to another, and everyone wanted in on the action, and here we are! If you want to run, I don't blame you, but I promise we're all harmless. Oh, sorry. I'm Caroline," she said belatedly, holding out her hand.

Bree shook it and gave her a genuine smile. "I'm happy to meet you. I've heard a lot about you."

"I'm sure you have. Not all of it good." She grinned as she said it, then stepped back and gestured inside with her arm. "Come in. Please. I've got plenty of appetizers and snacks. Do you want something to drink?"

"I'm good, thanks," Bree told her.

Smiley walked behind the women as they headed toward the living room. The second they entered the crowded space, Bree was surrounded. Everyone was very eager to meet the woman who'd been the talk of the SEAL gossip network for months now.

Keeping a close eye on her, Smiley backed up and let Caroline do her thing. From what he understood, she'd come a long way from the shy, nerdy woman Wolf had met all those years ago, when they were on a plane together and shit went south. She'd survived some pretty horrific stuff and had blossomed throughout the years. She was the one all the others looked up to, the unofficial leader of the wives.

"Sorry about this," Cookie said as he came up beside Smiley and leaned against the wall, watching the women welcome Bree into their fold.

"Are you?" he couldn't help but ask.

Cookie grinned. "Not really. You know this had to happen sooner or later. Might as well get it over with in one fell swoop. Besides, we're all going to be at Aces at Kevlar and Blink's wedding reception soon, it'll be more comfortable for everyone to meet now rather than then."

He wasn't wrong. But Smiley was still perturbed that he hadn't warned him everyone would be here for this little meet and greet.

"Come on, man. Lighten up. This is a good thing. Look, they're already all getting along so well!" Cookie said, gesturing to the women with his head.

They were. Bree was sitting on the couch between Fiona and Jessyka, and the others had pulled up chairs Caroline had strategically placed around the room, so everyone could have a seat. They were all laughing and talking exuberantly. He wasn't surprised Bree was fitting in so seamlessly.

"Hey," Wolf said as he approached, with the rest of his team following.

The men in this room really were legendary. Smiley hadn't lied when he'd told Bree that he looked up to them. The missions they'd been on, the things they'd survived against all odds, would make current Hollywood movies seem tame. And yet they were all down-to-earth and dismissive of what they'd done. And now that they were retired, their entire worlds were their families. Smiley had always been a little envious of what they had.

But now, maybe he was on the cusp of having the same thing.

With Bree.

He hoped.

Most would consider it a ridiculous idea, considering he'd known the woman for two-point-three seconds. How could he be thinking about a long-term relationship? But he was. He knew in his bones that she was *it* for him. His one chance to have what his friends had found. What all the men standing around Caroline's living room had found.

And he was scared shitless that he'd fuck it up.

"How's she holding up?" Benny asked.

"We've heard whoever's looking for her has been able to hide his tracks from Tex so far," Abe said.

"You need anything, we're here," Mozart added.

All of a sudden, Smiley felt the intense weight of the information he was keeping from these men. That Mateo Castillo might be involved in what had happened to Fiona and Julie all those years ago. They'd want to know...but he'd agreed to give Tex a little more time to be sure.

"I appreciate it," he told the others.

"For the record, I think this is a good thing," Patrick Hurt said. He was older than Wolf and the others, that team's previous commander. But he still looked younger than his years, and the silver in his hair gave him a distinguished vibe rather than an "old man" appearance. "Julie's been looking forward to talking with Bree."

Smiley nodded, but inside, he was having second thoughts. Suddenly, he wasn't sure what Fiona or Julie could tell Bree that wouldn't completely scare the shit out of her.

"Trust them," Cookie said, as if he could read Smiley's mind. "They aren't going to freak her out. They'll follow her lead and only talk about the things she's open to discussing."

"Caroline figured we could all mingle for a while first, let Bree get comfortable, meet all of us, then the others will head out, letting Fiona and Julie talk with her for a bit," Wolf told him.

"And I'm sure you probably have questions for me," Cookie told him. "I was there. I saw the condition they were both in. The compound. How they were being restrained. I thought you and I could talk while our women are getting acquainted."

Smiley looked at the older man. "You're okay with that? Talking about it?"

"Honestly? No. I hate even *thinking* about that day. About how I found Fee. How freaked out Julie was. It doesn't bring back good memories. But I figured it might help you to hear a firsthand account of their rescue from those scumbags."

It took all his legendary SEAL control not to blurt out that Cookie's info might come in handy even more than he thought. But he was able to keep his mouth shut.

Cookie and Hurt were going to lose their shit if Tex confirmed the man who'd bought Bree was also part of the organization that had held their women hostage years ago. He didn't want to be anywhere near them if that little tidbit of information was dropped into their laps.

"I appreciate it," Smiley managed to say.

Caroline called Wolf over then, and the other men eventually trailed after him, waiting their turn to be officially introduced to Bree.

Smiley kept a close watch on her and, to his relief, she seemed perfectly at ease with the other women and the former SEALs. Her manners were impeccable, she was charming and funny, and it was as if everyone in the room was drawn to her like a fly to honey.

And Bree seemed to blossom in front of his eyes. It was obvious she needed to be around other people. To be social. It struck Smiley not only how hard it must have been for her, living in her vehicle for months, no contact with anyone...but also how much his life was about to change. He wasn't too upset about it. Seeing Bree in her element made him forget about everything else.

It was surprising how fast the time went. Before he knew it, most of the group was saying their goodbyes to Bree and telling her they'd see her at Aces for the wedding reception. Soon, there were only Fiona, Julie, their husbands, Wolf and Caroline, and he and Bree left.

"I poured you all a glass of wine. Thought we could head out to the patio to talk," Caroline told the women.

"Thank you."

"I could use some for sure."

Bree stayed silent, but she followed the others into the kitchen for one of the glasses of wine Caroline had poured.

Smiley intercepted her as she was on her way to the backyard. "You good?"

"Yeah. You?"

"I'm good as long as you're good," he told her honestly.

Bree rolled her eyes. "Smiley, I don't want you staying if you're miserable."

"I'm not miserable. Not in the least," he reassured her. "Seeing you making friends, smiling, being a part of this close-knit group of people...it makes me happy."

"Me too. I've loved meeting everyone today, but I have to admit I can't wait to get to know your teammates' women better. They're closer to my age, and while it's obvious Caroline and the others have a lot of experience with life in general, I want to get to know Josie, Remi, Wren, and all the others more, because they're your best friends' best friends. If that makes sense."

"It does," Smiley said, feeling a warmth spread throughout his body. This woman, she constantly surprised and awed him. She'd been dealt a shitty hand, and yet she was still gracious and kind. He would protect that at all costs.

She smiled at him, then followed Fiona and Julie out the sliding glass door to the deck behind the house. They got settled into chairs and began to talk.

CHAPTER SIX

"With the way your man is watching you, I have a feeling we don't have all day to chat," Fiona said with a grin.

Bree looked toward the doors and saw Smiley standing where she'd left him. His gaze was fixed on her. She gave him a small smile, letting him know everything was fine, then turned back toward the two women sitting with her.

Julie Hurt was a tiny woman. Probably not too much above five feet tall, and slender to boot. Fiona Knox was tall, maybe just a couple inches shorter than Smiley. Both women had flawless skin and little wrinkles next to their eyes that made Bree assume they laughed a lot. They seemed happy and healthy, as if they didn't have a care in the world.

But Bree knew better. Knew the face people showed to the world could mask a lot of hurt in their past.

"I'll start. I don't know what you've been told about what happened to us," Julie said.

Bree shook her head. "Just that you were both

kidnapped and brought south of the border, with the intent of being sold into the sex slavery industry."

"That sounds so clinical," Fiona mused, taking a large swallow of wine.

"I'm sorry, I—"

"No, don't be sorry," Fiona interrupted quickly. "I just meant, that's right. That's exactly what happened, but it's kinda like saying a hurricane is a little storm. Or a tornado is a little wind." She took a deep breath. "Right, so...I was taken when I was in a club by myself in Florida. I was there on vacation. I was chained to the floor of a hut for my 'training period.' When I refused to do what my captors wanted, they drugged me. I mean, I guess they were drugging me before that, but they turned up the pressure big time. Denying me food, letting me sit in my own filth, raping me, chaining me to the floor by my neck...you name it, they did it. But I still refused to do what they wanted. I wasn't going to make it easy for them to sell me to some pervert for his sexual pleasure. I was determined to fight them the entire way."

"And then I entered the picture," Julie said, picking up the story. "I was raped as well, but unlike Fiona, I immediately did everything they told me to do. Ultimately, it didn't make them treat me any better. I was only there for five days or so, while Fiona was there for months. Thankfully, my father had connections and was able to hire a SEAL team to rescue me. And they found Fiona, as well. We had to hike through the jungle, which, I'll be honest, *sucked*, but we got out of there. And I was a total bitch—to Fiona. To Cookie. To all the guys. Thankfully, they eventually let me apologize to them, thank them, and I met Patrick."

The food Bree had eaten sat like a rock in her belly. She hated hearing what these two women had been through. It seemed so...unreal. Especially while sitting on the deck of this beautiful house, sipping wine, listening to the birds chirp in the trees and watching the first signs of the sun starting to set.

"I think what you need to know, to truly understand, is that we're here. We made it. We're married, with normal, healthy sex lives," Fiona said, sitting forward a little. "I had a hard time when I got home. Had some flashbacks, even had an episode where I was convinced the people who'd held me captive were here in Riverton, trying to take me back. Tex helped me get through that one, as did my amazing therapist. The point is...we survived. We made it. Because we didn't give up."

"Well, I kind of did," Julie said with a shrug. "I've come to terms with what I did and said, and thankfully, Fiona and the others forgave me for being a colossal bitch. If I have any advice for you, it's to *not* be like me. Don't ever give up. Don't give in. Whether that means going after some lifelong dream you have, or if something bad happens and shit hits the fan. Everyone you met tonight has been through hell and come through to the other side. Strangers you meet on the street are the same way. You have no idea looking at them who has been through an abusive marriage, miscarriage after miscarriage, horrible childhoods, accidents they should've died from."

"Being with a SEAL isn't easy. Every time they go on a mission, they might not come back," Fiona said softly. "And I'm not saying that to freak you out or to be a downer, it's simply the truth. And sometimes they come home moody and quiet because of the things they've seen and done. All you can really do is put one foot in front of the other. To keep going. Because it's a damn certainty that life isn't going to be easy. It's going to throw some horrible things at you, which you already know.

"You didn't give up back there in Vegas. You got away. You're here now. With Smiley. *Living*. That's what I've learned through my ordeal. To live. No matter what, to keep on living."

Bree nodded. She had already been in awe of these women, and now she felt that times ten.

"Lord, we've scared the hell out of her," Julie mumbled.

"No, I...I'm okay. I won't deny I'm scared, but not of what you said. Of the guy after me. Knowing what he wants me for is terrifying."

"It should be," Julie said succinctly. "And I'm not trying to be a bitch...although that seems to come natural to me. I think you need to use that feeling to motivate you to be more aware of your surroundings. To do what Smiley tells you to do, even if you think it's over the top. And if the worst happens, you—"

"Julie, no," Fiona said, interrupting her friend.

"She needs to hear it," she protested.

"I think she got the point," Fiona said with a shake of her head.

"I understand," Bree interjected, not liking that the women were arguing because of her. "If he gets me, I need to be strong. To stay alert. To look for my chance to get away. And if that doesn't happen, to not give up."

"Exactly," Julie said. "Because if the asshole after you succeeds, I have no doubt whatsoever that Smiley won't stop looking until he finds you."

"And knowing someone is out there doing what they

can to get to you...it's *everything*," Fiona said. "I didn't have that. And that made it even harder to stay strong. To keep fighting."

"But you did," Julie said, putting a hand over Fiona's. "You were so damn strong. It still humbles me to this day. All I'm saying is that if the worst happens, have no doubt that the cavalry is coming. And you have the best of the best with Tex on your side. The man is an angel. He'll figure out where you are, and Smiley and his entire team—hell, probably our men too—will come for you."

While Bree had already known that Smiley wasn't going to let her disappear into thin air, hearing Fiona and Julie also confirm it made a ball of tension she'd carried around for months ease just a bit.

"Thanks."

"Right, now that the bad stuff is out of the way...can we talk about you and Smiley?" Fiona asked with a grin.

Bree blinked. "Me and Smiley?"

"Uh-huh. Girl, I thought Dude was intense with the way he watches Cheyenne, but he's got *nothing* on your Smiley."

Bree wanted to correct her new friend. Say there was nothing between her and the man who'd taken her under his wing. Who'd decided it was his mission in life to keep her safe. But she really couldn't. Smiley was an intense man normally, but she'd caught him looking at her in a way that made her tingle from her head to her toes more than a few times.

"I don't know why," she admitted. "Or how to keep his attention. I'm afraid that once the threat to me is gone, any interest he has will disappear as well. I'll go back to Vegas and he'll continue doing his thing here."

"I think this is the point where a lot of women would say all you have to do is get naked or suck his dick and you'll keep his interest," Julie said bluntly. "But I have a feeling Smiley isn't like most men. That stuff...of course he'd love it. But I don't think you have to worry about doing anything to keep his attention. You being you is doing that just fine."

Bree shook her head. "But I'm not *doing* anything."

"Exactly," Fiona said with a nod. "I agree with Julie. There's something about you that draws people in. I feel as if we've been friends for ages rather than just meeting today. You have a vibe that makes me want to rage at anyone who dares look at you cross-eyed. And trust me, that's not me. That's more Caroline's habit. Or Jessyka's. She's good at that kind of thing. Comes with being a bar owner, I think."

"Smiley's...stoic," Julie said. "It's usually hard to figure out what he's thinking. But today? He's an open book. His attention has been laser focused on you all afternoon. Every time you so much as frowned, he shifted, as if he was going to storm across the room to find out what was wrong. He got you snacks, refilled your drink, and was basically so in tune with you, I'd be jealous if I wasn't already a happily married woman."

Bree blushed. Not sure if she should be embarrassed, defend Smiley, or be concerned he was so focused on her.

"None of that is bad," Julie was quick to say. "I'm just suggesting you go with the flow. That man would no sooner hurt a hair on your head than he'd run screaming down the street in the middle of a mission. You don't have to do anything to keep his attention, you already have it. He's a goner, Bree. If you want him, for good, he's yours.

Just tread carefully if he's *not* what you want. Because even though I don't know him all that well, it would suck if you broke his heart."

Bree blinked in surprise. Instinctively, she turned her head to look inside—and immediately met Smiley's gaze.

And in that moment, she saw what Julie was talking about. She'd either blocked it out or purposely misconstrued what she was seeing because of everything that was happening.

He wanted her.

Which was a heady feeling.

And she secretly admitted...she wanted him too. She'd already wondered what kind of lover he'd be, and now she couldn't think of anything other than his hands on her.

He'd thrust his hand into her hair earlier that afternoon, and now she couldn't help wondering if he'd do the same thing to hold her still as he kissed the hell out of her. Her mouth practically watered at the thought of getting her hands on him. Of him touching her in return.

Fiona chuckled. "I think you got through, Julie."

But Bree barely heard her. She only had eyes for her man. And there was no mistake, Smiley *was* hers. She'd been watching him for months, and he'd been with no one else.

She suddenly decided if she didn't experience everything that was Jude Stark, she was going to die.

Okay, that was a bit dramatic, but she didn't care.

She felt transfixed as Smiley stalked toward the door, still holding her gaze. He slid open the door and asked, "You ready to go?"

"Yes."

Bree felt no remorse that she was ditching her new

friends. That she was suddenly having a hard time talking at all.

Before she knew it, she was walking toward Smiley's truck. She didn't really remember saying goodbye to Julie, Fiona, and the others. She vaguely recalled promising to stop by My Sister's Closet to check out some outfits Julie said she'd put together for her, and Fiona agreeing to come too. Her entire focus was on the man next to her.

It was as if Smiley was in the same trance. He kept looking over at her while he drove, and eventually he reached out and took her hand in his. Bree jolted with the first touch, feeling as if she was truly living for the first time.

It was corny. Ridiculous. And yet that's how she felt.

Despite whatever had come over them, Smiley didn't skimp on her safety. His sharp gaze swept over every inch of the rapidly darkening parking lot before he walked them into his building. His fingers were tight around hers as he led her toward his apartment. He didn't relax until the door was locked behind them.

"You want to talk about what Julie and Fiona told you?" he asked.

Bree shook her head and licked her lips.

"Are you upset?" Smiley asked next, with a tilt of his head.

"No."

"Something's up. And I can't figure out what it is."

In response, Bree took a deep breath and stepped into his personal space, as she'd done earlier in front of Caroline's house. As she'd hoped, he immediately put his arms around her waist, holding her steady.

"I'm thirty-five years old," she said. "I've been with

men before. But I've never, in all my years, felt the way I do right now."

As soon as she mentioned other men, Smiley's muscles tightened under her hands. "And how's that?" he asked hesitatingly.

"As if I don't kiss you, feel you against me, inside me, I'm going to literally die."

He went completely still. "What?"

"I want you, Jude Stark. All of you. In every way. I've got an IUD, so pregnancy isn't an issue, and it's been almost a year since I've been with anyone else. You've gotten under my skin...and I need you more than I've ever needed anything in my life. I'm coming on too strong, and I know it, but this isn't me being desperate for any old dick. I'm desperate for *you*, Smiley. I need *you*. Your brand of intensity and broodiness. Need you to hold me close and remind me that you're here. If anything happens, you'll find me and make the bad guys pay. But if you're horrified by my forwardness, and wondering how the hell to get out of this situation, that's okay. I'll leave and—"

She didn't get to finish her statement before Smiley seemed to snap himself out of whatever shock he was in. His hand speared into her hair exactly like she'd imagined, and he slammed his mouth down onto hers.

This was no exploratory first kiss. It was a claiming. And Bree was more than happy to be claimed.

She moaned as Smiley bent her backward slightly, holding her up with an arm at her back. Her nipples hardened and her heartrate doubled. She felt a momentary ping of relief that she hadn't misinterpreted the look she'd seen in his eyes back at Caroline's house. He wanted her. As much as she wanted him, it seemed.

She hadn't felt this carefree, this sure of herself, since before she'd been kidnapped by the man her ex had hired and thrown into the back of his car. All her worries fled. The only thing she could think about was the man in her arms. Currently kissing the hell out of her.

Smiley moved, not taking his mouth from hers, and picked her up. Bree wrapped her arms around his neck and her legs around his waist and held on as he carried her down the hall toward his bedroom.

He didn't stop kissing her as he entered the room and dropped her on the bed, following her down.

What happened next was a scene worthy of the movies. He pulled back, stared down at her for a beat—then at the same time, they began to tear at their clothes, wanting to get them off as soon as humanly possible.

CHAPTER SEVEN

Smiley was having a hard time thinking. He couldn't believe this was happening. Bree wanted him. *Him*. At first, he'd thought he was dreaming. She couldn't be saying the things he'd longed to hear. Then her words sank in and he hadn't been able to hold back.

Seeing her on his bed made lust swim through his veins. He needed her. Right this second.

Thankfully she seemed to be in the same frame of mind, because she was undressing just as fast and desperately as he was. Then suddenly she was naked. There were clothes strewn across the bed, but Smiley barely noticed. All he could see were her perfect tits. Hard little nipples. The adorable pooch of her belly. Her pubic hair glistening from her arousal. Legs that didn't seem that long while she was dressed, but suddenly went on forever, stretched out naked on his sheets.

Moving his gaze back up her body, Smiley was suddenly afraid to touch her. Scared that this was a dream after all. Much like the ones he'd been having since she'd moved in.

But this one was in such vivid detail. He could hear her fast breaths, see her chest heaving, smell her arousal.

"Smiley?" she whispered, sounding uncertain.

Which wasn't fucking acceptable.

"So beautiful," he murmured. "I don't know where to start or to look."

"I'm having the same problem," Bree said, her gaze focused between his legs.

Smiley was hard. Fuck, he was already dripping precome. That wasn't like him. He was as controlled in bed as he was on the battlefield. But this woman had changed the game. Changed every fucking thing.

Her hand reached for his cock, but Smiley caught it before she could touch him.

She frowned, raising her gaze to his.

"If you touch me, I'm gonna lose it."

"So?" she said with a saucy grin.

"When I come, it's gonna be deep inside your body. I'm gonna fill you to the brim. Mark you. Claim you."

"*Yes*."

That was all Smiley needed to hear. He dropped onto her like a feral beast. One hand caressed her from chest to hip, hiking her leg up over his ass, opening her to him, and the other went straight to her tit, squeezing and kneading.

She moaned into his mouth as he kissed her once again. She wasn't still under him though, squirming and arching into his touch, pushing her hips up in a rhythmic motion that mimicked sex.

He needed inside her. Now.

But he had to make sure she could take him without pain. He'd rather cut off his own dick than hurt her.

Pulling her leg down, he pressed his fingers between

her thighs, barely holding off from spurting right then and there when he slid in without any resistance whatsoever. She was soaking wet. For *him*. Proof that she wanted him as badly as he wanted her.

Shifting, Smiley propped himself over her. "I want to take you bare. I haven't been with anyone in a long time either. And I was just tested by the Navy last month. May I?"

"Yes. Now, Smiley. Please!"

One second he was looking down at her, legs spread open and her pussy glistening, and the next, he was balls deep inside her body.

They both gasped.

Smiley moved to grab the base of his dick to prevent himself from prematurely coming. He'd never felt like this before. He'd had plenty of sex, but never had he felt as if he was going to explode from the inside out with just one thrust.

"Oh my God, you're huge!" she exclaimed, eyes wide.

Smiley couldn't help but chuckle. "You're good for my ego," he told her.

"I love your smile," she told him.

"I love yours more."

"Smiley?"

"Yeah?"

"You gonna move?"

"Not yet."

"*Why not?*" Her question came out more as a whine than words, and that made Smiley grin once more.

"Because if I move, I'm gonna come. And I don't want to yet. I want to feel your hot, wet pussy gripping me for as long as possible."

"I thought you wanted to fill me from the inside out. Mark me. Claim me," she retorted, throwing his words back at him.

That was pretty much all it took for Smiley to lose the little control he was barely hanging on to. He leaned over his woman and began to fuck her—hard.

Every time he bottomed out, she moaned in pleasure. He knew he was going too fast, too rough. But Bree wasn't complaining. He'd wanted to feel her orgasm on his dick before he filled her up, but he was too far gone. This was a dream come true, and he couldn't stop himself from taking what he'd previously only fantasized about.

It didn't take long. Smiley's moves became erratic, then he thrust just a few more times before holding as deep inside his woman's body as he could get—and he let loose.

It felt as if he came forever. His vision went dim as he orgasmed.

When he returned to the present, he was panting, one hand under Bree, gripping her ass cheek with enough force that he was probably leaving finger marks.

Lifting his head, Smiley looked down at the woman who'd become his entire world. If she asked him to quit the Navy and live on a commune with her and grow sunflowers, he'd say yes without any hesitation.

But his Bree wouldn't ask that of him. He knew without a doubt. She'd rather cut off her own hand than ask him to do anything he didn't want to do.

She smiled up at him. "That was amazing," she said softly.

"You think we're done?" Smiley blurted.

"Um...yes? You came."

"But *you* didn't. If you think I'm the kind of man who

climbs on his woman, pumps a few times, and rolls off, you're very wrong."

She looked bemused, which pissed Smiley off. It was obvious she'd been with selfish assholes in bed who didn't think about anything but their own pleasure. She was about to discover for herself that wasn't who he was. That her sex life had taken a turn for the better. Starting now.

"Don't move," he ordered, as he carefully got to his knees, pulling her hips until her ass was on his lap, making sure he didn't slip out of her body as he did so.

"Smiley..." she began hesitatingly.

"We aren't done. Not even close," he warned her. "Get ready to have your world rocked, sweetheart."

He heard her indrawn breath as he put his hands under her shoulder blades, forcing her to arch her back as he leaned over her.

* * *

Bree inhaled deeply as Smiley's lips closed around one of her nipples. How was he this flexible? How was *she*? She could still feel Smiley's cock twitching inside her body as he leaned over her...then she couldn't think about *anything* but how good his lips felt around her extremely sensitive nipple. They'd always been that way, but until now, none of her lovers have ever paid much attention to her chest. Preferring to get straight between her legs.

She'd honestly thought Smiley was done after he came. That's how it had always been in the past. But it seemed that she'd once again read him wrong. He wasn't done. Not even close.

Arching her back even more, Bree moaned as he used

his teeth to bite down a little on her nipple. Sparks flew from her chest to between her legs. Making her shake in his arms.

"Squirm for me, Bree," he murmured against her heated skin, before he bit her once more.

She couldn't think. What he was doing to her was...it was turning her inside out. "Smiley!" she moaned.

She felt him smile against her skin, which was a huge turn-on.

He held her with such authority. Bree felt herself relax, giving him full control.

"That's it," he murmured, obviously feeling her acquiesce.

It wasn't until that moment that Bree realized with every other sexual encounter she'd had, which really wasn't all that many, she'd held back. Gone through the motions. Let the man think he was the best she'd ever had to avoid hurt feelings. But she could honestly say that Smiley *was* the best. He outshone everyone else. He was making her feel things she'd never felt before.

He lifted his head and held her off the mattress as he stared down at her. His arm muscles bulged, and he had a naughty little smirk on his face. Her pussy spasmed.

"*Fuck*, that feels amazing. Time for more of that." He lowered her back down to the mattress then put his hands on her thighs, pushing her legs apart.

Bree felt exposed. Vulnerable. But safe. With Smiley, she was always safe.

"You have no idea how erotic this is. My cock buried deep inside your pussy, my come leaking out, your lips stretched wide to accept me."

Bree felt herself blushing. "Smiley," she protested. "Less talk, more action."

He chuckled, and she could feel it deep inside her body.

"Yes, ma'am," he growled.

But instead of fucking her, he pressed down on one thigh with his hand and brought his other between her legs.

Bree jolted almost violently when he strummed her clit.

"Oh yeah, you're sensitive," he murmured, his gaze glued to where they were joined.

Sensitive? Hell, she was more than sensitive.

"Oh!" she breathed, as she felt her orgasm approaching like a runaway freight train with no brakes.

Between one breath and the next, she was flying.

She'd had orgasms before, of course she had, most she'd given herself. But this one, with Smiley's rough, calloused fingers stroking her clit, his cock deep inside her body, the way he looked at her with such reverence and lust, left all the others in the dust.

Reaching down, Bree grabbed hold of Smiley's forearms and dug her fingernails in as she flew over the edge. Her entire body shook as pleasure flooded her. It was overwhelming, and she knew with certainty that he'd ruined her for any other man.

"So damn beautiful," Smiley whispered, and then, to Bree's immense pleasure and relief, he began to move.

His cock slid easily in and out of her soaked body, the sounds they created as he made love to her almost embarrassing.

"Look at me," he ordered.

Bree forced her eyes to open all the way as she met his gaze.

"That's it. Don't look away from me. I want to see you go over again."

"I don't think—"

"You will," he interrupted, obviously knowing what she was going to say.

Bree wanted to roll her eyes, call him cocky once more. But she lost all sense of what they were talking about when his thumb brushed against her clit again. She hadn't realized he still had one hand between them as he thrust in and out of her.

She couldn't help but jerk under his touch. She was sensitive. Almost painfully so. But he didn't let up. He played her like a professional pianist. A maestro. Like a rock star strumming his guitar. The metaphors shot through her brain, one after the other, as Smiley lasted a lot longer the second time around. And then she could no longer think at all.

Her second orgasm wasn't as powerful as the first, but when Smiley propped himself over her with both hands and began to fuck her hard and fast, it seemed to go on and on. Every time he bottomed out, the pressure on her clit prolonged her pleasure.

Throughout it all, Bree kept her gaze locked on Smiley's. There were so many emotions swirling in his eyes, she couldn't separate them all out. This was more intimate than anything she'd ever done before. Somehow looking into his eyes connected them on a level she'd never experienced with previous lovers.

Even as Smiley came, he didn't close his eyes. Didn't look away from her.

They only lost eye contact when he seemed to deflate like a popped balloon. He collapsed onto her chest but didn't crush her. Instead he immediately rolled, taking her with him.

She let out a small girly shriek of surprise, then nuzzled into him, loving being on top, using him as a pillow. One of his hands came to rest on her ass, holding her against him, keeping his cock from slipping out.

Bree felt exhausted. And almost embarrassed, for some reason. She'd never been that uninhibited before. That desperate to have a guy. Did he think less of her, now that she'd slept with him?

"That was...wow," Smiley murmured.

Bree grinned against his shoulder. It sounded like he was just as wrung out as she was, which made her feel a little better. Lifting her head so she could see his face, she noted his cheeks were pink and his chest was blotchy. His hair was mussed and he had a sheen of sweat on his brow.

He was beautiful.

"This isn't something I usually do," Bree blurted.

His brows furrowed. "What? Sleep?"

"Sleep with someone after only knowing them for such a short time. One-night stands."

Every muscle in his body tensed, and she knew that, because she could feel it happening all along her body.

"First, this isn't a one-night stand. That implies that it's a one-time thing. That's not what's happening here. Second, we know each other. You've been stalking me for a while now, and I've more than done my research on you. And third, I've never been a fan of having sex just for the sake of sex. I've got my fist, and that's enough when I need to get off.

"This is different. Special. And if you don't agree, if you just needed a tension reliever...you need to climb off me right this second, and I'll go sleep in the living room like I have been."

By the end of his little speech, Smiley sounded pissed. Any warm, fuzzy feelings he might've had after his orgasm, she'd obviously ruined.

But she couldn't help feeling a tiny bit relieved that he was so emotional. And happy about what he'd said.

In response, she lay her head back down on his shoulder and tightened her arms and legs—and inner muscles—around him as she said, "No."

After a heartbeat, he asked, "No?"

"No, I'm not climbing off. I'm comfy right where I am, thank you very much. I like you right here. Where I can keep an eye on you."

She felt him chuckle. The rumble reverberated down her body. "Okay."

"We good?" she felt the need to ask.

"More than." Then, after a moment, "I'm gonna need you to keep doing that."

"Doing what?" Bree asked, feeling more and more drowsy after the two orgasms she'd received.

"Not backing down when I'm an ass."

Bree lifted her head at that. "You weren't an ass," she said, feeling confused.

"I was. Don't let me get away with talking to you like that. I was rude. Instead of snapping at you, I should've had a calm, rational discussion."

Bree couldn't help it. She laughed. "Smiley, that *was* you having a calm, rational discussion. You said what you were feeling and gave me a choice. It was fine. You're fine.

I'm good." He stared at her for so long, Bree began to feel uneasy. "What?"

But he simply shook his head. "Nothing. It's just...nine out of ten women would've gotten pissed if I'd talked to them like that."

"I like doing the unexpected."

"Like stalk a Navy SEAL and his friends?"

"Yup, like that," she agreed breezily.

"By the way...I'm impressed," Smiley told her. "Not many people could've done what you did, for as long as you did it. I mean, I'm not happy about it, you should've just come out and told me you needed help as soon as you got to town, but the fact that you were able to stay under the radar, and not have me or any of my friends notice you watching us...it's impressive."

"Thanks."

"Do I dare ask how you learned that shit?"

She smiled and lay her head back down. "No."

"Fair enough."

Bree didn't want to think about her teenage years. She'd been a hellion. She'd tested every boundary her parents had set. Including sneaking out of the house at night, doing stuff a lot of stupid teenagers did. Smoking, drinking, partying. And while her friends inevitably got caught and grounded, her own parents never noticed.

She'd learned how to hide in plain sight. Like how to hide from the cops when they broke up a party, and she had to run into the woods to get away. And once she started driving, she became very adept at evading the police when running on foot turned into driving away from those same parties.

Bree wasn't proud of the things she'd done when she

was young and dumb, but staying under the radar had become second nature to her. So when she'd needed to hide for her own safety, she'd fallen back on old habits. Thankfully, she still seemed to have a knack for being invisible.

"I really liked Fiona and Julie. And everyone else," Bree said after a moment.

"We didn't have a chance to talk after your visit with them. That go okay?"

Remembering the look he'd given her while she was on the deck with the women made Bree blush. "Yeah. I hate what happened to them. But I'm so impressed with how they've coped."

"They're amazing. But then again, they'd be amazing even without the shit that happened to them."

He wasn't wrong. And his words made Bree like him all the more. "Yeah," she agreed.

His cock, which had been inside her this entire time, slipped out of her body.

They both groaned, which made Bree giggle.

"Fuck, that sucks," Smiley complained. Then he rolled, taking Bree with him once more.

"Smiley!" she exclaimed, surprised by the move.

"Gotta get up and get you a washcloth," he told her. Then he kissed her on the tip of her nose before climbing out of bed.

Bree didn't even have a chance to tell him not to bother. That she was fine. But the view of him from behind as he strode toward the bathroom was one she'd remember for the rest of her life. She hadn't had a chance to really check him out, since they'd been so desperate to get naked and make love.

He was a Greek god. Or at least sculpted like one. His ass was a work of art. The globes perfectly round, and she could see the muscles contract as he walked.

As she climbed under the covers, she heard running water in the bathroom, and when he walked back toward the bed, to her surprise, he was still naked.

And...Lord. His front was almost better than the back. Bree greedily ran her gaze up and down his body as he came toward her. His cock was flaccid now, and still she could hardly believe he'd fit all of it inside her. His chest had a sprinkling of hair, and he had that V thing going on with the muscles at his hips that all hetero women lusted after.

When her gaze made it back up to his face as he stopped by the side of the bed, he was smirking. "Done?" he asked.

"Not even close," she murmured.

To her surprise, Smiley didn't move to get back into the bed. Instead, he lifted his arms, then spun in a slow circle, letting her look her fill.

Giggling, she said, "Get back in here," as she started to lift the covers.

In response, he grabbed the sheet and blanket and whipped them off her body.

Bree screeched in surprise. But when she saw the look of awe and appreciation in his gaze, she stilled, realizing he was doing the same thing as *she'd* done. Looking his fill, now that desperation and lust wasn't clouding his vision.

"How'd I get so lucky?" he asked, putting a knee on the mattress. He settled himself next to her on his side and brought his hand with the washcloth between her legs.

"I can do that," Bree told him.

"I got it."

This should've been weird. Uncomfortable. But Smiley didn't linger. He wiped her clean, then tossed the wet washcloth onto the floor.

"Are you going to leave that there?" she asked.

"Yeah."

"But it could mildew. It'll get the carpet pad wet, and it'll mold."

He looked at her for a beat, then without a word, swung his legs back over the side of the bed. To Bree's amazement, he leaned down and grabbed the washcloth and went back to the bathroom without complaint.

He was back seconds later, turning off the overhead light and pulling the covers over them.

"I can't believe you did that," Bree said.

"Did what?"

"Got back up to put the wet washcloth away."

"Why wouldn't I? You had a good point. And the last thing I wanted was for you to be worrying about it all night."

"I wouldn't have worried about it *all* night," she protested.

In response, Smiley lifted a brow, which she could just see in the dim glow from the nightlight in his bathroom.

Damn. How did he know her so well already? "Okay, maybe I would've. But still. I didn't really expect you to get up right then and there and move it."

"You ask something of me, if it's in my power to do it, I will," Smiley said simply.

Bree stared at him. "Some women would abuse that power."

"Yeah. But you won't."

She wouldn't. Again, how he seemed to know her so well was almost startling. "You're kind of scary," she blurted, saying what she was thinking.

"Not to you," he retorted calmly. "Now can we stop talking about a fucking washcloth and get some sleep? We've had some early mornings, and tomorrow is no exception. We could use an early night to bed."

Bree took a deep breath and relaxed against Smiley. She was still a little confused about how she'd gotten here, but she was happier than she'd been in a very long time. She felt safe. Which wasn't a feeling she'd had much in her life.

"Smiley?"

"Lord, woman. What?"

She couldn't stop the chuckle that escaped. "Just... thank you for being you. For introducing me to your friends. For sharing your world with me. It means...well, it means a lot."

"You'll learn in time that they can be annoying. Showing up when you least expect it. Butting into your business. Giving you unsolicited advice."

"Not to mention having your back, giving you unconditional support and loyalty."

"Yeah, that too," Smiley agreed. "Sleep, woman."

Bree fell asleep with a smile on her face. Her life was anything but settled, Mateo was still a threat, but with Fiona and Julie's words of encouragement, and seeing how happy and well-adjusted they were, somehow he didn't seem quite as scary anymore.

She had her SEAL at her back, as well as his entire

circle of badass friends. If the worst happened, she'd fight to get back to Smiley. Because this was the life she wanted. Here in Riverton. With him.

CHAPTER EIGHT

"Wow, I've never seen this parking lot so full!" Bree exclaimed, as Smiley pulled into Aces Bar and Grill's lot a week and a half later.

Truthfully, Smiley hadn't either. But then again, this wasn't a usual Friday-night crowd.

Kevlar and Remi, and Josie and Blink were getting married. They'd decided to also have the ceremony here at the bar, rather than just the reception. Because once they'd started writing down the names of the people they wanted to witness the actual ceremony, the list had gotten too big for the courthouse or a simple backyard wedding.

Kelli and Flash had done the courthouse thing a few days ago—without telling anyone—and Remi and Josie had both declared that the party after their own ceremony would be for all of them. To celebrate everyone's weddings.

It looked like Smiley and Bree were late. Which wasn't surprising, because after Smiley had seen the dress Julie had sent over for Bree, he hadn't been able to resist putting his hands all over her.

He'd done his best not to muss up her hair, makeup, or the beautiful designer dress she was wearing, but after he'd fucked her on his kitchen table, she'd still needed a bit of time to "fix herself," as she'd called it. To Smiley, she was perfect. Though, after a bit of reflection, he decided Bree's just-fucked look wasn't one he wanted to share with the world.

Life with Bree had only gotten better since they'd begun their physical relationship. She didn't hold back, wasn't afraid to tell him what she wanted. And the other night, when she'd dropped to the floor when he was sitting at the dining room table and insisted she'd always wanted to give a guy a blowjob while he was eating...Who was he to protest?

He hadn't meant to come down her throat, but when she'd refused to stop, just clamped her mouth around him tight and sucked like a fucking Hoover, he hadn't been able to hold back. In retaliation, he'd hoisted her onto the kitchen counter, pulled up a stool, and hadn't let her back down until she'd come all over his face three times—then he'd fucked her hard and fast right there next to the dirty dishes from the preparation of their meal.

But it wasn't the sex that had him so wrapped around her little finger. It was Bree herself. She never complained. Did whatever was asked of her with a smile. Didn't seem to mind sitting in empty conference rooms on the naval base as he worked. And she'd spent the last few days helping Remi and Josie make decorations for the reception tonight.

The smiles that were so few and far between not too

long ago were almost constant now. And Smiley couldn't get enough.

"I hope the decorations are okay," she said, biting her lower lip in concern as Smiley parked his truck.

After turning off the engine, he leaned over and wrapped his hand around the back of her neck and pulled her across the seat so he could reach her mouth. He kissed her gently. "They're perfect."

She chuckled. "You haven't even seen them yet."

"Don't need to. You made them, so I know they're perfect."

She rolled her eyes. "Whatever."

He was clearly a sick man, as even her little attitude turned him on.

And he hated to ruin the mood, but he needed to remind her that even though things seemed to be quiet, that could change in a heartbeat. Tex still hadn't located Mateo Castillo—but he *had* gotten confirmation the man himself was in Riverton. Whether because of Bree or for some other nefarious reason had yet to be determined.

Tomorrow, Tex was also going to break the news to Cookie and Hurt—and the rest of Wolf's team—that Castillo indeed had ties to the same organization that had kidnapped Fiona and Julie. He was waiting until after the celebration tonight.

Smiley had no doubt that tomorrow, the men would be raising hell, wanting to meet to find out what he and the rest of his team knew. It would be an uncomfortable meeting, but long overdue.

"You know Aces will be closed tonight for the celebration. Only those on the invitation list will be allowed inside, so it should be safe. But, even so, don't let down your guard. With so many people, strangers could still get in."

Smiley still had his hand around her nape, so he felt Bree stiffen. But she nodded immediately. "Okay."

"We're all going to be on the lookout, and since many of the people there will be strangers to you, you won't be able to tell who's friend and who's foe. But we will."

She nodded again.

Smiley hated this. Fucking *hated* it. Today should be about celebration. About his favorite people finding their other halves and tying their lives together. Instead, he was worried about someone sneaking into the bar and stealing Bree out from under his nose.

Bree put her hand on his arm. "It's fine, Smiley. I understand. Trust me, I haven't forgotten he's out there. Watching and waiting. I feel it. Feel *him*."

Smiley frowned. "What? Have you seen anything?"

"No. Nothing like that. It's just a feeling I have. That I've had since I escaped from that car back in Vegas. He's always just there. In the back of my mind."

Smiley didn't like that. Not at all.

"It's okay. Now that I have the trackers Tex sent, and you, it's not as scary as it once was."

Smiley pulled her closer and rested his forehead against hers. "Fuck him. He's going down. He picked the wrong woman to fuck with because you are a badass, Bree."

To his surprise, Bree smiled. And not a small polite smile either. One that spread from ear-to-ear.

"That's the most romantic thing anyone has ever said to me. Thank you."

Smiley pulled back in surprise.

"It is," she insisted. "Knowing you think that way

about me? That I can handle whatever he might dish out... with your help, of course. It means the world to me."

Hell, this woman was way too easy to compliment, and Smiley made a mental note to do it more often.

"How about we get out of this parking lot and do this?"

"Yes!" Bree said.

They quickly entered Aces, stopped to have their names and IDs checked on a list that one of Jessyka's kids was manning—and taking her job extremely seriously. Benny was hovering nearby, just in case anyone gave her crap, which they wouldn't if they were a part of the group. He was there mainly to prevent any uninvited guests from coming in.

As soon as they entered, Bree was surrounded, everyone wanting to greet her. Smiley frowned as he gave her some space. He loved that she fit in so well with his friends, but he was also grumpy because he wanted all of her time to himself.

Which was stupid because he'd been with her practically every minute since the shit with Kelli went down. Except for when he was in meetings, he was by her side.

As if she could read his mind, Bree looked over her shoulder at him and smiled. Her acknowledging him went a long way toward making him feel better.

Smiley walked around the room, saying hello to his friends and meeting the people he didn't know.

Remi's parents were there. And surprisingly, Fernando Stephenson, the man who single-handedly made Crown Condoms a household name, looked right at home in the hole-in-the-wall bar. He was standing with his wife, Claire Crown-Stephenson, and they both had huge smiles on their faces.

He also met Remi's grandmother, who lived up to all the stories he'd heard about her from Remi. She was currently at the bar doing shots with two of the Night Stalkers who'd been invited by Blink and Josie. They were the teammates of Blink's brother, who was also one of the legendary Army helicopter pilots.

As he watched, one of the men surreptitiously nodded at the bartender as he carefully, and sneakily, watered down the next shots. It was one thing to have a good time, another to get Remi's grandmother falling-down-drunk at a wedding and reception.

Smiley heard a loud bark of laughter, and he glanced over and saw Marley, who was Remi's best friend, sitting in a corner with Blink's dad, who had come up from Florida. Everywhere he looked, Smiley saw people having a good time. Happy to have come together to celebrate with their friends and family.

For a moment, regret struck so hard, Smiley had to close his eyes to get his equilibrium back. He wished his own mother was still around. That he'd had a more normal relationship with both her and his father growing up.

"You good, Smiley?"

Opening his eyes and turning, Smiley saw Tate "Casper" Davis standing next to him. For a split second he thought it was Blink, and he'd been about to ask him what the hell he was doing out here and not in the back, getting ready for his wedding.

Blink and Casper were twins. One had gone into the Navy and the other into the Army. They had a competitive relationship, but when push came to shove, they'd do anything for each other.

"Yeah," Smiley told the other man a little belatedly. "It's good to see you."

"And it's good to see *you*," Casper returned. "How's Blink been doing? I didn't get much time to talk to him after that shit went down with him and Josie. At least not in person. And it's sometimes hard to gauge how someone's doing over the phone."

"He's good," Smiley said, not blowing smoke up Casper's ass. "Really good. Josie's been his rock, and while the man certainly doesn't talk a lot, he makes up for it by kicking some ass in the field."

Casper nodded. "That's my brother. He's never been a big talker, but he was always the first person to stand up and fight for what's right. I met Bree earlier."

It was an abrupt change of subject, and Smiley narrowed his eyes in question.

Casper laughed. "Don't go all squinty-eyed on me. All I was gonna say is that I like her. She's spunky. And friendly. The opposite of you. You're a good match."

Smiley wasn't sure if he should be offended or not, eventually deciding that since Casper wasn't saying anything he didn't already know, he couldn't exactly get pissed at him. "Just don't get any ideas," he warned the hotshot helicopter pilot.

Casper grinned. "Never. I've got my own woman. She's bummed she couldn't come out here with me, but maybe next time."

Smiley hadn't heard that Casper was dating anyone, but he was happy for him. Which was a weird emotion, since he'd never really thought much about the relationships the men around him were in. They were just something the men did...dated women, broke up, found someone else.

But after being surrounded by men in serious, healthy relationships, he had a different take on girlfriends and wives now.

"If I can have your attention!" Jessyka said loudly from where she was standing on the bar. "We're going to start, if you can please form an aisle leading from the front door to the pool table landing, it would be appreciated."

Looking around, Smiley searched for Bree. He was relieved to see her making her way toward him with a smile on her face.

"See you around," Casper told him, but Smiley barely heard him. All his attention was focused on Bree.

She looked happy. A little tipsy already. Her reddish-brown hair wasn't quite as perfectly made up as it had been when they'd arrived. As if she'd run her hand through it a few times. Her smile was crooked. And her hazel eyes bore into his as she approached.

"Isn't this awesome?" she asked, as she snuggled into him the second she got close enough. Her arm was wrapped around his back and she gave him her weight.

A feeling of...rightness settled in Smiley's chest. He held her against him and said, "Yeah."

The crowd shifted until there was a space wide enough for two people to walk side-by-side toward the makeshift ceremony area Jessyka had created, where one of the pool tables usually sat. There was a wooden arch decorated with flowers, which was where the couples would say their vows.

Neither couple had any bridesmaids or groomsmen, insisting they wanted to keep things simple. But Smiley knew it was also because neither wanted anyone to feel left out, and since they had so many friends, it would be impossible to pick anyway.

Everyone turned as the front doors opened, and Remi and Kevlar stepped into the bar. They were arm in arm, and smiling so wide it was almost blinding. Remi had on a cream dress with tiny sleeves, and Kevlar was wearing his dress white uniform with all his medals. They paused a moment, and then Queen's "Crazy Little Thing Called Love" blared from the speakers in the bar, and they started walking toward the arch.

Everyone clapped and whistled at the nontraditional song. It was a great choice for the two of them. It wasn't a terribly long distance from the door to the arch, but it took quite a while anyway, because Remi kept stopping to hug her friends and family lining the walkway.

When they finally reached the platform with the arch, they turned back toward the front door. It opened again, and this time Josie and Blink walked in. Josie looked so tiny next to Blink, and she positively glowed as she looked up at her husband-to-be. Blink was also wearing his dress whites, but instead of white or cream, Josie chose a pink dress that reached her ankles and made it seem as if she were floating rather than walking, as she and Blink made their way toward the platform.

"I barely know them, and I love this so much," Bree murmured from next to him.

They chose the chorus to Pink's song "Trustfall" for their walk down the aisle together. Which Smiley had to admit fit the pair perfectly.

They joined Remi and Kevlar at the altar, and once they were in place, Remi and Josie reached out and held hands, as their soon-to-be husbands wrapped their arms around their fiancées' waists.

To Smiley's surprise, Wolf stepped in front of them with an open folder. It *shouldn't* have surprised him that the couples had chosen one of their mentors to officiate, but it somehow still did. Wolf wasn't in his uniform, instead wearing a suit and tie. He looked distinguished and professional.

"I'd like to welcome all of Remi, Kevlar, Josie, and Blink's friends and family to this wonderful occasion. It's a chance for us to get together to celebrate love, friendship, strength, and resilience. Because without those things, these couples might not be joining their lives together with all of us as witnesses. Adversity is usually thought of as a negative thing. Something to get through. To survive. But I think most of us here would agree that sometimes it can be seen as a set of circumstances that allow our greatest strengths to shine.

"The four people in front of me met under the worst of circumstances. Many would say it was the worst days of their lives. But together, they persevered. I don't care what anyone says, life is full of bumps in the road, and hills and valleys. Things that can break a person if they aren't careful. But with the right partner at your side, you can weather those ups and downs. You can overcome whatever life throws at you. I think these four amazing human beings have proven that to us all.

"Together, Remi and Kevlar, and Josie and Blink, are stronger than they are individually. That's what today is all about. Joining two couples who were meant to be together.

"But look around you. The people here in this room

are *also* our strength. The ones who prop us up when we need it the most. The ones who are there when we need them. When we need a timeout. There's nothing more important than having a support system.

"Now, I could stand here and hog the spotlight all night, but no one's here to see me, or hear me blab on and on."

Everyone laughed.

"Kevlar...the floor is yours," Wolf said, nodding at his friend.

Remi let go of Josie's hand and turned to face her almost-husband.

"Remi, from the first day I met you, there was something about you that called to me. It wasn't just the way you dealt with the shit...er...sorry...the *stuff* that was happening. It was a connection I'd never felt before. To be honest, it was confusing, but I wasn't going to let you go without figuring out what was between us. Wolf said that might be the worst day of our lives, but I think it was one of my *best* days. Who forgets the day they meet the other half of their soul? The person who makes you want to get out of bed each day and makes you a better human being because they're at your side?

"I promise to always trust and value your opinions. To travel beside you in whatever adventures await us. To always fight for us, because that's what I feel as if I was born to do. Be by your side. I'll protect and honor you. Laugh with you. Sometimes *at* you, because let's face it... you're hilarious."

Everyone around them chuckled, and Kevlar smiled at his bride.

"Most of all, I promise to love you the way you deserve

to be loved. To brag about you to strangers in the grocery store, to keep you forever in my heart and mind whenever we're separated. And in good times and bad, I'll be there. *For* you and *with* you. Forever."

"Crap, I have to go after that?" Remi complained, as she wiped away a tear.

Once again, the room broke out into laughter.

Remi took a deep breath before speaking. "Can I just say ditto and be done?"

"Yes."

But Remi shook her head. "No, I can't. Okay, here goes. Vincent, I had no idea how much my life would change when I went to Hawaii on my own. When I went outside my comfort zone and decided to go on that snorkeling trip by myself. The truth is, I was terrified when I realized what was happening to us, but with you there, I found that it was easier to stay calm. You do that for me. You ground me. Make me feel as if I can do anything. You laugh at my Pecky the Traveling Taco comics, you support me, but most importantly, you love me. For who I am. And that's worth more than anything in the world.

"I love you. I'll *always* love you. I'll support and protect you if need be. And...I'll be there for your friends too..." She turned her head and looked at Blink. "I've learned the hard way that just because someone says they're your friend, doesn't mean they have your best interests at heart. But the true friends, the ones who will go to hell and back for you...they're gold."

Blink put his hand over his heart and nodded once at Remi.

By now, most of the women in the room were crying, and Smiley had to admit he was feeling a little emotional himself. Remi and Blink had a special bond, one born out of tragedy.

"Right, so…" Remi said, looking back up at Kevlar. "Vincent. I choose you. Today, tomorrow, and the rest of our days."

There was an awkward silence at the end of her declaration.

"Are you done?" Wolf asked quietly.

"That wasn't enough?" Remi asked.

Chuckles rang out around the room.

"It was perfect," Kevlar answered for her.

Wolf turned to Josie and Blink. "Your turn."

"I'm going first!" she blurted.

Blink's lips curled up in a huge grin.

"I love you, Nate. Exactly how you are. You're my everything. My light in an otherwise dark world. You swooped in and gave me back my humanity. My life. You're a man of few words, but each and every one is carefully chosen and has meaning. You make me laugh, you've taught me what love is. You've provided a safe place for me, unlike anything I've ever known. I can be myself with you, and that's more than I've had with anyone else. Ever. I've found my place. My home. You make me whole. I love you."

Blink stared at her for a long moment, as if trying to regain his equilibrium. Then he spoke. "Josie, I'm yours. You come first. Always. You need me, I'm there. No matter what it takes. I love you."

Then he looked at Wolf and nodded.

"Short and sweet. Not surprised, but damn if that wasn't the most heartfelt vow I've ever heard," Wolf said. Then he looked at both couples. "If you can please face each other, hold hands, and repeat after me."

The two couples did as he requested.

"Remi, Josie, do you take Vincent and Nate to be your husband? Do you promise to love, honor, cherish, and protect them, forsaking all others and holding on to them forevermore?"

"I do," both Remi and Josie said at the same time.

"Vincent, Nate, do you take Remi and Josie to be your wife? Do you promise to love, honor, cherish, and protect them, forsaking all others and holding on to them forevermore?"

"Hell yes."

"I definitely do."

Smiley wasn't surprised at his friends' enthusiastic agreement to the vows.

Wolf grinned as he continued. "The couples will now exchange rings as a symbol of the vows they made here in front of all of us today. A ring has no beginning or end. It's a promise of endless love and respect for each other. By placing these rings on each other's fingers, you are vowing to not only love each other, but to honor, be compassionate, patient, and understanding as you build your futures together.

"Josie and Remi, if you'd each place the ring on your partner's finger and repeat after me. I give you this ring... as a symbol of my love...with the pledge to love and support you...today, tomorrow, always, and forever."

Wolf paused as he spoke, giving the women time to repeat his words.

"Kevlar and Blink, each of you place the ring on your partner's finger and repeat after me. I give you this ring...

as a symbol of my love...with the pledge to love and support you...today, tomorrow, always, and forever."

Both couples turned to face Wolf once more.

"And now, by the power vested in me by the State of California, it's my honor and pleasure to declare you husbands and wives. You may seal this declaration with a kiss!"

Both Kevlar and Blink had bent their newly wedded wives over their arms before he'd even finished speaking. The kisses they shared were passionate and deep. The room broke out into raucous catcalls and whistles as the kisses went on and on.

"It's not a contest," Wolf finally said dryly.

Kevlar and Blink were both grinning by the time they straightened. Remi and Josie were blushing, which only added to their beauty and the perfection of the moment.

"I'm pleased to present to you, Remi Stephenson-Hill, Vincent Hill, and Josie and Nate Davis."

Once again, everyone cheered and clapped. The newlyweds were swarmed as people were eager to be among the first to congratulate them.

Smiley stood back with Bree and looked down at her. She was beaming as if *she'd* been the one getting married. If he could bottle this moment, he would. He always wanted to see his woman this happy. She'd had a hell of a time recently, and giving her this, this opportunity to be completely relaxed and happy for her new friends, was something Smiley would always cherish.

"That was awesome," Bree said as she looked up at him.

"Yeah." It was a lame response, but Smiley was feeling tongue-tied. It was difficult to think about anything other than how badly he wanted to keep that smile on her face.

"First round of drinks are on me!" Remi's dad shouted.

The rest of the night was nothing but pure happiness. Everyone was overjoyed for the two couples, and for Kelli and Flash, who'd recently gotten married at the courthouse themselves. Jessyka had mock cocktails for the women who were pregnant and for those who didn't drink alcohol. And the champagne and beer flowed as everyone celebrated soul mates and love.

The music was loud and Smiley's ears were ringing by the end of the night. But he couldn't deny that he'd had a great time. Hanging out with the older SEALs and their women was fun, and he enjoyed spending time outside of work with his own friends. The Night Stalker crew was the life of the party, and Smiley approved of how they went out of their way to interact with all the women, asking them to dance and generally acting as if they'd known everyone their entire lives.

And while Smiley had heard stories about Remi's infamous grandmother, he hadn't really believed half of them. But he'd be the first to admit that the woman was a firecracker. Said what she thought without any kind of filter. It was hard not to love her, and he could see where Remi got her sense of humor.

Smiley's feet hurt—hell, his face hurt from smiling, which was definitely a new thing for him. And most of those smiles were because he'd watched Bree all night. Without a threat hanging over her head, she blossomed. She danced, drank, and laughed with everyone.

Thankfully, he and his team had the next day off, so they could sleep in for once. As Smiley led Bree to his truck at two in the morning, he didn't forget to check his surroundings. To his relief, he saw no one suspicious. No one lurking around in the parking lot. No strangers sitting in a car watching the bar. He had no doubt Castillo or his goons were still out there, but for tonight, it seemed as if things were quiet.

Once he had Bree settled into the passenger side of his truck, he ran around to the driver's side and started the engine.

"Smiley?" she said, her voice slurring a little.

"Yeah?"

"That was awesome. I love your friends. Aces. Remi's grandmother. Marley. The condom king. Blink's brother...I can't believe how alike they are. The rest of the Night Walkers."

Smiley snorted. "Night Stalkers."

She waved her hand. "Whatever. I haven't danced like that since...well, it's been a long time. And I had too much to drink."

"I noticed. You feel okay?" Smiley asked.

"I feel awesome," she said with a breathy sigh.

And just like that, the erection he'd been fighting all night sprang to life in his pants.

"What is it about a man in uniform that is *so* hot?" Bree asked, her gaze boring into his.

Smiley and the rest of his team, as well as the former SEALs, hadn't worn their uniforms. Kevlar and Blink insisted everyone be as comfortable as possible. So the thought of his woman ogling another man in his dress whites didn't sit well with him.

He frowned.

"No frowning allowed!" she admonished.

"Not sure I like you thinking my friends in their uniforms are hot," he admitted truthfully.

"Well, maybe you should put yours on when we get home so I can think *you're* hot," Bree countered. "Not that I don't think that already. You in that polo shirt and dress slacks tonight? *Woo-wee*...you're lucky I didn't jump you on the dance floor. But I think seeing you in that white uniform, with that hat and all the medals I'm sure you have? You'd be getting lucky for sure," she giggled.

Smiley couldn't stand it a moment longer. He needed to get his woman home. In bed. Now. He backed out of the parking spot and headed down the dark, empty streets toward his apartment complex.

"Yeah?" he finally managed to say.

"Oh yeah," she said in that breathy tone that did nothing to control his erection.

Smiley drove a little faster.

He got them home safely, then rushed her up to the apartment. Once safely locked inside, he took Bree's hand and led her to the bedroom. He put his hands on her shoulders when she was in the middle of the room and said, "Stay here. *Right* here. Do not move. Not an inch, understand?"

She nodded eagerly. The lust was easy to see in her face and the way she licked her lips.

Thankful for the large walk-in closet, and the room it provided for him to change, it didn't take long for Smiley to strip off the clothes he was wearing and put on his dress whites.

His Bree wanted a man in uniform? She'd get a man in uniform.

He strode back into his bedroom.

Bree hadn't moved, and as he stalked out of the closet, her mouth fell open.

"Holy crap," she whispered.

"Ma'am," Smiley said, giving her a little bow as he reached her.

He wasn't sure what to expect—but it wasn't for Bree to fall to her knees and swiftly start tugging at his belt.

Before he could take his next breath, his cock was engulfed in her mouth. It was all Smiley could do to stay standing. His fingers flew into her hair, totally ruining her hairdo for good, and he held on as he received the most intense blowjob he'd ever had in his life.

He tried to pull her off his cock at one point, desperate to be inside her, but she was having none of that. Bree's head tilted up as she sucked him, and seeing her lips stretched around his dick, her gaze locked on his own, was more than Smiley could take.

"Let go if you don't want my load in your mouth," he warned.

In response, Bree sucked harder.

Smiley blew. And his Bree did her best to swallow every drop of come he gave her, but some still leaked out the sides of her mouth. It was the most erotic thing Smiley had ever experienced.

He pulled her up and yanked her dress over her hips. He ripped her underwear trying to get it off then lifted her into his arms.

His cock, which had just been drained seconds earlier, was already back at full mast. He plunged deep inside her body without a second's hesitation.

They both moaned. Smiley stumbled forward, bracing Bree against the wall as he took her hard and fast. Both her hands went into his hair, knocking off his hat. Neither noticed.

Smiley had no idea how long he'd been thrusting hard into his woman, lost to the pleasure, when she began to shake, squeezing the hell out of his cock from the inside. She let out a small scream as she came, taking Smiley down with her.

When he could breathe again, he felt rung out. Staggering, he aimed for the bed, dropping Bree onto her back as soon as he reached it.

She smiled up at him lazily and lowed her legs from around his waist, stretching like a cat in a beam of sunlight. "Oh yeah, you're hot in your uniform, Jude Stark."

Her words sent goose bumps down both arms. "Glad you think so," he said, before he began to take off the uniform he'd put on minutes earlier.

"A strip tease to boot? Lucky me," Bree sassed as she came up on her elbows to watch him disrobe.

She hadn't tugged her skirt down to cover herself, and as Smiley got undressed as fast as humanly possible, he saw her pussy glistening in the overhead light from his come and her own juices.

"Fuck," he muttered, feeling his cock twitch.

"Goody," she said, as she saw him thicken, licking her lips.

"You're going to kill me," he mock-complained as he leaned over her.

"But what a way to go," she countered, lifting her arms to wrap them around his neck.

In less than a minute, Smiley had removed Bree's dress

and they were both naked in his bed and ready for another round.

Later, much later, when they were both exhausted, the covers were totally askew, and he felt as if he were eighty rather than the thirty he actually was, Smiley found himself grinning up at the ceiling. That wasn't him. He never randomly lay in bed and smiled as he stared at the light above his head.

But with Bree snoring lightly in his ear as she lay bonelessly on top of him, sweaty and smelling like sex, he couldn't do anything *but* smile. For now, he was as content as he'd ever been in his life.

He'd die for this woman. For the right to experience this moment over and over again. Not the sex exactly—though that was great—but lying with Bree in his arms, hearing her snore, which meant she was completely relaxed. That she trusted him with her life.

He'd kill to have this for the rest of his life.

The tension of knowing someone was hunting her had obviously gotten to Bree. She'd let down her guard tonight. And Smiley realized how much of herself she'd been hiding from him. He wanted *tonight's* Bree to be the woman he had every day. And he'd do whatever it took to make that happen.

* * *

Mateo Castillo glared at the apartment complex his property had entered. This had to end. He knew where she was, and he was tired of this country. He needed to get back to his compound. Word was, things were falling apart without him. Four days ago, one of his girls had escaped—

which was inexcusable. Those responsible would die for allowing it to happen. He had to set an example.

He'd wanted to take Bree Haynes along with the other two bitches, the ones who'd escaped all those years ago, but he'd yet to find an opportunity to make that happen. He'd thought that moment was tonight. The women were all together. And he'd tried to get into the piece-of-shit bar, thinking while everyone was drunk and paying little attention, he could steal one, even all three of them out the back. But it turned out to be some private party. He couldn't get past the asshole at the door.

He'd pretended to be a tourist just passing by, hoping for a drink, but no matter what he said, he wasn't allowed inside. And when he'd seen all three of his targets dancing, drinks in hand, out on the dance floor, it had taken all his control to turn around and leave.

He'd been so close—and yet denied his prize.

Fuck that.

It was time to act. Time to get back to Ecuador. He had transport all arranged. For three, but he'd take one if he had to. The youngest. The one he'd paid for, who could earn him the most money in return. His buyers in Russia and North Korea might have to wait for another shipment.

Looking at his watch and seeing it was three in the morning, Mateo reached forward and started the engine. Within a week, he'd be home. Counting his money and making sure no other bitch thought it was a good idea to escape. He was their master, and they did what he demanded. Period.

Bree Haynes would learn that the hard way. Learn that running only delayed the inevitable. After she was trained, she'd spend the rest of her days locked in the very special box he was having built just for her. One she'd only be allowed out of twice a day to use the bathroom...or when it was time for her to take whatever a man wanted to give her.

Mateo smirked. Women were good for one thing only. Spreading their legs and letting men take what they wanted. She'd learn that or die. It was that simple. He'd spent good money on the bitch, and he'd get that money out of her one way or another. That's how his operation worked. Training the bitches was the fun part. Breaking them. He loved to see the life drain out of their eyes as they accepted their new reality.

Bree Haynes would be no different. She was *his*—and he always got what he paid for.

CHAPTER NINE

Bree was cautiously optimistic. She and the rest of Smiley's team had a phone call with the mysterious Tex yesterday afternoon, and he'd confirmed again that he and his crew of computer geniuses not only had proof that Mateo Castillo was in Riverton, but now, they also knew where he was staying—and had relayed that information to the FBI, the Riverton PD, and the sheriff's office.

Today, the Fugitive Apprehension Tactical Enforcement Unit, part of the FBI Violent Crimes Task Force, had been preparing to apprehend him, and that was supposed to go down any moment now. Castillo was apparently wanted in several countries for kidnapping and for his involvement in the sex trade. The various police forces were surprised he was in the United States, but they weren't going to waste time wondering why.

Hopefully by tonight, Bree's nightmare would be over and she could get her life back on track. Of course, that was kind of scary too...because she'd been enjoying living with Smiley here in Riverton. She was becoming closer to

Kelli, Remi, and all the women, and honestly, she didn't want to go back to Las Vegas.

But while things with Smiley were going well, or at least she thought so, she wasn't sure either of them were at the point where they wanted to move in with each other permanently.

Well...Bree was pretty sure that's what *she* wanted, but she wasn't going to assume anything when it came to Smiley. He'd taken her in out of necessity. *Her* necessity. And from what she understood, he'd been somewhat obsessed with finding her ever since she'd snuck away from his truck that awful night when he, Preacher, and Blink had come to rescue Josie from her ex-boyfriend's mother and sister.

The truth was, Bree was a little torn. A small part of her missed her old life, the one that was predictable and boring...but safe. A bigger part was loving *this* life. Being with Smiley every minute of every day. Cooking with him. Watching TV. Laughing. Making love. She didn't like that she had no money of her own coming in, but she was confident she could find a job here in Southern California.

Shaking her head, she reined in her wayward thoughts. She had no business planning a life here in Riverton until her current shitshow of a life was figured out. With luck, Tex and the law enforcement officers would get in touch in a few hours and let them know Mateo had been apprehended and her life on the run and in hiding was done.

"Are you sure this is okay?" Bree blurted.

Smiley looked over at her from behind the wheel of his truck and frowned. "Sure what is okay?"

"You bringing me to My Sister's Closet to meet up with

Fiona and Julie. It has to be old, shuttling me around everywhere."

"Why wouldn't it be okay?" Smiley asked, instead of directly answering her question.

She shrugged. "Because I can't imagine hanging out at a woman's boutique is your idea of a good time. And again, because you're a badass Navy SEAL who should probably be making plans with your teammates to go off and save the world or something. And instead of doing that, you're driving me around like you're my chauffeur or something."

To her surprise, Smiley pulled over and stopped his truck. He reached out and put his palm on the side of her neck as he spoke. "I told you when this all started that I wasn't letting you out of my sight, and I meant that. You want to go visit with Julie and Fiona and find some more clothes, that's what we'll do. I've been trying to get more clothes in my closet for you since you got there. As far as work...I have so much leave time saved up it isn't funny. Which doesn't even matter in this case, because we only left thirty minutes early. And the commander and the team know that at the moment, *you're* my priority."

"Not sure taking me shopping counts as a priority," Bree mumbled, dropping her gaze from his. "Especially now that Mateo is about to be caught. I can go access my storage unit in Vegas again."

"Look at me," Smiley ordered.

Bree lifted her eyes.

"This isn't about clothes," he said, in a tone that was in direct contrast to the grumpy exterior he always showed the world. "It's about you needing to do something while we wait to hear from Tex. It's about you connecting with two women who lived through an experience like the one you've been running from for months. It's about me proving that *you* come first, that I support you unequivocally. All right?"

Bree's belly churned, her breathing sped up, and all she wanted to do was throw herself at the man next to her. He made her feel seen. Important. Wanted. It was a heady feeling. And she so wanted to show Smiley her appreciation.

"Later," he said with a twitch of his lips, proving that he really was a mind reader.

"Thank you, Smiley. Seriously. I'm really anxious about Mateo. About finding out what happens. I don't want anyone to be hurt, but I definitely want to hear he's in custody. Do you really think I'll be safe if he's caught? Won't there be others on my trail? Like, people he works with?"

Smiley's fingers caressed her cheek for a moment before he dropped his hand and turned back to face forward. Checking for vehicles coming up behind them, and seeing it was clear, he pulled back onto the road and continued toward downtown Riverton and Julie's secondhand clothing shop.

"Tex went over this. He doesn't think so. For some reason, it's Castillo himself who seems determined to complete the sale your asshole ex made. I'm guessing the rest of his crew sees you as a liability. They could get their hands on other women much more easily."

Bree frowned. She hated the sound of that, even if it was true.

"How about we worry over what comes next *after* we hear back from Tex."

"Okay," Bree agreed.

Smiley deftly pulled into a parking spot in the public lot down the street from Julie's store. He took Bree's hand as they walked toward My Sister's Closet.

"I'll try not to be too long," she told him, still thinking about how he couldn't possibly want to spend time at a women's boutique.

"Take as long as you want. I know Julie usually has snacks and stuff, and coffee. You guys can shop and chat. I'm not going to leave you alone, sorry, but I'll try to be as nonintrusive as possible."

Bree smiled at him while they walked. "I don't mind you being there, Smiley. I have nothing to hide from you."

"Still, you might want to talk about girl shit."

She laughed. "Girl shit? Like what?"

"I don't know. Periods, giving birth, hemorrhoids..."

Bree stopped in her tracks and stared at him for a beat, before bursting into laughter. Smiley simply smiled at her in return. She realized he was messing with her but couldn't stop giggling. She was still chuckling when they reached My Sister's Closet. The bell over the door tinkled as they entered.

Almost immediately, Julie and Fiona appeared from a room at the back of the store.

"Hi!"

"It's so good to see you again!"

Both women came forward and hugged Bree warmly. She was well aware of Smiley still standing at her back.

"What's so funny?" Fiona asked, after she'd greeted both Bree and Smiley.

"Smiley's idea of girl talk."

Julie hooked an arm around Bree's and led her toward the coffee bar set up against one of the walls of the store, near the cash register. "Let me guess. That time of the month, which tampons are the best, and boobs."

Bree giggled again. "Close enough."

Smiley didn't seem perturbed that he was the butt of the joke. He simply shrugged, then turned and went to sit in one of the comfortable high-back chairs scattered around the store. Julie had likely bought them for situations just like this, when a guy accompanied his girlfriend or wife and needed a place to get off his feet for a while.

"Smiley, you want a coffee?" Julie asked.

"I'm good. Thanks."

"How much time do we have?" Fiona asked Bree.

"As much as we need," she said. "Smiley's done working for the day, so we're just heading home after this."

"Awesome. I received a pile of donations that I haven't had time to sort through yet. You guys want to help? Or, Bree, do you want to check out the things I put aside for you to try?" Julie asked.

"Ooooh, tough choice. Can we do both?" she asked.

"Both for sure. How about we start with the new stuff?"

"Sounds like a plan."

"They're in the back room. But a warning, they'll probably be wrinkled and stuff, so sometimes something might look like a mess right out of the plastic bags they're usually dropped off in, but it's a gem once cleaned and ironed."

"I can't wait to dig in," Bree said with a smile.

"You want to come to the back with us?" Julie asked Smiley.

"I'm good out here. I'll move the chair so I can see you guys back there, if that's okay."

"Of course it is."

Bree couldn't stop herself from walking over to where Smiley was sitting. She literally couldn't think of any previous boyfriends who would've done what this man was doing. Spending time babysitting her, keeping her safe, while she did something frivolous like look for clothes. Especially when she literally had a storage unit full of them back in Vegas.

She put her hands on the arms of the chair and leaned over him. "Thank you," she whispered before kissing him lightly.

His hand came up and clamped around the back of her neck when she went to stand up. "This isn't a hardship," he told her sternly. "Seeing you laughing and happy...it's my pleasure, Bree."

He was killing her.

"I'll show you tonight how much I appreciate you," she told him.

"Tonight? I'm thinking maybe we can get started as soon as we're home..."

She chuckled. "You're such a guy," she told him.

"Yeah, I am. A guy who appreciates a good thing when he has it. In case you're confused, *you're* that good thing."

"You're so getting some," she whispered, before leaning down once again. This time the kiss wasn't short *or* sweet.

"You two can make out later, we have bags to sort through!" Fiona called out, the amusement easy to hear in her tone.

Bree stood, Smiley caressing her hip as she did. She had a feeling she was blushing, but for the first time in a long time, she felt utterly carefree.

Today felt like the first day of the rest of her life, and

she was going to make the most of it. Go after what she wanted. And what she wanted most was Smiley.

"Go on. If you need anything, let me know," he said, shifting in the seat.

Bree's gaze went between his legs, and she saw his erection. She wrinkled her nose; that couldn't be comfortable. But Smiley physically turned her and gave her a little push toward the other two women before she could comment.

"Go. Do your thing."

"Yes, sir," she sassed.

The second she crossed the threshold between the outer store and the backroom, Fiona and Julie began to giggle.

"Girl, you two are hot together!" Fiona exclaimed.

Julie waved a hand in front of her face like a fan. "Scorching."

"Whatever," Bree said with a roll of her eyes, even though deep down, she agreed with both women. "Where are we starting?"

"Right. The new stuff is over there," Julie said, pointing at four large trash bags along one of the walls.

The back room was full of several racks of clothes, mostly dresses. Some had dry-cleaning tags on them and others were wrinkled, as if waiting to be brought to the cleaners. There were other boxes of supplies stacked up in the space as well. It was a crowded room, but organized and clean. There was a door that probably led to the alley that ran behind the row of stores along Main Street, and what Bree could see was a small bathroom as well.

"The first step is to take everything out of the bags and hang it up. Once it's all out, I usually look at each piece, try to validate the authenticity of the brand, you know, see if it's a knockoff or real, and then separate out what I think will sell and what I'll bring over to one of the general goodwill stores," Julie explained, as she headed toward the bags.

Bree followed, strangely excited to see what had been donated. It was like Christmas and her birthday rolled into one.

Forgetting about the arrest of Mateo Castillo for the moment, she lost herself in the pleasure of working alongside new friends.

* * *

Smiley watched the women with a small smile as they worked in the back room. If any of his teammates could see him now, they'd probably think he was sick and needed to consult a doctor. He didn't usually sit around and do nothing...much less sit around and watch a woman shop.

But listening to Bree and the others giggle and gasp in surprise and delight when they uncovered something special was an experience he'd never had, and never expected to actually enjoy.

Bree might think this was a waste of his time, but the more he was around her, the more he discovered the joys of simple pleasures.

The ringing of his cell made Smiley jerk in surprise, and he chuckled under his breath. Some badass SEAL *he* was, scared by his own damn phone.

Looking down, he saw it was Cookie—and he tensed. This couldn't be good.

Tex's call with Wolf's team about Castillo had been postponed. Smiley didn't know why and he hadn't asked—

but it was taking place today. There could only be one reason why Cookie was calling him now, and it wasn't to say hi.

"Smiley," he said as he answered.

"What the motherfucking *fuck*?" Cookie said in a low, pissed-off tone.

Smiley sighed as he studied the floor, frowning. Yup. Tex had definitely talked with Cookie and the others about Mateo Castillo. And the former SEAL clearly wasn't happy that he'd been kept in the dark, which Smiley didn't blame him for one bit.

As the days went by, Smiley had felt worse and worse about keeping intel from Wolf's team. It wasn't right, but he'd felt as if his hands were tied because of everything Tex was doing to help with Bree's situation.

But not telling his friends was the wrong decision. Period.

"I told Tex it wasn't a good idea not to tell you," Smiley said.

"Damn right it wasn't. I can't believe he—and you and your team—kept this from me! My wife went through *hell* at the hands of Castillo! Well, maybe not him specifically, but the damn organization he worked for, and you all thought it was a good idea to *not* tell me that he might not only be in the US, but in motherfucking *Riverton*?"

Cookie's voice had risen as he spoke, and Smiley worried the women could actually hear him, even though his cell wasn't on speaker.

"I'm going to step out front for a second," he called out to the women.

"Okay!"

"We'll be here."

"No problem!"

Smiley quickly stepped toward the front door of the shop and stood outside on the sidewalk as he spoke to Cookie.

"As I said, it wasn't my idea. I told Tex that you and Hurt deserved to know."

"Fiona continued to go through hell when she got back. Tex *knew* how badly she struggled. Hell, he kept her calm when she was lost in the delusion that her kidnappers had come for her. And now, despite the possibility they really *might have* come for her, he stays silent? It's bullshit!"

"It is," Smiley agreed. "But there's no evidence that Castillo knows anything about Fiona. Or Julie, for that matter. From what Tex was able to find out, he wasn't even in the jungle when you rescued them."

"I don't care," Cookie said, still sounding pissed off. "If there's a one percent chance that anyone from that fucking organization even knows my wife's *name*, I should've been informed."

"And I've agreed with you," Smiley told him. "Tex truly doesn't think Castillo is here for your wife or Julie. He wants Bree. Paid money for her. I told Tex he should talk to you, but he asked for more time to confirm whether Castillo was even part of that organization from years ago to begin with. He didn't want to alarm you for no reason if he was wrong. I gave him that time. It wasn't the right decision, and I'm sorry."

He heard Cookie take a deep breath, could practically picture him running a hand through his hair in agitation.

"Anything that has to do with my wife and that time in her life brings out the worst in me," he finally admitted.

"Actually, I think it brings out the best in you."

"Right. Talk to me, Smiley. Tex already gave me the deets about the hopeful apprehension of Castillo today, but I need to know what *you* think. Everything you know about the man. Why he's so determined to get his hands on Bree. All of it."

Smiley wasn't surprised by Cookie's demand. He'd ask the same if the roles were reversed.

Ten minutes later, he'd told Cookie everything. All his concerns about the situation, his opinions, and by the time he hung up the phone, his friend was much calmer than he'd been when he'd first called. But he was on his way to the store to pick up Fiona, just in case. He also said he'd call Patrick Hurt, his former commander, and give him the rundown of what was going on, which Smiley appreciated. The last thing he wanted was to get his ass chewed by Hurt as well, after being on the receiving end of Cookie's ire.

He re-entered My Sister's Closet and called out, "It's just me!" He didn't want the women to interrupt what they were doing, thinking a customer had walked in.

But to his surprise, he didn't get any kind of response.

The hair on the back of his neck immediately stood up, and Smiley reached for the KA-BAR knife he always carried. He walked quickly to the open door to the back room and looked inside.

His adrenaline spiked even higher when he saw the back door was wide open and the women were nowhere to be seen.

"*Fuck!* Shit, shit, shit!" he swore, as he pulled out his cell.

As he pressed on Cookie's name in his contacts, Smiley knew he'd fucked up. He'd sworn that Bree wouldn't be out of his sight until Castillo was caught—and yet he'd willingly walked out of the store, leaving not only his woman alone, but Fiona and Julie too.

It hit him hard as the phone rang in his ear.

Bree was gone. As was Julie and Fiona. The three women Mateo Castillo had every reason to want to kidnap. He was reclaiming what he felt was his. His friend's fears were justified...

And Smiley had been standing fifty feet away when it happened.

Cookie was going to lose his mind. He had every right to be even more pissed than he'd been before.

Smiley knew down to his bones that Castillo wasn't currently being apprehended by the special task force. He'd finally made his move.

So the hunt was on. *No one* fucked with the Navy SEALs and their women.

Castillo might think he'd won, but in reality, he'd just signed his own death warrant.

CHAPTER TEN

"Ooooh, look at this one!" Fiona exclaimed as she held up a sparkly dress. "The tag says it's a Versace."

Bree couldn't believe how fun this was. Each bag was a treasure trove of satin and lace. There were some duds mixed in, but for the most part, everything was beautiful. The donations would make so many girls and women happy. She hadn't found anything appropriate for herself yet, not for everyday living, but that was more than all right. She was having an amazing time anyway.

Looking through the door to the front, Bree could see Smiley pacing back and forth outside with his phone to his ear. He didn't look happy. Well, he looked unhappier than normal. Whoever he was talking to, and whatever they were talking about, it seemed intense. For a split second, she wondered if it was about her, but then she mentally rolled her eyes at herself. Just because Smiley was having what looked like an important phone call, that didn't mean it was about her.

Besides, if it was about Mateo hopefully being captured, surely he wouldn't hesitate to let her know. He knew how stressed she was about what was going down today.

She'd just turned to dig back into the bag she'd been assigned when suddenly the door that led into the alley slammed open.

Shocked, Bree didn't have time to do anything but gape before three men stormed in. They each made a beeline for a woman. The largest of the men came toward her, and Bree tried to back away, only to trip over one of the bags sitting on the floor behind her.

"No!" Julie yelled. "Let—"

The rest of her words were cut off abruptly as the man who'd grabbed her slapped a hand over her mouth.

Fiona was struggling with another man, who'd lifted her completely off her feet and was already walking toward the door.

The man nearest Bree reached down and grabbed her upper arm, yanking her back onto her feet roughly.

Then he wrapped an arm around her neck and squeezed.

Bree grabbed his arm, trying to wrench it away from her neck so she could breathe, with no luck. He force-marched her out the back door, following the other two men.

The entire abduction took less than thirty seconds. And aside from the door banging open, it was eerily silent. The men hadn't said a word, and Bree—and Julie and Fiona too—had been too surprised and overpowered to scream. To try to alert Smiley that something was terribly wrong.

The kidnappers dragged them toward a large black SUV and opened the back hatch. Bree's vision was going dark, as the man who held her hadn't loosened his arm even a fraction. She took in gulps of air when he finally let go to shove her into the cargo area of the vehicle.

Her arms and legs tangled with Julie and Fiona's, and before they could untangle themselves, the back hatch slammed shut.

"Fuck!" Julie exclaimed, as she began to desperately fumble for any kind of latch or handle that would open the back hatch again.

Sparing a glance at Fiona, Bree saw that she was huddled in on herself, staring into space.

"Help me!" Julie cried, as the vehicle began to move.

Bree scrambled to her side, and when she didn't see any kind of handle, she went to her ass and began to kick at the glass with all her strength. Julie followed suit, but the glass refused to break.

That's when Bree realized her vision was going foggy.

Looking around, she discovered it wasn't her vision. There was *literally* fog filling the back area of the vehicle! It was only then she noticed the clear partition between the cargo area where she, Julie, and Fiona had been placed, and the backseat.

Two of the men who'd grabbed them were staring back through the Plexiglas, grinning manically.

Bree coughed and felt the world start to spin.

"Oh, shit," Julie muttered, as she brought her shirt up to cover her nose and mouth.

But it was no use. The fog was thick and it was getting harder and harder to think. They were being drugged. She could only think of one person who'd have a vehicle made with unbreakable glass, a partition between the cargo area and the rest of the car, and a way to gas the occupants.

Mateo Castillo.

He wasn't being handcuffed and taken to jail. He was *here*. Now. And he'd found her.

Not only her, but he'd taken Julie and Fiona as well.

It wasn't fair! They'd already been through hell.

Crawling over to Fiona, Bree wrapped her arms around the woman and held on as tightly as she could, even as she felt herself losing consciousness. Whatever Mateo had in store for them wouldn't be good. She knew that as well as she knew her own name. But she vowed to do whatever it took to get Fiona and Julie out of this. Mateo was after *her*. Not them.

The last thought she had before passing out was how pissed Smiley was going to be. The guilt he'd feel would be overwhelming. He'd assigned himself as her protector, and yet she'd been taken right out from under his nose.

She had no idea how Mateo had known where and when to strike, but that didn't matter anymore. All that mattered was surviving until Smiley and his friends could find them.

* * *

Thirty minutes later, Safe's house was packed to the gills, but Smiley barely noticed. He couldn't get the sight of that empty back room out of his head. He hadn't heard a damn thing. No screams. Nothing. Castillo had swooped in and somehow taken all three women without making a sound.

Hurt had already given Tex access to the store's security camera footage. He was already working on tracking

Castillo through other CCTV cameras in the area. Meanwhile, Hurt was trying to connect the security camera app for Julie's system to the television at Safe's house, so they could view the footage.

Even knowing Tex was on this, Smiley felt sick. He couldn't help but feel as if this was his fault.

"What the fuck went wrong with the task force?" Cookie bit out. He wasn't asking anyone in particular, but the room in general.

All of Cookie's former teammates were there. As were Smiley's friends. Everyone wanted to *do* something, but they didn't have a direction to take yet. So they had to wait. Which normally wouldn't be a problem, they were all used to waiting, but this time things were personal. Not only was Bree's life in danger, but Fiona and Julie's too.

And everyone was more than aware of what had happened all those years ago in Mexico. How badly the women had been abused. How Fiona had been drugged. And how she'd had that relapse when she'd come back to California. This was literally her worst nightmare come true.

And Julie...she hadn't exactly dealt well with being a captive last time, although she was definitely a different person now than she was all those years ago.

Then there was Bree. Yes, she'd been taken from her apartment back in Vegas, but she'd been rescued pretty quickly. How was she holding up?

Smiley couldn't stop thinking about what he should've done. How he should've kept her on base or at his apartment until he'd gotten confirmation that Castillo was taken into custody.

Minutes later, Hurt had finally gotten the security

footage pulled up from My Sister's Closet, and everyone gathered around the TV to watch.

Kevlar sidled up next to Smiley and put his arm around his shoulders. He needed the support, and didn't push his team leader's arm away. He wasn't sure he could handle seeing Bree being taken.

As he leaned against Kevlar, Hurt clicked play. Holding his breath, Smiley watched as the girls smiled and chatted. Fiona held up a dress she'd just taken out of one of the garbage bags full of clothing. Then the back door slammed open, and all three women spun around as three men stormed inside.

To Smiley's shock, Castillo himself was among the three kidnappers. He stood out amongst the others, as he was quite large, both in height and weight. He stormed toward Bree, who stumbled backward and tripped over one of the bags.

Fiona and Julie were struggling with the other two men as Castillo grabbed Bree. He wrapped his arm around her neck, and Smiley could barely breathe himself as he imagined the panic Bree must've been feeling.

And just like that, the back room was empty.

The entire kidnapping had taken no more than thirty seconds.

Twenty-four seconds, to be exact.

The view changed to the camera in the back alley, and Smiley watched as the women were forced into the cargo area of a large SUV. He could see Julie pounding on the back glass as the vehicle sped out of the alley.

To everyone's dismay, they could clearly see the license plate on the SUV had been blacked out. No doubt they would pull over somewhere and take the tape off so they wouldn't be stopped by the cops.

After watching the video, the room was silent as the men absorbed what they'd seen.

Smiley didn't know what to say. To do. His first instinct was to get in his car and start looking for that black SUV. But he didn't know where to start. Riverton itself wasn't a huge city, but it was close to others in Southern California. They could be anywhere by now.

Tex had notified border control, and they were on the lookout for the vehicle and the men who'd taken the women. But Castillo wasn't stupid. He wouldn't attempt to simply drive across the border in the same car he'd used to abduct the women. Also, Smiley knew for a fact that Bree wouldn't just sit in the back and not scream her head off if there was a chance someone could hear her. He figured Fiona and Julie would do the same.

No, Castillo would have to subdue the women in some way—and that was what worried him the most.

"*Fuck*," he swore.

Kevlar tightened his grip around Smiley for a moment, then straightened.

"All right. Tex already confirmed the damn trackers are malfunctioning—which means the kidnappers almost definitely did something to them, since all three women were wearing at least one, and no way in hell do several trackers malfunction at once—we can't just head straight to their location. Which fucking *sucks*. But we also can't stand around with our thumbs up our asses either. So we split up. Some of us will check out the roads leading to the border, others will go to the coast and the shipyards. We should also take a look at the truck stops. He's going to try to take them out of the country, we all agree on that, right?"

Everyone nodded.

"He could go east until he gets to a crossing that he feels is less hot," Dude suggested.

"What about airports? This asshole has the funds to be able to hire a pilot, right?" Preacher asked.

Smiley hadn't even thought about that. With every word out of his colleagues' mouths, his tension increased tenfold.

"We have to find them. Fiona can't go through this again," Cookie said, sounding distraught.

"We're going to find her. All of them," Wolf said sternly, clapping a hand on Cookie's shoulder and holding on.

"You heard Tex. He's pissed. Mostly at himself. He fucked up, and he knows it. If we'd known about Castillo before today, we could've locked down the women," Benny said.

Smiley was done. He couldn't think about what Bree and the others might be going through as they all stood around and talked about how fucked up this was. He had to *do* something. Turning, he headed for the door.

"Where are you going?" Mozart called out.

"To look for Bree," Smiley barked without slowing down.

He heard footsteps, and he braced himself to fight whoever was coming after him if they tried to stop him.

Instead, he heard Cookie say, "I'm going with him."

"I'm driving," Blink told them.

"Give me one second, Smiley," Kevlar said.

"No."

"Damn it! Stop for a fucking second. We need to be methodical about this. We don't want to miss them!"

Kevlar sounded pissed, and Smiley heard the order in his tone. Taking a deep breath, he stopped, turning to look at his friend. He'd give him one more minute, out of respect, but after that he was out of here.

Kevlar quickly grabbed a notepad that was sitting on Safe's counter. "Okay, Smiley—you, Cookie, and Blink head east and check out the truck stops on the way to I-8. Hurt, Wolf, and Flash, you go south, look at the stops near I-5 heading toward Tijuana. Safe, Preacher, Dude, and Benny will head to the shipyard. See if you can talk to a foreman and look at security tapes. I'm sure Tex and his crew will get to them eventually, but if we can get a head start looking at them to see if a black SUV unloaded anything into a shipping container, that'll be good.

"MacGyver, Mozart, Abe, and I will check out the regional airports. *Everyone* stays in control. We're all pissed off about this, but going off half-cocked isn't going to help Fiona, Julie, or Bree. Got it?" Kevlar asked.

"What are we telling the women? Caroline's been blowing up my phone. She knows something's up because of the way I left the house so abruptly," Wolf said.

"The truth," Smiley said, before anyone else could offer their opinions. "They need to stay alert. We have no idea if Castillo has eyes on any of them."

"Fuck!"

"Shit!"

"Damn it!"

It was obvious no one else had thought about that. They'd been so focused on figuring out where Castillo might be taking Fiona, Julie, and Bree, they hadn't even considered he might try to grab anyone else.

As one, everyone in the room—except Smiley, Cookie, and Hurt—brought their cells to their ears as they called their wives and girlfriends.

Five minutes later, everyone had frowns on their faces and the tension in the air was so thick it was almost hard to breathe. "Jessyka's getting in touch with the others and telling them to come to our house," Benny said to his teammates. "It's large enough to accommodate everyone, including the kids."

"And Wren's having everyone meet her here," Safe added.

"Do we think having the women and kids all in one place is a good idea?" Preacher asked.

"Yes," Dude said firmly. "There's power and safety in numbers. And now that everyone knows what's going on, they aren't going to be surprised like Fiona, Julie, and Bree were. Cheyenne will be armed. No one is going to get close to her or the others."

"Same with Remi," Kevlar agreed. "She's pissed. Scared, but angry as hell."

Smiley was done. He was glad the women would be protected, but he couldn't stop thinking about Bree and how scared *she* was. He didn't want to imagine what she was going through.

Turning, he headed for the door once again, Cookie and Blink at his heels. Searching truck stops felt like a futile mission. But it had been an hour now since they'd been taken, and doing *something* was better than sitting around, waiting on Tex or one of the women he was working with to get back to them. If they found out any info, they'd be in touch and could move to plan B. Or C, D, F, Q. Whatever.

All that mattered was finding the women before Castillo got them out of the country. Things would get much more complicated if that happened.

Complicated, but not impossible.

For the first time, Smiley understood Phantom a little better.

Phantom was a SEAL who'd gone rogue and traveled on his own out of the country to rescue a woman he'd never spoken to in person, had only seen once—at the bottom of a pit filled with dead bodies, where rebels had thrown her after allegedly killing the woman. But she wasn't dead. After his team had left Timor-Leste, Phantom thought he remembered seeing her foot move...but no one believed him. He'd been determined to rescue her, with or without his commander's or the Navy's permission.

Smiley hadn't approved when he'd heard what the SEAL had done. He couldn't understand why the man would risk his career and jail time to rescue a woman he didn't even know. Hell, even if he *had* known her, he didn't understand the desire to risk everything he'd worked so hard for, without concrete proof she was even alive.

But now he did.

If Bree was taken out of the US, nothing would stop him from going after her. He'd promised that if anything happened, he'd come for her. And by damn, he wouldn't break that vow. No fucking way. He had a feeling Cookie and Hurt would be right there at his side. They might not have as much to lose as he did when it came to their professions, but they were still risking their retirements.

"I'm driving," Blink announced, as they headed out of

the house. Smiley lobbed his keys toward his friend without comment. He didn't mind if Blink drove, the man might not talk much, but he could be a psycho behind the wheel. He'd learned as much during one of their missions.

As he, Cookie, and Blink piled into his truck, Smiley took a deep breath. Bree had to be all right. She had to. He'd just found her. He couldn't lose her now.

CHAPTER ELEVEN

Bree was having a dream that she was late for school and running through a snowstorm to get there. She'd just opened the door to the school, only to find she'd entered some kind of barn instead. She was freezing. Looking down, she saw she didn't have any shoes on. Or clothes.

Damn, she was having one of those "naked" dreams. She hated those.

Shivering, she opened her eyes...and realized she wasn't dreaming. She really *was* freezing. Her hands felt like ice, and whatever she was lying on was hard as a rock.

Confused, Bree turned her head, wondering why Smiley wasn't in bed next to her, keeping her warm.

But instead of seeing Smiley, she saw bars.

Bars?

Scrambling to her knees too fast, she yelped when her head hit something hard. Bending again, Bree tried to understand what was happening. Where she was.

There was a weird red light above her head, giving her the ability to see, but things were almost distorted. The rods and cones in her eyes were having a hard time adjusting to her surroundings. Whimpering in confusion, she turned her head the other way—and froze.

"What the hell?" she whispered. It was comforting somehow to hear her own voice. "Fiona?" she said a little louder.

And just like that, she remembered everything.

Well, not everything, obviously, but enough. She, Julie, and Fiona had been in My Sister's Closet, looking at the newest donations, when three men had come in and grabbed them. The last thing she remembered was being shoved into the back of that black SUV and realizing the fog in the air was actually some sort of gas or sedative.

"Fiona!" she said again, louder, getting as close to the bars of her cage as she could. She was in what looked like some sort of dog crate. Metal bars all around her, plastic tray under her ass. Looking down, Bree saw why she was so cold, as well. All she had on was a spaghetti-strap gown. A negligee or slip. She wasn't sure *what* it was, just that it barely covered her ass and wasn't nearly enough material to keep her warm.

But for the moment, she was more concerned about Fiona. She was lying unmoving in the cage next to Bree's. Stretching her arm through the bars as much as she could, Bree couldn't reach her.

"Fiona!" she yelled, desperately wanting the other woman to wake up.

"Bree?"

Looking past Fiona's cage, Bree saw Julie on the other side, also in a cage of her own.

"Julie!" The relief she felt at not being alone in this hell was almost overwhelming. Julie wore the same skimpy outfit. Of course on her, since she was so petite, it came down almost to her knees.

Fiona groaned, and Bree turned her attention back to the other woman.

"Fiona! Wake up! It's me, Bree. Julie's here too. Please, wake up."

It took a little bit, but eventually Fiona regained consciousness. Bree wasn't sure how the other woman was going to handle the situation. She'd kind of frozen when they'd been locked in the back of that SUV. Shut down. Bree didn't blame her. How could she, when she was literally reliving her worst nightmare.

"Where are we?" Fiona croaked.

"From what it feels like, we're in a truck or something," Julie said.

"What's that smell?"

Bree had been so focused on waking Fiona and trying to get her brain to catch up to what was happening, she hadn't realized how bad it smelled in whatever container they were being held in.

"Look around. Chickens."

Bree did just that, and she realized Julie was right. They were surrounded by cages filled with chickens. She'd obviously pushed the sounds of the birds to the back of her head as she processed everything else. But now, as reality set in, the stench of excrement from all the animals surrounding them registered. She gagged.

"I can't believe this is fucking happening again!" Fiona seethed.

Surprised at the venom in her voice, Bree looked at her once more. She was sitting cross-legged in her cage now, her head bent since she couldn't sit up straight, and glaring at nothing.

"Fiona?" Bree asked, worried about her mental health.

"What?" she barked, turning to look at her. "Fucking kidnapped. *Again*! As if once wasn't bad enough. Fuck!"

Relieved she wasn't sobbing her heart out and completely on the verge of a mental breakdown, Bree still wasn't sure how to respond to the pissed-off woman. She considered her a friend, but hadn't known her long enough to know if her current emotions were a precursor to losing it altogether or not.

"Fiona, are your earrings in?" Julie asked.

Fiona reached a hand up to touch her ears, then swore again. "Shit, no. You?"

"No. They also took my barrettes."

"And our clothes. All of them," Fiona said.

Bree was confused. They were in some sort of truck filled with livestock after being kidnapped and gassed and stuffed in cages...and Fiona and Julie were worried about their accessories?

"And my ring too. The one Cookie gave me," Fiona said, sounding sad for the first time since she woke up.

"Mine too. Bree, do you have any of Tex's trackers on you?" Julie asked.

Finally, understanding dawned. They weren't upset about losing jewelry. Taking a mental inventory, and feeling her throat for the necklace she'd chosen to wear this morning—and not finding it—she said softly, "No."

Without the trackers, how was Smiley going to find her? How were *any* of the SEALs going to find them? As much as she tried to tamp it down, panic began to creep in.

"Okay, nobody panic," Fiona ordered, as if she could feel Bree's downward slide. "Anyone know who these assholes are who took us?"

Bree hated that Fiona didn't know this already—and she was terrified to be the one to have to break the news. But it was too late to try to protect them now. They were in deep shit. Taking a resigned breath, she said, "Mateo Castillo. I'm so sorry you two got caught up in this. He's the guy who bought me from my ex. He's the one who's been looking for me for so long, who I've been trying to hide from. He was supposed to be taken into custody today. Tex said there were all these task force people who were going to surround his hotel and get him."

"That was obviously a major fail," Julie said sarcastically.

Bree wasn't tempted to laugh at that. Not even a little. "And there's more," she said a little reluctantly. So far, Julie and Fiona were handling this situation better than she was...but they didn't know the rest.

"More?" Fiona asked.

Bree forced herself to meet the other woman's gaze. "Yeah. Mateo? He was a part of the group that took you guys, all those years ago. He wasn't in charge, and he wasn't there when you were rescued, but he was a low-level player in that group. Tex said that he rose in the ranks over the years, and then started his own organization."

"Are you *shitting* me?" Julie asked.

Bree didn't take her eyes from Fiona's. "No. Tex didn't want to tell Cookie and Hurt until he knew for certain and had more intel on the guy." She held her breath, praying Fiona wasn't going to completely lose it.

To her surprise, Fiona shifted to the side of her cage

closest to Bree's. She reached her fingers through the bars and wiggled them impatiently.

Bree's hand came up without thought, and she gripped Fiona's fingers.

"This isn't like the last time," she said firmly. "First off, we aren't alone. We have each other. And even if these assholes separate us, we have an ace up our sleeves."

"What's that?" Bree asked, the thought of being separated from these women enough to make her want to have a complete breakdown. The only reason she was handling this as well as she was, for the moment, was because she wasn't alone.

"Our guys. Cookie said something to me once, back after I was rescued and when I had that little...episode, where I thought my kidnappers had found me. He told me, and I quote, 'I'll always come for you.' I've never forgotten it. Ever. Cookie is never, ever going to give up until he finds me. Of that I have no doubt."

"Our SEALs are probably turning Riverton upside down right about now," Julie agreed.

"But I'm guessing we aren't in Riverton," Bree whispered. "And we don't have Tex's trackers anymore. We could be anywhere. How will they find us?"

"I don't know. But I trust Hurt. And Tex. And Cookie. And Smiley and his team. All we have to do is hold on. No matter what happens, we have to hold on. They're coming for us," Julie promised.

Fiona squeezed Bree's fingers, hard. "Positive thinking, Bree. You have to stay positive."

"I don't know if I can," she admitted, suddenly terrified of what was to come. All these months she'd been hiding, living out of her car, she hadn't ever really thought about what would happen if she was caught. Intellectually, she was aware of what Fiona, Julie, and countless other women went through when they were forced into sexual slavery. But it had all been an abstract concept.

Now? Sitting in this cage, surrounded by livestock, on their way to who knew where...reality was hitting home. Hard.

"You can," Fiona told her sternly. "*Nothing* they can do to us will make our men love us any less."

Bree let her words sink in. Fiona and Julie were married. Had been for years. Were in committed relationships. She and Smiley...what were they? They were still practically strangers. She didn't even know what his favorite color was. Or if he was allergic to any kinds of foods. Or where his favorite place to vacation was!

Just then, the truck lurched and the women were all thrown against the sides of their cages, as were the birds all around them. A cacophony of sound erupted, making Bree put her hands over her ears to try to drown it out. Putting them in with all these live animals was a smart move. Any noise they tried to make would set off the birds and drown out their cries and screams.

As the ruckus continued, Bree had an epiphany. She didn't need to know all the trivial things about Smiley to know she loved him. She wouldn't have moved in with him if she didn't. Wouldn't be sleeping with him every night.

She *knew* Smiley. And she loved him. Was pretty sure that a man like him, who could have any woman he wanted, never would have moved her into his home if he didn't love her right back.

The three of them weren't alone in the world. Not only did they have some badass Navy SEALs who loved them, their men had others who'd have *their* backs. Bree had a feeling if they asked, the entire SEAL network would be activated. No one was going to stop looking for them until they were found and returned home, safe and sound.

It was a powerful thought. It gave Bree the strength to take a deep breath—and then she promptly choked on the feathers, the smell of excrement, and the sense of danger in the air.

That hadn't been a great idea, but she still felt stronger.

No matter what happened. What Mateo might have in store for her, she wouldn't break. She might not have told Smiley that she loved him, and she might not have heard the words in return, but that didn't mean she didn't know down to her soul that she and Smiley were meant to be together. He was out there. Losing his mind, scowling, barking at people, doing whatever needed to be done to find her. She simply had to hang on until that happened.

"Bree? Are you okay?" Fiona asked from the next cage.

"I'm okay. Julie, are you all right?" Bree asked.

"Pissed, but hanging in there," the other woman responded.

"Right. So we're all okay," Fiona said. "Surrounded by shit, choking on the stench, freezing in these fucking ridiculous slips, but okay. Now—how are we going to get the hell out of here?"

Bree was surprised to feel a smile forming on her face. Never in a million years would she have thought Fiona would step up to be their leader. Not after how broken she'd been when this same thing had happened to her all those years ago, or after she'd curled into a fetal position in the back of that SUV. But time, and true love, had a way of giving you strength.

Bree just hoped it was enough. That Mateo wouldn't simply decide to kill them all. Alive, they could handle whatever he had planned long enough for their men to swoop in and save the day. But if they were dead—

Bree cut off the thought.

No. Mateo wouldn't have gone to the lengths he had if he was just going to kill them. He could've done that at the store. Or while they were unconscious. He had a plan for them.

What he didn't realize was that by taking them, he was as good as dead.

Smiley wouldn't let him live after this, of that Bree had no doubt. And Cookie, Hurt, and the rest of the SEALs would be lining up to make sure the deed was done. She, Julie, and Fiona simply had to figure out a way to make their job easier. If they could escape Mateo and his goons, and these damn chickens, it would make the SEALs' job a hell of a lot easier.

It was time to plan.

* * *

"Anything?" Cookie barked into his phone as they pulled into the fourth truck stop east of Riverton to search for any sign of the black SUV and the women.

"No. You guys?" Wolf asked, his voice echoing around the cab of the truck through the cellphone speaker.

"No. And I spoke with Dude and Mozart and they've struck out too. Any word from Tex?"

"Not yet," Wolf said.

Smiley clenched his teeth as Blink drove slowly through the maze of trucks parked at the truck stop. It was fully dark now. The women had been gone for nearly four hours. Thoughts of what they could be going through ate at him. He'd never felt like this before. As if his insides were being slowly pulled out of his body one inch at a time.

He'd been concerned when he couldn't find Bree during all those trips to Vegas, when he was hunting for her. And that was before he'd gotten to know her. Before he'd connected with her on both a physical and emotional level.

He'd spent almost every moment with her for the last few weeks. To not have her there now...it physically hurt. But underlying the pain was an anger that was festering. Bubbling. Ready to overflow.

Even with his job as a SEAL, he'd never felt he was a particularly violent man. Yes, he did some violent things as part of his job, but he was able to turn the other cheek when it came to the assholes he encountered in his regular life. People who thought their needs and wants were more important than those of everyone around them. Fuckers who had no problem cutting him off in traffic or butting in front of others in a line, simply because *they* were in a hurry.

But right now? Smiley was itching to hurt someone. No, not someone. Mateo Castillo and the other assholes who dared break into My Sister's Closet and take what didn't belong to them. Not that Julie, Fiona, and Bree *belonged* to anyone but themselves.

The anger and violence simmering under the surface of his skin should've worried him. But it didn't. He was more than ready to kill the men for touching Bree. He'd watched the video. Had seen the panic in her eyes when her oxygen was cut off. Watched how she'd clawed at Castillo's arm. The vision in his head made his hands clench as he strained to see any hint that the women had been at the truck stop. Maybe they were still there.

He didn't know what he was looking for though. The black SUV, yes, but by now the women had certainly been transferred to some other mode of transportation. Truck, train, boat...the shitty thing was, they had no idea how Castillo was planning on getting them out of the country. They just had no doubt that he *was*. His operation was out of Ecuador. Surely that's where he was heading.

"Fuck! This is hopeless," Cookie swore, as he hung up with Wolf. "We should just go to fucking Ecuador already. Meet the asshole at *his* house."

"If we can't find how he's getting them out of the country, that's what we'll do," Blink said calmly. "But if at all possible, we want to intercept him now. Save the women the trauma of that transport."

He was right. Of course he was. But his words made Smiley feel even sicker than he did already.

They were driving past a row of semi-trucks that were all backed into designated parking spaces at the truck stop, but there was one empty space between a semi from a big-box store and a logistics company truck.

If he hadn't been focusing right on the area behind the trucks, he would've missed it. As it was, Smiley wasn't sure *what* he'd seen.

"Wait! Stop!"

All three men were thrown forward as Blink stomped on the brake.

"Back up! I saw something!" Smiley exclaimed.

Putting the truck in reverse, Blink gunned it backward until they were parallel to the empty parking space. Squinting, trying to see what was lying in the grass under the trees behind the line of trucks, Smiley reached for the door handle.

Blink and Cookie were at his heels as he raced toward the tree line.

Unfortunately—or fortunately—the object on the ground wasn't one of the women. It was a pile of clothing. To anyone else it might look like garbage.

But Smiley recognized the blouse Bree had been wearing.

It was one of her four outfits she'd brought with her from Vegas, and she'd told him it was a favorite because it had sunflowers all over it that made her smile when she wore it. How many times had he already folded that blouse after washing it?

Turning abruptly, Smiley managed just three steps away from the mound of clothing, doubled over, and threw up.

Seeing Bree's clothes in a heap on the ground, in the dirt, hammered home that whatever had happened to her, whatever was *still* happening, wasn't good.

"That's Fiona's," Cookie said, pointing out another shirt.

"You okay?" Blink asked quietly, putting a hand on Smiley's back.

He stood and wiped his mouth with the sleeve of his shirt. "No," he said succinctly, turning back to the pile of clothing. He crouched next to it, not sure if he should touch anything or not. Leaning closer, he swore again.

"Cookie, tell me those aren't the earrings your wife was wearing...the ones you told me have trackers in them?"

"*Fuck*. And her wedding rings. And those are the barrettes and earrings Hurt said Julie was wearing, also from Tex."

Smiley nodded. "Bree was wearing that necklace. It was her favorite thing Tex had sent." He looked over at Cookie, who was crouched on the opposite side of the discarded items. "They stripped them," he whispered.

Cookie's jaw was ticking in his cheek. He looked like Smiley felt. As if he was two seconds away from losing his shit. He stood and looked around. "They were here. A truck was probably backed into this spot. Their belongings were taken before they were loaded. So we know they're in a truck."

"But not *which* truck, or where they're going!" Smiley exclaimed, feeling extremely agitated. He began to pace back and forth, not able to look at Bree's belongings thrown away like trash. He wasn't sure what to do next.

"Blink here. Where's Tex?"

Looking up, Smiley saw that Blink was holding his cell. He had the phone on speaker, so he and Cookie could hear his conversation, which Smiley appreciated. He would've probably done or said something he'd regret later if Blink had tried to keep any scrap of information from him. Even if what they heard was bad news, he needed to know.

"Hey, I'm Ryleigh," a woman said on the other end of the line.

"Where's Tex? I called his number," Blink repeated.

"And I answered. It's not a hard thing to do—at least not for me—you know, reroute phone calls from one number to another."

"I don't care if you're the President of the United States or the Queen of England. I need to talk to Tex. *Now*," Blink said in a harsh voice.

Any other time, Smiley would've been impressed. Blink wasn't the kind of man who was terribly assertive. He let others be the bad guy, while he backed them up.

"He's not available. You know how long it takes to search CCTV cameras in a city the size of Riverton? This isn't like the TV shows, where it happens in the blink of an eye."

"We found the trackers the women were wearing."

"At the EZ On-and-Off Truck Stop east of Riverton. I know."

"You fucking know? Why weren't we told?! We're wasting time and resources looking all over the fucking city, and you *know*?" Blink asked in an outraged tone.

"The trackers had been disabled, but there was one, a ring, that wasn't quite destroyed. It had a very faint signal. It took me a while to track it and by then, the women were long gone. I was still going to call to tell you the location but...you're there now. And I figured you'd rather know where they *are*, not where they *aren't*. So I've been busy trying to follow the truck that was parked where the three of you are now standing," the woman, Ryleigh, said. "By scrolling through hours and hours of freaking security video."

Looking around, Smiley didn't see any cameras, but that obviously meant nothing. If Ryleigh knew there were three of them, she was obviously watching them right now.

"And?" Blink bit out.

"And it was a Perry Fried Chicken truck. It went east,

which is a shame, because once it left the city limits it became much harder to track. But I know it went east on I-8, then headed south on State Route 94 toward Tecate."

"Where is it now? Can we intercept before it crosses into Mexico?"

"Too late. I hacked into the cameras at the border crossing, and after a short wait in line, it went through without any issues over an hour ago."

Smiley swore viciously.

"I don't know for sure, but if Castillo really is headed for Ecuador, it's unlikely he'd drive all the way there. He'd put his cargo on a ship. Probably in Ensenada."

Smiley was still pissed. That they'd missed the women and they were no longer in the US. He also wanted to know where the hell Tex was. He'd been extremely pissed when he'd learned the task force failed and the women had been taken. Why hadn't his ass been in front of his computer, doing all he could to rescue them before they crossed into Mexico? Or working with the Mexican authorities to intercept this fucking Perry truck and rescue the women?

He had too many questions and no answers.

"Look, I made the best call I could under the circumstances. Yes, I could've contacted you sooner about the trackers, but the women were already gone, and I thought my time was better used finding the truck. I'll be in touch when I have more intel, like if they're definitely going to Ensenada, what sort of vessel they're transferred to, and if I can capture any video clips of the women. But until then...you're going to have to trust that I know what I'm doing, and there's no way I'm going to let this asshole get away with this."

The steel in her tone went a long way toward making Smiley feel better. He still wasn't happy, far from it, but the fact that this Ryleigh person was stressed and pissed off on their behalf actually helped.

"In the meantime, get back to the base. Your commander is already working to get approval to send a team to Ensenada to intercept that truck."

"*What?* Why didn't you start with that?" Cookie barked in disgust.

"I should've," Ryleigh said simply. "But you had questions."

Blink handed his phone to Cookie and hurried back toward the truck without a word, but Smiley felt rooted to the spot. This was the last place he knew for sure Bree had been. For some reason, he didn't want to leave. It was ridiculous, she wasn't there any longer, but his brain was screaming that he needed to stay right there in case she returned.

Again, that wasn't happening, she was already in Mexico, but he couldn't help but wish for the impossible.

"Go to the base, Smiley," Ryleigh ordered, reminding him that she was watching them, even now. "And the last thing anyone needs is you guys getting into an accident. Fiona and Bree are gonna want to see their men, so Blink, you better fucking drive safely."

"Yes, ma'am," Blink said, as he knelt on the ground. He'd returned with a reusable bag from the truck, one of the ones Smiley used when he went to the grocery store. He began to gather the women's clothes and jewelry.

"Hang up, Cookie," Ryleigh said in a gentler tone. "I'm on this, and I'll be in touch."

He did as ordered, and held Blink's phone out to him.

He took it, and held his other hand up toward Cookie. "Here."

Cookie closed his eyes as he wrapped his fingers around his wife's jewelry.

"Smiley," Blink said, getting his attention.

Turning, he saw Blink holding the necklace Bree had been wearing.

This felt...wrong. Permanent, somehow.

Clenching his teeth together so hard it felt as if they'd break, Smiley took the necklace and slipped it into his pocket. He'd hold on to the necklace until he could give it back to Bree in person. The tracker might not work anymore, but she loved the piece of jewelry. And when he found her, and got her home, he'd fix it. Or have Tex fix it.

Smiley was sure that Castillo wasn't going to kill Bree or the other women. He had plans for them. He and his friends would just have to make sure he didn't get a chance to finalize those plans.

Castillo had signed his death warrant by taking the women. He was a dead man walking. Smiley might not know how this would ultimately play out, but Castillo's death was one outcome that was guaran-fucking-teed.

* * *

The smell of chicken shit was making Bree nauseous. And the air blowing through the back of the truck they were in, swirling the chicken feathers and dander in the air, along with the stench, was enough to make it hard to breathe.

Not to mention the skimpy piece of cloth they'd each been given to wear wasn't nearly enough to keep them warm. The red light on the ceiling above allowed them to see, but it was also seriously messing with Bree's eyesight. The shadows seemed to be moving all around them and it was impossible to focus.

She sat in the corner of her cage with her head leaning against the side closest to Fiona, feeling as if she was hovering on the ceiling, watching what was happening from above.

Fiona and Julie were...well, they were amazing. They had every right to be hysterical, to have shut down completely because they were experiencing the same thing they had years ago. Who got kidnapped *twice* in one lifetime? By someone from the same organization? By people who wanted to use and abuse their bodies simply because they were women?

Fiona and Julie, that's who.

But they weren't crying, bemoaning their fate. They were angry. And doing their best to bend the bars of their cages.

What was Bree doing? Sitting there feeling sorry for herself.

She was hungry, and thirsty, and she had to pee earlier in the corner of her cage, which was humiliating and demoralizing. And to top things off, that pee hadn't stayed in the damn corner, no—the motion of the truck helped the liquid make its way to where she was sitting. So now the bottom of her skimpy slip was soaked in her own urine, and she was also sitting in it.

"Bree! Talk to us," Fiona ordered in a bossy tone Bree hadn't heard from her before. Not that she'd spent a lot of time with the older woman, but she'd seemed pretty even-keeled and not like one to boss people around.

"About what?" Bree asked a little belligerently. "You want to talk about the weather or something?"

"Don't," Julie warned.

"Don't *what*?" Bree asked.

"Be a bitch. Trust me, it'll eat at you later. I know from experience. The first time I was taken, I was the biggest bitch in the world. And I still regret it all these years later."

"We've all forgiven you," Fiona said in a gentler tone.

"I know. And you'll never know how much that means to me. But it doesn't change anything that I did. I'll never forget how horrible I was. How I begged Cookie to leave you behind in that hut."

Bree looked over at the woman. "You did?" She hadn't heard that part of the story.

"I did," Julie confirmed. "And I complained during every single step we took as we escaped. Whined about the food Cookie brought for us, about how Fiona coped with everything that happened to her by counting backward, and a million other things."

Bree couldn't imagine Julie doing any of that. The woman she knew wasn't cruel.

"I was absolutely horrible, and I said things that I regret to this day. So I'm telling you to take a deep breath and think before you speak. Don't be like me. This sucks, make no mistake. I'm terrified and pissed off and a hundred other emotions. But I'll never do the same things I did in my past. This time will be different. I'm stronger. And most importantly, I have a man who will have my back. I can just imagine what Patrick is doing right this minute. He'll be trying to take control, even though he's retired and not in charge anymore. He'll be yelling at people, ordering them around."

"And Cookie will be scowling, telling everyone to hurry the fuck up. And when he comes for us, he'll have more than a few granola bars this time. He'll bring me real shoes and mosquito repellent, just in case," Fiona said.

"Damn right, he will," Julie agreed.

It was obvious the two women had a bond. They also had a good point. She and Smiley weren't married. But they were together. And from everything she knew about him, he wasn't going to sit back and let others do all the work in finding her. Hell, when he didn't even know her, he'd done everything he *could* to find her. Now that they were sleeping together? Living together? That he seemed to like her as more than a casual hookup?

Yeah, he'd go to the ends of the Earth looking for her.

"Smiley has a teddy bear that he used to sleep with. It's tattered and looks as if it's been through the wringer, one arm is barely hanging on by a thread, the material is all torn and worn, and the stuffing is coming out of one of the ears, but it's sitting on a shelf in his bedroom, and he told me that it's one of his prized possessions. That when his dad used to beat his mom, he'd bury his face in its fur and pretend he was far, far away," Bree blurted.

Fiona and Julie both turned to stare at her.

Bree went on. "He feels guilty that he never did anything to help his mother. I tried to tell him that he was just a kid. That there wasn't anything he *could* have done, but he doesn't agree. I want to change what it represents. Make it so it's not a symbol of his shame, a reminder that he hid while his mom was being hurt. I want to fix it up.

Repair it. Maybe symbolically, it'll be like repairing his psyche. But I'm not sure it's a good idea. He might get mad that I dared to touch something so meaningful to him."

Fiona sat close to the bars of her cage and reached out for Bree's hand. "I think it's a great idea. But maybe you can talk to him about it first. Make sure it's okay."

"Yeah."

"Watching Patrick with our son is beautiful," Julie said. "He's this macho former Navy SEAL, and yet he has no problem going to musicals and talking about fashion with him. Many fathers would resent having a son who's not exactly like him, who doesn't want to go hunting and fishing and do all those so-called manly kinds of things. I caught the two of them the other day talking about relationships. Patrick was telling our son that respect was one of the most important factor in any kind of relationship. It was sweet. And it made me realize the day I called Patrick and begged him to let me apologize to his SEAL team was the best day of my life."

"Hunter is...he's my rock," Fiona admitted. "Without him, I'd probably be in a mental hospital right now. He's stood by me since the first day I met him. He's stubborn and annoying sometimes, but I knew from the second he refused to leave me in that hut what kind of man he was. Fierce. Loyal. And so damn sweet it actually makes me feel a little guilty that he's mine, and so many women out there can't experience what I have with him."

Bree nodded. Tears filled her eyes. She was so scared. But if Julie and Fiona could be strong, so could she.

"They're coming," Fiona whispered. "But that doesn't

mean that we should sit here and do nothing. We have to help ourselves."

"I'm not sure wasting our energy trying to bend the bars of these cages is smart though," Bree told her.

"This isn't the first time they've done this," Julie said from Fiona's other side. "They've had other women in these cages, I'm sure of it. They think they're smarter than us. They're counting on us being so scared we can't fight back. But they have no idea who they've messed with. Patrick has taught me a thing or two over our years together. Taking them by surprise is the best advantage we have.

"We might not be able to bend the bars, but maybe there's some weakness somewhere. All this chicken shit might've weakened the joints of these cages. Or maybe we can break off a piece of the plastic trays we're sitting on. I don't know. But we have to do *something*. I learned my lesson all those years ago. I'm no longer willing to be complacent. To sit around and take whatever they want to dish out. They can drug us, force us to do things we don't want to do, but they can't take our willpower. Our strength. Fiona taught me that."

"Love you, Julie," Fiona whispered.

"And I love you too. Bree, can you maybe check out your cage? See if you can find any weaknesses we can exploit?"

She wanted to stay right where she was. Sitting on her ass, feeling sorry for herself. But Julie and Fiona were right. That wouldn't accomplish anything. Besides, Mateo wanted *her*. She was his main target. The other women had just been in the wrong place at the wrong time. It would be awful of her to let them do all the work when they were truly innocent victims in all this.

No, not victims...innocent bystanders. She in no way saw either Julie or Fiona as a victim.

Which got her thinking. If *they* weren't victims, why was *she*? She hadn't done anything wrong either. Carl, her ex, had been the one to freaking *sell* her. As if she were a piece of property.

She wasn't. She was Bree Haynes, and she'd managed to elude Mateo and his goons for months. And she had Smiley on her side. And his friends. She had an army at her back, or would that be a Navy? She grinned at her own joke.

"Bree? You aren't losing it over there, are you?" Julie asked worriedly.

To her surprise, Bree found herself chuckling. "No. Just thinking something that made me laugh. I have to say it... I'm terrified. This is a nightmare, and I don't want to think about what's going to happen when we get to wherever we're going. I know Mateo is from Ecuador, but surely we aren't going to be driven all the way there. And they can't keep us in these crates the whole way either, right? They have to stop and feed us. At the very least give us water. I'm thinking that's our chance. To take them by surprise, like you said, Julie."

"I agree," Fiona replied with a firm nod.

"Me too. So we need a weapon. Something we can use when they let us out of these cages."

Taking a deep breath, and immediately regretting it *again* because of the contaminated air she'd just sucked into her lungs, Bree coughed, then nodded. Shifting to her knees, her head brushing against the top of the cage, she shuffled to the end of the plastic tray. Methodically, inch by inch, she tested the plastic. Looking for weaknesses, anything that could be exploited and might help them escape.

CHAPTER TWELVE

Smiley leaned against the wall of the conference room back on the naval base. It was nearly one in the morning—and they were no closer to finding the missing women than they'd been earlier. Smiley hadn't slept, but neither had anyone else. Everyone was on edge and tense, and tempers were short.

Putting over a dozen amped-up, stressed-out Navy SEALs in a room with no clear objective or plan wasn't a great idea. And yet no one was going to leave. Not without having some intel on the whereabouts of three of their own.

Someone had ordered takeout, but hardly anyone had touched the food. Just the smell was making Smiley sick. Besides, all he could think about was what Bree might be eating—or *not* eating, as he feared was the case. How could he eat when he knew she was hungry and hurting?

They'd spoken a couple times to Ryleigh via phone, but she didn't have updated intel to share yet. A woman named Beth was working to try to track Castillo to any connections he might have at shipyards in Ensenada. They needed to narrow down where that chicken truck might end up before a team headed into Mexico.

The commander was making calls to get emergency approval to send Smiley and his team into that country, but there was a lot of red tape to work through with both the US and Mexican governments. Obviously, the authorities south of the border weren't thrilled about a group of armed-to-the-teeth SEALs coming into their country, but because of Fiona and Julie's past history in Mexico, the commander was slowly making headway.

Not quick enough for Smiley, Cookie, and Hurt though.

The older men looked as if they'd aged a decade overnight. Smiley had a feeling he probably looked the same. Just because he and Bree weren't married didn't mean he was any less affected.

He loved her.

There was no doubt in his mind that Bree Haynes was the person he wanted to spend the rest of his life with. She was his perfect match. He had a feeling he'd known it back when he was desperately looking for her after meeting her that night in Vegas. Something about her just hit home. It made no sense, and a lot of people would scoff at the idea of soul mates. But without Bree, Smiley had no doubt he'd revert back to the grumpy asshole everyone thought he was before he'd met her.

And that wasn't who Smiley wanted to be. Not anymore. He laughed more, tolerated the idiocy of his fellow humans better when he was around her. She made him want to be the kind of man she could rely on, who could make her laugh and smile every single day.

His future was a deep dark hole without her. Smiley knew that without a doubt. And if he lost her...

No. He couldn't go there. Not while also staying focused on what he needed to do.

Jerking in surprise when the door to the conference room slammed open, Smiley glanced over to see who'd entered so abruptly. All conversation stopped, and it was so quiet, the ticking of the second hand from the clock on the wall was loud in the silent room.

"Well?" the man boomed, his slight southern accent clear even in that one word. "What's happened since I've been trapped on that fucking plane? I was working with Ryleigh before I left, helping her go through video feeds, but the Wi-Fi on the plane wasn't working so I had no way of communicating with anyone. Then we were delayed not once, but *three* fucking times. I'm irritated beyond belief and I feel as I'm way behind. Someone fill me in. Stat."

Tex.

Smiley couldn't believe it. Tex fucking Keegan was here. In the flesh. He couldn't remember a time when the man had personally involved himself in...a situation. He usually communicated via phone and stayed glued to his computer as he did what he could to help. For him to be here, in person, said a lot about what was happening. Smiley didn't know whether to be impressed or fucking terrified.

"Well?" Tex demanded again.

Wolf broke out of his shock first and strode toward the man, hugging him. Hard.

The rest of Wolf's team followed, and soon Tex was surrounded by his oldest and dearest friends. They had a lot of history together, and it wasn't surprising the SEALs were so happy to see the man.

Then it was Kevlar's turn. Safe, Blink, Preacher, MacGyver, and Flash followed suit. Smiley was honored to meet the legend in person, but he hated the reason he was there in the first place.

Tex broke away from the others and walked toward him. He hadn't moved from his place near the wall.

"Smiley," he said, with a nod of his head.

"Tex," he returned.

"Fuckers disabled the trackers," Tex said next.

"Yeah."

"I agree with Ryleigh's assessment that the truck is headed for the coast, likely for Ensenada. Wheels going up in two hours. Can you be ready?"

Smiley blinked in surprise. "The commander's working on getting clearance."

"He can continue working on it all he wants. I've already got it. But there's only room for four."

Smiley's heart was in his throat. He shouldn't have been surprised Tex had already arranged transportation and gotten clearance, and yet he still was.

"So...who's going?" Tex asked.

Smiley blinked again. "What?"

"Who's going?" he repeated.

Smiley looked from the legendary former SEAL to the anxious faces behind him. *He* was supposed to choose who'd be going south to try to find and rescue the women? He didn't want to leave *anyone* behind. His team was his rock. They all had different and vital skills.

And then there was Wolf's team. They weren't active

duty anymore, but they were just as capable as they'd been before they retired.

Taking a deep breath, Smiley went with his gut. "Me, Cookie, Kevlar, and...you, Tex."

"Me? Shit, man. I'm the least capable of everyone in this room," he told him.

"Bullshit," Smiley countered, even as everyone else voiced their disbelief at the same time. "You have more skills on your fucking phone than most people do with an entire bank of servers at their disposal. Yes, the woman who's working with you is good, but she's not *you*. You have the combat experience, and you've been in the heads of assholes like Castillo for longer than Ryleigh's probably been alive." Smiley turned to Hurt. "I'm sorry, Sir, but—"

Hurt cut him off. "No. You're right. As much as it kills me, I'm not the best person for this mission. I've been out too long. I trust you to take care of my wife. To get her home."

Smiley nodded, respect filling him.

"I'm gonna call Tate," Blink said. "I should've done it last night. I know this isn't an official mission, and he and his Night Stalker team are on the other coast, but they have connections. Former Night Stalkers who've retired to Mexico. If needed, maybe one of them could be useful."

Gratitude threatened to overwhelm Smiley. He'd spent so much of his life keeping people at arm's length, for his own self-preservation, he hadn't even realized it was no use. They were already under his skin. Still had his back regardless. These men were his brothers, his family, in every sense of the word. When he hurt, they hurt. When the woman he loved was threatened, they all took it personally. Just as he had when *their* loved ones were in trouble.

They were a team, they banded together. And if that meant staying behind and holding down the fort while he was gone, that's what they'd do.

Relieved no one was upset with his choices, Smiley turned to Cookie, who hadn't said a word.

"Cookie?" He wasn't even sure what he was asking, but he supposed he wanted reassurance that he'd chosen correctly. That Cookie was up to the task. That he could control his emotions in order to be an asset rather than a liability.

Smiley's own emotions were all over the place, but he was channeling them into a single focus. Finding Bree and the other women, and killing anyone who dared stand in his way. He'd chosen Tex for his technological skills, yes, but he'd also be an asset in case there was any bloodshed. The last thing he wanted was to spend the rest of his life in some shitty Mexican prison, and he knew Tex would be the man who'd be able to spin whatever happened and get them cleared.

Cookie approached Smiley and put a hand on his shoulder. The determination in his facial expression matched what Smiley felt in his soul. "Let's do this. Let's go get our women back."

"Two hours," Tex said firmly.

"Make it one," Smiley countered.

"One," Cookie agreed.

"That work for you, Kevlar? Assuming you want to go see Remi before we leave?" Tex asked.

"One is more than enough time," Kevlar reassured the others.

The only people who headed for the door were the four who would soon be on their way to Ensenada. The others stayed where they were in the room. It was obvious no one was leaving until the women were located and rescued. Most of the men had brought their phones up to their ears, probably to call their wives, but Smiley was already focused on the task ahead of him.

"Smiley?" Kevlar asked as they stepped outside the room. "Got a sec?"

"See you at the base airport," Tex said, as he continued down the hall with Cookie at his heels.

"You need to get going if you're gonna see Remi before we leave," Smiley warned.

"Already texted her. She's coming to the base. I'll be with you before the plane leaves. I just wanted to say...I'm not going to let you down."

"I know."

"I mean it. You could've picked anyone to go with you, and I'm honored that you chose me."

"Kevlar, you're my team leader. You've proven time and time again that you aren't afraid to get your hands dirty. You aren't going to back down from a firefight. And you don't give a shit about morally gray if it means helping an innocent civilian or bystander. But that's not the only reason I chose you. I need you to make sure I don't lose my shit. If things don't work out..."

Smiley paused and swallowed hard, not wanting to say the words, but needing to all the same.

"If Bree's already been moved, or killed, or if she's too traumatized to even know who I am, I need you to rein me in. Because if I lose her...I don't know how I'll respond. But it won't be good."

Kevlar squeezed his shoulder. "You don't need me for any of that, Smiley. Out of everyone on our team, you're the one who I know will *always* be our rock. You've always had our best interests at heart and you do what needs to be done. Others might think you're an unfeeling machine, but I know differently. And Bree has helped bring out that part of you even more.

"You're the biggest protector of all of us. And it's because of your mom. Because you want to atone for something that you never needed to atone for. If she was around today, she'd tell you the same thing. You think your mom wasn't protecting *you*? And I'd bet everything I have that the guilt she felt over the situation she put you in as a child ate at her, even more than your guilt eats at *you*.

"We're going to find the women. Of that I have no doubt. Whether that's in Ensenada or Ecuador, I don't know. But we aren't going to stop until they're safe and back home where they belong. Whatever you need, whenever you need it—it's yours."

Smiley nodded, Kevlar's words hitting him hard.

His mom probably *had* felt guilty that she couldn't find her way out of her marriage, and that he'd suffered right alongside her.

It was something he'd never considered. Couldn't see while buried under his own guilt for so many years. And it was past time to let that go. Kevlar and Bree were both right...he'd been a kid. There really wasn't anything he could've done.

It was his mother's responsibility to leave her husband. And she couldn't or wouldn't.

"Thanks," he told Kevlar in a quiet tone.

"You're welcome. Let's go get your woman. Remi and

the rest of the girls aren't going to be happy until one of their flock is back in the nest. I'll check in with her and meet you at the hangar."

Smiley nodded and followed Kevlar as he strode down the hall toward the stairs. He took a moment once he was outside to look at the clear, star-filled sky.

He thought about Bree. Wondered if she was seeing the same stars he was. He'd found out through his job that the world was a smaller place than most people realized. What happened in one corner would eventually trickle down and affect someone thousands of miles away.

"I'm coming, Bree. Stay strong. You can do this."

Simply saying the words aloud and putting them out into the world made him feel better. He had no idea how things would turn out, but no one would ever be able to say he hadn't done everything possible.

* * *

"Stay strong. You can do this."

Bree stopped tugging at the plastic piece and tilted her head. She'd heard the words as if they were whispered in her ear. It was a weird feeling. To hear Smiley's voice yet know for a fact he wasn't anywhere near her.

But...even if she was having hallucinations, the words made her feel better. It was something Smiley would absolutely say to her if he could. He'd always believed in her. Thought she was stronger than she was.

"Any luck?" Julie asked.

"Almost," Bree told her, grabbing hold of the plastic tray once more and pulling as hard as she could.

The piece snapped off so quickly, she flew up then back on her ass, bumping her head on the top of the cage.

Bree stared at the long piece of plastic in her hand. She'd done it!

"Wooooo!" Fiona cheered.

"Good job!" Julie exclaimed.

Holding up the jagged piece, Bree was shocked to see that it was the perfect size for a weapon. One end pointed and sharp, it was about the length of a butcher knife. She needed to make some sort of handle though, so it didn't cut her palm.

"Here, let me see it for a second," Julie requested, holding out her hand.

Bree didn't hesitate, handing it to Fiona, who passed it through the bars on her other side to Julie.

Squinting to see Julie through the hazy air and dim red light, Bree watched the other woman use the sharp edge to cut a swath off the bottom of her slip. "Since I'm so much shorter than either of you, I have more material to work with," she said matter-of-factly. When she was done, she passed the makeshift knife and the material she'd cut from her own clothing back to Fiona, who gave it back to Bree.

Looking down at it, Bree felt like crying. Either of the women could've kept the plastic for themselves. Having a weapon felt like a huge advantage. And yet neither even seemed to think twice about giving it up. And Julie had sacrificed part of her clothing—which there wasn't much of to begin—to help make the plastic more useable.

Fumbling with the material, Bree tried to figure out how to wrap it around the plastic and get it to stay. Frustrated with her lack of success, she huffed out a breath.

"I can cut some more," Julie said quietly. "Maybe it can be used to tie around the material you already have."

Sitting up straighter, Bree nodded to herself. That's what she needed. Something she could use to tie around the material.

Without thinking twice, she raised the plastic and, before either of the women could say anything, she'd cut off a chunk of her long hair.

Looking up at Fiona, she said, "I needed a haircut anyway."

For a moment, no one said anything—then both Fiona and Julie burst out laughing.

Smiling, Bree leaned over the locks of hair she'd hacked off and carefully began to separate them into three sections. If she'd thought about this for a second, she would've been smarter and braided her hair *before* she'd cut it off, but it was too late now.

By the time she was done, her back hurt from hunching over, her eyes ached from trying to concentrate on her task in the funky red light and make sure she didn't lose any of the hair, and her fingers were sore from a task that was *way* harder when the hair was no longer attached to her head.

But she'd done it. She'd braided the hair and wound it around the material, tying it off to create her odd-looking handle.

It wouldn't stand up to much vigorous use, but it felt good to have some sort of weapon.

"Now to get one of us out of these fucking cages," Fiona muttered, as she sat on her ass, leaned back on her hands, and began to kick at the bars on the front of her cage.

But no matter how hard she kicked, or how desperately she tried to pry them apart with her hands, the bars wouldn't budge. Bree had no idea what they were made of...titanium? It was frustrating. How could they escape their captors if they were stuck in the damn cages?

While the other women struggled with their cages, Bree did her best to hone the edges of her makeshift knife so it was as sharp as possible. At some point, she'd get a chance to use it, and she had to make the most of whatever opportunity arose.

"What do you think the guys are doing?" Julie asked, sitting back with a frustrated huff when it became clear their efforts were futile.

"Stressing. Planning. Arming themselves," Fiona said without hesitation.

That made Bree smile a little. She could picture Smiley and his team hunched over a table at the base, studying maps and swearing revenge on Mateo and anyone else who'd had a hand in kidnapping them.

Then she sobered. She hated to think about Smiley or any of his friends stressed out because of this situation. And poor Remi, Caroline, and the others. Were Maggie and Addison all right with this added stress? It couldn't be good for their babies.

She *hated* this. Hated being the reason the closest friends she'd had since high school were probably not eating well, stressed out, and worried.

Hell, she was worried too. There was no telling what Mateo had planned for them.

No, that wasn't true. She knew *exactly* what he had planned, and it made her want to stick the plastic knife she'd made into her own heart. She'd rather die than be used as nothing more than a way for a man to get off.

As soon as she had the thought, Bree felt horrible. She wanted to live through this so she could go back to building a life with Smiley. Besides, Fiona and Julie were living, breathing proof that it was possible to survive what many people would think was the worst thing that could ever happen to a woman.

Bree mentally vowed to do whatever she could to help herself out of this situation. And if the worst happened, if she was assaulted, she wouldn't break. Smiley and the others were out there. Desperately doing what they could to find them. She had to believe that they'd succeed.

"You guys feel that?" Fiona asked, a sense of urgency in her tone.

Bree sat up inside her cage as she looked over at the other woman.

"Yes!" Julie added. "We're slowing down."

The truck they were in had slowed down before, and nothing came of it. At one point, they'd slowed for what seemed a considerable amount of time, inching along, then stopping briefly.

All three women got excited, thinking they were very likely at a border crossing. They tried shouting, praying someone would hear them and inspect the truck. But a cacophony of honking horns from other vehicles had already driven the chickens into a squawking frenzy.

No one heard them. No one checked the back of the truck. And soon they were speeding along again. It felt like it took an hour, though the entire process was probably only fifteen or twenty minutes.

But now, Bree couldn't stop the spike of adrenaline

from coursing through her body. She wrapped her hand tighter around her makeshift weapon. They had to be ready for anything.

"Look, I've been thinking. We can't do anything from inside these cages," Fiona said quickly. "We have to get out somehow. If someone does come for us, we have to do whatever it takes to convince them to let us out."

Bree nodded. She agreed.

"Fake an illness?" Julie asked.

"Do we think they'd care?" Fiona countered.

"Hmm, probably not. But maybe? I mean, I'm guessing they want us well enough to...you know," Julie said quietly.

Bree didn't want to think about *you know*, but she couldn't help it. She couldn't think of any scenario where their captors would open all three of their cages. "Really, only one of us needs to escape. That person can free the other two."

"I don't know. The padlocks on these cages aren't going to be easy to get open, especially if there's more than one asshole who comes for us. Even if they're carrying the keys to the locks, we have to find them, figure out which goes to which lock, then unlock the damn things," Julie said pessimistically.

"I'll do it," Bree told the others.

"Do what?" Fiona asked.

"Get them to open my cage."

"How?" Julie asked.

Bree had no idea. She just knew it was her responsibility to get her friends out of this. She still felt as if it was her fault they were here in the first place. If she'd gone east, away from Riverton and Smiley, Julie and Fiona wouldn't be locked in cages inside this horrible truck.

All three women held their breaths as the truck slowed even further. The floor rumbled under them as it crept along. Bree prayed this was different from other times when they'd slowed down. She'd lost track of how often that had happened. It was impossible to gauge time in this truck. She didn't know how long they were inside before waking up in the cages. Since then, it felt like they'd been trapped for days, but she knew it was actually just a matter of hours.

In any case, she realized it couldn't have been too long, because without water at least, they wouldn't be in as good of shape as they were.

Still, they were all beginning to feel the effects of lack of sustenance. And Bree had gotten over the humiliation of smelling like pee and sitting in her own waste. All around them was nothing but chicken shit. It wasn't as if she could smell herself through all that stink, although if she could, she'd probably be horrified.

She had the thought that maybe her condition would make their captors keep their distance. Being dirty and disgusting might be the best thing for them right now.

The truck came to a jerking halt, making Bree fall forward and knock her head against the bars of the cage once more.

"Ow!" Fiona complained. "Asshole needs to learn how to drive."

The chickens around them obviously agreed, because they all began to cluck in agitation.

Several minutes went by, and Bree held her breath. She still had no plan. If someone came for them, she'd have to think of something. Fast.

Then a loud clanking noise sounded from the rear of

the truck, making the chickens flap their wings in the too-crowded cages and the noise level in the enclosed space once more increase to a painful level.

The light that suddenly shone through the open door at the other end of the truck almost hurt Bree's eyes. It was artificial, coming from streetlights of some sort, shining dimly in the darkness beyond the open door. Which was probably good, because after being in the gloomy truck with only red light for so long, the three of them would probably be blinded if they saw sunlight right now.

As it was, Bree had to blink rapidly to try to get her eyes to adjust. She saw a blurry form climb into the back and walk between the stacked chicken cages. He had a respirator over his nose and mouth so he could breathe. Asshole. Of *course* he had a respirator, but he didn't give a shit if she, Julie, or Fiona could breathe.

"Time to go," he announced, his voice muffled from behind the mask.

Bree took stock of the man. He wasn't big. Maybe around Fiona's height. And he was skinny, not hugely muscular. It was obvious he didn't consider any of them a threat, which she hoped would be his downfall.

More importantly, her eyes homed in on the keys in his hand. She needed to get a hold of those somehow. Get them to Fiona and Julie, who could then open the locks holding them captive in their cages. But how?

Just as she opened her mouth to pretend she was having cramps or some other womanly affliction—guys always seemed to get flustered when confronted with talk of periods or cramps—the man leaned down to her cage and grabbed the lock.

He was letting her out? Just like that? Without her having to make a scene?

Glancing over at Julie and Fiona, she saw their eyes were huge and they looked both confused and thrilled at the same time.

This was it. Her chance. It might be the only one they had.

"You first," the man told her. "Boss has special plans for you. The others are being shipped off to Russia and North Korea. Their buyers have already arranged for transportation. But *you're* going to his compound in Ecuador. A personal slave for his employees, he's decided...to use whenever and however they want. Free of charge. Kind of perk for their hard work." He chuckled. "They'll enjoy it—but I'm guessing you won't. That doesn't matter though, does it? You belong to the boss. You're his to do as he pleases. The sooner you come to terms with that, the better. You want food? Water? A place to shit and piss that isn't your own bed? You better behave. The more you do what he wants, the better your life will be."

"I'll do anything!" Bree whined, trying to sound cowed and meek. "I'm so thirsty! Do you have any water?"

"What are you going to give *me* if I give you water?" the man asked, straightening and grabbing his crotch suggestively. "Maybe I should have you suck me off before I bring you to the boss."

Bree wanted to gag. Instead, she forced herself to keep her eyes downward and sit with her shoulders slumped submissively. Her fingers clutched the knife harder as she waited for him to open the cage door. She could hear her heart beating hard in her chest. The *thump thump thump* a loud reminder that she was alive. And that it was up to her to help Fiona and Julie.

"Nothing to say to that? Not a yes, sir? Please, sir?" the man asked. "Guess you aren't getting that water then. You'll learn. Boss is big on respect. As long as you do as he says, you'll live. If not..." He shrugged.

He turned the key in the lock, and even over the clucking of the chickens, Bree heard it snick open. Licking her lips, she waited.

The man swung the door open and reached for her. Bree kept her muscles loose as the man grabbed her upper arm and dragged her out of her cage. It hurt to stand, and for a moment she was afraid her legs wouldn't hold her upright. She didn't have to fake the unstable wobble before she locked her knees.

The guy swept his gaze down her body, and it was all Bree could do not to move to shield herself from his leer. The pastel slip she was wearing didn't hide anything. It was sheer, and she could feel her nipples tighten against the cold air coming in from behind the man.

Without a word, he brought his free hand up, the one not holding her arm—and the keys—and grabbed one of her breasts. Fondling her as if he had every right in the world.

Fuck this.

Fuck *him*.

She moved without thought. Swinging the plastic knife and stabbing him in the neck as hard as she could.

His eyes widened almost comically as he instantly let go of her arm, clutching his neck with his hands.

Bree brought her knee up next, hitting him in the crotch. He reacted like any male in the same situation would—he dropped to his knees. Hard, as he groaned loudly.

The keys fell to the floor of the truck. Bree snatched them up, turning and tossing them toward Fiona's cage in one fluid movement.

Then without hesitation, she swung the knife again, thrusting it once more into the man's neck.

She guessed that was the most vulnerable part of his body right now, figuring the knife wouldn't be able to penetrate his clothes into his chest, his heart. She needed to do her best to incapacitate him—if she was lucky, kill him. But at the very least, do as much damage to his throat as possible, so he couldn't call for help.

How many times she stabbed the man, Bree had no idea. But she felt his blood on her fingers. On her face. Stabbing someone was a messy business. She'd kind of gone into a trance while taking out her frustration, terror, and fury on this asshole who'd taunted the three of them with what was in store for each woman. No way were Julie and Fiona being shipped off to North Korea and Russia. Not if she could help it!

"You sampling the goods in there?" a voice called out from the back of the truck, snapping Bree out of her daze.

She was breathing hard, as if she'd just run for miles. And her legs felt like jelly.

A touch on her arm had her spinning around violently, knife at the ready.

"It's just me!" Fiona told her, taking a step backward with her hands up.

"Shit, sorry," Bree said, lowering the knife.

Then it hit her. Fiona was out. And Julie too. They

stood there, looking bedraggled and pathetic, but they were free.

Well...not free yet.

"Carlos?"

Shit. They still had to get past whoever was waiting outside the truck. "I'm going to distract them, you two slip out while I lead them away," Bree said.

"No," Fiona said with a firm shake of her head. "We stick together."

"That's not going to work. In a few seconds, whoever's calling for Carlos is going to come in here looking for him. You wouldn't be here if it wasn't for me! I'm doing this," Bree insisted. "*Run.* Get away. Find a way to contact the guys. Tell Smiley..." Her voice cracked. "Tell him I love him. And that he's the best thing that ever happened to me."

With that, she gripped the knife tighter and quickly made her way toward the other end of the truck. Every time she passed a cage full of chickens, she shook it slightly, making the animals squawk and complain. Her heart hurt for the birds. She'd probably never eat chicken again. But for now, she needed them loud and annoying.

Taking a deep breath, she paused—then ran straight toward the open door.

She saw a man step in front of the door just as she jumped. The timing wasn't great. But then again, maybe it was perfect. She landed on the man, and they both fell to the ground. He basically broke her fall and softened her landing.

Bree scrambled off him, cursing the fact she'd dropped her weapon. But there was no time to find it. There were two other men staring at them with wide, surprised eyes.

She let out a feral scream and ran.

"Get her!"

Glancing over her shoulder as she ran, Bree was both terrified and relieved to see all three men chasing her.

She had to get as far away from that truck as she could, give Julie and Fiona time to slip out and hide. To get away.

Her heart in her throat, Bree ran. Her legs felt wobbly from lack of use and because she hadn't had anything to eat or drink. But she refused to give up.

Thoughts of Fiona were in the forefront of her mind. *She* hadn't given up. All those years ago when she was a captive, she'd never given in. Hadn't done what her captors wanted. She'd been held for months, walked through the jungle in flip-flops. Saved Cookie from drug runners who were shooting at them. If she could do all that, Bree could evade her pursuers for the little time it would take for Fiona and Julie to get away.

She'd hoped for a jungle to be able to run into. Or some huge city where she could get lost in back alleys. Instead, she found herself running along a tall chain-link fence in the dark, only the dim lights behind her guiding the way.

Her breaths came faster and faster. Bree had no idea where she was, some sort of shipping facility—which was ironic. On the run from someone, in another shipyard, for the second time in just months. She could smell the water, but otherwise she couldn't see much other than what was directly in front of her.

"Go to the right, John!"

Shit. They were going to box her in. Bree tried to run faster, but it was no use. She was exhausted. Her muscles were shaking. The adrenaline coursing through her veins had kept her going until now, but it seemed as if her body was failing her.

Refusing to cry, Bree let out a small scream as one of the men got close enough to try to grab her. His hand brushed against her arm, but she jerked away and put on one last burst of speed. Only to come up against the corner of the property.

She slammed into the fence and immediately began to climb.

Two of the men grabbed her legs. She did her best to kick at them, but it was no use. She clung to the chain-link for as long as she could, until one of her captors slammed his fist down on her wrist, making her cry out in pain. She found herself on her back in the dirt, with all the three men holding her arms and legs.

"*Fuck*, is that blood?" one of them asked.

Bree bared her teeth and growled at him.

"Damn, she's practically feral!" a second man exclaimed.

"It'll make her even more fun to tame," the last man said, an evil grin on his face. "Hold her down. Time for this bitch to learn her place. Me first, then you two can have a go." He reached for the belt at his waist.

No. This wasn't happening. She knew it was inevitable that she'd eventually be violated. But this wasn't that moment. Not if she could help it.

Bree fought. She bucked and squirmed and bit. She refused to just lie there and let herself be raped.

It seemed as if she had some adrenaline left after all, because the men were having an extremely hard time holding her down. She screamed until her voice was hoarse, doing everything in her power to prevent these assholes from taking what she didn't want to give.

"Shit! We don't have time for this," one of the men barked, after several minutes of wrestling with her.

"Boss expects her at the dock in Ecuador at the time he specified," another pointed out.

The man who'd reached for his pants finally growled, stood up, and kicked her.

Bree tried to curl into a ball, but the other men were holding her too tightly. Soon, however, they joined their buddy in punching the crap out of her. Unfortunately, this was also familiar. She was beaten at that other shipyard, as well, back when she'd helped Ellory and Yana.

Bree would take a beating over a rape any day of the week.

Doing her best to protect her most vulnerable parts, she was relieved that the men were concentrating on her, despite the pain. Hopefully that meant Julie and Fiona had gotten away. Had found a place to hide. She refused to think her sacrifice was for nothing.

She was strong. She could do this.

Repeating the words she'd heard from Smiley, over and over in her head, Bree didn't even notice when the men had stopped hurting her, and she'd been thrown over one of their shoulders.

She lay there, stunned and bleeding. All the fight gone out of her now. If they decided to assault her, she wouldn't be able to do much to stop them. But it seemed the men who'd chased her down were more scared of their boss—Mateo, she assumed—to do anything other than take her to wherever she'd been ordered to go.

Blood dripped down her temple and fell to the ground

as she was carried back to the truck with the chickens. She could hear their shouts as they got near.

"Carlos!" one of the men yelled. "Quit fucking around...literally. Get your ass out here *now*!"

But of course, Carlos didn't appear from inside the truck.

"Damn it! Go get him," the man holding her ordered the others.

They hopped into the truck, sending the chickens into another round of loud squawking. Bree couldn't hold back a small smile, knowing what they were about to find.

"He's dead!" one of the men exclaimed, quickly reappearing in the open doorway.

"*What*? How?"

"Don't know. He's covered in blood, still wearing the respirator."

"And the other girls are gone," the second man said grimly, coming up beside the first.

The man holding her swore so long and viciously, Bree's smile grew.

Fuck him. Fuck them all.

"How the fuck did this bitch kill him?" one of the men asked, jumping out of the truck.

"I don't know. But Boss is gonna be furious. We need to come up with a story. Otherwise, we're screwed."

Bree didn't feel the least bit sorry for these assholes.

"Give her to me," one of the other two ordered, his tone lethal.

"No. Back off, John," said the man holding her. "I know you're pissed but if we kill her, the boss'll fucking kill *us*. You know how much time and money he's spent tracking her down. And he's already paid to bring her to Ecuador."

The man, John, grabbed Bree's hair and forced her head up, where it hung over the shoulder of his colleague.

"You *bitch*," he growled, his teeth bared. "Where are the others?"

"Gone," she rasped. "And their Navy SEAL husbands are on their way right this second to take you assholes out."

"Yeah, right," the man scoffed. But Bree could hear the concern in his tone.

She had a moment to feel proud of herself before he pulled his arm back, still holding her hair, and brought his fist forward.

That was the last thing she remembered before the world went blissfully dark and she felt no more pain.

CHAPTER THIRTEEN

It was closing in on four o'clock in the morning as Kevlar raced toward the shipyard Tex had confirmed Castillo would mostly likely use in Ensenada. How he'd deduced that, Smiley had no idea. But if Tex said this was where the women would probably be, he wouldn't question him. He supposed Ryleigh or Beth had traced payments Castillo had made to others or bribes he'd paid to the area.

"Gate's shut," Cookie called out, as Kevlar drove the Jeep they'd obtained from another one of Tex's contacts, when they'd landed at the airport twenty minutes earlier.

Choosing Tex to come with them was one of the best decisions Smiley had ever made. He might not be the best man if they had a foot chase, or if they had to spend days in the jungle, but the intel the man was able to obtain, and the connections he had, were better than any other asset they could claim at the moment.

"Kevlar!" Cookie yelled again. "Gate."

"I see it," he returned, not sounding concerned in the least.

He hit the gate at speed and all four men inside rocked forward, but otherwise didn't blink at the fact they'd just obliterated the metal gate as they barreled their way into the shipyard. There were no huge container ships here, as there'd been back in Riverton when they'd looked for Ellory and Yana. This was essentially a private shipyard, used by people who wanted to stay under the radar from the governmental shipping rules.

But the government had to know what happened here. That goods moving through the gates weren't exactly legal, but they likely looked the other way because of bribes. It disgusted Smiley, but it was a part of life, and wasn't anything they hadn't seen over and over in other countries.

There were 18-wheelers parked along one end of the huge dirt parking area, along with pickup trucks and at least a hundred passenger cars. Smiley had no idea where to start looking for Bree and the other women.

But of course, that's why he'd chosen Tex.

"There. Go right, Kevlar. Toward the trucks. There are three on the end that have Perry Fried Chicken logos."

The Jeep went up on two wheels briefly as Kevlar turned sharply in the direction Tex indicated.

It was eerie how deserted the shipyard was. No one came running to see what the commotion at the gate might have been. There weren't any workers around this late. The silence made the hair on the back of Smiley's neck stand up.

Kevlar brought the Jeep to an abrupt stop, dust swirling around the wheels as all four men leapt out of the vehicle.

"Tex, you and Cookie take that one, Smiley and I will

check this one," Kevlar ordered, pointing to the two trucks nearest the end of the row.

The doors to the trucks weren't locked, which made Smiley's hopes wither a little. If the women were inside, surely the doors would be secured.

Pulling out one of the pistols Tex had also arranged to be delivered when they'd landed in Mexico, Smiley held it at the ready as Kevlar grabbed the handle and nodded.

As soon as Smiley nodded back, Kevlar wrenched open the back door.

The stench that greeted them almost took Smiley to his knees. The inside of the truck was lined from floor to ceiling with cages. Some were empty, but there were quite a few with carcasses of dead chickens. Excrement covered the cages, as well as every inch of the floor and even portions of the walls.

If this was how Perry Fried Chicken transported the birds they used to supply grocery stores, he was never eating chicken again. Ever.

Without hesitation, even with his eyes watering and his lungs screaming for fresh air, Smiley jumped into the back of the truck. He used a flashlight in one hand and held the pistol in the other as he made his way through the cargo area.

"Clear!" he called to Kevlar, then turned and quickly made his way back to the doors. He didn't even want to think about Bree being in this truck.

By the time he jumped down, Cookie was emerging from the other truck, obviously not having found anything either. The four of them moved to the third truck, the last one with the Perry Fried Chicken logo on the side.

Bree had to be inside. She *had* to. Tex couldn't be wrong about this, too many lives depended on it.

Tex and Kevlar opened the doors, and Cookie and Smiley made their way inside together. This one was much like the last truck he'd been in, the stench overwhelming, and the thought of chickens being transported in such filth and inhumane conditions making Smiley sick.

But that was nothing compared to what greeted him and Cookie when they made their way to the very back of the cargo area.

"Motherfucker."

"Shit!"

Cages. Which wasn't anything different from the rest of the truck...but these were bigger. Human-sized. They were side-by-side in the very back, out of sight of anyone who might open the door to give a cursory inspection of the truck's cargo.

"They were here," Cookie said, fury in his voice.

Smiley agreed—but more important in the moment was the large dark spot in front of one of the cages. His heart stopped beating in his chest as he pointed his flashlight at the floor. He knew blood when he saw it. He'd certainly seen enough of it in his lifetime.

Cookie knelt next to the bloodstain with his head dipped low.

The women had been here...but who'd been hurt. Julie? Fiona? Bree? None of the scenarios in Smiley's head were good.

Suddenly, he needed out of that truck.

Smiley spun and hurried toward the door, jumping out and leaning over with his hands on his knees as he struggled to gain control over his rioting emotions.

He heard Cookie jump down and join him on the ground.

"Smiley, look," he said, pointing with his flashlight at something lying in the dirt.

Turning to see what he'd found, Smiley crouched and reached for the object, picking up a crude-looking piece of plastic covered in material and...hair?

Adrenaline shot through him so fast and hard, Smiley felt light-headed.

"It's not their blood!" he exclaimed with absolute conviction. "In the truck. It's not theirs!"

"We don't know that," Cookie said.

"Look—this is Bree's hair. I'd bet my life on it. She used it to bind the material around the plastic to make a handle." His gaze went back to the truck, and he remembered seeing something, in one of the cages. "The plastic came from those cages. One of the trays was missing a chunk near the back edge."

If Smiley held the shank next to the tray, he knew it would fit perfectly.

"It's not their blood," he repeated. "They made a weapon. Used it on at least one of their captors. Probably waited until he opened their cage and attacked him. I'm guessing he didn't even see it coming. Figured they were weak and scared. Fucker underestimated our women."

"Okay, but where are they now?"

"I don't know." But Smiley couldn't help but feel proud. They had to be terrified, but they hadn't given up. From all the stories he'd heard from Cookie about Fiona, he wasn't all that surprised. He'd also seen firsthand Bree's stubbornness when it came to staying under the radar and doing what she needed to do in order to remain safe. And Julie had come a long way from the woman she'd been in that jungle in Mexico.

Smiley pocketed the shank the women had made—and used effectively, if the blood on the floor of the truck and on the plastic was any indication. It was tangible proof of the strength of the woman he loved.

He wasn't losing Bree. Not if he could help it. He'd follow her to the ends of the Earth, and then fight the devil himself to bring her home. Together, they'd get through whatever difficulties she suffered from being kidnapped.

He had no illusions. By now, she'd most likely been violated in the worst way a woman *could* be violated. He'd get her all the help she needed. And he'd make sure she understood that he loved her no matter what she'd been forced to do. Bree Haynes was his match, and he'd be damned if someone took her away from him without a fight.

"You found blood in the truck?" Kevlar asked, sounding alarmed.

He'd completely forgotten Kevlar and Tex were standing nearby. They didn't know about the cages. Hadn't seen the blood.

"Yeah," Cookie said grimly. "They were here. There are three cages in the back, big enough to hold the women. There's also blood on the floor. Smiley doesn't think it's from any of the women, but we have no way of knowing."

"If Smiley doesn't think it's theirs, it's not," Kevlar said firmly. "What now? Tex? What do you think?"

Tex frowned, and Smiley felt a black cloud move over him. Shit. If Tex was frowning, things were bad.

"I'm sure Castillo brought them here for transport.

He's based in Ecuador, so he could be bringing them there, but there's also no telling who he sold them to. He could be shipping one, two, or even all three of them off to different places from here. Ryleigh is trying to track money trails, but there are so many of them. Russia, India, China...North Korea even."

"What are you saying? That they're gone? That we can't find them?" Cookie asked in a cold, hard tone.

"No. That this search just got bigger than I expected. We can start with his compound in Ecuador, but we also need to regroup. Call for more assistance. We can't search every boat on the sea, we need the Coast Guard's help, and the Mexican authorities. We need to put the word out about the missing women, get as much assistance as we can from the countries Ryleigh has tracked Castillo's money to."

Smiley felt as if he had a four-hundred-pound weight on his heart. All his talk about finding Bree and making sure she came home seemed to go up in smoke. How the hell was he supposed to find her if the women were already on their way to some far-flung country? They were *so close* —and yet they'd still taken too long. The women were gone.

His failure and guilt weighed on him even more than it had every time his mom was beaten. He didn't have the excuse of being "just a kid" anymore. He was a grown man. A Navy SEAL. And yet his woman had been taken right out from under his nose and disappeared into thin air without a trace.

A noise from nearby had all four men spinning around with their weapons drawn. But what was it? Had it come from one of the hundred cars haphazardly parked around the trucks?

Cookie was the first to move. He holstered his weapon and hurried toward a nondescript brown hatchback parked in the middle of a row of other vehicles.

Smiley rushed after him, his weapon still drawn and ready to be used. He had no idea what the other man had seen, but he wasn't taking any chances. The last thing they needed was one of them to get hurt.

To Smiley's shock, a woman's head emerged from beneath the car.

It was Fiona.

Cookie dropped to his knees, carefully pulling her out from under the car then taking his wife in his arms, rocking her back and forth.

A second head popped out from where Fiona had emerged—Julie.

Tex also dropped to a knee, and engulfed Julie in a huge hug when she was safely out from under the vehicle.

His heart beating hard in expectation, Smiley waited for Bree to slide out from under the car, or another one nearby. But after several long seconds, when she didn't appear, his chest tightened and emotion clogged his throat.

Fiona looked up from where she was still held tightly in Cookie's arms. As if she could read his mind, she whispered, "She's not here."

Smiley wanted to ask where the hell Bree *was*. What had happened. But he couldn't get any words past the lump in his throat. The disappointment and fear were crushing.

Cookie shifted then, not letting go of Fiona but

inching back enough that he could remove his T-shirt. He tenderly put it over his wife's head. The slips she and Julie were wearing were sheer and left nothing to the imagination. Seeing what they'd been forced to put on was infuriating. And it only proved how much danger they'd been in.

Smiley shifted impatiently...but he couldn't bring himself to interrupt Cookie's reunion with his wife. If Bree had been there, if he'd had his arms around her, Smiley would've exploded in anger at anyone who dared rush him.

Tex pulled out his cell, hit a few buttons, then handed it to Julie, all without removing his arm from around her waist.

"Patrick?" she said in a wobbly tone.

Smiley turned away. The emotional reunion of the women with their husbands was too much. He was thrilled for his friends, but...

Kevlar's hand came down on Smiley's shoulder, but he didn't say anything. He didn't have to. The disappointment and fear in the air was palpable. Where was Bree? Why wasn't she with Julie and Fiona? How had they gotten away? How long had they been hiding? Smiley had so many questions, but he'd have to wait for answers.

He scanned the shipyard, hoping against hope he'd see Bree coming toward him. Maybe she'd gotten away too. Maybe she'd simply gotten separated from the other women and was too scared to come out of hiding.

"Holster your weapon," Kevlar said softly.

Looking down, Smiley saw he was still clutching his pistol in his right hand. One of the worst sins a SEAL could commit was losing track of his weapon. And even though his finger wasn't on the trigger, he didn't remember anything about the last few minutes in regard to the gun.

Moving slowly, as if mired in quicksand, Smiley put the pistol back in the holster at the small of his back. Taking a deep breath, then another, he turned toward the others. Bree wasn't here. He knew that as well as he knew his name. He felt empty, hollow.

It was as if he was watching the scene in front of him from a great distance. Or was simply an observer watching a play. He felt cold. Numb.

Stepping toward Tex and Julie, who was wiping tears from her eyes after just hanging up with her husband, Smiley removed his T-shirt. He held it out to the petite woman, who took it with a grateful smile.

Cookie got to his feet, his arm not leaving Fiona's waist, holding her against him.

"Are you *sure* Bree isn't here?" Kevlar asked gently.

Smiley held his breath waiting for the answer. He already knew what it would be, but maybe he'd get a miracle.

"We need to hear what happened, and we need to get you two somewhere safe," Kevlar told them. "But if there's even a one-percent chance Bree is here, hiding, we need to know."

Fiona shook her head. "We saw her being carried over that way," she said, pointing to a large dock. An *empty* dock. There was no boat waiting to be loaded. No cars idling. The area was deserted.

"They got onto a boat and left. We've been hiding ever since, just to make sure the guys who took Bree didn't call for others to come find us."

"How long ago did the boat leave?" Tex asked.

Smiley was grateful for his friends. He couldn't get a

word out. If he opened his mouth, he'd either start screaming, swearing, or moaning. He wasn't sure which.

"I'm not sure. It feels like forever. But probably at least...four or five hours," Julie speculated.

"Fuck. All right. While we get the hell out of here, I need the two of you to think really hard on any details about the boat, the men, anything that we might be able to use to track her down," Tex said.

Cookie leaned down and picked up Fiona, carrying her against his chest as he headed for the Jeep.

Kevlar offered to carry Julie, and she shyly took him up on his offer, since she wasn't wearing shoes.

Seeing her toes in the dirt made the ache in Smiley's heart grow. Bree probably wasn't wearing shoes either. His desire to know what the hell happened here, how she'd gotten separated from the other women, was gnawing at him. But he wouldn't deny the women the time they needed to process that they were safe.

Tex and Cookie climbed into the backseat with the women. Fiona sitting on her husband's lap, and Julie between them and Tex.

"I knew you'd come," Fiona said softly, when they were all settled into the Jeep and Kevlar was pulling out of the shipyard.

Everything within Smiley was urging him to stay, same as he'd felt after seeing her clothes at the truck stop. Once again, this was where Bree was last known to be. It physically hurt to leave. He rubbed his chest as he stared straight ahead.

"I told you once that I'd always come for you, and I meant it," Cookie told Fiona.

"Hurt wanted to come but—"

"But it's been a very long time since he's been in the field," Julie said, interrupting Tex. "It's fine. Being able to talk to him, reassure him that I'm okay...it was enough for now."

"Fuck," Smiley swore under his breath. He felt more than saw Kevlar look over at him from behind the steering wheel. But he kept his gaze straight ahead. He was holding on to his control by a thread.

"Bree," Fiona whispered.

"We aren't leaving her," Tex said in a low tone, full of emotion.

"She...we wouldn't have been able to escape without her."

"Hold that thought," Cookie said. "We're going to a hotel where you can shower, eat, and change into some clean clothes. Then we'll sit down and you can tell us the whole story. Unless you have intel that we need right this second about where she is so we can go get her."

Smiley looked back and saw both Fiona and Julie sadly shaking their heads. Julie reached over and took one of Fiona's hands in hers. He didn't like the look that passed between the two women.

He clenched his teeth so hard they started to ache. He wanted to disagree. Tell Kevlar to pull over so they could hear what Fiona and Julie had to say right then and there. But Cookie was right. They needed to get them to the hotel and do what they could to make them feel safe and comfortable.

Knowing there was nothing they could do right this moment for Bree was more painful than any injury he'd ever gotten while on a mission. Smiley would rather be shot than feel this.

"Smiley? Are you okay?" Fiona asked.

His first instinct was to lash out. To tell her of *course* he wasn't okay. Bree was in the hands of a fucking sadistic madman who wanted to defile and hurt her both mentally and physically.

Instead, he simply shook his head and continued staring out the front windshield.

He heard Cookie murmuring to his wife, telling her not to push, to give him some time. But time wasn't going to fix this. It would only take Bree farther and farther away from him. And give Castillo more chances to hurt her.

Closing his eyes, Smiley prayed for patience. And he prayed Bree was strong enough to withstand anything the assholes who took her had planned.

CHAPTER FOURTEEN

Bree lay on the floor of yet another fucking cage and did her best not to move a muscle. She was curled into a ball, trying not to throw up or moan from the motion of the boat. They were moving incredibly fast, and every time the boat went over a wave and came down hard on the water, her bones ached.

She was pretty sure she had at least one broken or cracked rib from being kicked. And one of her eyes was swollen shut. She had to be covered from head to toe in bruises. She hurt...everywhere. But she was alive.

And Fiona and Julie had escaped. She'd overheard the men on the boat worrying about that. Clearly concerned about how "unhappy" the boss was going to be when he found out. A search of the shipyard was being planned at daylight, and she could only hope her friends were able to get out, get beyond the fence before that happened.

Even though she wanted to rage and cuss out the men who were on the boat with her, Bree instinctively knew that her best option was to pretend to be unconscious. So far that had worked, as far as the men leaving her alone. The last thing she wanted was to bring their attention to her again. She had no idea if they were the kind of men who would rape a woman while she was passed out, but she had to continue hoping they weren't, as they hadn't touched her so far.

So she lay on the floor of the cage and did her best to act as if she was completely out of it. All the while, trying to remember the Spanish she'd learned during her college days to glean any information she could.

Honestly, even though she'd been beaten to a pulp, Bree wouldn't have changed anything she'd done. She wasn't upset for killing that guy back in the truck. She wouldn't spend another second thinking about him. He'd chosen his path, kidnapping innocent women to sell in the sex trade, and his death was a direct result of his life choices.

But most importantly, Julie and Fiona had benefitted from her sacrifice. Anything that happened to her now would be worth it.

Bree *did* worry a little about what they'd do now, after getting out of the truck. Especially without proper clothes. Would a kindhearted stranger in the area take them in? Give them food, water, clothes? Or would they run into someone Mateo or someone else was paying to look the other direction when illegal stuff went down at the shipyard?

Mentally shaking her head, Bree refused to be pessimistic. Julie and Fiona were smart. They'd be careful. They'd figure out a way to get to a phone, to contact their husbands. To tell them everything that had happened.

They'd do whatever it took to give the guys the info they needed to find *her*.

She just had to stay alive until that happened. Every painful breath reminded her that staying alive might be easier said than done, but Bree was determined to live long enough to let Smiley know how much he'd come to mean to her. That she'd been intrigued by him even from that first meeting. From the first time she'd heard his name, Jude Stark, something within her had sat up and taken notice.

She was going to campaign hard for either Addison or Maggie to name their kid Jude, if it was a boy. It was a kick-ass name, and Smiley had certainly lived up to the feeling of safety it evoked in her.

Thinking about him made her want to cry. How she wished she was back in his apartment, cuddled up against his side, talking about their plans for the day. He had to be freaking out right now.

No, not freaking out, that wasn't Smiley's style. He'd be frowning, that furrow in his brow would be super-prominent. He'd be barking at everyone when they didn't answer his questions fast enough, and he'd be pacing. She had no doubt about that.

Before pretending to pass out from the pain of her injuries, her captors let her have a small amount of water and a piece of stale bread when she feigned delirium and begged for something to eat and drink. But they didn't give her anything else to put on. The slip she'd been dressed in back in the States was filthy. And one of the straps had broken in her desperate fight for her freedom. She felt lucky not to be completely naked at this point.

She smelled horrible, like chicken shit, pee, and the dirt she'd lain in when she'd been beaten. Her hair was greasy, and now uneven since she'd cut some of it to use on her knife. Thinking about the piece of plastic that had allowed her to distract the asshole who'd been groping her made Bree sad. She was proud of that weapon. Even MacGyver would probably tell her good job. And now it was gone. She wasn't going to get a chance to make something else like it, since the cage she was in had a metal tray instead of plastic.

Her best defense right now was time. To stay quiet. To try to let her body rest so it would be ready for whatever was to come. She'd heard the man in the truck. She was being taken to Ecuador. To Mateo's private compound. Nothing good was going to happen to her there, but maybe, after a while, those around her would let down their guard and she'd be able to escape. She wasn't going to comply with anything asked of her, but in the long run, that might be the only way she was going to be able to escape.

Just the thought of what she'd have to do in order to make Mateo think he'd won was abhorrent. But she wouldn't stop fighting. Ever. Her only goal was to live. Then to escape. If she had to hike through hundreds of miles of jungle, she'd do it. If Fiona and Julie had been able to endure, so could she.

* * *

Smiley couldn't stand still. Adrenaline was still coursing through him. He needed to be *doing* something. Not just standing in this hotel room. Bree was out there, she needed him, and yet here he was.

But he was also well aware that he needed intel. He couldn't just run around like a chicken with its head cut off. He needed a plan. And he needed to hear Fiona and Julie's story in order to formulate one.

The sun was just starting to rise, and the two women had showered, eaten, and were wearing the clothes the men had brought for them. Smiley refused to think about the pants, shirt, underwear, and toiletries that were sitting in his own bag for Bree, unused. It hurt too much.

"Start at the beginning," Kevlar said gently. Julie was in a chair covered by a blanket, her legs drawn up in a somewhat defensive position. As much as she said she understood why her husband wasn't there, Smiley still felt a twinge of guilt for not choosing Patrick Hurt to accompany them.

Fiona was in Cookie's lap on the bed. He was leaning against the headboard covered by another blanket. She was sitting sideways with one arm around his shoulders and her head resting against his. Cookie literally hadn't let her out of his sight since she'd crawled out from under that car.

Tex was sitting in a chair next to a small circular table with his laptop open in front of him. He'd been clicking away at the keys ever since they'd returned to the hotel, and Smiley could only hope he was sending, and getting, information about Bree from the women he was working with.

Kevlar was leaning against one of the walls, looking relaxed. But his jaw was ticking and it was obvious he was just as anxious to hear the entire story as everyone else.

"So, we were in the back of my store looking through

the bags of donations, when the door slammed open and three men barged in," Julie said, starting things off.

"Yeah, we saw the surveillance video. What happened after you were put in the SUV?" Tex asked.

Smiley was glad that he was moving things along. He felt bad, because there was probably some therapeutic benefit for Julie and Fiona to give them every detail, but he needed new info.

"They used some sort of gas. The back of the SUV we were in was separated from the rest of the seats by Plexiglas," Fiona told them. "This fog appeared, and I don't remember even leaving the downtown area of Riverton."

"We woke up in that chicken truck," Julie picked up the narrative. "We were in cages, side by side, all the way at the back. It smelled horrible, and we didn't have any of our trackers or clothes, only those slip things."

"The chickens were loud, and I'm guessing the smell was meant to hide our own scents," Fiona said. "We could tell we were in a truck, but that's all we knew."

"And Bree? How was she?" Smiley couldn't help asking.

"Scared. We all were. It was my idea to see if we could find a way to break the plastic trays we were sitting on. But she was the only one able to actually do it. I guess there was a crack or something in hers, which she was able to get her fingers under and break off," Julie said.

Smiley fingered the knife Bree had fashioned, which was still in his pocket. He was proud of her, despite being pissed that she'd been in that situation in the first place. "I'm sorry," he blurted.

Everyone turned confused gazes toward him.

"For what?" Fiona asked.

"I was supposed to be watching over you guys. And I

left the store. I left you alone. Which was the exact chance those assholes needed to grab you."

"Smiley, you couldn't have known they were waiting for a moment to make their move. It was a *coincidence* that you were even out front, taking that call. If you were inside, you could've gotten hurt."

Smiley snorted. She was being very magnanimous. Those men did what they did, *when* they did it, one hundred percent because he was distracted. Of that, he had no doubt.

"He was talking to me," Cookie told his wife. "I was pissed that my team and I hadn't been told that the man after Bree had connections to your own abduction, years ago. I was chewing him a new asshole."

Fiona straightened to look at her husband. "Bree told us about that. About how the man after her had worked for the same organization responsible for holding us in Mexico."

"And?"

"And what?" Fiona asked.

"Did you have any flashbacks? Panic attacks?"

"No," Fiona said. "I won't deny it was a shock. But I was more pissed than anything else. Bree was the one who was having the hardest time with what was happening."

Smiley's heart ached at hearing those words.

"So what happened next? Bree made the knife...?" Kevlar asked.

"I cut off some of my slip, since I'm the shortest and it was the longest on me. Bree used the piece of plastic to cut some of her hair, to secure the cloth to the handle. Then we waited."

"It seemed to take forever," Fiona said, the women

going back and forth, telling the story. "We stopped, and for some reason it felt different that time. As if we'd made it to wherever we were going."

"There was this red light inside the truck, and when the door finally opened, it was dark outside. The light from some kind of streetlamps hurt our eyes. A man got into the truck and walked through the cages of chickens, who were squawking up a storm, not happy to be disturbed. Or maybe they just knew evil was walking amongst them. Who knows."

"Our plan was to somehow get someone to open our cages, to give us a chance to get away. It wasn't *much* of a plan, but Bree said she'd fake being sick or something. I wasn't sure it would do much good, it wasn't as if anyone gave a shit about our well-being up until that point as it was."

Smiley's gaze went back and forth between Fiona and Julie as they recounted their ordeal. Hatred welled inside him, and it took all his training to tamp it down. He couldn't afford to be emotional right now. He needed to be impassive, take in every scrap of info he could.

"He told Bree that Fiona and I had been sold to men in Russia and North Korea, but that she was being taken to their boss's compound in Ecuador. She was a gift to the employees to use however they wanted." Julie shuddered.

"She begged for water. Pretended to be terrified, although she probably wasn't really faking it, now that I think about it. But she acted submissive, as if she was already broken. It made the guy drop his guard, I think. He unlocked her cage and dragged her out. He touched her...squeezed her breast...and that's when she made her move."

The pride and awe in Fiona's voice couldn't remove the fury coursing through Smiley's body at the thought of someone touching Bree without her consent.

"She stabbed him. Right in the neck," Julie said, sounding bloodthirsty and not at all traumatized by what had happened right in front of her eyes.

"And then she kneed him in the balls," Fiona added.

"He dropped his keys, and she threw them to Fiona. Then she stabbed the guy in the neck again while he was down. Blood went everywhere but she kept doing it. Making sure he wasn't going to get up or call for help."

"I unlocked the padlock on my cage, crawled out, and freed Julie."

"Then we heard another guy calling for the one who was lying at our feet, bloody and dying. Bree told us she was going to distract them. That we should run," Julie said, her voice breaking for the first time.

"We refused. But she insisted," Fiona added.

"She told us to tell you..." Julie paused, as if she couldn't get the words out.

"That she loves you," Fiona finished quietly for her friend. "And that you're the best thing that ever happened to her."

Smiley's first thought was happiness. It hit him hard and fast. But terror overrode it in an instant. He could see his Bree standing there, in that same damn slip the others had worn, holding her makeshift weapon, probably splattered with her victim's blood. Looking like a Valkyrie. Willing to sacrifice herself so her new friends could get away.

He *hated* that she'd sacrificed herself...but he was also never as proud of anyone as he was of her in that moment.

"She ran out of the truck, jumped right on top of one of the men outside the door, screamed like a banshee, then ran away as fast as she could," Julie said.

"And everyone followed her," Fiona said with a sad nod. "Just as she hoped. Her actions allowed us to sneak out of that truck and hide."

"Did anyone look for you?" Cookie asked gently.

"Yeah, but we just kept slithering under different cars. They were parked so close together, it wasn't hard to stay ahead of them. And it was dark, so that helped big time. They got impatient, and I think they were scared of something happening and Bree getting away again, even though the one guy had her over his shoulder, and it seemed as if she was unconscious. Eventually, they gave up and headed for the dock. I don't think they looked for more than maybe thirty minutes or so. They got onto a boat and left."

"What kind of boat?" Tex asked, speaking up for the first time. "What did it look like? What color? Did you see any kind of name on it?"

"Um...it wasn't huge," Fiona said uncertainly.

"But it wasn't small either," Julie argued.

"True. It was pointy. The front."

"And dark. Maybe a navy blue? Or black?"

"I thought it was green," Fiona said, with a shake of her head.

"I didn't see any kind of name, sorry," Julie said.

Smiley's hopes fell. How could they track a boat if they didn't know anything about it?

"It's okay," Tex said. He'd been typing nonstop since the women started talking.

"How is this *okay*?" he blurted. "We don't know where she is. Which boat to track. How can we get to her if we have no idea which boat she's on out of the thousands that are probably on the water?"

"Because we know where she's going," Tex said calmly, pausing to look up at Smiley. "I know you want to swoop in and rescue her while she's on that boat, but you're right. We have no idea which one she's on. But since we know where Castillo is taking her, we can go there and intercept them."

Fuck. Smiley should've thought of that. His only consolation for the lack of foresight was that this mission was personal. He couldn't think objectively. He could barely *think*, period. All he could picture was an unconscious Bree slung over some asshole's shoulder.

He turned to Cookie. "You need to take Fiona and Julie home."

It was easy to see how torn Cookie was. "Call your team. Get them to join you," he said. "It'll take a while for that boat to reach Ecuador, even if it's a speedboat—and it sounds like it is—it won't be a one-day journey. Three at a minimum."

He wasn't wrong.

"I've already started that in motion," Tex said. "Been texting with your commander, he was already on standby. Your team can go wheels up by two p.m. They'll meet you there."

"We need you too, Tex," Smiley argued.

The older man shook his head. "I'm too old for this crap anymore. I'm heading back with Cookie, Fiona, and Julie. I'll head to base and work with your commander, Ryleigh, and Beth. With your team as boots on the ground, and my eyes from the air and on Castillo's digital footprint, we'll get her back and shut down that entire fucking operation. Oh, and I've made contact with someone who you're going to want to talk to as well."

"Who?" Kevlar asked.

"His name is Rex. He's with the Mountain Mercenaries."

"That guy whose wife was taken by del Rio?" Cookie asked.

"One and the same. He's not happy Castillo has taken up basically where his nemesis left off. He thought that organization was done, once and for all. But hearing Castillo basically took over that operation, and moved it from Peru to Ecuador, has him seriously riled up. He'll be calling to give you as much intel as he can when you get to Educator and set up an HQ."

Smiley would be happy to talk to the man. It was unfathomable that Rex had found his wife alive after a decade, but it gave Smiley hope. Bree was stronger than she knew; if anyone could survive a similar ordeal, it was his woman.

"I've got tickets for the two of you for seven o'clock this evening. That'll give you time to plan and rest," Tex told them. "Our flight for Southern California leaves around the same time."

"I'm assuming the fact that we weren't kidnapped with our passports isn't an issue?" Fiona asked with a small smile.

"Of course not," Tex told her calmly.

"I remember thinking that same thing...before," Fiona said.

"It wasn't an issue then and it's not an issue now. Speaking of which, Bree's passport will be waiting for you at the airport," Tex told Smiley. "I have a guy waiting for us. He'll take the Jeep, the weapons, and trade us for the IDs. When you get to Ecuador, I'll have another contact waiting for you outside customs. He'll have a sign with Mr. Hill written on it. Go with him, and he'll give you everything you need while you're there."

Tex was kind of scary, but Smiley was never as glad to have someone on his side as he was right this moment.

"Trackers?" Kevlar asked.

Tex sighed and his brows furrowed. "I don't have any with me. As you can probably guess, I left home in a hurry. Then things happened so fast with coming here to Ensenada that I wasn't able to get some backups from Wolf, which I'm sure he has hanging around his house."

"I've got mine," Smiley said.

"Did you find our trackers? When we woke up, all of our jewelry was gone," Fiona said.

Cookie nodded. "They were mostly destroyed, but I do have your rings. The signal is faint but still there, at least that's what Ryleigh said." He reached into his pocket and pulled out her wedding rings. "Give me your hand," he ordered.

Fiona did, and Cookie slid her rings back onto her finger. Then he brought her hand up to his mouth and kissed the back.

Julie took her earrings from Kevlar, frowning a little sadly at them, since they were so bent and broken.

"I'll make sure your teammates have their trackers with them before they head down to South America," Tex said, looking back at his computer screen. "Castillo's going down," he muttered. "He picked on the wrong woman. *Women*. Team. He should've known that he didn't get away with this all those years ago, and there's no damn way he's getting away with it a second time. Don't mess with Navy SEALs. *Period*."

"Hoo-ah," Cookie and Kevlar said under their breaths.

But Smiley was thinking too hard about what was to come to bother with the typical Navy cheer. Making a plan felt like a step forward, but having to wait until that afternoon to leave Mexico didn't sit well. Even knowing that the boat Bree was on couldn't magically levitate to Ecuador didn't make him feel any better.

They had to figure out where the boat would make landfall. Ecuador wasn't a small country. And knowing where Castillo's compound was wouldn't make narrowing down the boat's location any easier. Tex was good, but he wasn't *that* good.

Or was he? Maybe luck would be on their side, and they'd be able to meet the boat at a shipyard when it docked. They could end this once and for all, without having to hike into the fucking jungle.

Smiley would never admit it, but he hated the jungle. Bugs gave him the creeps. And snakes? Forget about it. But he'd face a million snakes if it meant getting Bree back safely.

Excusing himself after telling Fiona and Julie how relieved he was that they were all right, Smiley went back to his room. He didn't feel like being around anyone right now. He needed to think. To plan. To stress the fuck out. Once he got it out of his system, he could fly to Ecuador and be the kick-ass Navy SEAL he'd trained to be for years. Because this mission? It was the most important of his life. And he had no intention of failing.

CHAPTER FIFTEEN

It was official. Bree was seasick. She felt awful. Escaping was the last thing she was thinking about. Since she no longer had anything in her belly, all she could do was dry heave...which might've been a blessing in disguise, because her captors wanted nothing to do with her. She was grossing them out.

They left her alone, for the most part. Preferring to stay out of the small cabin where her cage was located, which now smelled like vomit and body odor. To her surprise, they'd also left her water, which was more than they'd done for her and the others when they were in that damn truck filled with chickens.

But she couldn't even really appreciate it much. She tried to drink, but it usually came right back up. Bree was weak, disoriented, and so sick of being on this boat, she was actually looking forward to when they arrived in Ecuador. And that was just sad, because arriving in the country meant her suffering would *really* start. Mateo would be there, and he probably wouldn't care that she was seasick.

The only thing that kept Bree from completely giving up was the thought of Smiley. And of Fiona and Julie being rescued. She had no way of knowing that they'd gotten away, but given the way the men who'd beaten her had been acting, and the snippets of conversation she'd been able to translate, they seemed scared shitless to see Mateo. And she hoped that meant the other women hadn't been found.

Surely the SEALs would've gotten to them by now. Maybe Julie and Fiona had found someone who'd let them use a phone, and they were able to call Wolf, or Tex, or somebody to come get them. The thought made Bree smile, even though it hurt her face to do so.

She was swollen and bruised all to hell. Maybe her appearance would be a turn-off to Mateo's employees. Then she huffed out an exasperated breath. No, it wouldn't. Men who had no problem sexually assaulting women being held against their will wouldn't give a shit if said woman was covered in bruises or begging for them to leave her alone. They'd take what they wanted, damn the consequences.

Turning her mind away from that, Bree's stomach tightened once more as they dropped off another big wave, and she began to dry heave again. She was a mess. Tears leaked out of her eye that wasn't swollen shut and rolled down her cheek. Right about now, she'd kill for a toothbrush. And for the room to stop rocking.

Time had no meaning. Bree had no idea how long she'd been on the boat, or how much longer they had to go. She could only close her eyes and pray this torture would be over soon. Of course, she had to be careful what she wished for...because what was waiting for her on dry land was most likely a hundred times worse than what she was experiencing right now.

Not able to wrap her mind around the fact that she could ever feel worse than she did right now, Bree did the only thing she was capable of at the moment. She closed her good eye, curled into a ball, and prayed to sleep. To escape the hell she was in. Even if just for a moment.

* * *

Smiley was nervous. No, he was internally freaking out. He and Kevlar were in Ecuador. The city of Guayaquil, to be precise. It was where Tex thought Castillo would mostly likely be waiting for Bree. But if he was wrong...

Smiley didn't want to even think about that possibility. Guayaquil was the largest city in the country, with about two-point-two million inhabitants. But it was also where most of the import and export trade was conducted. It was home to the country's chief port, where the majority of the ships entered and exited. Making it ideal for Castillo. It was likely many of the workers had been given bribes to ignore anything illegal they might see or hear.

Port Guayaquil itself was responsible for ninety percent of the commercial flow that affected the national economy, but there were also other, smaller seaports and marinas. They had no way of knowing where the boat Bree was on would be docking.

When Smiley and Kevlar had arrived, it was almost three in the morning, and they'd met up with Tex's contact, waiting for them outside of customs as promised.

The man didn't speak much, simply nodded at them and led them out to his truck. As he drove them through the city, it was obvious the country was in the middle of a crisis.

Men with rifles openly prowled the dark streets and signs of recent violence were everywhere. Very few people were out and about, owing to the late hour...and likely the state of nervousness from civilians.

Their contact drove into an underground parking area beneath a large building, after someone appeared out of nowhere to pull back a metal gate. Smiley had the thought that it was possible he and Kevlar would disappear themselves, become a casualty of the violence the nation was facing, but at that moment, he'd take his chances. He'd risk anything for a chance at finding Bree.

The man got out of the vehicle and led them through a door. The hallway they entered was dark, and Smiley couldn't help feeling uneasy. But nothing happened, other than their contact opening another door and gesturing for them to enter.

Inside the room was a virtual treasure trove of weapons.

"Choose," the man told them.

Kevlar and Smiley didn't waste time. They found serrated knives that they immediately strapped to their thighs by the included holsters. Pistols went in every available pocket, and they slung as many rifles over their shoulders as they could carry. They needed enough weapons for both themselves and the rest of the team, when they arrived. And if the men on the streets were any indication, they'd need all the firepower they could get.

Their escort nodded at their choices, then picked up a

crate Smiley had noticed when he'd been inspecting the weapons. It was full of ammunition, which was also vital if they were forced to storm Castillo's compound.

From what Tex had shown them, Castillo had set up his operation in the Amazon jungle. The closest city was Coca, which had a small airport. If they weren't able to find Bree in Guayaquil, Tex had already arranged for a flight to the Francisco de Orellana Airport. From there, they'd trek to Castillo's compound. Smiley wasn't looking forward to heading into the jungle, but he'd literally go to hell and back if it meant finding Bree.

Once they had as many weapons as they could carry, they were led back to the parking garage toward what looked like a freaking tank. It was an SUV on steroids. The tires were larger than normal, and Smiley realized the outside had been reinforced with steel plates. Someone had outfitted this vehicle to withstand almost anything.

He was impressed.

They swiftly loaded the weapons, their bags, the ammunition, and a large crate of food. Smiley wasn't sure what their contact thought they'd be doing or how long they'd be gone, but he wasn't going to complain about the latter. Neither he nor Kevlar had stopped to eat since arriving in Ensenada. They'd been too focused on searching the shipyard, then planning and trying to anticipate where Castillo's boat would make landfall.

It would be easier—from a human trafficking standpoint—to come into the country at a small city like Manta, travel to Quito, then to Coca from there. But Guayaquil had the benefit of being a city of unrest at the moment. Castillo likely had connections who would look the other way when an unwilling woman, or *women*, were unloaded from a boat.

For all Smiley and Kevlar knew, Castillo had arranged for a few others to be picked up on their way south. There was no telling how many women he may have kidnapped for his nefarious purposes.

Just as they were done loading the vehicle, the sound of the metal gate opening had both Smiley and Kevlar whipping around, each with a hand on the pistols at their hips. But since their escort didn't seem surprised at the van arriving, Smiley did his best not to jump to conclusions.

When the doors opened and the rest of his team hopped out, Smiley was incredibly relieved.

Blink made a beeline for them—and shocked the hell out of him by pulling Smiley into a long, tight hug. Then he pulled back, grasped his shoulders, locked eyes with him and said, "We're going to get her back. She's ours, and no fucker is going to take what's ours."

Some people might've questioned Blink's choice of words, but Smiley was having a hard time keeping control over his emotions. He'd felt the same way about Josie when she'd disappeared. About all his friends' women. They were as much a part of his family as his team.

"Thanks," he choked out.

Then the rest of the guys were there. They'd circled around, and all of them had at least one hand on him. His shoulder. His back. His arm. No one said anything, but their support at that moment was what Smiley needed. Together, *no one* was better than their team. They'd been through hell and made it through to the other side. They would find Bree and kill that motherfucking Castillo so he couldn't ruin any other women's lives.

"Pistols and knives are in the SUV," Kevlar said after a long moment.

Safe, MacGyver, and Flash nodded at Smiley, then turned their attention to the vehicle. Once everyone was armed, they piled inside.

"Where to first?" Safe asked.

"Motel. Drop off our stuff and tell you what we know. Then the port at sunrise. We'll go in pairs and get the lay of the land. Tex sent a list of all the speedboats headed toward Guayaquil. We don't know which one might be our target, but knowing where they're going to dock will be helpful. As far as he figures, they should be arriving tomorrow or the day after. If they made any stops, it could be as much as three or four days from now. If we don't find Bree within four days, we'll head to the Amazon. Go straight to his compound."

Smiley didn't want to think about what condition Bree might be in four days from now, and what might happen to her if Castillo got her to his compound. But he forced his mind away from those thoughts. He might not be able to function if he dwelled too long on what she was going through. His Bree was strong, but even the strongest woman could break.

Kevlar got behind the wheel of the SUV and glanced over his shoulder. "See if you can get Smiley to eat something, will you, Flash?"

Annoyed, Smiley glared at the back of his team leader's head. He didn't want to eat. In fact, the thought of food made him sick. But Flash wasn't going to take no for an answer. He dug into the box of food and pulled out a protein shake. Opening it, he held it out to Smiley.

He thought about refusing, but knew his teammates

were just as stubborn as he was. They wouldn't stop badgering until he'd consumed the damn thing. Snatching it out of his friend's hand, Smiley brought it to his lips and chugged.

It tasted like shit, but he couldn't deny that once he had something in his belly, the churning and rolling it had been doing began to wane.

MacGyver grabbed a protein bar and handed it to Kevlar as he pulled out from under the building. The metal gate closed behind them with an audible clank. Taking a deep breath, and hoping they wouldn't run into any trouble on the way to the motel, Smiley stared out the front windshield and prayed luck would be on their side, and they'd be able to find some sign that would point them to what boat Bree would be on and when she'd arrive.

* * *

Two days later, Smiley's prayers hadn't been answered. The seven of them had prowled the port, searching for any signs of Bree on any of the speedboats that had come in and generally keeping an eye on things as best they could. Their job was made more difficult by not knowing exactly what they were looking for. But nothing they'd seen so far had given them any indication that a woman was being smuggled onshore.

Three of them were now holed up in what would be considered a one-star motel back in the States. The other four teammates were back at the port, watching and waiting.

Kevlar, Smiley, and Blink were supposed to be sleeping

so they could trade off with the rest of the team when their watch ended, but none of them were even close to feeling sleepy. The part of the city where the port was located was one of those places the State Department—and anyone with half a brain in their head—would warn Americans against visiting, or even traveling through.

It was poor, and violence had taken a firm hold. Every twenty minutes or so, the sound of gunfire could be heard through the thin walls of the room they were in just a few blocks away from the port entrance. Every so often, they could hear screams and even the occasional explosion. Smiley had seen several children as they made their way back and forth to the rundown building that called itself a motel, and their condition made him incredibly sad. All they'd ever known was poverty. Life wasn't fair, that was for sure.

The sound of Kevlar's phone ringing seemed loud in the otherwise silent room. None of them were talking. There was no idle chitchat going on. All three men were lost in their heads, thinking about the upcoming search and what they could do to make it successful.

"Kevlar here. Yeah, okay, let me put you on speaker. Okay, go ahead."

"As I said, my name is Rex. I'm in charge of the Mountain Mercenaries out of Colorado. Tex tells me you and your team are in Ecuador hunting a man named Mateo Castillo?"

"Yes. He kidnapped Smiley's woman. Had been after her for a while now. Bought her from her ex out of Las Vegas."

"Vegas. Figures. That was del Rio's favorite hunting

ground. Tex also said that Castillo has, for all intents and purposes, taken over del Rio's operation, moved it to Ecuador. Is that right?"

"From what we understand, that's correct," Kevlar told him.

"Motherfucker. Right. Okay, I'm going to tell you what I know about how del Rio did things. How his operation was set up. The schedule of the guards, how the women were kept and where. Everything I can. Hopefully, you'll be able to use the intel to take this Castillo fucker down once and for all. You need to send a message that if anyone tries to pick up where he left off after his balls are cut off and shoved down his throat, the same thing will happen to them, no matter *what* hole they crawl into to try to hide."

Smiley approved of Rex's barely held-in-check violence. His hatred for anyone who worked in the sex trade came through loud and clear. And why wouldn't it? His wife had been held captive and tortured for years.

An hour later, Smiley was sick to his stomach, and his sense of urgency to find and kill Castillo was higher than ever.

But he also had a better understanding of the business side of the sex trade. How customers were contacted, how they paid, where the money went, things like that. Tex and the women he was working with were surely following the money trail right that moment. They'd want to catch as many men as they could who were using Castillo's services and buying women from him, as well as finding Bree.

At the moment, all Smiley could think of was his woman. Yes, he cared about the others who might be under Castillo's thumb, but he was desperate to prevent his Bree from spending even one more second than necessary as a captive.

Rex had offered the services of his mercenaries, but Kevlar declined. As it was, they were conspicuous enough. Adding six more large men to their group would make it almost impossible for the government and the police to overlook their presence.

By the time Kevlar said goodbye to Rex, Smiley was keyed up. He wanted to go back to the port right that moment. Needed to do something other than sit around and worry and imagine all the bad things that might be happening to the woman he loved.

Without a word to the others, Kevlar's fingers tapped on the screen of his phone. Then he looked up and said, "Our turn."

Thank fuck.

Glad his team leader was on the same page as he was, Smiley stood. Making sure his weapons were still secure, he strode toward the door, more determined than ever to find the boat Bree was on and liberate her from the men dumb enough to make their living kidnapping innocent women.

And if one hair on her head was harmed...so help those men. Their deaths would be long and painful instead of quick and humane. He needed them to hurt as much as he was right now. As much as they'd made Bree suffer.

* * *

Bree didn't think she'd ever feel normal again. She'd been sick for so long, she could barely see straight...or maybe that was because her eye was still swollen shut. And her ribs hurt like crazy; dry heaving wasn't the best thing for a cracked rib.

But thankfully, it had been at least a day since she'd last puked, and she'd been able to keep down the water and crackers she'd been given. She was still hungry, but she could practically feel her cells soaking up the water as she drank tiny sips.

She still felt a little green, and was still in pain from the beating she'd received, but as the boat slowed, and as she saw lights twinkling from the small porthole in the side of the vessel, her heart began to beat faster.

They were here.

Where *here* was, she had no idea. No, that wasn't true. She assumed they were finally in Ecuador. But she didn't know exactly where in the country. Regardless, her only chance to evade the hell Castillo had planned for her was to escape before she arrived at his compound.

From what she understood from her captors, that compound was in the Amazon jungle. Far from civilization. Men...customers...flew into the nearest city under the guise of taking a vacation or some such bullshit. Then they were escorted to the compound, where they could indulge in all the sex they wanted—for a price. The more they paid, the more they were free to do with the women.

It was disgusting and vile, and scary as hell. Even though the man she'd killed had said that she was to be a reward for the workers at the compound, and not the paying customers, it didn't make her feel any better. It almost felt worse to Bree.

Hell, who was she kidding? It was all bad. Terrible. Awful. Horrifying.

She had to figure out how to get away before they arrived in the jungle. Because she was *not* a jungle girl. Bugs freaked her out. And snakes? Nope ropes? Forget about it.

The men were busy on the deck, readying the boat to dock, and Bree frantically looked around for anything that might help her. The men would have to remove her from the cage, because she could tell it was permanently attached to the floor of the boat. There were bolts holding the bottom down so it wouldn't slide across the floor in rough seas.

That would work in her favor. As long as they didn't bring in *another* cage to put her in, before taking her off the boat.

The men believed her to be totally weak and terrified, especially since she'd been so sick for the entire trip. She didn't feel great still, but seasickness wasn't going to keep her from doing everything in her power to get away from these assholes. She'd swim back to the States if she had to.

Okay, no she wouldn't. She wasn't the strongest swimmer in the world.

Raised voices outside had her heart beating faster still. This was it. They were docking. For a moment, Bree panicked. Who did she think she was? She wasn't Superwoman. She couldn't fight off three men, that much was obvious, given what had already happened. She didn't have her plastic knife anymore to use against anyone, and her ribs hurt like hell. She probably couldn't even walk after being cooped up in this cage for who knew how many days. And with little caloric intake, she'd probably fall on her face as soon as she tried to take a step.

Then she pictured Smiley. Him grinning at her. Telling her how strong she was. How proud he was of her. Then scowling and telling her to stop fucking feeling sorry for herself and to do what needed to be done.

That did the trick. She wanted Smiley to be proud of her, and if she had to rescue her damn self, that's what she'd do.

Before long, one of the men who'd gleefully beaten her back in Ensenada entered the small area of the boat she was being held in. Without a word, he reached for the padlock on her cage.

Bree's heart was racing so fast, she felt light-headed as adrenaline coursed through her body, enough to make her shaky. He reached into her cage and yanked her out as if he were handling an inanimate object.

She stumbled, but locked her knees to stay on her feet. She was dragged out of the small cabin into a star-filled night, and the first breath of fresh air in days invigorated Bree. The man hauled her to the side of the boat, then handed her off to another, someone she'd never seen before. As this new guy force-marched her toward the shore, Bree looked back to see the three men preparing the boat to leave again.

Internally, she smiled. She had no idea what her captors had told this new guy, but hopefully he would underestimate her. She looked like shit, she knew she did. Bree could only hope he didn't think she was any kind of threat.

Looking around as he walked her down a long pier toward a van, Bree's mind spun. This was it. Her one and only chance. If he got her in that van, it was over.

Wishing she had shoes, or even a freaking shirt, Bree winced as she stepped on something sharp.

While she was wishing for things, she might as well

wish that Smiley would step out from behind the wall of the small building up ahead and shoot this asshole holding her in the forehead.

With every step toward the end of the pier, Bree's pulse kicked up a notch. It had to be in the danger zone by now. Her vision narrowed as she went over and over the best way to yank her arm out of this guy's grasp.

When they reached the end of the pier and stepped into the parking lot, once again, Bree's foot landed on something sharp. She gasped and instinctively stopped, reaching down to her foot to dislodge whatever she'd stepped on.

To her surprise, the man holding her stopped too.

And now she was leaning over—and her head was level with his crotch.

She hadn't planned things this way, but her body was moving before her brain had given the command. Her fist flew and she punched the man's dick as hard as she could.

Her knuckles throbbed, but to her amazement, it worked. The man howled and brought both hands between his legs.

She couldn't believe punching a guy in the nuts had worked a second time!

And Bree was off and running. She had no idea where she was running *to*, her only goal was to get away from that fucking van. It signified a slow, painful, humiliating death, and she wasn't ready to die yet.

She didn't feel the pain of the rocks and glass in the parking lot under her feet. She didn't feel the throbbing of her side as her ribs were jostled as she ran. She simply acted like a cornered animal, desperate to get away.

Luck was on her side, as the port wasn't well lit and

there was no one around that she could see. She had no idea if it was night or early morning, but it didn't matter. Her captors thought to use the cover of darkness to hide their despicable deals and illegal cargo, and she would use it to *her* advantage.

The man shouted from behind her, but Bree didn't stop. She ran as if her life depended on it—and it did. Weaving in and out of cars parked in the lot and ducking behind shacks made out of tin and wood, Bree never stopped. It felt as if she ran forever.

And before she could stop herself, she careened headlong into *another* freaking chain-link fence.

Cursing, she looked to her right, then left. There was fence as far as she could see. Which admittingly wasn't very far, since it was dark out.

Fucking fences! This was the second time a fence was keeping her from escaping.

Despair hit hard and fast. It didn't look as if she could crawl under the thing, and she couldn't go up and over either, because the top had a spiral of nasty, sharp-looking concertina wire. The kind of deterrent prisons used to keep people from climbing out...or in, for that matter.

Holding back a sob, Bree turned left. There had to be an opening somewhere. A place for cars to come and go from the port. But the longer she ran, the more worried she got. Just how big *was* this place anyway?

She could still hear shouts behind her, and it sounded like there were several men after her now. Shit! She wasn't going back. No way in hell.

As her initial adrenaline waned, she felt pain now with every step. It was difficult to breathe and every inhalation felt as if she were swallowing nails. Her limbs were shaking and it was only a matter of time before her body failed her.

No! She couldn't get this close only to break now.

But her mind could no longer overpower her body. Bree fell to her knees, hard. A squeak of pain escaped her lips as she scraped the hell out of her legs. She stayed there a beat, on her hands and knees, panting.

She was so tired. She'd tried *so hard*. And it looked as if she was going to fail after all. And that sucked! She considered getting up and running some more, but even as she gave her body the order, her limbs refused to move.

With a last-ditch will to live, to escape, Bree dragged herself toward a large pile of debris. It was rocks, leaves, and dirt, piled up as if moved by a bulldozer or something. Maybe she could hide herself behind it.

As she neared it, the male voices got louder. They were right on her tail.

To her surprise, the pile was pliant. Crumbly. Turning so her legs were toward the pile, she crawled backward. Her legs were quickly swallowed up by the debris.

Wiggling and squirming, Bree frantically tried to cover as much of her body as she could. To push her way inside the pile. She was able to get all but her head and shoulders into the dirt.

It occurred to her that she was basically burying herself alive. That she was making it easier for the men searching for her to conk her on the head, then use the pile as her actual grave, hiding their misdeed from the authorities and anyone who might come looking for her.

And that made her think about Smiley once more.

Determined to do whatever she could to help herself, grave or not, Bree scooped up some of the dirt around her and rubbed it into her hair and shoulders, trying to blend in more with the dark pile of dirt and rubble.

Then when the voices were perilously close, just on the other side of her hiding place, she lowered her forehead to the ground and held her breath, praying she was sufficiently hidden and her pursuers would walk right by.

CHAPTER SIXTEEN

At the first man's shout, Smiley's head whipped around in the direction the sound had come from. Blink and Kevlar had headed south to one of the smaller docks, and he'd stayed behind to watch a larger one. It was starting to sink in that they might not find Bree. The thought was almost debilitating. They'd been so close back in Ensenada. So close to finding her and ending this once and for all.

But a part of Smiley, deep down, refused to give up. The same way he'd relentlessly searched for Bree back in the States. And she'd been there, right under his nose, the entire time. He just needed a break. A tiny little break. He could take it from there.

The shouting from someone not too far from him could possibly be that break he was waiting for. It was late...or early...and even though this was a working port, he hadn't heard shouting in the middle of the night before.

Racing quickly toward the sound, Smiley moved silently through the crates, vehicles, and Conex containers strewn around the many docks and ports. Unlike in the

United States, it didn't seem as if there was much oversight, as far as maintenance went. Bulldozers sat abandoned and there were piles of construction debris everywhere. It seemed to him that a major project had been in the works, then stopped suddenly.

Dodging around random piles of wood, concrete, and dirt, Smiley searched for the man who'd let out the pained shout...but as he moved farther away from the water, he had second thoughts. Was he on a wild goose chase? Would he miss the boat Bree arrived on if he took his eyes off the water?

He should turn back, at least contact Kevlar and Blink, work with his teammates to find out what was going on.

But something kept him running. Kept him moving away from the dock he'd been watching.

He was near the edge of the port now, where a tall chain-link fence had been erected for security purposes. Suddenly, three men came into sight, and they were obviously looking for something—which had Smiley's heart beating extra hard in his chest. There was no light back here except for the small beams coming from the flashlights carried by the three men he was now stalking.

Smiley barely prevented himself from announcing his presence by stumbling around a large mound of debris, directly into the men's line of sight. They were walking up and down the fence line, shining their lights around the area.

Squinting to try to see what they were pointing at, Smiley spotted footprints in the dirt.

Hope rose within him, even though he had no reason to think the men were looking at *Bree's* footprints. He hadn't seen any boats come in, although there were dozens of docks in the huge port that he and his team weren't able to monitor, not every moment of every day and night.

The men seemed agitated, almost frantic. Just when he was pulling out his phone to notify Kevlar that he needed assistance, one of the men let out a shout of triumph.

He ran over to a mound of what looked like mostly dirt and began rooting around.

The next sound Smiley heard almost stopped his heart. It was a heart-wrenching wail of despair and frustration. And he'd never forget it as long as he lived.

Bree!

He was racing toward the three men before he thought about what he was doing.

The man who'd found her grabbed hold of Bree's arms and was dragging her out from where she'd attempted to conceal herself. She was struggling and doing her best to wrench free, without success, clouds of dirt flying from her body.

The other two men were laughing, standing off to the side and not helping their friend, assuming he could handle Bree on his own.

Smiley targeted them first. He silently snuck up behind the larger of the two men and, using the knife strapped to his thigh, quickly slit his throat. Even as he was falling to the ground, Smiley had already turned to the second man.

Losing the element of surprise meant the next man was a little more prepared. But he was no match for Smiley. He was a pissed-off Navy SEAL with his woman's wail of fright still echoing in his head.

Smiley sacrificed the knife as it embedded deeply into the man's chest, right over his heart, when he fell face down into the dirt.

He turned toward the last man. The one who dared to touch Bree.

Every muscle in his body tensed. The third man had Bree in a headlock. He was wrenching her head back so far, she was looking straight up instead of at Smiley. She was making choking noises in the back of her throat and standing on her tiptoes.

Smiley's senses were on overload. The sounds from Bree, the briny smell of the ocean and dead fish, the blood he could feel on his hands, the bitter taste of fear in his mouth—and finally the sight of the woman he loved, practically naked, wearing nothing but that damn slip, both the material and her body covered in dirt. The slip was hanging off one shoulder because of a broken strap, exposing one of her breasts. Like Fiona and Julie, there were no shoes on her feet.

Out of everything, it was the lack of shoes that hit Smiley the hardest.

"Get back!" the man ordered.

But Smiley had no intention of doing any such thing. He also wasn't going to stand there and have a fucking conversation with this asshole or give him a chance to hurt Bree any more than he already had.

In one fluid movement, Smiley grabbed the pistol from the holster at his back and swung it up. He fired one shot.

It went right through the man's forehead.

He fell like a stone, taking Bree with him.

Smiley rushed forward and desperately tried to untangle her from the dead man's grip. On his knees, he pulled Bree into his arms and held her so tight, it had to be painful, but he couldn't seem to loosen his arms.

That is, until he heard a slight whimper from her lips.

That had him pulling back faster than anything she might have said to him.

"Bree?"

"Smiley... You're here," she croaked.

"Of course I am. I told you that I'd come for you no matter what."

"How...how are you here?" she asked.

Smiley frowned. She sounded out of it. "Where are you hurt?" he barked, wincing at his tone. But she didn't seem to even notice. She blinked, and it was only then he realized that one of her eyes was swollen shut.

He'd killed these assholes too quickly.

"Bree? Talk to me. Where are you hurt?"

"Um...everywhere. Do you have any food? I'm so hungry."

His heart broke again. Smiley didn't think anything could be more painful than seeing the woman he loved so damaged. But hearing the desperation and fear in her voice was like a physical blow.

"I have some in the car. Come on, I need to get you out of here and somewhere safe."

Just as he finished saying the words, loud shouts echoed through the port, coming from the direction of the water. He reached for his phone but came up empty. *Fuck.* He remembered holding it, getting ready to text Kevlar when Bree's hiding place was discovered. He must've dropped it.

Moving quickly, Smiley acted on instinct. He picked up Bree, holding her against his chest, and began moving quickly away from the dead men.

He still had his pistol, but not enough bullets to take down an entire group of bad guys. His teammates would've heard the shot, but it would take too long for them to figure out exactly where it came from. He had no way of communicating with Kevlar and Blink without his phone, and Bree was seriously hurt.

He needed to get them out of here. *Now*.

He ran, with no destination in mind except getting away from the yelling he heard behind him. Unfortunately, the team's vehicle was in the other direction, but at the moment, getting Bree away from the men he heard shouting back and forth—a dozen or so, at his guess—was his only mission.

"Smiley?" she asked, the fear and uncertainty easy to hear in that one word.

"I've got you," he told her, seeing exactly what he needed. Up ahead, there was a gate in the perimeter fence. Upon closer inspection, he saw there was a small lock holding it closed. Reluctantly, Smiley put Bree on her feet. "Hold on to the fence for a second, sweetheart."

Her arm tightened around his neck. "Don't leave me!" she exclaimed, panicking.

Smiley turned to her, put his hands on her face, and leaned down so his forehead was resting against her. "I'm not leaving you. I'm *never* fucking leaving you. I just need to get this gate open, then we'll be on our way again."

He'd never been so proud of Bree as he was in that moment, when she took a deep breath, nodded, and took a step to the side, putting her back against the fence. "I'm sorry. I know you aren't going to leave. I just...I can't believe you're here."

Moving slowly, Smiley lifted the scrap of material on her chest and tried to cover up her exposed breast. She looked down, then brought her hand up to hold the slip in place.

Feeling anger course through his veins, Smiley turned toward the fence before he did something stupid, like turn around and hunt the men looking for her and kill them one by one with his bare hands. He had no doubt he could do it. With the way he was feeling, they'd be dead before they knew what hit them. But he'd promised not to leave Bree, and no way in hell was he breaking that promise.

He turned toward the gate and took a deep breath, then lifted his leg and kicked at the lock with his boot as hard as he could. The small, flimsy lock broke upon impact, metal parts flying in all directions. Then it was a simple matter of lifting the latch and pushing the gate open. He turned back to Bree and picked her up again without a word.

He walked through the gate, intending on not looking back, but Bree stopped him.

"We should close it. So they don't know for sure we came this way."

She was right. Adrenaline was making it difficult for Smiley to think. That, and holding a wounded and hurting Bree.

Turning back toward the gate, he went to put her down, but once again she was thinking more clearly than he was.

"Just get close, I'll shut and latch it."

Leaning down, Smiley did just that, and Bree pulled the gate closed then reached out and lowered the latch.

If anyone looked closely enough they'd see the broken lock on the ground, but closing it might give them a few precious minutes to lose themselves in the slums surrounding the port.

Smiley wasn't happy about not being able to take Bree immediately to a doctor, or hell, straight to the airport to get her out of Ecuador. Still, *nothing* could dim the immense relief he felt at finding Bree.

Taking her back to the motel for now would be ideal. But it was on the opposite side of the port. He wouldn't risk taking her back through the dockyard, nor could he possibly know if the assholes searching for them had enough manpower to spread out to the nearest streets...

He needed to find a place to hole up. To wait for Tex to find him using the fucking tracker in his underwear and come to his aid.

Any other time, in any other situation, Smiley would resent having to go to ground, but right now, Bree was his only focus. He absolutely would not risk her safety after everything she'd been through. He'd hide for years if it meant keeping her safe and secure.

Smiley began to jog once more. The small forested area on this side of the shipyard gave way to dirt roads, then asphalt. They began to pass more buildings and cars until they were in the midst of civilization once more. But that didn't mean they were safe. There was no telling where the loyalties of anyone they came into contact with might lie. Ecuador was full of honest, hardworking people, without a doubt, but like any country in the midst of a violent uprising, people did what they had to do in order to survive. And this neighborhood wasn't in good shape. Even as he jogged with Bree in his arms, Smiley could hear gunfire in the distance.

They weren't safe here. Castillo could have spies everywhere, people who would be more than willing to give up two Americans for a hefty payday.

Kicking himself for dropping his phone, Smiley looked around for a place to hole up. To check on Bree. To breathe for a moment before meeting up with his team.

The sun was just beginning to light up the world around them, which would soon mean more people out and about and more eyes on them—and Bree was in no condition for anyone to be looking at her. She was practically naked. That could result in a whole *different* set of worries if he didn't find a place to hide pronto.

Then, he found what he was looking for. Down an alley was a dilapidated building. Actually, it could hardly be called a "building" anymore, from the looks of it. The roof was half caved in, but from the street, Smiley couldn't see past the wall that had fallen inward.

Praying they could get inside and hide from any prying eyes, Smiley carried Bree down the dark alley toward the structure. Checking to make sure there wasn't any glass to cut her more than she was already, Smiley put Bree on her feet.

"Give me a second," he told her.

She nodded, and he didn't like the faraway look in her eyes. Moving quickly, he ducked under the partially collapsed doorway and looked around. There was nothing of value in the small space, just rubble and glass. But it would work for now. At least until Kevlar and the rest of his team could pick them up.

Returning to Bree, Smiley saw her weaving on her feet with her eye shut.

"Come on," he said, kicking himself when she jerked violently. "It's me, Bree. Just me."

"Sorry," she told him.

"Nothing to be sorry about. Let's get you inside." He didn't give her time to take even one step before picking her up once more.

Ducking down again, he brought Bree into the small island of safety—at least, he hoped that's what it was—under a section of ceiling that remained intact. He leaned over and gently set her on a wide board. Then he went to work, trying to shuffle away the worst of the glass and debris out of the area immediately around her.

"Smiley? Will you sit?"

He shouldn't. There were a million things he needed to do. Further secure the area, go out and find something for Bree to eat and drink—if she felt secure enough to allow him out of her sight—and contact his team. But he couldn't deny this woman anything.

He sat, then picked up Bree and placed her on his lap.

She inhaled sharply, and he froze. "Fuck. Did I hurt you?"

She shook her head. "No. My ribs are a little sore though."

A little sore, his ass.

Smiley began to gently probe her side, noting when she flinched, where he was touching when she did so. Then he held her head in his hands once more and studied her bruised face, the eye that was still swollen shut.

Honestly, she looked like hell. She had black circles under her eyes, her lips were chapped and peeling, she had bruises everywhere, and he could tell she'd lost weight in just the few days it had been since he'd last seen her.

"You found me," she whispered, staring into his eyes. "I'm okay now that you're here," she told him.

Smiley swallowed hard. He didn't want to ask this next question, but he had to. Had to know what he was dealing with. What *they* were dealing with. "Did they rape you?" he asked quietly, not beating around the bush.

She shook her head.

"Be honest with me," he pleaded. "Nothing between us changes if they did. I love you so much, and *nothing* those assholes did will ever change that."

Her expression shifted then. Any pain she was feeling seemed to disappear. "What?" she whispered.

"If they violated you, that's a stain on *their* soul, not yours. We'll get you some help when we get home, so you can talk it out, process it. I want you to understand that nothing that happened to you is your fault. You did nothing wrong."

Bree laid her palm on the side of his face as she shook her head. "No. You love me?"

Understanding dawned. "Love seems like such a tame word for what I feel for you. Nothing in my life scared me as badly as when I realized you'd been taken. Did you mean what you told Julie and Fiona? What you asked them to tell me?"

"They're okay?" she asked urgently. "You found them?"

"Yes. Cookie and Tex took them back to California. I came here with the rest of my team to find you. They told us you'd been taken on a boat, and I think I lost ten years of my life, wondering if we'd be able to find you."

"Where are we? Ecuador?"

"Yes. Guayaquil."

She sighed.

"Bree? Did you mean it?" Smiley repeated. It didn't matter, not right now. Not when she was almost naked, hurting, and starving. But he couldn't stop himself from asking. He felt exposed. Vulnerable. And didn't like it one bit. He needed the words from her own lips.

"If that was going to be the last time anyone saw me, I wanted to be sure you knew what you meant to me. How much I loved you."

Smiley's world turned upside down once more. He knew how much this woman meant to *him*, but hearing from her own lips that she felt the same made him all the more determined to get them home so he could spoil the hell out of her. To give her as easy a life as he could. He never wanted to let her down. Never wanted her to regret loving him.

He gathered her into his arms gently and rocked back and forth.

As soon as the sun dropped below the horizon again, if his team hadn't found him by then, they'd venture out and attempt to make their way to the motel. The sooner he got Bree on a plane back to the States, the better.

CHAPTER SEVENTEEN

Bree was lightheaded and feeling quite sick. She needed food. And water. But it wasn't as if Smiley could produce those things out of thin air. He'd explained that he didn't have anything with him, any supplies, because he and the rest of his team expected that if they found her, they'd go straight to the motel, and then the airport.

And he'd left his pack in the vehicle they were using.

Her mouth watered at the thought of what he had in that backpack. Clothes. Socks. Shoes. Food. Water. Chapstick...all the things a girl who'd been kidnapped could ever want.

Instead, she was sitting on Smiley's lap in a building that felt as if it was going to completely collapse on top of them at any second, still in the nasty slip—but at least now, also in the shirt Smiley had literally given her from his own back—and so hungry she thought she was going to pass out.

But she wasn't in a cage. Wasn't on her way to

becoming anyone's sex slave. And Smiley's team was going to find them hopefully sooner rather than later. She could hang on for a little while longer.

"At least it's not the jungle," Bree said out of the blue. She should be sleeping, but she was too keyed up. And sensing Smiley's tension made her too nervous to close her eyes...er, *eye*. Every sound she heard made her wonder if that was it, if Mateo's goons had found them. "I hate bugs. And snakes. And itchy plants. For the record...I'm not a camping girl."

Smiley chuckled, and she felt it along every inch of her body. "Noted."

"Smiley?"

"Yeah, sweetheart?"

"He's not going to give up."

His entire body went hard. She hadn't meant to blurt that out, but she couldn't stop thinking about it. Mateo Castillo had gone to extraordinary lengths to find and recapture her. Just because she'd gotten away a second time didn't mean he was going to let her go. For some reason, he was determined to add her to his collection of women. She had no idea why. She wasn't anything special. She was just...her.

"I know."

Bree wasn't expecting that response. She met his gaze and bit her lip.

"But he's not going to win. He's on the radar now. Mine, yours, the team's, Tex, Wolf and his friends. A guy from Colorado named Rex. He's going down, Bree. I guarantee you that."

Bree believed him. It would be easy for her to blow

him off or get upset, because *he* wasn't the one Mateo was after. But he was in this as much as she was. His being here, right now, proved that. "Okay."

"Okay?" he repeated, dipping his head so he could look into her good eye better.

"Yeah. I'm scared, Smiley. I won't deny that. But I got away not once, but twice. I'm not the stupid, weak woman he obviously thinks I am. Of course, me getting away means he'll be more careful next time, but whatever."

"There won't be a next time," Smiley said gruffly.

"I hope you're right."

"There won't," he insisted. "This is gonna end. Sooner rather than later."

Bree prayed that was the case.

"I need to talk to you about something else."

She braced even as she nodded.

"I need to go out and find you something to eat and drink. Maybe get you something more appropriate to wear."

Her first instinct was to say no. *Hell no.* But she seriously didn't feel well. Was feeling sicker by the minute. If she wanted to be any kind of help, or just not have to be carried everywhere, Bree knew he was right.

It was one of the most difficult things she'd ever done, giving him a nod of agreement, but she did it anyway.

"Fuck, Bree. You amaze me."

She shook her head firmly. "No. Don't tell me how strong I am or how impressed you are. Everything within me is screaming to say no. To hold on and refuse to let you leave. But I'm not in good shape. I don't know if I can even stand up on my own anymore. I feel like shit, and I know it's because I'm hungry and dehydrated. And if you can find anything for my feet, I'd be extremely grateful. Even flip-flops."

"You *are* strong, and I *am* impressed with you," Smiley countered. "And the fact that you want to tell me to stay but aren't, just solidifies your strength."

Bree rolled her eyes and huffed out a breath. "Whatever," she mumbled.

"I'm not going far. I'll be back before you can miss me."

She snorted at that. "I *already* miss you, and you haven't even left yet."

Smiley looked into her eyes. "I'm not losing you again," he declared, somewhat dramatically.

Bree couldn't stop the small smile that formed on her lips.

He looked confused. "What? That wasn't funny in the least."

"You didn't lose me the first time. I was kidnapped. By assholes."

It was his turn for his lips to twitch. "Semantics."

"Go, Smiley. Before I change my mind and become someone I don't like. A weak, begging, pathetic woman who can't function without her man in sight."

"Don't do that again," Smiley said sternly, all humor gone from his expression and his tone.

"Do what?"

"Denigrate yourself. You aren't weak or pathetic. And if you *did* beg me not to go, I'd never hold it against you. Not after everything you've been through."

Bree swallowed hard and nodded.

Carefully, Smiley moved her to the side and put her ass

on the wooden board he'd been using as a seat. Then he began to move other boards and debris around the small area.

"What are you doing?" she couldn't help but ask.

"Arranging things so if someone does happen to look in here, all they'll see is junk. If you hear something, don't move. Stay as silent and still as possible. But if someone discovers you, scream. As loud as you can. I'll hear you and come running and kill whoever it is who dared put their hands on you."

Bree frowned. That made her remember what he'd done back at the port. "I'm sorry you had to kill those men."

"Why? I'm not."

The three words made Bree blink. Why *was* she apologizing? Yes, those men might have families, people who relied on them. But they were also working for Mateo. Were going to take her to his jungle compound and most likely take part in sexually assaulting her.

"I have no remorse over killing anyone who puts one fucking hand on you. If that's not something you can live with...I'm sorry, but...tough. And I'm not saying I'll lose my shit in the future if someone does something stupid in a bar. I'm talking if they hurt you. If they try to force themselves on you. They're dead."

Smiley was definitely not the easygoing, fun kind of guy the rest of his teammates seemed to be. Yes, they were all Navy SEALs and had probably killed bad guys. But Smiley had an edge the others didn't. And Bree might be crazy, but she loved him all the more for it. Because when he *did* show his gentler side...it made her melt. "All right."

He stared at her for a beat, then asked, "All right?"

"Yes," she told him with a nod. She wanted to smile at the ridiculousness of their conversation. How so much could be shared with a few simple words was beyond her. But with Smiley, nothing surprised her.

"I'll be back," he told her firmly.

Bree's first instinct was once again to protest, but she took a deep breath instead and simply nodded.

But he hesitated. "I only have one tracker on me," he said softly.

Bree frowned.

"I'd give it to you in a heartbeat, but it's sewn into my boxers."

"It's okay, Smiley."

"It's not. The team brought extras but they're in my pack. *Fuck*. I'm such an idiot."

Bree hated how hard he was being on himself. "You're not an idiot. You're my man. My SEAL. And you found me. I trust you, Smiley."

"I love you," he whispered, running the backs of his fingers down her cheek in a barely there caress.

"I love you too," she said, tilting her head into his fingers.

"I'll be back," he said again.

Between one blink and the next, he was gone. Disappeared into thin air.

She almost yelled for him to come back immediately, but refrained.

Wrapping her arms around herself, Bree carefully lowered to her side. She closed her good eye, giving herself permission to shut down for a moment. It had taken all her strength to stay upright for Smiley. But now that he was gone, she could be weak. For just a little while. When he returned, she'd sit up and put on a brave face once more.

All she wanted was to be back in Smiley's apartment. In his bed. Looking up at him as he made love to her. As she drifted, that was the image she took with her. One of love and comfort and without the threat of kidnappings, starving to death, or broken bones.

* * *

As Smiley made his way through the rough neighborhood, he realized it wasn't going to be as easy as he hoped to get Bree out of there and back to the motel. For one, he had no idea where he was. All the buildings looked the same. And two, the desperation and distrust on the faces of many people he passed made it clear that he and Bree stuck out like sore thumbs.

And to make matters worse, he saw a crude "Missing Person" poster tacked up on a pole...with Bree's picture.

It was homemade, and the picture was grainy and looked as if it was taken with a first-generation digital camera, but there was no mistaking that it was Bree. He could understand a few words on the flier...American, Guayaquil Port, and Mateo Castillo's name.

And the amount of money listed under the image was enough to change the life of anyone in the area who found her.

For a moment, Smiley wished they *were* in the jungle. At least then he could easily find Bree water, get her some food, and they would know who their enemies were. Here, the woman on the corner could be calling the number on the flier as he walked by, or the kids kicking a ball back and forth could blow their cover by recognizing Bree and pointing her out to their parents. Or the men prowling the streets with their rifles could all be Castillo's henchmen.

The situation was dire, and all Smiley wanted to do was get to his team and get the hell out of there. Rex had promised that he'd call in some favors and end Castillo's operation once and for all, so leaving without killing the man who'd made his and Bree's life a living hell wouldn't be an issue. The outrage and fury coming from the Mountain Mercenaries leader was loud and clear when they'd spoken on the phone. Smiley trusted him to be true to his word.

Determination rose hard and fast. Bree had been through enough. *No one* was going to take her from him. No damn way. He hadn't learned all he had as a SEAL to fail the most important person in his life. And while he would've preferred having his team at his back, he could protect Bree on his own. Especially the way he was feeling right this moment. Pissed way the hell off.

Thankfully, Smiley had some local currency on him; Kevlar insisted on everyone carrying a few bills on every single mission. They'd learned through their job that sometimes having a buck or two could mean the difference between living and dying.

He used the money to purchase some bottled water and food, but Smiley had no qualms about stealing the other things he needed. He found some tattered shoes that would be better than nothing. He also pulled a shirt and a pair of pants right off a clothesline hanging behind a three-story building. Then he nabbed a bag to hold all of the things he'd accumulated.

He was on his way back to Bree when he turned a corner and came to an immediate halt. There were about a dozen people standing around a shop window, watching something on a television. Cautious, Smiley walked closer...and saw images of tanks in the streets and masked men standing in a TV studio, holding the news anchors hostage.

He didn't understand what they were saying, but he didn't need words to know that getting himself and Bree out of the country just became a hell of a lot harder. Not to mention his entire team.

Ecuador had been politically unstable before they'd arrived, but it seemed as if it was on the verge of a full-out conflict now.

Just as he had the thought, a loud explosion sounded a few streets over. The people around him panicked and ran away from the noise.

Smiley ran toward it—because it came from the direction of the abandoned building where he'd stashed Bree.

His heart in his throat, Smiley ignored the civilians running in the streets, his only concern for his woman. Shots began to ring out as the coup expanded to the streets. This was no longer a capital city issue. At the moment, Smiley wasn't sure who was on the side of "right," if there even was such a thing.

Regretting leaving Bree, even if it had been necessary to get what she needed quickly, Smiley made his way back to the alley.

To his alarm, when he turned the final corner, there were two armed militants no more than a couple yards away, standing between him and Bree's hiding place.

They saw him immediately, of course. But it didn't matter, because Smiley wasn't leaving. Not without Bree.

They said something to him in Spanish, and guessing

what they wanted, Smiley lifted both his hands, trying to show that he was unarmed. The pistol in the holster at his back felt heavy and way too obvious, but he did his best not to act rashly. He didn't know what the men were looking for, but maybe, just maybe, he could get out of this without any violence.

Almost as soon as he had the thought, one of the men walked toward him and swung the rifle right at Smiley's face.

So much for no violence.

The last few days had been some of the most stressful of Smiley's life, and he was done. D.O.N.E.

Easily grabbing the rifle, he tore it out of the man's grip and backhanded him with his own weapon, making him drop like a stone.

Smiley was aiming the rifle at the other man's head before his friend had even hit the ground, ignoring the fact that he had a weapon pointed at *him* too.

"Don't do it, man," he muttered, as he and the militant had a stare-down. All it would take was one wrong move and Bree would be on her own again. Something Smiley wasn't willing to risk.

The man gestured to the bag of supplies Smiley had draped around his chest.

He shook his head. In any other situation, he would've handed over the water, food, and clothes in a heartbeat. But Bree needed what he'd managed to acquire. He wasn't giving it up.

He could practically hear Kevlar's voice in his head, telling him to wait. To go easy. But Smiley was done with that shit. Nothing had gone right, and he and Bree should be at the airport right that moment, getting ready to fly back to California.

Instead, the country was quickly falling into chaos, she was hurt, they were out of communication with his team and lost in the worst part of the city. Smiley was *beyond* pissed, and no punk was going to get the better of him. No way.

They were at an impasse. Neither willing to back down. Smiley was sorting through his options in his head. Shooting this man was at the bottom of those options, he really didn't want to kill him—for one, it would bring too much attention to the alley. Attention he didn't need. Not with those posters of Bree tacked up in the area, with that exorbitant bounty on her head.

Suddenly, a loud crashing noise echoed through the alley—from Bree's building—and the militant jerked his head instinctively toward the sound, giving Smiley the opportunity he needed.

Rushing forward, he was already swinging the butt of the rifle toward the man's head when he turned back around.

It hit him square in the face, and just like his friend, he fell to the ground bonelessly.

Panting, Smiley ran toward the opening in the dilapidated building. He was making more noise than a hippo in heat but didn't check his movements. Throwing a few pieces of debris aside that he'd strategically placed across the opening when he'd left, Smiley could feel his panic to reach Bree rising.

When he finally entered the room, relief made his knees weak.

She was there, looking much as she had when he'd left.

Except instead of sitting on the floor, trying valiantly to keep her eyes open, she was standing behind a three-foot pile of bricks with a four-by-four in her hands. Holding it like a baseball bat, on guard and ready to swing.

Smiley had never been so glad to see anyone in his entire life. He was physically shaking as he stepped over the wood, rocks, and bricks on the ground to get to her. She moved at the same time, coming around the new pile of debris that he had a feeling she'd deliberately knocked over to cause a distraction. He didn't drop the rifle in his hand, and she didn't let go of the piece of wood. They collided and held each other with one arm tightly.

"Are you all right?" she asked.

"Me? Yes. Are *you*?" he countered.

"Of course. I heard those guys rooting around out there and almost panicked. But they weren't coming in here yet. So I just stayed quiet, hoping they'd leave. Then *you* showed up. I nearly had a heart attack when they pointed their guns at you."

Smiley didn't want to let her go. Time and again, she was proving how tough she was. He was proud to be by her side. But they could no longer stay here. The men he'd knocked out would regain consciousness soon enough, and they needed to be gone when that happened.

He had no time to waste, but Smiley couldn't stop himself from lowering his head and kissing Bree hard and fast on the lips. "I love you. So damn much," he told her.

The smile he loved spread across her lips. "I love you too," she responded.

It took all the strength he had to let go of her and focus on the bag he'd draped across his body. He pulled out the shirt and pants and held them up. "I have no idea if they'll fit."

The pleasure in her eyes hit Smiley hard. She was so excited to get a ripped, stained shirt and pair of pants. Anger rose within him once more. He wanted to give her the world, but if all he could manage was some fabric to cover her body and make her feel less vulnerable, he'd take it at the moment.

Bree pulled her arms inside his shirt and shimmied her hips, obviously removing the slip she'd been forced to wear. For a moment, she was naked beneath his T-shirt, and Smiley hated that for her. Hated even more to think about what could've happened. What Castillo had planned for her. It was a struggle to contain his fury.

As Bree braced herself on his shoulder to put one foot through one of the legs of the pants, Smiley reached for the shoes he'd found.

The pants were a little short and loose, but Bree gave him a huge smile as she tied the drawstring around her waist. "They're perfect!"

They weren't. Not even close, but the pleasure she felt in being covered was easy to see and hear in her voice.

She turned her back and took off the T-shirt he'd given her, then quickly pulled the stolen long-sleeve shirt over her head. When she turned back around, Smiley picked up one of her feet and held his breath as he helped her don one of the shoes he'd found.

He had no socks, but amazingly, the shoes fit reasonably well. They were slip-on Keds. At one time they'd probably been white, but now they were a dingy gray, stained from the dirt and filth of the city. They were just a touch large, but Bree obviously didn't seem to mind. "Thank you," she breathed, staring at her covered feet.

Again, Smiley had to force himself not to show any emotion. He was ready to scorch the Earth for what Bree had been through. She'd been to hell and back, and the security of shoes on her feet and a covered body was enough to make her extremely grateful. When they got home, Smiley was going to pamper the hell out of his woman.

"We need to go," he told her, after he put his shirt back on, still warm from her body, before handing her a bottle of water from the bag.

Her eyes lit up again, and she grabbed the bottle without a word, but she didn't have the strength to crack the seal on the lid. It was one more thing to blame on Castillo. Smiley reached over and, without taking the water from her, twisted the top off.

She brought the rim to her mouth and drank several gulps of the clean, cool water.

"Easy, Bree."

She nodded as she lowered the bottle. He could see the desire to chug the entire contents, but she smartly took the lid from him and secured it in place.

Smiley reached back into the bag and pulled out the loaf of bread he'd purchased. It was still slightly warm. He broke off a piece and held it out to her.

She reached for it, and he noticed her hand shaking. It was all Smiley could do not to turn around and start breaking shit. His woman was hungry. *Starving.* And he could practically see her salivating.

She took a large bite of the bread, smiling at him as she chewed.

As much as Smiley wanted to stay there, waiting until she'd had her fill of both food and water, they needed to find another, hopefully safer place to hole up. If such a place existed.

Grabbing her hand to help her over the rubble, Smiley watched her closely. She wasn't limping and seemed steady on her feet. Just another testament to how fucking strong she was. After what she'd been through, he wouldn't have been surprised if she told him she couldn't move. Instead, she was putting one foot in front of the other.

"I'm so proud of you," Smiley blurted.

"Why?"

Why? She was asking *why*? Smiley shook his head in exasperation.

"Smiley, what choice do I have right now? I can't exactly refuse to move. You can't carry me and protect us from men like the ones outside at the same time. Later, I'm sure I'll collapse and probably have a major crying fit. But right now, we need to get out of here and find your team. And stay two steps ahead of Mateo and his goons in the process. I don't have the luxury of having a mental or physical breakdown."

She was right. And that kind of sucked.

"I'm going to make this up to you," he promised, as he continued toward the alley.

"That's fine, but it's not yours to make up to me," she said calmly. "None of what happened is your fault. It was all put in motion before we even met. Besides, without you...I'd be in deep shit."

Smiley snorted. They were in deep shit right now.

Bree squeezed his hand. "The truth is, I'm scared. I'm hurting. I still feel a little sick. But none of that matters right now. Besides, *you're* here. I feel as if I can handle anything else life decides to throw at me now."

She was too good for him.

Smiley peered out of the makeshift door and saw the two men still lying on the ground where he'd left them. Glad they hadn't woken up and fled, he let go of Bree's hand and stalked over to the closest man. He rifled through his pockets, coming up with a bit of money, a knife, and some ammunition for the rifle lying on the ground next to him.

The second man had much of the same, but he also had a packet of some sort of crackers or cookies. Neither had a cellphone, which sucked, as Smiley could've really used one right about now.

But he still had his tracker. Any moment, his team would come toward them in typical V-shape formation, swooping in to save the day.

But a niggling doubt crept in. Why hadn't they *already* appeared? Tex should've tracked him by now. Had they been caught in the unrest going on around them?

He hated to think of his team in trouble, but Smiley turned his attention back to the task at hand. His team could take care of themselves. His job right now was Bree. Keeping her safe, out of the hands of desperate civilians who would see her as a payday and nothing more.

Holding his hand out, he gestured for her to come to his side. She stepped out of the rubble of the building and quickly walked toward him. The second his fingers closed around hers, a calm settled in Smiley. They were in this together.

* * *

Mateo Castillo was furious. His men had bungled the retrieval of his property from the get-go. Not only had they lost the old broads who were supposed to go to customers in Russia and North Korea, they'd let the bitch he'd been forced to personally hunt down escape!

He'd also gotten word that the Navy SEALs were in Ecuador. In the port area. Their presence certainly complicated the reacquisition of his property.

He couldn't understand how the hell she'd been able to escape in the first place. He'd given strict orders for her to be confined at all times, yet clearly someone had fucked up and let her out of her travel cage. Now, he would have to make an example of everyone involved, so those who worked for him in the future followed his instructions to the letter.

If he was smart, Mateo would write the bitch off. Move on to other acquisitions. Those who were easier to control. Ones he could add to his stable of women without so much hassle. Bree Haynes was a huge pain in his ass—but one he refused to let go. She had to learn who was in charge. *Him.*

The current state of Ecuador would work in his favor. The militia was spreading fear with their stunt at the television studio. The bands of armed men looting and killing anyone they suspected of supporting the current political party. Which would make it easier for his men to move around Guayaquil, also armed...and ready to take his property back into custody.

When he got the bitch to his compound, she would never see the light of day again. He'd tie her down and keep her so weak, she wouldn't be able to even *think* about escaping. She was his to do with as he pleased—and what he wanted now was for Bree Haynes to suffer.

Making a split-second decision, Mateo leaned forward and tapped on the glass separating him from his driver. The soundproof window rolled down, allowing Mateo to talk with the man. "Turn around."

"Yes, sir." The limo immediately pulled to the side of the road as the driver prepared to make a wide U-turn.

This was the kind of obedience Mateo insisted upon. How he trained both the men who worked for him and the women he owned to act.

"Back to Guayaquil. I have unfinished business I need to attend to."

"Yes, sir," the driver said again, with no emotion whatsoever.

Mateo rolled the window back up as the vehicle headed toward the city. He'd left the retrieval of his property to others, and they'd fucked it up time and time again. This was one job he obviously needed to continue to do himself. He'd let his men find her, then he'd personally escort her to his compound. The long trip—in the trunk of his car, naked except for a ball gag and cuffs—should make her a little more compliant.

Then he'd introduce his most loyal employees at the compound to their new toy.

Within a week, the bitch would be calling him Sir and doing as he ordered with no disobedience whatsoever. Then he could turn his attention to fulfilling the orders of customers around the globe that he'd been putting off for far too long.

Bree Haynes had taken up way too much of his time, but that was about to change. Once she learned her place, things could go on as always. He'd continue bribing government officials to look the other way, paying off the locals around the compound, and living his best life.

Reaching into his pocket for a cigar, Mateo lit the end and took a deep puff. Yes, things were about to go back to normal, which meant pussy whenever he wanted it, however he wanted it, and money rolling into his bank accounts. Life was good...and was about to get much better.

CHAPTER EIGHTEEN

"This is bullshit!" Safe swore. "I can't believe Tex can't track him."

Kevlar was just as frustrated as the rest of his team. When he and Blink had lost track of Smiley at the port, they'd contacted the others, but even with their help searching, it seemed as if their teammate had disappeared into thin air.

The only good thing about the situation was that they were pretty sure Smiley had found Bree, and the two were together.

They'd seen the "Missing Person" signs around the port, and deduced that Smiley must have come across Bree at one of the docks, and wasn't able to contact Kevlar or Blink before being forced to disappear for their own safety.

Kevlar had thought it would be a simple matter of getting with Tex and having him direct them to where the two had holed up. But there was something wrong with the tracker Smiley had on him. It wasn't transmitting.

The swear words that had come out of Tex's mouth had been impressive. He was apparently done with external trackers, threatening to have every SEAL and Delta operative injected with tiny microchips that wouldn't malfunction just when he needed them to work the most. But that wouldn't help them at the moment.

And now, the violence in the country had ramped up a thousandfold. Stepping outside the motel put all their lives at risk, especially since they were obviously foreigners and didn't belong in the neighborhood. That didn't keep any of the SEALs from doing what they could to search for their teammate, but it definitely made it more challenging.

And to top it off, Smiley had no equipment with him. Clearly no comms to talk to the rest of them, no extra ammunition, no food or water. As far as Kevlar knew, Smiley and Bree were literally on some of the most dangerous streets the team had seen in quite a while, with only a knife, a pistol, and years of experience.

It would have to be enough.

"It *is* bullshit," Kevlar agreed. "But we all know Smiley is the toughest son-of-a-bitch on the team. If anyone can navigate this FUBAR'd situation, it's him."

"But we have no idea what condition Bree is in," MacGyver countered. "Of course Smiley can handle himself, but having Bree with him is a liability."

"That's fucked up," Preacher said in a pissed-off tone.

"I don't mean it in a disrespectful way. But think about Julie and Fiona, what Kevlar said they were wearing when they found them. They didn't have any fucking *shoes* on. And if Smiley *did* find Bree, she'd been captive on a fucking boat for days. We have no idea what her mental state is, never mind her physical one. And we all know

Smiley will do whatever he has to in order to make sure she's safe. *That* makes her a liability."

MacGyver was right. And that sucked. Kevlar sighed. "We need to go out again. See if we can cover more ground. Start south of the port and work our way outward."

"It's gotten worse out there just since this morning," Flash stated unnecessarily.

"The government has declared a state of emergency," Blink added.

"I *know!*" Kevlar snapped. "You think I don't? We don't have a choice. We're flying blind but I'm not leaving Smiley out there to find his way back on his own. We didn't get a chance to go over maps of the area and we all know he has the worst sense of direction. For all we know, he's halfway to fucking Quito by now."

Not surprisingly, all the men in the room chuckled. Kevlar wasn't saying anything the rest of them didn't know. Smiley was a mean asshole, and he was an amazing shot. He had more bravery in his little finger than most men did in their entire bodies.

But he had zero sense of direction.

"No one goes out alone. Stay together. And for God's sake, keep your tracker on you at all times. The last thing I need is any of *you* guys going missing with no way to fucking track you," Kevlar bitched.

Everyone nodded their agreement.

"Everyone takes a pack with medical supplies and extra food and water. When we do find them, we have no idea what condition they'll be in. Stay in the shadows. We don't want to come on the militia's radar. We don't need to be their targets, along with every-fucking-thing else we have going on. Find Smiley and Bree and get the hell out. That's our mission. Understood?"

"Hoo-ah!"

"Affirmative."

"Hell yeah!"

Kevlar had confidence in his team, but this situation was way too fluid for his liking. They had no idea where to start looking for Smiley and Bree. The atmosphere in the streets was volatile. And the last thing they wanted was to get in the middle of a hostile takeover of the government. Tex and the women working with him could get them out of the country, but if things continued in the direction they were going, it was likely planes would be grounded and it would become more and more difficult to be extracted.

As the men got ready to head out and continue their search, Kevlar sighed. "Where are you, Smiley?" he murmured.

* * *

Smiley was frustrated. He had no clue where he was. He had a feeling he was walking in circles. No, it wasn't a feeling. He *knew* he was going in circles, as he recognized a building he'd passed for the second time.

His team would be giving him so much shit right now. He'd never wished so hard for a compass, or to have Preacher or MacGyver at his back. Feeling as if he was letting Bree down completely—any one of his teammates would have found the motel they were staying at by now—

Smiley's responses to her infrequent questions had gotten more and more curt.

She hadn't spoken for the last twenty minutes or so, as Smiley tried to figure out if they'd already been down the current street yet or not. Nothing looked familiar, so he had to hope that he hadn't gotten them turned around, *again*.

A quiet noise to his left had him looking over at Bree. He was appalled to see tears on her cheeks. Her swollen eye had looked a little better earlier, but he imagined it was still difficult to see out of. And now she was crying? *Fuck*.

"Bree?" he asked, stopping in his tracks.

"I'm fine," she told him, trying to tug him forward, to no avail.

Smiley backed her up against the wall of a building and bent his head, trying to catch her gaze. But she was staring at his chest and refused to look at him.

"Talk to me," he ordered gruffly.

She sighed and wiped her cheek with her shoulder. "Why? You'll just get madder."

"Mad? I'm not mad."

She snorted.

"Okay, I'm not mad at *you*."

"I'm sorry, Smiley. You shouldn't be here at all. I don't know what I could've done differently, but maybe if I was smarter, or stronger, or *something*...we wouldn't be here now. Lost in the middle of some kind of uprising. You wouldn't have had to kill those people at the port or conked those other men on the head. You wouldn't have had to steal these clothes from someone who probably needs them more than me. Your stomach wouldn't be growling because you made me eat that entire loaf of bread by myself."

Smiley was distraught by what he was hearing. Looking around, he desperately searched for a place where they could sit and rest. And talk. He'd fucked this up, obviously, and he needed to fix it. Immediately.

Without a word, he picked up Bree and held her against his chest. It was unconscionable that he was wandering around fucking lost while Bree, who was weak from lack of food and water, and *injured*, had to stumble around after him.

"Smiley!" she protested, even as she looped her arm around his neck.

As he walked toward what he thought was an apartment building, Smiley got an idea. He wasn't getting anywhere walking around on the streets; the only thing he was doing was exposing both of them to the eyes of civilians who could make a call to the number on that fucking flier. Smiley wasn't going to let anyone take Bree. No way in hell.

He needed to get off the streets, figure out where the hell they were and which direction to go, while staying under Castillo's radar. He needed to get a lay of the land. Figure out a plan. And let Bree get some stress-free rest.

So...he was going up.

He should've done this hours ago. He'd get to the top of this building, where hopefully there'd be access to the roof.

"Smiley!" Bree said again. "I can walk."

"But you aren't going to," he said.

He entered the lobby of the building and grimaced. It was trashed. Broken glass, refuse, rotting food. This obviously wasn't a five-star apartment building, but then again, he hadn't expected it to be in this neighborhood. Thankfully, no one was in the lobby as Smiley strode toward a door with a sign over it, depicting a stick figure seeming to float above a set of stairs.

He kicked open the door, relieved that it really was a stairwell.

"Where are we going?" Bree asked.

"Somewhere we can regroup. Sit and rest in peace," Smiley told her.

"I'm too heavy for you to carry. Put me down," she insisted.

Smiley snorted as he recalled the weight of the packs he'd carried on some of his missions. Not to mention the gear they always wore. He barely felt the two rifles he had slung across his back. Carrying Bree was no hardship.

He hoped it was a good sign that they didn't run into anyone on the way up. When they reached the top, there was a single door. He lowered Bree's legs and held on to her for a moment, making sure she wouldn't stumble or fall. Then he pushed her behind him as he reached for the door handle.

Holding his pistol in his free hand, ready for trouble, Smiley held his breath as he opened the door. Sunlight streamed into the stairwell, momentarily blinding them both.

Blinking...Smiley's heart dropped.

He'd hoped to find an empty place to hole up, but instead, the rooftop seemed to be just as crowded as some of the streets filled with the homeless. There were tarps and makeshift "homes" built with boxes and other trash. The people he spotted were all lying down in shade they'd created with their dwellings.

"Fuck," he muttered.

He felt Bree shift behind him. She steadied herself with a hand on his back as she leaned around his body. "Over there," she said, pointing to their right.

He saw immediately what she meant, and mentally nodded. There was a small space between two other dwellings that was shaded, where they should be able to lie down. It was also at the edge of the roof, so he'd be able to get a good visual of the city and hopefully figure out which direction they needed to go.

The only wildcards were the woman and child to the right of the space, and the older man to the left. Would they be all right with them crashing there for a while?

There was only one way to find out.

He was just opening his mouth to tell Bree to hang back, to wait here for him while he scoped out the situation, when she began to walk forward.

Catching her by the hand, he pulled her to a stop. "You can't just walk over there," he said.

"Why not?"

Why not, indeed. At first glance, the people on the roof looked harmless. They were either elderly or mothers with children. Everyone looked down and out. Tired. Beaten down by circumstances. But that didn't mean they weren't a threat. Smiley pretty much thought everyone was a threat, while it was obvious Bree wasn't quite that cynical.

The more he thought about it, the better it would be for Bree to make first contact. He was carrying weapons, and was *definitely* a threat. But Bree, in her ill-fitting clothes, limping slightly, with one eye almost swollen shut…she didn't look as if she could harm a flea.

Keeping his eye on the people all around them—who were all keeping a very close eye on them, as well—Smiley and Bree made their way toward the small sliver of unoccupied space.

Bree gave the man a smile, and then turned to the woman holding a baby.

"*Hola*," she said, gesturing to herself, and then to the space. She held her palms together as if pleading.

Smiley held his breath.

First the woman nodded, then the man.

Was it really that easy? He was skeptical. Nothing had been easy recently, but then again, he'd found Bree before she'd been shipped to the jungle, so maybe, just maybe, their luck was changing.

Turning, Bree beamed at him. Her obvious pleasure in having succeeded shining through loud and clear. Smiley nodded at their new neighbors, then put his hand on the small of Bree's back and urged her forward. They had no padding, nothing soft to sit on, but at the moment, all Smiley was concerned about was getting Bree out of the sun and getting her off her feet.

He got her seated, then took a moment to look over the edge of the roof. All around him were buildings as far as he could see. In the distance, he saw the ocean. It was hard to believe he and Bree had gotten as far inland as they had. Shit, he'd obviously walked longer and faster than he'd thought when he'd first left the port.

"Smiley, get off your feet for a moment," Bree begged, tugging at the leg of his pants.

PROTECTING BREE

It was hot out, and while he wanted to continue to study the landscape in the hopes that something would stick and he'd be able to figure out how to get back to the motel and his team, Smiley couldn't deny Bree her request.

He sat, then pulled Bree into his arms, moving her carefully, aware that her ribs were sore. She put her head on his shoulder and relaxed into him.

Moving slowly, Smiley shifted around the bag he was carrying so it was sitting next to him. It was still slung over his chest, but now he could reach into it and pull out a bottle of water for Bree and some crackers. She gave him a grateful smile as she took them. He was encouraged by the fact that she could crack the seal of the water bottle by herself this time. She'd scared him when she didn't have the strength to do such a small task earlier.

"How do you feel?" he asked softly, as she ate and drank.

"Better."

"Give me a rundown of where you hurt," he ordered.

"Smiley, I'm okay."

"Not what I asked. I need to know your limitations, Bree."

She sighed. "My side hurts. My eye. My feet. Walking helped work out some of the kinks I had from being scrunched inside that cage on the boat."

"Can you talk about it? It might help." As much as Smiley didn't want to know what she'd been through, conversely, he *needed* to know.

"Honestly, there's not much to tell. I assume Julie and Fiona told you how we got to Ensenada?" When he nodded, she continued. "I surprised them by leaping out of the back of that chicken truck. They were expecting their buddy, not me. I ran, hoping they'd all chase me, and they did. Giving Julie and Fiona a chance to get away. But it wasn't fast enough. They caught me, beat me up, then I woke up on the boat, in another cage. I was pretty sure we were on our way here, to Ecuador, because I heard snippets of their conversation.

"I got seasick. Threw up a few times. The men didn't want to be around me then, so they mostly stayed outside the small cabin. When I felt a little better, I pretended to still be sick because I didn't want them getting any ideas about what they might do with me to pass the time. It worked. They left me alone. When we got to the dock, they took me out, handed me off to another guy, and as he was leading me toward a van—and probably another cage for a ride to the jungle—I punched him in the balls and ran. Then you found me...and here we are."

It was a very abbreviated edition of the reality, but Smiley was more relieved than he could say that she'd managed to escape not once, but twice.

Then he remembered something.

Sitting forward a bit, he reached behind him to the holster at the small of his back. He pulled out the plastic knife she'd used in Ensenada to help Fiona and Julie escape, holding it up as he sat back.

Bree gasped. "Where did you get that?"

"Where do you think? It was on the ground outside that fucking chicken truck."

There were still smears of reddish-brown stains on it, and now that he was looking at the thing, Smiley figured he probably should've just left it where he'd found it. Why did he think it was a good idea to keep it? Or to even bring it out now?

She reached for it and, ducking his chin, Smiley saw a small smile on her face. "Bree?"

"I can't believe you found it." She fingered the hilt. The hair she'd used to bind the material from Julie's slip was fraying, but it still held. Bree looked up at him. "Can I keep it?"

Relief swam through Smiley. She wasn't disgusted by seeing it, or by what she'd done out of necessity. "For the record...MacGyver was impressed."

She blushed. "It's not *that* impressive."

"Are you kidding? It did its job. That's all that matters, not what it looks like. The most effective weapons are sometimes the most random things you find around you. Not fancy guns or knives. I don't have a sheath for you to put it in, and I don't want you to hurt yourself by simply sticking it in your pocket. Would you be okay with me continuing to hold it for you?"

"Yes. Smiley? Can I ask you something?"

"You just did," he joked, as he put the makeshift knife back into the holster at his back. Most people wouldn't understand either of them wanting to keep something that could potentially bring back such horrific memories. But it was just another thing that proved Bree was made for him.

At his response, instead of smiling, Bree simply stared at him.

"What?"

"You made a joke."

"Apparently not a very good one," he said with a shrug.

"It's just...you aren't a joker. We're going to die, aren't we?"

She sounded completely serious. "No!" he barked, louder than he'd intended. Taking a deep breath to try to control his emotions, he said a little softer. "No, we aren't. If you think Kevlar and the rest of the guys are gonna let me off the team that easily, you're wrong."

"I think that was also a joke. Lord, Smiley, what's gotten into you?" Bree asked.

"You. You make me want to be a better man. Not so grumpy all the time."

She put her hand on his cheek and caressed him with her thumb. "I love you exactly how you are. Be grumpy, Smiley. Be an asshole. Because I don't ever want you to change who you are for me."

"You had a question?" he asked a little hoarsely. He was overwhelmed by this woman. Here she was, in a foreign country, filthy, hungry, thirsty, hurting, and yet she was the one reassuring *him*. He didn't deserve her, but he was going to do everything in his power to try to keep the look of love in her eyes that he saw right that moment. The belief in her gaze that said she trusted him to take care of her. To get them out of this fucked-up position they were in.

"Are we lost?"

Smiley blinked. That wasn't what he thought she was going to ask. He felt his cheeks heat with embarrassment. He hated to admit his shortcomings to this woman, but he wasn't about to lie to her. Not now, after everything she'd suffered.

He shrugged. "I'm not the best at directions. I'm an expert marksman, I can swim for miles without tiring, can outrun all of my teammates. But I suck at figuring out which way to go."

To his surprise, Bree smiled. "So I guess I'm going to have to be our navigator when we go on road trips, huh?"

The thought of the two of them sitting in a car

together, with her telling him which way to turn, sent a shaft of pleasure shooting through his system. "Yeah, sweetheart. You are."

"So what's the plan? Did you figure out where we are when you looked over the edge of the roof?"

His woman didn't miss much. "Just that we're headed in the wrong direction," he admitted a little sheepishly. "We want to head back *toward* the water, not away from it."

"But isn't that where Mateo's men will be looking for us?" she asked, her brow furrowing.

"You saw the fliers. They're looking for us everywhere. But my team and I were at a motel near the water, the port. I'm sure they've fanned out, trying to find us, but the closer we can get to my team's perimeter, the better."

"What about your computer friend, Tex? Can't he tell them where we are?"

"He should be able to. But if he had, they'd have found us by now. I have a tracker on me, but it must be malfunctioning."

"Oh. I have a feeling Tex isn't going to be happy about that."

"You have no idea," Smiley agreed, thinking about what the computer genius was doing right that second. Having a temper tantrum to end all tantrums, probably. He wasn't exactly thrilled himself. If ever he'd needed an assist, it was now.

"Maybe if *I* got the lay of the land, I could help," Bree suggested.

Smiley's first reaction was to say no, she needed to rest. But he reconsidered. He was obviously useless when it came to navigation. She couldn't be worse than he was.

"In a while. For now, we need to rest. When the sun sets, we'll set out again."

"In the dark?" Bree questioned.

"We're too conspicuous. The bounty on your head is too much for the people in this part of the city to ignore. It would be like someone offering two million dollars for the return of their runaway dog back home. Everyone would be on the lookout and wouldn't hesitate to make a call for that kind of money if they spotted the animal."

"I don't understand why he wants me so badly," Bree mused.

"I'm not saying this to be a dick, but I don't think it's you, per se," Smiley said. He'd been thinking about this. "I think it's more the principle at this point. He paid a good chunk of money for you, and as time went on, stubbornness set in and he became more and more determined to get you."

"So it's a pride thing?" Bree asked with a frown.

"Something like that."

"That's stupid," she said with a huff.

"It is," Smiley agreed.

"So...what happens when we find your team and get the hell out of here? What then? Is he going to come back to California? Send more people after me? Will I have to hide out for the rest of my life because of his stupid pride?"

"No!" Smiley exclaimed. Again, too loud.

He heard the woman with the baby make a noise of disapproval, and he glanced at her and shrugged apologetically. There was a gap in the cardboard boxes that were stacked around her little area, allowing her to see them, and vice versa.

"Remember what Tex said, about the group that took out Castillo's predecessor?" Smiley asked Bree.

"That Rex guy?"

"Yeah. So, needless to say, Rex isn't happy. He's going to make sure Castillo isn't a threat to you, or any other woman, ever again. Once we get home, the only thing we have to worry about is our future. Together."

Bree looked up at him. "I want to stay with you."

"Good. Because I want that too."

"Don't hurt me, Smiley. Because I think it would destroy me."

"I'm not going to hurt you. I think you could hurt *me* way worse than anything I could do to you."

She snorted. "Whatever."

"I mean it. You think I usually spend months looking for women I meet while on an op? I don't. There was something about you that wouldn't let me quit. You got under my skin, Bree. And now you're in so deep, I can't imagine you *not* being there. You once asked me why I was helping you."

Bree nodded. "And you said you'd tell me after Mateo was caught."

"Right," Smiley said, pleased she remembered the conversation. "He hasn't been caught yet, but he's as good as dead. I think I loved you from the second I saw you. Which sounds impossible, but I can't think of any other reason why I was so obsessed with finding you, making sure no harm came to you."

Bree stared at him with an expression he couldn't read.

He blurted, "If you come to your senses and change your mind about being with me, it would destroy me."

"I'm not going anywhere. Why do you think I went to

Riverton when I left Vegas? I could've gone anywhere. But for some reason, I went straight to where *you* were. I think we were meant to be together. I somehow realized you were someone who wouldn't let me down. I don't know about love at first sight, but there was definitely something about you that drew me in. That's why I found you in Riverton, why you were able to track me to Mexico, and why we're here now. We're going to get back to home, I just know it."

Smiley's throat was so tight, he couldn't speak. All he could do was gather Bree closer to his chest and close his eyes and pray she was right.

As Bree fell asleep in his arms, Smiley stayed awake and on alert. He wasn't tired. Not even close. When he was sure they were safe, and they were on their way out of the country, he'd crash hard. But for now, he was wired.

Bree slept for two hours in his arms, but when more and more people started coming and going from the roof, he decided it was in their best interest to head out. It wasn't dark yet, but Smiley didn't like the looks he was getting from some of the men, and even some of the women. His analogy about the lost dog and the massive reward kept replaying in his head. All it would take was for one person making a phone call, and they'd be in big trouble.

"Bree," he said softly.

She woke in an instant, as if his voice was all she'd been waiting for.

"What? What's wrong?"

"Nothing," Smiley soothed, hoping against hope he wasn't lying. "It's time for us to get going. You want to check out the area, make mental notes so you can get us going in the right direction?"

She nodded and went to climb off his lap, but Smiley held her still. "Hang on, sweetheart. Let me get up first."

He helped her slide off to his side, then stood. Reaching down, Smiley helped her stand as gently as he could, then stood behind her as she looked out over the city.

In Smiley's estimation, it was probably around five or so in the afternoon. The sun was still up, but much lower in the sky.

Bree scanned the area, and Smiley could practically see the wheels turning in her head as she did her best to memorize landmarks and plot a path toward the ocean. Once the sun went down, he'd be lost, but Smiley had confidence in his Bree. He should've asked her way before now for help. He'd gotten used to his teammates taking charge of navigation without having to be asked.

She looked up at him. Even with the bruises and scrapes all over her body, she was the most beautiful woman he'd ever laid eyes on. She shone with an inner strength and kindness that called to him.

The woman with the child began speaking, and Smiley turned to glance at her through the opening in the boxes. He thought she was talking to them...then he realized she was actually using a cellphone.

He was somewhat alarmed, praying that she wasn't calling someone to alert them to the foreigners who were so out of place on the roof. But she didn't look worried, or concerned, or shifty in any way...

The woman's baby began to cry, and she hung up the phone to try to console the child.

Feeling like an idiot for not even considering that someone on the roof might have a phone, he asked Bree, "You good?"

She nodded. "Yeah. I've memorized a few landmarks, and if we start out now, while the sun is up, that'll help a lot."

Smiley grabbed her hand, then took a few steps away from the edge of the roof. "Okay?" he asked. "Your legs feel good?"

"Yeah. The nap helped a lot. Thank you."

Shaking his head, Smiley wanted to tell her that she never had to thank him for giving her what she needed, but he was too focused on what he should've done way sooner. Circling around to the front of the woman's makeshift shelter, he stopped. Shit, how did he ask for what he wanted?

"I took Spanish in college," Bree said softly. "What do you want to ask her?"

Once again, Bree was saving his ass. "She has a cellphone. We can use it to call Kevlar."

Bree's eyes widened. "Holy shit, that would be much better than walking all the way back to the coast."

She turned and asked the woman what her baby's name was.

Smiley understood that much Spanish, and while he didn't know why she wasn't asking about the phone, he trusted her to do the right thing.

As Bree and the woman had a stilted conversation, considering Bree's rusty Spanish and the woman's obvious mistrust of the foreigners, the hair on the back of Smiley's neck prickled. Looking around, he didn't see anything out of the ordinary, but experience had taught him not to discount the uneasy feelings he got while on a mission.

"We need to go," he told Bree.

She nodded, and her voice changed as she spoke with the woman. Got softer, as if she was pleading for something. They said a few things back and forth, then Bree turned to Smiley. "She wants to know what we'll exchange for the use of her phone."

Smiley didn't hesitate. He ducked his head and removed the small bag he'd been carrying and held it out to Bree. "There's a couple bottles of water left. A candy bar, another loaf of bread and two cans of vegetables."

Bree's eyes widened. "You have a candy bar?"

He felt like shit for not giving it to her earlier. "Yeah. But I figured you needed something more nutritious first. Then you fell asleep and..." His voice trailed off.

"You're never going to live this down," she muttered, as she took the bag and turned back to the woman.

Smiley watched Bree negotiate, and once again was struck with pride. She was still probably starving, and yet she didn't hesitate to offer up all they had in order to use the phone.

"She wants the rifles too," Bree said, biting her lip as she looked up at him.

"No. Not negotiable. We need to get going, Bree. It's important." Urgency was hitting Smiley hard. They needed to get off this roof before they were cornered.

Apparently, they'd called the woman's bluff, because within twenty seconds, she was clutching their bag and Bree was holding the cellphone.

Smiley took it and quickly dialed Kevlar's number. He might not be the best navigator, but he had a knack for memorizing numbers. He knew all of his teammates' digits by heart.

"What?"

Smiley couldn't help but grin at his team leader's greeting.

"Hey, if you aren't busy, I could use some assistance," he said.

"Smiley? Holy shit! Where are you? Are you all right? Is Bree with you?"

"No clue, yes, and yes."

"Figures you're lost. Asshole, I'm putting your ass in the beginners navigation courses the second we're home. Give me something to work with here."

"I take it my tracker is busted?"

"Yeah. Tex is pissed. Said it wasn't transmitting for some reason."

"Right. We're on a roof. My estimate is probably about five or so miles from the coast."

"How the fuck did you get all the way out there?"

"Again, no clue."

"I need more than a roof. Describe the area."

"We're in an apartment building of some sort. Ten stories." Smiley walked back to the edge of the roof and looked out, describing as many buildings and landmarks as he could make out.

"Right. I think MacGyver and Safe have you pinpointed on the map. Can you stay put while we come to you? The roads here suck and the violence out there has ramped up more and more throughout the day. It'll take at least thirty minutes before we can get to your location."

"Negative. My Spidey senses are screaming at me to move. Castillo has flyers out with Bree's picture on them.

He's offering more money than anyone here could make in a lifetime for information on her whereabouts."

"Yeah, we saw," Kevlar said, disgust heavy in his tone. "Right. Can you see a statue of a guy riding a horse to your southwest?"

"Um..." Smiley said, searching the area for what Kevlar described. Then he turned to Bree. "Is there a big statue of a horse and a guy near here?"

Without pause, Bree pointed to their left.

"Let me guess, your woman is a master navigator."

"Way better than me," Smiley told him.

"*Everyone* is better than you," his team leader joked. Then got serious. "Get moving. We'll meet you there. Keep your head down. We'll find you. Glad you're all right, Smiley. We were worried."

For some reason, Smiley got choked up hearing that. He and his teammates were used to being in danger. To looking in the eyes of death and not flinching. But this situation definitely felt different.

"Thirty minutes, Smiley. Don't stand us up or we'll be pissed."

The line went silent.

Smiley stepped around to the front of the woman's shelter and handed the phone back to her with a smile and a nod.

"Um...Smiley?"

"Yeah?" he said, not liking Bree's tone. He quickly stepped back to her side and wrapped an arm around her waist as she leaned over the side of the building a little too much for his liking.

"I'm thinking that's not a good thing."

Smiley leaned over to see where Bree was pointing. "Fuck!"

A military-style truck had pulled up in front of the apartment building and armed men were jumping out of the back, running toward the front door.

Without a word, he took Bree's hand and hurried toward the door to the stairwell. They needed to get off this roof. Before those men made it up here. For some reason, Smiley had no doubt they were there for them.

Someone had obviously made a phone call to Castillo to report that they'd found the missing American. Using the stairs to get to the first floor was out. They'd have to find another way.

"Smiley?"

"Thirty minutes, Bree. All we have to do is keep ahead of them for thirty minutes. Then Kevlar and the rest of the gang will be here. Can you do that?"

"Piece of cake," she said, her voice shaking.

Usually while in the middle of a mission, when bullets were flying and one wrong step could make the difference between life and death, Smiley felt at his most untouchable. He'd laughed in the face of death more than once. But at this moment, all he felt was dread. It wasn't just *his* life on the line.

He'd always known dying for his country was a possibility. But Bree had done nothing wrong. Had simply dated the wrong man. And here she was, kidnapped twice, beaten, and in the middle of an attempted military takeover and trapped like a rat in a maze.

Desperation made Smiley move faster. He held Bree's hand with an iron grip as he ran down to the floor below the roof. He needed to find a place to hide, to let Castillo's henchmen run past them and waste their time searching the roof. Surely one of the inhabitants up there would tell them that they'd left, but they'd have no idea which floor of the building they were on, or which apartment they might be in.

Smiley just hoped they'd be able to find an unlocked door. If they were in the hallway when Castillo's men searched the floors, they'd be sitting ducks. And Smiley would do whatever it took to make sure Bree got away, even if that meant taking a bullet.

CHAPTER NINETEEN

Bree's heart was beating way too fast. She'd been scared more than once in the last few days, but nothing like this. They were trapped. Smiley was being optimistic, but she could see the worry in his eyes. Thirty minutes for his team to arrive seemed like a lifetime. She wasn't sure how they were supposed to hide from the men coming up the stairs for that long.

But she didn't voice any of her concerns out loud. It was taking all her control to stay on her feet and keep up with Smiley. As they walked down the dark and dingy hallway that smelled a little funky, he tried each door they passed. They were all locked.

Then, finally, they came to one that opened when Smiley turned the knob.

Looking back at the door to the stairwell, Bree was relieved it stayed shut. She couldn't help but picture a bunch of men running up the stairs, weapons at the ready, willing to do whatever it took to get their hands on her.

And getting their hands on her meant Smiley would die. She knew better than her own name that the only way he'd ever let anyone take her again was over his dead body. And she couldn't live with his death on her hands.

Thankfully, the apartment they'd entered was empty. The last thing Bree wanted was to bring someone else into the shitshow that was her life at the moment. The place was surprisingly clean and tidy. The occupants were obviously poor, but they took pride in the few belongings they had.

The apartment was literally one room with a curtain in the corner, which Bree assumed was where the occupants used the bathroom. There was a mattress on the floor against one wall, two chairs and a rickety table, a love seat of sorts that had definitely seen better days. The stuffing was coming out of the cushions and she could see a few springs through a hole in the backrest. But there was what looked like a homemade crocheted blanket folded neatly over the back.

The kitchen area was tiny, consisting of a small sink with rusted knobs. A bucket sat under it to catch the water. Bree had no idea if there was running water, but she guessed not, since there were large buckets of water sitting alongside the sink. There weren't any cabinets, instead just some boxes of rice and other food items stacked in a few crates to the left of the sink. Dishes were in a box next to the makeshift pantry, and a hot plate was plugged into the wall on a large piece of wood fashioned into a kind of countertop.

It would've been a sad little living area if it wasn't for the personal touches the owners had added to make it a home. There were drawings done by children on the walls. A few books neatly lined up on another makeshift piece of furniture, a bookshelf. A few photographs were tacked around the space as well, showing a man and a woman, each holding a small child. The thought that four people lived in this tiny room, in this piece-of-crap building, made Bree sad...but at least they weren't on the roof, having to live in the elements and heat.

Smiley didn't let go of her hand as he tugged her toward a window in the kitchen, behind the sink. He looked out, scowled, then turned without a word to the only other window in the small space. It was on the same wall as the other window, but closer to the bed.

He made a pleased noise in his throat then turned to look at Bree. "If we need to, we can go out this way."

Bree's eyes widened. "What? Out the window? Smiley, we're nine stories up."

"And there's a gutter right outside this window. Piece of cake," he said, echoing her earlier sentiment.

He was crazy. That was the only explanation for his nonchalant announcement.

Stepping into her space, Smiley took her face in his hands. "Do you trust me?"

That was a no-brainer. "Yes."

His head tilted as he continued to hold her. "You didn't even hesitate," he said softly.

Bree's hands came up and she grabbed his wrists. "Smiley, you're a lot of things. Introverted, not a people person for sure, kind of a jerk when it comes to being around others, in fact. But the one thing you *aren't*, is reckless. If you say we can get out of this building by going out the window, I trust you one thousand percent."

He stared at her for so long, Bree began to worry.

Just when she opened her mouth to apologize for her flippant response, to insist that of *course* she trusted him, he spoke.

"I didn't understand what love was. When my teammates fell one by one, I didn't get it. I was happy for them, of course, but was still cynical about their relationships. And then you appeared...and disappeared. I was consumed with finding you, but I kept telling myself it was only because I wanted to make sure you were safe. But it was way more than that. That short encounter in Vegas made me want what *they* had. And now, here we are."

Bree wasn't sure where he was going with this. "Here we are," she echoed.

"Trust is hard for me. I was let down by the people I should have relied on most in my life, my parents. My dad because he was an abusive asshole, and my mom because she didn't get the fuck out of that relationship. She stayed, even knowing how horrible my father was. I slowly learned to trust Kevlar, Safe, Blink, Preacher, MacGyver, and Flash...but that was it, and it wasn't easy. And then you exploded into my life. I've never been happier for someone to know me, *truly* know me, than I am right this second. No matter what happens, I know you've got my back, just as I have yours."

He was making Bree's heart hurt. "I love you," she whispered. "And I don't think I even knew what those words meant until right this second."

"Same," Smiley said with a nod. Then he leaned forward and kissed her gently. "When we get home, you're definitely going to move to Riverton, right? Stay with me?"

"Yes. If you want me to."

"I want you to."

They were just four words, but the emotion behind them was loud and clear. Bree loved how confident he was. And he hadn't said *if* we get home, but when. They were in the middle of a very precarious situation. They could be discovered any second. They were definitely in big trouble, and yet he had no problem standing there having an emotional conversation as if they had all the time in the world.

"Shouldn't we be getting out of here?"

Smiley shrugged. "The second we go out that window, we'll be sitting ducks. Visible to anyone and everyone. I'd rather stay here, hunker down, see if they'll think we escaped and run off looking for us before we purposely put ourselves out there."

That made sense, but waiting wasn't Bree's strong suit. It felt as if the boogeyman was just outside the door. Salivating, purposely torturing them by not coming inside. But she'd said she trusted Smiley, and she'd do whatever it took to prove she was a woman of her word.

Every minute that passed felt like an eternity. They heard stomping over their heads, and it amazed and worried Bree how thin the ceiling seemed to be. Without a watch, she had no idea how much time had passed, but it wasn't enough. It hadn't been thirty minutes yet, of that she was sure.

But when they heard voices in the hallway, then the unmistakable sound of doors being kicked in, it was obvious their time had run out.

"Time to go," Smiley confirmed, sounding calm.

She was seeing her man in a new light. This was the deadly Navy SEAL. Focused. Intent. Decisive.

Swallowing hard, she let him lead her to the window. He raised the glass and looked out. Then he turned to her. "I think it's best if I carry you. You can climb onto my back and hold on as I get us down. Unless you think you have the strength to hold on to the gutter and slide down yourself."

The concern in his voice was easy to hear. And he was right. She was shaky, hadn't had nearly enough sleep or calories in her to be able to do something so physical. She wanted to question if he could get down with the added weight on his back, but she'd said she trusted him. If he was suggesting he carry her, then he was sure he could get them to the ground safely.

"Turn around," she said in response.

He stared at her for a moment, before removing the rifles strapped around his back and placing them on the floor. Then he turned his back to her and crouched. Biting her lip, Bree climbed onto his back, hooking her ankles together at his belly and doing her best not to strangle him with her arms as he stood.

She didn't like that he was leaving the weapons behind, but she wasn't sure how this would work if he had to carry her *and* the weapons.

Without hesitation, Smiley slung one leg over the window ledge. Bree squeezed her eyes shut and held her breath as he asked, "Ready?"

With the men kicking in what sounded like the door right next to where they were hiding, Bree made some sort of affirmative noise. They couldn't stay where they were, there was literally no place to hide in the tiny apartment, but sliding down a questionably secure gutter didn't seem super-smart either.

"Hold on," he said—then they were moving. Sliding downward at a brisk pace.

The sound of Smiley's boots creating friction along the gutter was scarily loud, even with the noise of the city all around them. She felt the wind in her hair as he raced down the gutter...

Then the jolt when his feet hit the ground seconds later.

She heard a shout from above. Glancing up, she saw a man looking down at them from the apartment they'd been in moments before. Without putting her down, Smiley began to move—but before he took more than a few steps, he stopped abruptly.

To her utter horror, Mateo Castillo and two of the men who'd been on the boat to Ecuador were standing in front of them.

Mateo had a smirk on his face, while his men pointed what looked like freaking machine guns at their heads.

Bree's blood ran cold. She didn't want to think about going through everything she had, yet *still* ending up in some jungle prison after all. But she also couldn't let Smiley lose his life because of her either.

She'd surrender to Mateo. Give herself up, if he let Smiley live.

In the back of her mind, she knew that was never going to happen. For some reason, the movie *The Princess Bride* flashed in her head. When Buttercup had done what Bree was contemplating. Gave herself up so Wesley could live...except the bad guy instead had her love taken to an underground lair and tortured him to almost-death.

Very slowly, Smiley crouched slightly and tapped one of her legs. Assuming that meant he wanted her to get off his back, Bree slid off but stayed right behind him. She held on to his shirt with white knuckles.

"So...you're the Navy SEAL who thinks you can take what's mine," Mateo said, that smirk still on his face, sounding like a man who was sure he'd won.

"Bree doesn't belong to anyone, least of all you," Smiley told him in a tone Bree had never heard from him before. It was full of derision and hate. She shivered.

"That's where you're wrong. I bought her fair and square."

"You can't *buy* human beings."

"Wrong again," Mateo said calmly.

It felt weird to be standing there having what looked on the surface like a civilized conversation. The street around them was suddenly empty, the civilians in the area had apparently been smart enough to get the hell out of what was obviously a volatile situation.

"I've been doing this a long time, and I'll continue to do it for years to come. You can't stop me. No one can."

Smiley laughed. It wasn't a humorous sound though. It was rough, harsh, and condescending. "You're an idiot."

Mateo's eyes narrowed, his lips pressing together in irritation.

Bree wasn't sure it was best to antagonize this guy, but as she'd said in the apartment, she trusted Smiley.

"By the way, your friend Rex told me to say hello," Smiley continued, standing with his arms crossed over his chest, as if he didn't have two automatic weapons pointed at his head and probably a contingent of more armed assholes racing down nine flights of stairs to join in the fun, even as he spoke.

Mateo straightened out of the fake relaxed pose he'd assumed.

"That's right. I know you've heard of him. He was responsible for taking out del Rio. And now he's got his sights on *you*. You fucked up, Castillo. Got yourself on his radar. And the only outcome is death and the end of your reign of terror."

The man's smirk was back. "Yes. I know Rex. And the boy he raised as his own? He is most likely my biological son."

Bree nearly let a gasp escape. She'd heard about the child Rex's wife had while she was in captivity. That boy was Mateo's?

"How do you figure?"

Smiley was still outwardly relaxed, but Bree could feel how tense his muscles were under her hands.

"Del Rio let me have her as often I wished. She was my favorite. I loved the fear in her eyes, even as she willingly spread her legs while I did whatever I wanted. With how many times I took her, there's no way the brat *wasn't* mine. Your precious Rex is raising *my* child." Mateo laughed. An evil sound that made Bree shiver. "How do you think he's going to feel when he hears?"

"If you think you'll even live long enough for your lies to make it back to him through your slimy underground network, you're wrong."

Mateo looked pissed now. And even...a little scared? It was nice to see, but it also worried Bree. For good reason.

His next words proved he was done with this little conversation.

"Kill him," he ordered his men. "But she's mine."

The two men took a step forward.

Bree acted without thought, dashing around Smiley and standing in front of him with her arms outstretched. "No!" Her only thought that, since Mateo didn't want her dead—at least not yet—she could guard Smiley with her own body.

But Smiley was having none of it. He shoved her to the side and ran *toward* the men with guns, all in the same motion.

It obviously surprised the two assholes, because they didn't even manage to pull the triggers before Smiley was on them. He kicked the gun out of one man's hands even as punched the other guy in the face.

The fight was on. Smiley didn't give either man a chance to grab hold of his weapon again. He was like a man possessed. Shifting his attention back and forth from one man to the next, not giving either an opportunity to get the upper hand.

It would've been beautiful to watch, if Mateo hadn't rushed forward and grabbed Bree.

She struggled against him, but her ribs still hurt like hell and she was no match physically for the taller, stronger man.

"You've been a pain in my ass!" Mateo hissed. "You're going to regret defying me."

"Fuck you!" she spat, fighting for all she was worth. She wasn't going to go with him willingly. Broken or cracked ribs be damned. If she didn't get away this time, she was as good as dead. And the life she'd envisioned with Smiley would go up in a puff of smoke. She'd never get to meet Addison or Maggie's babies. Wouldn't get to see Julie or Fiona again. Wouldn't get to know Remi, Kelli, Wren, or

Josie better. Wouldn't get to watch Yana and her brothers grow up.

Fuck that. She wasn't ready to die. She'd fight for herself and for Smiley.

While she'd been standing behind him, she hadn't just been cowering. She'd tried to get the pistol out of the holster at the small of his back, but he'd felt what she was doing...and had subtly stepped forward, clearly sending a message. Which was probably smart; she'd never shot a gun before, and the last thing she wanted was anyone to overpower her and use the weapon against her or Smiley. Besides, she didn't want to take away his only weapon.

So, she'd done the next best thing.

The long-sleeve shirt Smiley had found for her was plenty big enough to hide the plastic knife she'd made while in that chicken truck. That seemed so long ago, but now, the makeshift weapon felt right in her hand.

She'd used it once to kill, she'd use it again if she had the chance.

Attempting to maneuver in a way that would allow her to plunge the knife into Castillo's throat, like she'd done to the man back in Ensenada, Bree thrashed in his hold. With a growl, Mateo shifted until his arm wrapped around her neck. He wasn't cutting off her air, but he definitely had better control of her now.

An anger so hot and fierce swept over Bree. *No!* This wasn't how her and Smiley's story ended. He was still fighting the other two men, and as she watched, one of them broke away and scrambled for the weapon that had been kicked out of his grasp.

He was on his hands and knees in the dirt, and had just grabbed the rifle when Bree made her move.

She swung the makeshift knife and stabbed Mateo as hard as she could in the arm wrapped around her neck. It wouldn't kill him, but if she could make him let go long enough for her to run, that's what she'd do. Smiley had found her once, he'd find her again.

Mateo let out a pained roar, which made Bree's ears ring—and amazingly his arm dropped from around her neck.

When she tried to run, Bree's legs collapsed under her. She fell to the dirt like a sack of potatoes. Even as her brain told her legs to get up, to run, gunshots echoed off the buildings surrounding them.

Horrified, Bree whipped her head up to see if Smiley was all right, but a heavy weight fell on top of her, making her surge forward, face-first onto the ground.

Grunting, she desperately tried to get out from under whatever or whoever had tackled her, with little success.

Meanwhile more shots rang out. It sounded like World War III was going on all around her.

A sob escaped. Smiley couldn't be dead. He couldn't be! If he was, she'd never forgive herself. He was the best thing that had ever happened to her—and she'd gotten him killed!

Suddenly things went eerily quiet. Bree was almost afraid to move. Maybe if she stayed really still, the assholes after her would think she was dead and they'd flee.

The weight on top of her was suddenly removed, and she was flipped onto her back. Blinking, Bree had trouble focusing on what she was seeing. Then strong arms lifted her, wrapping around her in a painful grip.

For a second, Bree thought she was being restrained by

Mateo's men—but after one inhalation, she knew the arms around her belonged to Smiley.

She latched onto him with more strength than she thought she had.

"Are you hurt? Fuck!"

She shook her head against him, then a thought occurred to her. The men from the apartment building... They had to get out of there!

Lifting her head to tell Smiley they had to run, she blinked in confusion. Her eye was still pretty swollen, but in the last few hours, she'd been able to see out of it a little. But she couldn't be seeing what she thought she was.

Crouched next to her and Smiley was Blink. And at *his* side was MacGyver.

"She's got blood on her. Where did he get you, honey?" Blink asked gently.

This felt surreal. Bree was confused. She tried to look down at herself, but Smiley wasn't relaxing his grip.

"Smiley, ease up, man, we need to check her out," Kevlar ordered.

Ever so slowly, his grip around her loosened, and Bree leaned back far enough not to look at herself, but to check Smiley for injuries. "Did you get shot?" she asked.

"No. You?"

She shook her head.

"Is this what I think it is?" Preacher asked, holding up the plastic knife Bree had used on Mateo. When she glanced to the side, she saw Mateo Castillo lying still in the dirt, a large puddle of blood forming around him and a hole in the center of his forehead.

"I felt you taking it out of my holster," Smiley said, bringing her attention back to him.

"Good job on distracting him," Safe added.

Looking over her shoulder at him, she saw the men Smiley had been fighting lying on the ground, bullet holes in their heads as well. "What...how?" she stammered.

"Twenty-two minutes and forty seconds," Kevlar said. "Not thirty minutes...my bad. Was never very good at estimations."

It finally sank in. Kevlar and his team had arrived at just the right moment. She didn't know how, didn't really care. They probably heard Mateo's goon yelling at them or something.

"Hate to interrupt, but we need to scoot," Flash said. "The natives are getting restless."

The men Mateo had sent after them exited the apartment building, but after taking one look at their dead boss on the ground, and the armed men standing around him—now with guns at the ready—they took off for the other end of the alley. Probably back to their truck.

But the civilians were curious too. Now that bullets had stopped flying, locals were coming out from wherever they'd holed up to see what was going on.

Preacher and Kevlar took hold of Smiley's arms and, in one fluid motion, pulled him to his feet, with Bree still in his arms.

She let out a small squeak of surprise, but Smiley shushed her. "I've got you."

And he did. Smiley had her. That's all she needed to know. Her aches and pains returned with a vengeance, and all she could do was close her eyes and relax into Smiley's arms when he adjusted his grip and put an arm under her legs, cradling her. He walked them, surrounded by his team, toward an SUV parked haphazardly against the curb a block away. It was a miracle no one had stolen it in the short time it had been sitting there.

It was a tight fit, but Bree didn't care. Mateo was dead. She was free.

A lightness came over her then, a feeling of having her entire life ahead of her. It was both scary and exciting at the same time.

"We can go back to the motel, or we can go straight to the airport," Kevlar said.

Bree lifted her head and looked into Smiley's eyes.

"Airport," they said at the same time.

She grinned, and the look of love he gave her was so intense it felt as if they were the only two people on the planet.

"We don't have your bag," Preacher warned. "We left in too big a hurry to grab it."

"Don't need anything in there. I've got everything I need right here," Smiley said, not breaking eye contact with Bree.

"Oh, but what about you guys?" she asked, reluctantly looking away from Smiley. "Do you have your stuff?"

"Nope," Preacher answered. "Don't care though. I'm guessing all our crap is infested with bedbugs anyway. Let the people who work at that piece-of-shit motel have it."

"We'll return the car and the weapons to the man we borrowed them from. We have our identification—yours and Bree's included, Smiley," Kevlar said. "I, for one, will be glad to get home."

"I'm sure Julie and Fiona will be anxious to see you," Safe added.

"As will the rest of the girls," MacGyver added.

Bree desperately wanted a shower. And a huge bowl of

mac and cheese. And a gallon of water. Maybe a painkiller. But she'd get all that and more soon enough. Other than Smiley being unharmed, her biggest wish at that moment was to go home. To the apartment in Riverton that felt more like a home than any place she'd ever lived...simply because she shared it with the man she loved.

Closing her eyes, she relaxed against Smiley once more as Blink drove them toward freedom.

CHAPTER TWENTY

After what had been a very stressful experience, the flight back to the United States was ridiculously mundane. The private plane was waiting for them at the airport in Guayaquil, and after meeting with a mysterious contact in the parking lot to return the vehicle and borrowed weapons, Smiley carried Bree into a hangar and onto the plane.

He and his teammates had remained quiet and on alert. The atmosphere was tense, since the bands of roving militants were still causing havoc in the city.

It wasn't until they were wheels up that Smiley relaxed. The trip home was spent hovering over Bree, who'd been given an IV by MacGyver, and as much protein and other food as Smiley could get her to eat.

They landed at a private regional airport in Southern California, and it shouldn't have surprised him to find his Ford Ranger waiting for him in the parking lot, as well as Kevlar's Crosstrek and MacGyver's Explorer...and yet he was still surprised. He wasn't sure who had arranged to deliver their vehicles—probably Tex, working with Wolf's team—but he was grateful.

That was two days ago. After a visit to the doctor, he and Bree had holed up in his apartment. Truthfully, Smiley had needed the one-on-one time. They'd talked a lot. About what she'd been through, how Smiley had found her, and about what had happened there at the end.

Smiley had been afraid Bree would be emotionally damaged because of the violence, but she admitted she was a little worried about how *okay* she was with the way everything went down. That led to a discussion of how he coped with some of the things he did on missions, and he'd arranged for a Zoom call for her with the psychologist he sometimes used after especially difficult deployments.

He'd spent the last two days pampering her, making sure she was eating healthy and drinking water constantly. Their phones had been exploding with voicemails, emails, and texts, but neither had been eager to do anything but soak in the other's presence.

But it was time. Smiley noticed that Bree was already getting restless. He wanted nothing more than to keep her to himself, to continue to hole up here in his apartment, hidden from the rest of the world, spoiling her, making sure she healed completely with no complications. But his Bree was an extrovert. She needed to see Fiona and Julie, see for herself that they were okay. Thank his teammates and Wolf's team, who'd had a hand in finding her. And she desperately wanted to meet Tex.

Smiley knew the man was still in Southern California. He was giving Bree the time she needed to regain her equilibrium. Everyone was. They might be texting and emailing, but they were respecting their need for space by not knocking down his door.

"I thought we could go down to Aces this afternoon," Smiley suggested.

The smile on her face when she whipped around to look at him was all the reassurance he needed that he was doing the right thing.

"Yes! I'd love that!" Bree said happily.

"You sure you feel up to it? You had that headache yesterday." Even though he'd suggested the outing, all of a sudden, Smiley worried that it would be too much, too fast.

"Yes. But...are *you* okay with it?" Bree asked with a small frown.

They were sitting on the couch next to each other, and Smiley turned so he could see her more easily. He put a hand on her cheek. "I want what you want," he told her.

"That's not fair," she protested.

"I love you, Bree Haynes. I made myself a promise while searching for you that if I found you, I'd spend the rest of my days bending over backward to give you the life you deserved. And you deserve to be surrounded by friends. Laughing. Living in the moment with joy."

But Bree stubbornly shook her head. "Don't you get it? I can't live in *any* moment with joy if I'm worried about you. If you're hating what we're doing. If you're miserable."

"I will never, *ever* be miserable with you by my side. That sounds like a line, but it isn't. Seeing you happy, your smile, that makes *me* happy. Makes me want to do everything in my power to keep putting that smile on your face. If you want to eat out, we'll eat out. If you want to go to a movie, we'll go to a movie. If you need some girl time, I'll give you space to do what you need to do.

"We haven't talked about our long-term future much, but I want to marry you, Bree. I want to grow old with you by my side. I want to go on vacations with you, babysit our friends' kids, and laugh because they're hyper when we send them home. And I want to spoil you."

Tears filled her eyes, but she was smiling, so he didn't panic.

"I want all that too. But only if I get to spoil you right back."

"Deal. And you should know..." He paused.

"Yeah?" she asked.

"Everyone's gonna be there. At Aces."

She giggled. "I assumed."

"You still want to go?"

"Yes. Absolutely. We've holed up long enough. It's time to get back to living. He's not an issue anymore, right?"

Smiley knew exactly which *he* she was referring to. "I'm sure. You know that I spoke to Tex when we got home and told him everything that went down. He sent me a message this morning, after looking into the situation in Ecuador. Castillo's compound was raided. All the women found there were rescued. They're getting assistance from private women's rights groups so they can get back on their feet. Those who aren't from Ecuador are being flown back to their countries, their families. Castillo's organization is done. You're safe. I give you my promise on that."

"It's going to feel a little strange to not have to look over my shoulder all the time."

"You'll get used to it," he told her firmly.

She gave him a small smile. "Have I told you today that I love you?"

"No," Smiley said, giving her an exaggerated pout.

She giggled. "Whatever. I did too. After you made me that Tater Tot bacon cheesy casserole this morning. And when you helped me trim my hair so it wasn't so uneven."

"*Hmmm*, I don't remember," he teased.

Bree beamed. "This," she said, the one word filled with emotion. "This is what I thought about when I was locked in those cages. Sitting here with you, teasing each other, feeling safe and loved."

The reminder of what she'd been through, even the damn word "cage" brought so many visceral emotions to the surface. But Smiley tamped them down and concentrated instead on the feelings of love her words evoked. "I love you," he whispered.

"It's a good thing, because I think you're stuck with me now," she told him with another smile.

He leaned forward and kissed her. It was meant to be a short kiss to let her know how much he adored her, but it turned into something more. Deeper. Longer. Almost desperate.

Pulling back reluctantly, he ignored the whine of complaint from Bree. "When your ribs are completely healed, I'll show you exactly how *stuck* with me you are," he told her.

Bree pouted. "This sucks."

It was Smiley's turn to chuckle. "At least you don't have to deal with this," he said, nodding at his erection.

Bree reached for him as she said, "I can do something about that."

But he caught her hand in his and brought it to his lips.

"I can wait for you," he told her. "I waited my whole life for you, I can wait a little longer."

Her eyes widened. "That was so sweet. Who are you and what have you done with my boyfriend?"

He huffed out a laugh.

Then Bree leaned closer and wrapped her arms around him. Smiley immediately shifted her until she was sitting across his lap. The position was much more comfortable for them both, and he could feel her warmth all along his body.

They sat like that for a few long minutes, both enjoying the closeness and comfort of being in each other's arms. Then Bree lifted her head. "So...when are we going to Aces?"

Smiley chuckled again, realizing he'd laughed more in the last two days than he had in probably the last ten years. Bree had brought light into his otherwise dim life. It was a huge change, and one he didn't hate.

Looking at his watch, he said nonchalantly, "Everyone will be there in about fifteen minutes."

"Fifteen minutes!" Bree exclaimed, trying to leap off his lap.

But Smiley held on to her.

"Smiley! Let me go. I need to get ready!"

"You're ready enough," he told her.

But Bree rolled her eyes. "I need to change, figure out what to do with my crazy hair, put on some makeup to hide some of these bruises a little better. I'm not *ready*!"

He put a finger on her cheek and turned her head until he could rest his forehead against hers. "You're perfect exactly how you are. And your friends will tell you the same thing."

She stilled. "I don't want them to look at me and feel sorry for me. Or remember all the bad things that happened. I want them to be happy for me. For *us*. That we're together now without Mateo hanging over our heads."

When she put it that way, Smiley understood. He nodded and straightened as he loosened his grip around her waist.

"I love that you think I'm fine exactly how I am though."

"You're more than fine," Smiley said with conviction. "Go do what you need to do. I'll let Wolf and Kevlar know we'll be late. They can let everyone else know."

"We aren't going to be late," Bree protested.

He simply smiled and nodded. They were totally going to be late. But he didn't care. And neither would their friends. They were extremely anxious to see her. To see for themselves that she was all right after her ordeal. And Fiona and Julie were apparently chomping at the bit to talk to her. Smiley had managed to keep them from showing up on his doorstep, but it was time. All the women needed to be reunited.

After he watched Bree hurry down the hall toward their room, he sat back against the couch and closed his eyes. A few days ago, this moment seemed almost impossible. And now, he was home with the woman he loved, she wasn't broken or even all that bent. She was a miracle. *His* miracle. And he'd spend his life working his ass off to make the rest of her days a hundred percent better than the last week had been.

* * *

Bree was nervous. She wasn't sure exactly why. Maybe it was because she desperately didn't want anyone to treat her any differently than they had before she'd been taken. Or because she was worried Julie and Fiona would blame her for what had happened. She didn't know. All she knew was that what seemed like the best idea ever a while ago, now seemed like a mistake.

"Relax," Smiley ordered as he grabbed her hand and led her toward the door to Aces Bar and Grill.

Bree stuck her tongue out at Smiley behind his back and quickly shifted her expression to a smile when he suddenly turned to look at her.

He grinned. "Did you just stick your tongue out at me?"

"No," she lied.

When he chuckled, Bree actually relaxed. She loved being able to make this man laugh. He didn't do it enough so when it happened, it felt like a major victory.

She didn't have any more time to stress about what was to come because Smiley was opening the door.

For a moment, silence greeted them when they walked in—but then it felt as if the entire room exploded in greeting.

It was overwhelming, but a warm feeling filled Bree's heart at all the people who'd come to Aces. Who were there for *her*.

Remi was the first person to get to her, and she hugged Bree hard. Then she was passed from person to person, as everyone wanted to make sure she knew how much she'd been missed and how worried they'd been.

Surprisingly, the mood of the room was celebratory instead of solemn, which was a relief. The last thing she wanted was to have to recount what she'd been through, or for people to feel sorry for her. She was alive, and she was well aware that many women who'd been in her same situation hadn't been so lucky.

Then the moment she'd both been dreading and looking forward to happened. Julie and Fiona approached, both looking as nervous as Bree felt.

To cover up her unsteady emotions, Bree said, "You two look like someone stole your last Christmas Tree Cake or something."

They looked startled for a moment—then they both lunged at her at the same time.

Bree went back on a foot to keep her balance. Thankful Smiley hadn't left her side, and he braced her with a hand on her back.

Then all she could think of was how close she, Fiona, and Julie had come to never seeing each other again.

All three burst into tears. For Bree, the emotional release was a combination of relief, delayed fear, and pride that she could call these women friends.

Fiona was the first to pull back, but she didn't remove her arms from around Julie and Bree. "Don't you ever do that again!" she practically yelled in Bree's face.

"Yeah, that wasn't cool at all," Julie agreed.

To her amazement, Bree found herself smiling. "You would've preferred that I sat back and did nothing as we were all shipped away?"

"You could've *died*!" Fiona snapped.

"And you were hurt because of us!" Julie added.

Bree sobered, looked from Julie to Fiona, then said, "If I could go back and do it all over again, I wouldn't change a damn thing. You two were there because of me. There was *no way* I was going to allow you two to go through the worst experience of your life *again*."

"We weren't there because of you," Julie insisted. "We were there because of an asshole who thought he had the right to take away our freedom."

"If something happened to you, if you had disappeared, or had to go through what we did…" Fiona's voice cracked but she forced herself to continue. "I think that would've been worse than what happened all those years ago."

Bree was appalled. "Fiona, no."

"*Yes*," she insisted. "That was one of the most unselfish things I've ever seen in my life, and I can't decide if I want to hit you or hug you again."

"I choose hugs," Bree told her.

And then the three women were once again huddled in a three-way embrace.

"If I may," a deep voice said from behind Fiona.

She pulled back, and Bree looked into Cookie's eyes.

His lips were pressed together as stared down at her. Then he said, "I'd like to give you a hug too…if that's okay. If it won't cause you any angst."

Bree practically threw herself at the older man, her nose buried in his chest as she hugged him. His tight hug hurt her ribs, but she didn't complain. One of his hands rested on the back of her head, and he lowered his lips to her ear and said, "Thank you."

It was just two words, but they settled deep in Bree's soul.

"My turn," another deep voice said.

And before she knew it, she was engulfed in Patrick Hurt's embrace. He too thanked her, with deep emotion swirling in his words.

Bree was beginning to feel a little embarrassed by all the attention. She truly believed she hadn't done anything the other two women wouldn't have done themselves, if they'd had the chance. She was just the one who'd been let out of her cage first.

"Right, so...I think we all know why we're here!" Turning toward Jessyka's voice, Bree found herself once more in Smiley's arms. She snuggled in, feeling content to be with him and all her friends.

The owner of Aces was standing behind the bar, addressing the crowd.

"Tonight, there is no chicken on the menu, for obvious reasons."

Bree laughed along with everyone else. She shared a look with Julie and Fiona, who both wrinkled their noses at the same time, making Bree laugh even harder.

"There'll be trays of hors d'oeuvres carried around for a few hours. If you want something different...too bad."

Everyone laughed again.

"Champagne is on the house as well, everyone grab a glass from the servers and let's raise a toast. To Bree, Julie, and Fiona being home. For our SEALs being the best of the best. And...to Tex!"

Bree blinked, twisting her head to look in the direction everyone else was looking. Standing alongside the far wall was a man she'd never met. But she'd know him anywhere. For one, he was wearing shorts, and it was easy to see his prosthetic leg. But also, he gave off confusing vibes. Fatherly and pissed off at the same time.

Without hesitation, Bree headed his way. She felt Smiley at her back, but she only had eyes for the man who'd gone out of his way to help her. Who'd helped so many others in his lifetime. It was *him* she had to thank for doing the legwork to find out they were in Ensenada. And even though Smiley's tracker had failed, she had no doubt he hadn't slept while he tried to discover where they'd disappeared to while in Guayaquil. Not to mention his role in the plane ride home, and the passport for her that Kevlar had pulled out of his pocket after they'd landed.

She'd heard the larger-than-life stories about this man, and it was almost surreal that she was about to meet him. From Remi to Wren, Josie, Maggie, Addison, and Kelli... this man had played a part in all of them being happy and healthy today.

The first tear fell as she approached him, and they didn't stop as she practically fell into his arms. Tex held her as she completely lost her composure. How long she stood in his arms crying, she had no idea, but he didn't seem uncomfortable holding a hysterical woman he'd never met.

When she finally got control over herself, Bree eased out of his hold.

"Hi," she said a little sheepishly, as she wiped tears off her cheeks. Her makeup was certainly ruined, but that was the last thing on her mind at the moment. She had so many questions, but couldn't remember a single one.

Tex smirked. "Hi."

"I...you...Dang it!" Bree complained, hating her inability to speak.

"I'm Tex," he said. "It's nice to meet you."

"I'm Bree." It seemed a little surreal to be introducing themselves to each other when they were both more than aware who the other was.

Suddenly, all the things Bree wanted to say came back to her at once, and she tripped over her words trying to get them out. "Thank you. And please thank the women you work with too. If it wasn't for you...I don't know how Smiley would've found us. How did you know where the boat was going to dock? Which city and port? Were you tracking me all the way from Ensenada? I'm sorry the tracker Smiley gave me got taken away, that must've made your job a lot harder. Fiona and Julie told me all about you. I already knew about you from Remi and the others, but we had some time to chat on that truck, and they told me how awesome you were when they were taken the first time, and what you did for Fiona...calling her every four hours even though you had your own stuff going on. And I don't know how you got a copy of my passport, but I appreciate that too. And the plane ride home. I just—"

"You're welcome," Tex said, interrupting her and effectively stopping her word vomit.

Then he pulled her into a tight hug once more. As he let go, he said, "I need to get home to my wife and kids. And dog. And I need to figure out why the hell Smiley's tracker failed. I've got his underwear in a plastic bag in my suitcase—I'm sure that'll look weird as hell if someone searches my luggage. But I hate when technology fails me. I'll figure out what happened, even though it'll mean having to touch Smiley's fucking dirty underwear."

Bree couldn't help it, she laughed. Hard. She'd expected this man to be...stiff and nerdy. But he was anything but. He felt like a favorite uncle. Someone she could tell all her secrets to and know they'd be safe.

He gave her a small grin that she felt down to her toes. "You moving in with Smiley?" he asked out of the blue.

Bree shyly looked behind her at the man in question, then back to Tex as she nodded.

"Figured. I've arranged to have your things in the Vegas storage facility shipped here to Riverton. You might want to think about where everything is gonna go."

Bree blinked in surprise.

"Thanks, man," Smiley said, reaching around her to shake Tex's hand.

Then the older man nodded at her, gave Smiley a chin lift, and strode across the room toward Fiona. If she hadn't known it before, it was obvious that woman was a favorite of his. They had a lot of intimate history, and the love they had for each other was a beautiful thing.

"You good?" Smiley asked, as he wrapped his arms around her from behind and rested his chin on her shoulder.

"Did you arrange that?" she asked.

"Nope. He texted me and asked what the plan was for your stuff. I told him we'd deal with it later. Guess he decided *not* to let us worry about it. Again, you good?"

"Yeah. I'm more than good, Smiley," Bree said. She looked over the crowd. Her friends. She'd almost lost this. That thought upset her more than everything that had actually happened to her. Yes, it had been horrible. She'd been locked up, treated as less than human, threatened, beaten, and scared out of her mind. And yet...she was here. Alive. With more friends than she'd ever had in her life.

She could act like a victim. Let what happened overwhelm her and turn her into a different person. Someone who was scared of her own shadow. Who stayed inside so she didn't have to interact with strangers who may or may not hurt her.

The truth was, life was full of ups and downs. And she preferred to concentrate on the ups rather than the downs. Turning in Smiley's arms, she grinned at him.

"What?" he asked with furrowed brows. "What's that smile for?"

"I'm happy," she informed him.

He didn't look appeased. If anything, he looked even more concerned. "It's only been two days. Everything that happened could hit you hard when you least expect it."

Bree shrugged. "You're right. But you'll be there. And I can talk to Julie and Fiona about it. Or Remi or Kelli. Or go spend some time with Yana, to remind myself of how appreciative she is for all she has and how well she's dealing with what happened to her too. I was lucky, I know that. But I'll take lucky over dead any day of the week. I want to *live*, Smiley. Look forward, not back."

"I love you," he told her.

"And I love you too. One day, we'll stand in this place when we're old and gray. All our friends' kids will be here, cutting up and saying stuff we don't understand and talking about technology that's over our heads. And we'll look back over our life with no regrets."

A look of such longing flashed on Smiley's face, Bree's heart ached.

"I want that," he said.

"So we'll do what we have to in order to make it happen."

"Yeah."

A waiter walked over and held out a tray full of champagne glasses filled to the rim. Bree took two and handed one to Smiley.

"To us," she said quietly.

"To us," he repeated. Instead of taking a sip, Smiley put the glass on a nearby table without looking and pulled her closer.

He kissed her long, hard, and with all the love she knew he felt in his heart.

Bree felt it down to her toes. She was the luckiest woman in the world, and she vowed to live life to its fullest from that day forward.

* * *

Hours later, Smiley couldn't sleep. He held Bree until she'd drifted off, but his brain wouldn't shut down. After everything that happened, he couldn't stop thinking about something Castillo had said. The man was dead, and what he'd said was most likely bullshit, but he couldn't rest until he'd gotten it off his chest.

Turning, he gently kissed Bree on the forehead, amazed that she was here with him. Not only because of what she'd been through, but because he was a grumpy asshole. He knew it, but somehow Bree didn't seem to care. It was baffling, but he wasn't about to let her go now. He needed her too much.

Staying as silent as possible, he slipped out from under the covers, standing by the bed for a moment to make sure Bree hadn't woken up. She shifted a little after losing his body heat, but settled again. Just looking at her shorter hair, her eyelashes against her bruised skin, made him wish he could go back and kill Castillo all over again.

Smiley forced himself to walk out of the bedroom and into the living room. He sat on the couch and stared down at his phone. Taking a deep breath, he dialed a number he'd asked Tex for before he'd left Aces.

It was the middle of the night, but the man on the other end answered after only one ring.

"Rex."

"I'm sorry for calling so late. It's Smiley." The urge to talk to this man had been overwhelming, but now that he had him on the line, Smiley wasn't sure he'd made the right decision.

"What's up? Is Bree all right?"

"She's good. Amazing, really. She constantly surprises me with her resilience."

"Our women are stronger than we think," Rex agreed. "Every day, I wonder how Raven survived what she did with her personality intact. I still have no idea how she did it."

"I need to tell you something," Smiley blurted. "If it was me, I'd want to know, but...it's not good news."

"It's about Castillo, isn't it?"

"Yeah. I know you're aware that he worked with del Rio. But he said something. Bragged about it, actually."

"He's dead, right?"

"Yeah."

"Thank you for that," Rex said. "You saved me from calling in a marker to take care of that myself."

Smiley nodded, even though the other man couldn't see him. "You can forget I called if you'd prefer."

"I'd prefer you said what you need to say, what's keeping you up in the middle of the night and taking you away from Bree's side," Rex said matter-of-factly.

"Right. So, I was stalling. Back in Guayaquil. Trying to kill time so my team could arrive and lend a hand. I taunted Castillo. Brought up your name. Goaded him with the fact you were going to hunt him down, and his impending death would be at your hands," Smiley admitted. "It probably wasn't my finest moment, but I was doing anything I could to give Kevlar and my team time to get there."

He was stalling again *now*, dragging out this conversation more than necessary. He got to the point.

"Castillo claimed he was your son's biological father. Said he'd been with your wife enough to be certain David was his."

To his immense surprise, Rex laughed.

"My son is just that—*mine*. And Raven's. He isn't, and never was, that asshole's."

Smiley wasn't sure what to say.

"Look. I've made peace with what happened to Raven. Does it make me want to kill every motherfucker who dared lay a hand on her? Of course. But I can't. I choose instead to concentrate on the life we have now. On the amazing, brilliant, compassionate, and kind son we're raising. And David *is* mine. One hundred percent. I might not have any DNA in common with him, but that doesn't make him any less my son."

"Right."

"I respect you, Smiley. It couldn't have been an easy thing to tell me. But it means the world that you cared enough to pass on what that asshole claimed. You know it wasn't smart to antagonize him, right?"

"Yeah. Right after he made that claim, he ordered his

men to shoot me. I would've been better off talking about the fucking weather or something."

Rex chuckled. "I've learned that it's always better to put a bullet in someone's head rather than hang around and have a fucking conversation. It's just easier."

"I'll remember that for next time," Smiley told him.

"See that you do."

"What you did, what you do...it's important," he told Rex, with as much sincerity in his tone as he could muster.

"I think so too. Every woman and child we save is a victory. And I'll never lose sleep over killing a man who thinks he owns women and can do with them what he pleases."

"Amen to that," he agreed.

"Thanks again for the call. Fuck him. Fuck them all. I'm gonna live my life, be happy, laugh, and enjoy the shit out of every day...that's enough for me."

He was right. Rex had been to hell and back, as had his family. If he could be happy, Smiley could too. "If you and your family ever get to Southern California, Bree and I would love to get together."

"I'll make sure that happens. Go back to bed, Smiley. Sleep with a clear conscience. That's an order."

Smiley snorted. "You aren't my commander."

Rex simply chuckled. Then the line went silent.

Feeling better now that he'd gotten that off his chest, Smiley stood, turned—and paused when he saw Bree leaning against the wall near the hallway.

"I didn't mean to wake you up," he told her.

"You didn't. Well, not really. I missed the feel of you next to me." She padded over to the couch and pulled him back down to sit with her, snuggling into his side, her knees pulled up with her feet on the cushion next to her. "It sounded like he took that okay."

Smiley wasn't surprised she figured out who he was talking to. She'd been there. She heard what Castillo had claimed.

"Yeah."

"For the record, I think he was lying," Bree said.

Smiley wasn't so sure, but he didn't contradict her.

"That had to have been really hard. Telling him, I mean."

"It wasn't easy."

"That's one of the many things I love about you, Jude Stark," Bree said, looking up at him. "You do what's right no matter how hard it is on you."

Her compliment soothed his soul in a way no one else had ever been able to. "Thanks."

"You're welcome. Now...it's the middle of the night. And even though it's too soon for me to jump your bones, can we go back to bed anyway?"

In response, Smiley stood and leaned over to pick her up.

She giggled but didn't protest. "I think I like you carrying me around."

"Good, because I like *carrying* you around," Smiley told her.

He got them both settled under the covers once more, and the contentment he felt when Bree put her head on his shoulder and threw a leg over his thighs was almost scary.

"I love you, Smiley. I always knew Jude Stark was a superhero name, and you prove it to me time and time again. And I'm not just talking about you sliding down a gutter nine stories with me on your back, or acting as if having two guns pointed at your head is no big deal, or any of the larger-than-life things you do on your missions. I'm talking about you calling a friend because a rumor you heard that involves him was bothering you. Or carrying me around because it makes you happy. Or making me dinner. Or arranging for all my friends to come to a bar to welcome me home. Or any of the other hundreds of things you do every day to make my life easier and happier. You're my superhero, Smiley. And I love you so much."

"I'm just a man who wants to do everything in his power to make his woman's life easier," he protested.

"Well, you do. And I appreciate it. And you."

"Love you," Smiley said, turning and kissing the top of her head.

She kissed his chest. "Love you back. When I'm healed, you better watch out...I'm gonna show you *exactly* how much I love and appreciate you."

"Looking forward to it," Smiley said with a sappy grin.

"Can I ask you something?"

"You can ask me anything you want, whenever you want," he told her.

He saw her gaze was fixed on something across the room. Following her line of sight, he realized she was staring at a bookshelf against the wall.

"I want to fix up your bear," she blurted.

Smiley couldn't help but chuckle.

"That wasn't meant to be funny," she protested.

"How long have you been thinking about that? Here we are, in bed, sleepy and talking about superpowers, and you're worried about Beary."

"I love that name," Bree told him with a huge smile.

It was ridiculous. Something only a kid could come up with. Smiley had such complicated feelings about his childhood stuffed animal. There were some good memories associated with the toy, but also some not-so-good ones. It was the only thing he took when he left his house for good.

"I just think that he deserves a face-lift," Bree went on. "You both went through some tough times, but those are over now. You're both free of all that."

She could be talking about herself...or him. And she was right. It would be cathartic to restore Beary. To see him shine again. "Okay," Smiley said.

"Really?" Bree asked with excitement.

"Really," Smiley said.

"Yay!"

His girlfriend was a goof...and he wouldn't change one damn thing about her. "Can we sleep now?" he asked, pretending to be grumpy.

She sighed with contentment and snuggled into him. "Yeah."

It was amazing how fast Bree fell asleep. He would've accused her of faking it, except he knew firsthand how she could be awake one second and snoring the next. He wouldn't have it any other way though. It meant she wasn't kept awake thinking about the awful things that had happened to her in the recent past.

Knowing that she could let down her guard, and that she trusted him when she was at her most vulnerable, when she was sleeping, made Smiley grin up at the ceiling.

He fell asleep with that smile on his face and woke up the same way. Because he held in his arms the one person who made him put aside the guilt he'd carried all his life about his parents. Who loved him for who he was, warts and all.

This was what life was about...not how much money you could amass, how big your car or house, or even how many friends you had—although friends were super important. It was about finding someone who could overlook your faults and love you anyway. Bree was that person for him...and he'd remind her every single day how important she was to him, and how much she was loved.

EPILOGUE

Ten years later

"Are you nervous about next week?" Bree asked Addison, as they stood at the edge of the trampolines and did their best to keep an eye on all the kids leaping from one platform to the next.

"No," Addison said firmly. "It's way past time."

"MacGyver's been super-reluctant, hasn't he?"

Addison chuckled. "That's putting it mildly. But Artem has been wanting to do this for years. It's the only thing he asked for as a graduation present. He knows once he starts college, he's going to be too busy to go."

"How overboard has Tex gone with the tracker thing?" Bree asked with a huge grin.

Addison rolled her eyes. "Good Lord. I love the man, but I'm thinking four trackers for each of us is a bit much."

"You can't blame him. Things in the Ukraine have been calm for years, but there will always be that small chance something could happen while you're there."

"I understand that. But MacGyver has everything under control. Kevlar is coming with us, as is Dude. Did you know my husband also hired a security guard to come with us too? I guess the man in charge of the tour group is a former Marine and fluent in Ukrainian."

Bree smiled at her friend, then swung her head around when she heard someone scream from nearby. She saw Violet sitting on one of the trampolines, holding her leg, but she already had five kids around her, plus Preacher and Safe heading her way. She didn't look hurt, but she was clearly soaking up the attention from her best friends.

"That girl is so spoiled," Addison said with a chuckle.

"She's used to all the boys' attention."

"I know you aren't badmouthing my baby," Maggie joked, as she and Josie joined Addison and Bree where they were watching the craziness from the trampoline platform.

"Your baby is spoiled rotten," Bree told her.

"Yup," Maggie said, not sounding the least bit bothered.

"Where's Amelia?" Addison asked Josie.

"With her dad. She got tired," Josie said, pointing to where Blink was sitting at a table with their two-year-old daughter in his arms.

"How're you holding up? Having triplets in the terrible twos isn't exactly the easiest thing in the world," Addison said.

"I can't imagine having three that age," Remi said,

approaching the group. "I remember when Vinny was that age. I swore I wouldn't have another kid because I was so stressed out, trying to keep up with him."

"You obviously got over it," Bree said with a laugh. "Because Mason came along two years later."

"And *his* terrible twos were definitely when I called it quits," Remi said. "My dad was disappointed. I think he would've loved it if I'd had eight kids, but two is enough."

"Blink's awesome with our brood," Josie said.

"I can't believe you had twins, then *triplets*," Addison said with a shake of her head. "You're crazy."

"It's not as if I planned it! And so says the woman with five kids of her own," Josie fired back.

"Yeah, but four of mine are older," Addison said.

"Speaking of...how's Ellory?"

"She's awesome. Just finished up her first year in the Peace Corps. We worry about her a lot, being in Gabon. I thought MacGyver was going to have a heart attack when he found out she'd be going to Africa to teach, but she loves it so much."

"She's going to the Ukraine with you guys, right?" Remi asked.

"Yeah. We're all going. I'm looking forward to it. Artem, Borysko, and Yana deserve to see where they came from. Yana doesn't remember much at all, but Artem and Borysko do."

"I'm really impressed that Artem is going into pre-law in the fall."

"He's always said that he wants to help people who don't have the means or ability to help themselves."

"I can't believe he decided to have his graduation party

here," Maggie said. "He could be hanging with his buds. Instead he chose a trampoline park, so all his little cousins could have the time of their life on his special day. He's such a good kid."

"He is," Addison agreed, sounding extremely proud.

"Oh! Here comes Kelli. My turn to hold her!" Wren exclaimed, stepping toward the other woman. Her daughter had just turned six months old, the youngest of all their kids. And she was extra-special because of everything Kelli and Flash had gone through to have her. Years of fertility treatments and trying and failing to conceive. Just when they'd given up, deciding to be content with the older dogs and cats they'd adopted from the local shelter, she'd found out she was pregnant.

She'd had to spend the last three months of her pregnancy in bed, to make sure she didn't lose the baby, and when Desiree was born, it had been a joyous day for everyone.

"No fair!" Bree whined. "I haven't gotten to hold her yet today."

"Too bad," Wren sang with a grin, as she reached for baby Desiree.

"Look at us," Remi said with a small shake of her head. "Who would've thought we'd be where we are today. How many kids are there now?"

"You and Kevlar have two," Wren said. "I have one. Josie and Blink have five, three for Maggie and Preacher, Addison and MacGyver also have five, Kelli and Flash have their little Des, and Bree is the only smart one with none."

"Seventeen kids. That's insane," Maggie said with a laugh.

"No, what's insane is how most of them are boys. What did we do to deserve that?" Wren asked.

Bree beamed at her friends. The happy shrieks and squeals from the kids bouncing on the trampolines echoed around them. They'd rented out the entire place so they could have it to themselves for Artem's graduation party. He'd invited a few of his close friends, and the older kids were keeping an eye on the younger ones. Especially Logan and Violet, who were four and five, respectively.

Brody and Cody, Josie's twins, were bossing everyone around, as they usually did when they got together with their cousins. Arlo, MacGyver and Addison's son, and Ben, who belonged to Maggie and Preacher, who were both the oldest at ten, were ignoring most of the other kids, pairing up and probably planning something outrageous and dangerous.

Borysko was chilling with two of his friends from school at one of the tables, eating hamburgers...something that didn't surprise Bree in the least. The kid was a bottomless pit. He could eat a full meal, then twenty minutes later claim he was hungry again.

Yana was fifteen and a typical teenager. Most days she barely tolerated the craziness that was her cousins, preferring to watch videos on her phone and chat with her girlfriends, but today she seemed happy to entertain Tony and Walker, two of Josie's two-year-old triplets.

Looking around the room, Bree saw the men who'd become some of her best friends, doing what they could to both entertain and rein in their overexuberant progeny. The retirement date for the SEAL team was quickly approaching and none of them were ready. They loved the

Navy. Loved what they'd done for a living for so long. It felt weird that they would be retiring and yet still have such young children at home.

But none of them would stop working altogether. Everyone had plans for the future. They weren't the kinds of men to sit at home and drink beer and watch television.

Kevlar was jumping on a trampoline with Vinny and Mason, his eight- and six-year-old boys. Safe was still hovering over Violet, making sure she was all right, and his son, four-year-old Logan, was right at his side, holding Violet's hand.

Blink was still sitting off to the side holding Amelia, now asleep in his arms, as he watched over the group in general. His boys were hellions, but most of the time all it took was one warning look from Dad to make them behave.

Preacher had left Violet in Safe's capable hands and was now standing next to Blink, holding his one-year-old adopted boy, Milo. He had Down syndrome, and was almost as spoiled as Desiree and Violet.

MacGyver had stopped by the table where Borysko was sitting with his friends, laughing with them about something, and was now heading back to the trampolines to join in the fun.

Flash joined Yana to help with the twins, giving chase as they ran from them, giggling maniacally.

And then there was Smiley. Over the last decade, he'd loosened up a lot. He'd never be called gregarious by any stretch of the imagination, but seeing him jumping up and down on a trampoline, acting as the judge as Ben and Arlo tried to see who could jump the highest? It filled Bree with joy.

As if he could feel her gaze on him, Smiley glanced in the direction of all the women. His gaze met Bree's, and she could practically feel him trying to figure out if she was good. If she needed anything.

He was extremely intuitive when it came to her. When she was crampy and bloated from her period, he brought her a heating pad. When she was hangry, he'd make her a snack without having to ask if she wanted one. And even after all this time, he was just as amorous in bed as he'd been when they'd first started dating.

They'd followed in the footsteps of their friends and had a small, intimate wedding ceremony on the beach, and then a huge party at Aces to celebrate. Becoming Smiley's wife was wonderful, but it hadn't changed how Bree felt about him. She loved him so much it was almost scary. His deployments were always stressful for her, but she put on a brave face and tried not to let him know how much she hated each and every time he left home.

But he knew anyway. He'd apologized once, and Bree had lit into him. Demanding he never do that again. Told him that he was an amazing SEAL, and she knew he loved what he did. How she felt about his deployments wasn't *his* problem, it was *hers*.

Of course, he'd immediately disagreed.

The bottom line was that Bree was as proud as she could be of her husband. He was very good at his job, but the thought of losing him was almost overwhelming. It had taken a long conversation with Caroline Steel to help her come to terms with her fears. To understand that he had six of the best men he could ever have at his back, and now that he had Bree, he'd do anything possible in order to come home to her.

And he had. Every time.

They didn't have any children, because neither wanted any. They were kept busy with their friends' kids. Of course, they all loved staying at Aunt Bree and Uncle Smiley's house because they got to stay up late, eat junk food, and play video games that their own parents wouldn't usually let them play. They were the "fun" aunt and uncle, and Bree was content with that.

Her life was full. Being kidnapped by a sex slaver seemed like it had happened to someone else. As if it was a lifetime ago.

As if Smiley could read her thoughts, he said something to Ben and Arlo and bounced his way toward her and the other women.

"Uh-oh, Smiley's headed this way," Remi teased. "Guess that's our cue to disperse."

"You don't have to go," Bree protested, but it was easy to see her friends didn't mind heading to their own husbands. Even after a decade, they were all just as in love with their spouses as they'd been when they were first married.

"Did I chase everyone away with my grumpiness?" Smiley asked as he reached her side.

Bree laughed. "You aren't so grumpy anymore."

"Whatever," he harumphed, making Bree laugh even harder.

"That's what I love to see and hear...you laughing. Did you know when I first met you, I privately made it my mission in life to make you smile more often?"

"I smiled back then," Bree protested.

"Not enough. But now? You're the light to my dark. When I'm feeling grumpy, all I have to do is look at you, see your smile, and I remember everything I have to be thankful for."

Bree couldn't stop grinning. "You're so sappy. What happened to the badass Navy SEAL I married?"

"Oh, he's still here. But I've learned over the years not to give a shit what other people think about me. If they want to think I'm pussy-whipped, they can. I mean, they aren't wrong."

"Shut up," Bree complained.

He grinned. Then sobered. "You're happy."

It wasn't a question. "How could I not be? I'm surrounded by my best friends, who've become my family. The kids are healthy and well-adjusted. Life sure gave us all some hard knocks, but we've made it through. We're here. Together. Celebrating Artem's graduation and the fact he's going to law school. Next year, Borysko will follow in his footsteps, although not to be a lawyer. The kid told me he wants to be a doctor. A lawyer and a doctor...who woulda thunk it?"

Smiley brushed his fingers against Bree's cheek. "I love you."

She felt her cheeks heat. "I love you too."

"How much longer do you think we have to stay?"

"Why?" Bree asked, feeling concerned. "Do you feel all right? Is something wrong?"

"I'm fine. I just have the urge to make love to my wife, and I'm thinking doing so in the bathroom of a trampoline park wouldn't be appropriate."

Bree rolled her eyes. "No, it definitely would *not* be appropriate."

"One of the benefits of not having any children is being able to fuck my wife whenever and wherever I want, without having to worry about a tiny human cockblocking me."

"Uncle Smiley! Guess what!" Arlo exclaimed, as he came bouncing over to the trampoline nearest where Bree was standing with her husband.

The heat in Smiley's eyes was searing, but he took a deep breath and turned to the little boy. "What's up, kiddo?"

"Dad said me and Ben could spend the night with you and Aunt Bree! Isn't that cool!?"

"It's Ben and I," Smiley corrected, with a long sigh.

Bree giggled. "So much for tiny humans not being cockblockers," she muttered under her breath.

"That's awesome," he told Arlo. The boy bounced away, yelling at the top of his lungs to Ben that Uncle Smiley said it was all right.

"I've changed my mind about sex in the bathroom," he told her.

Bree hugged him hard. "Not happening, but I love that you want to," she told him.

Smiley pulled back and stared down at her with an expression Bree couldn't interpret. "What?" she asked.

"You've given me a life I couldn't have pictured in my wildest fantasies. A perfect life. Yes, we argue, you hog the covers, we have stress, but I get to wake up to you and go to sleep with you at my side. I can't imagine anything better."

Bree melted into him. "You're *so* getting some tonight, buster," she told him.

He grinned. "Yay."

And that made her giggle all over again. Hearing her badass husband say "yay" was funny as hell.

Two hours later, everyone made their way out of the building. They'd overstayed their scheduled time by an hour, but everyone was having so much fun they hadn't been able to cut things short. Not to mention, getting their group to do *anything* on time was never going to happen. Too many kids, too many goodbyes and hellos. It was chaos wherever they went. And Bree loved it.

By the time she was able to get Arlo and Ben to bed that night, it was hours later than they usually went to sleep and she was exhausted. Even though the two boys were well behaved, they were still exuberant and full of energy.

Bree walked into her and Smiley's bedroom and found her husband already waiting for her in their bed. She quickly did what she needed to do in the bathroom and joined him under the covers. Even though she was tired, desire swam through her body. She'd never get enough of her husband, and she loved showing him how much she still loved and wanted him.

Pushing the covers off him, she grinned when she saw Smiley didn't have a stitch of clothing on. Not wasting time, she wrapped her hand around his cock and leaned down. His long, pleasurable moan went straight between her legs. She needed him. Now.

After he was fully hard, his hips subtly lifting every time she bobbed down on him, Bree shifted. She pulled up her nightgown and straddled him. Taking hold of his cock and sinking down in one hard and fast motion.

They both groaned that time.

"Shhhh," she admonished softly. "The last thing we need is either of the boys coming in here to find out what's wrong."

"I wanted to taste you," Smiley said with a pout.

Seeing that hangdog look on her normally stoic husband made Bree giggle.

"What? I do."

"Later," she told him. "I need my husband now."

No matter how many times she made love to Smiley in this position, or how many times she tried to be in charge, he took over within a few thrusts. Tonight was no exception. His hands moved to her hips, and he began to slam her down on him hard, then harder. The slap of their skin making contact was loud. *Too* loud.

Just as she opened her mouth to protest, Smiley rolled them so she was on her back. He continued to move in and out of her, as he stared into her eyes.

"Love you," he said.

"I love you too."

They made love silently after that. Lost in the love and lust they saw in each other's eyes, and the pleasure they took from each other's bodies. It didn't take long for Smiley to gasp out the adorable little grunting sound he made right before he came, holding himself deep inside her body.

Bree wasn't disappointed that she hadn't come yet. She knew her time was coming. Literally.

Smiley pulled out and immediately reached down to stroke her clit. After ten years, he knew exactly how to make her come.

Afterward, he pulled the covers back over them and lay mostly on top of her, his head on her chest as they both tried to regain their equilibrium.

Bree loved their cuddle time after they'd both

orgasmed. Stroking Smiley's hair as he lay on her breast made her feel loved. And desired.

No matter what he'd said earlier, their marriage wasn't perfect. They disagreed about things. Got irritated with each other. But at the end of each day, they managed to talk things through and go to sleep together. She couldn't ask for anything more.

"I saw this, you know," Smiley said out of the blue.

"What? What did you see?"

"This. Us. I saw it as clear as if it was a movie playing behind my eyes when I opened the door to that car and saw you tied up in that backseat. It's why I couldn't let you go."

Bree's eyes immediately filled with tears.

"I know most people don't believe in love at first sight. But for me, it happened."

They'd talked about this before. But it never failed to give Bree goose bumps, hearing her husband talk about how he'd fallen head over heels for her the first time he'd seen her. "It wasn't as fast for me, but I couldn't get your name out of my head. Jude Stark. It made me think of safety. It's why I was drawn here...to you."

Smiley lifted his head and rested his chin on his hands. "I've never liked my name. It was a reminder of a father who beat my mother. That I had his DNA running through my veins. But you make me proud of who I am now."

"You've *always* been a person you should've been proud of."

Her husband simply shrugged. "Maybe. Maybe not. But with you at my side, I feel as if I can do anything. Thank you for that."

This man. His outer shell might be tough as nails, but deep down, he was a freaking marshmallow. And she loved him so damn much.

He smirked at her, and just as he began to inch his way down her body, the sound of someone throwing up in the hall bathroom made them both freeze.

"Fuck," Smiley swore, dropping his head to her stomach.

This wasn't funny. Not in the least...but Bree found herself smiling anyway. "The cockblocker strikes again. I'll go."

"No, you stay here. I'll go see what's up."

"I'm thinking it was probably the bowl of popcorn, the s'mores, and the huge banana split they had tonight that's not sitting well."

Smiley grimaced. "Yeah, none of that was probably the best idea, but fuck it. We're the cool aunt and uncle. They'll learn some moderation in the future."

Bree lifted a brow.

Smiley chuckled. "Or not." He leaned up and kissed her on the forehead. "Go to sleep, sweetheart. If anything is seriously wrong, I'll let you know."

"I love you," Bree told him.

"Love you too."

She watched as her husband got out of bed, grabbed a pair of flannel pajama pants lying on the floor, and then pulled a T-shirt over his head before he strode confidently toward the door. She turned on her side as she listened to the low sounds of Smiley talking to whichever one of the boys had emptied his stomach into the toilet.

She fell asleep thinking she was the luckiest woman in the world. She had the best friends with some of the best kids on the planet. If she had any questions about the Navy or life in general, she could go to Caroline and all her friends. Her husband was generous, kind, and the best lover she'd ever had. And he had friends who were like family that always had their backs.

She never would've thought this was where she'd end up all those years ago, when she was scared out of her mind in the back of that car, about to be taken to who knows where, to become a sex toy for countless men. Or when she was in that cage in the back of the truck or on that boat, about to suffer the same fate.

Life was funny. It could suck, be terrifying, then change on a dime and become glorious. The highs and lows were sometimes hard to take, but in the end, the people you surrounded yourself with were the key to getting through each and every day.

And Bree had some of the best people around her. She wouldn't change a thing about anything she'd experienced...because it all brought her to Smiley.

* * *

I realize I always thank you, my loyal reader, after each series, but I genuinely am grateful that you've stuck it out throughout the series and gotten to the last book. This one was kind of fun since I got to bring back so many of my original characters. And I know it was a little mean of me to go ALL the way back to *Protecting Fiona* and bring back a bad guy from that story. But as always, my heroines are tough as nails and love wins over evil.

If you haven't started my new series, Rescue Angels, I'd

love if you gave it a shot. It features a team of hotshot Night Stalker Army helicopter pilots and book one is *Keeping Laryn* (the hero is the twin to Blink who you met in this series).

Stay strong, be happy, be kind, and read on!

-Susan

Scan the QR code below for signed books, swag, T-shirts and more!

Also by Susan Stoker

SEAL of Protection: Alliance Series
Protecting Remi
Protecting Wren
Protecting Josie
Protecting Maggie
Protecting Addison
Protecting Kelli
Protecting Bree (Jan 6, 2026)

Rescue Angels Series
Keeping Laryn
Keeping Amanda (Nov 4, 2025)
Keeping Zita (Feb 10, 2026)
Keeping Penny (May 5, 2026)
Keeping Kara (July 7, 2026)
Keeping Jennifer (Nov 10, 2026)

Alpha Cove Series
The Soldier
The Sailor (Mar 3, 2026)
The Pilot (Aug 4, 2026)
The Guardsman (Mar 9, 2027)

SEAL Team Hawaii Series
Finding Elodie
Finding Lexie
Finding Kenna
Finding Monica
Finding Carly

ALSO BY SUSAN STOKER

Finding Ashlyn
Finding Jodelle

Eagle Point Search & Rescue
Searching for Lilly
Searching for Elsie
Searching for Bristol
Searching for Caryn
Searching for Finley
Searching for Heather
Searching for Khloe

The Refuge Series
Deserving Alaska
Deserving Henley
Deserving Reese
Deserving Cora
Deserving Lara
Deserving Maisy
Deserving Ryleigh

Game of Chance Series
The Protector
The Royal
The Hero
The Lumberjack

SEAL of Protection: Legacy Series
Securing Caite
Securing Brenae (novella)
Securing Sidney
Securing Piper

ALSO BY SUSAN STOKER

Securing Zoey
Securing Avery
Securing Kalee
Securing Jane

Delta Force Heroes Series

Rescuing Rayne
Rescuing Aimee (novella)
Rescuing Emily
Rescuing Harley
Marrying Emily (novella)
Rescuing Kassie
Rescuing Bryn
Rescuing Casey
Rescuing Sadie (novella)
Rescuing Wendy
Rescuing Mary
Rescuing Macie (novella)
Rescuing Annie

SEAL of Protection Series

Protecting Caroline
Protecting Alabama
Protecting Fiona
Marrying Caroline (novella)
Protecting Summer
Protecting Cheyenne
Protecting Jessyka
Protecting Julie (novella)
Protecting Melody
Protecting the Future
Protecting Kiera (novella)

ALSO BY SUSAN STOKER

Protecting Alabama's Kids (novella)
Protecting Dakota
Protecting Tex

Delta Team Two Series
Shielding Gillian
Shielding Kinley
Shielding Aspen
Shielding Jayme (novella)
Shielding Riley
Shielding Devyn
Shielding Ember
Shielding Sierra

Badge of Honor: Texas Heroes Series
Justice for Mackenzie
Justice for Mickie
Justice for Corrie
Justice for Laine (novella)
Shelter for Elizabeth
Justice for Boone
Shelter for Adeline
Shelter for Sophie
Justice for Erin
Justice for Milena
Shelter for Blythe
Justice for Hope
Shelter for Quinn
Shelter for Koren
Shelter for Penelope

Ace Security Series

ALSO BY SUSAN STOKER

Claiming Grace
Claiming Alexis
Claiming Bailey
Claiming Felicity
Claiming Sarah

Mountain Mercenaries Series
Defending Allye
Defending Chloe
Defending Morgan
Defending Harlow
Defending Everly
Defending Zara
Defending Raven

Silverstone Series
Trusting Skylar
Trusting Taylor
Trusting Molly
Trusting Cassidy

Stand Alone
Falling for the Delta
The Guardian Mist
Nature's Rift
A Princess for Cale
A Moment in Time- A Collection of Short Stories
Another Moment in Time- A Collection of Short Stories
A Third Moment in Time- A Collection of Short Stories
Lambert's Lady

Special Operations Fan Fiction

ALSO BY SUSAN STOKER

http://www.AcesPress.com

Beyond Reality Series
Outback Hearts
Flaming Hearts
Frozen Hearts

Writing as Annie George:
Stepbrother Virgin (erotic novella)

ABOUT THE AUTHOR

New York Times, *USA Today*, #1 Amazon Bestseller, and #1 *Wall Street Journal* Bestselling Author, Susan Stoker has spent the last twenty-three years living in Missouri, California, Colorado, Indiana, Texas, and Tennessee and is currently living in the wilds of Maine. She's married to a retired Army man (and current firefighter/EMT) who now gets to follow *her* around the country.

She debuted her first series in 2014 and quickly followed that up with the SEAL of Protection Series, which solidified her love of writing and creating stories readers can get lost in.

If you enjoyed this book, or any book, please consider leaving a review. It's appreciated by authors more than you'll know.

www.stokeraces.com
www.AcesPress.com
susan@stokeraces.com

- facebook.com/authorsusanstoker
- x.com/Susan_Stoker
- instagram.com/authorsusanstoker
- goodreads.com/SusanStoker
- bookbub.com/authors/susan-stoker
- amazon.com/author/susanstoker

www.ingramcontent.com/pod-product-compliance
Lightning Source LLC
Chambersburg PA
CBHW020956060126
37782CB00015B/350